Andrew McCoy was  the University of St business he embark Since then he has adviser, an industr sional polo player ir yachtsman and a political organize

By the same author

Atrocity Week
The Insurrectionist
African Revenge
Cain's Courage
Iditarod

ANDREW McCOY

Blood Ivory

PANTHER
Granada Publishing

Panther Books
Granada Publishing Ltd
8 Grafton Street, London W1X 3LA

Published by Panther Books 1985

First published in Great Britain by
Martin Secker & Warburg Limited 1983

Copyright © Andrew McCoy 1983

ISBN 0-586-06100-2

Printed and bound in Great Britain by
Collins, Glasgow

Set in Times

For
JOHN
and
THE ELEPHANTS
in his bonnet

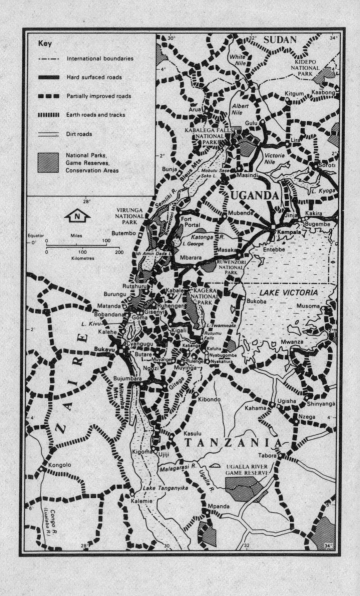

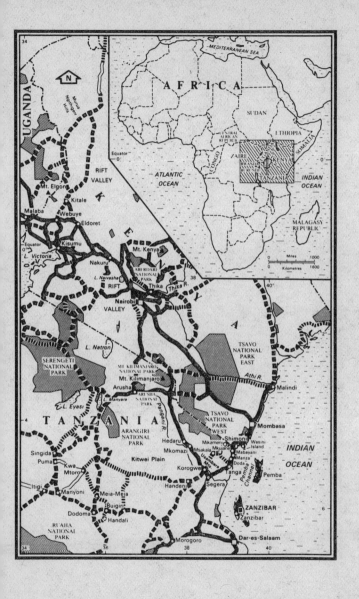

Kenya

It did not occur to Mpengi that men would die in Macao, the China Seas, Brussels, Tokyo, the Burmese jungles, Africa and the Kent countryside because the bellies of his children were empty. If it had, the knowledge would not have changed his course one whit. He did not know of these places, nor of the men who lived in them. They would have to look out for their own children, their own lives.

Lance Weber did not know Mpengi. It was true that, in general, he knew of the poachers and had beaten several he had caught quite severely, then let them go rather than hand them over to the police. For this they thought him soft but, remembering the beatings, they kept clear of his twenty-one-thousand-acre reserve. He had also killed two poachers, one a white man, who had had the temerity to raise their rifles against him on his own land. The reason he had not handed the black poachers over to the police was that there were strict laws about game protection in Kenya and they were rigorously applied. A black man who could not pay the fine – and he poached in the first instance because he had no money – would be sent to gaol with the inevitable result that his family starved or, at the very least, was broken up. Lance, a bachelor, was keen on the concept of family. He had set his parents up in a house on the beach in the sleepy little resort of Kleinmond with the first money he had ever earned, and he visited them at least twice every year.

What Mpengi did that would have such disastrous effects around the world, what he did to relieve the gnawing mouse in the bellies of his children, was simplicity itself. He

11

went to the camp of the Englishman with the red face and the luxuriant white moustache and told him where to find the last six elephants in the world. It was common knowledge that the Englishman would pay, and pay well – in golden Theresas, Victoria sovereigns, Krugerrands, to the choice of his informant – for knowledge of the whereabouts of an elephant. Even a small elephant or a one-tusk elephant or an old elephant with worn and broken tusks. The English bwana would pay. He would take you to show him the elephant and when he had seen the elephant, he would pay. Then he would kill the elephant.

He even, it was said, killed one elephant that had no tusks at all. This not even the old men could understand for the Englishman would not, of course not, eat elephant meat or even elephant liver, a delicacy.

The Englishman was touched by the sun. That was not unusual. All Englishmen were touched by the sun. This one had probably been bitten by a mad dog as well. But he paid in gold.

Mpengi travelled on foot, living off the land. On the third day he entered another country, but he did not know it. (He had voted for Daniel Arap Moi, because the elders of his tribe had shown him against which symbol to make his mark. He did not even know his country was called Kenya. This did not make him stupid: his skills were simply different.) Late in the afternoon he reached the camp of the white man who paid gold for the sight of an elephant. He squatted on the periphery of the camp and waited patiently.

At sunset the Englishman came from his tent and sat down in a canvas chair under the wing of his tethered aeroplane. He looked alertly around him and saw Mpengi. He did not nod or otherwise greet Mpengi. Instead he spoke to a servant, who took Mpengi a bottle of beer, cold and uncapped. Mpengi drank it in one draught and placed the empty bottle in front of him. Later, as darkness fell, he was brought a tin plate of food and another beer. One of the servants came and spoke to him but Mpengi shook his head: he did not understand. When the white man had finished his own meal, he approached. Mpengi remained seated as a sign of respect. The Englishman offered Mpengi a cigarette, and lit it for him. He tried snatches of greeting in several languages until he hit on Mpengi's. Before independence he had been a district officer, a good one.

'Approach the fire,' he invited Mpengi. Mpengi squatted near the man's chair. 'You bring news?'

'They say the Bwana likes to hear of elephants.'

'I do. I pay well for news of elephants.'

'There are only a few left.'

'That is true. That is why I pay gold for news. It is the law of economics that drives prices up when scarcity occurs.'

It was another far-off place Mpengi had never heard of; they were welcome to their own tribal laws.

The Englishman stopped chuckling at his own wit, quite aware that the black man had not understood but unperturbed by the knowledge. 'Where is this elephant you know of?'

Mpengi was shocked by the rude suddenness, the discourteous directness of the question, and the repulsive greed in the man's voice. But his children were hungry.

'Elephants,' he said. 'Six elephants, Bwana.'

'If I want to hear comedy, I can listen to the World News on my radio,' the Englishman said abruptly.

Mpengi said nothing, hoping that this had not been a wasted journey. But others had definitely been paid gold coins for lesser news than his. One gold coin, exchanged at the bank in Nairobi, would be more silver coins than a man could carry away in three trips from the bank. Mpengi and his family could live for nearly two years on one such gold coin.

The Englishman tasted his gin and tonic and wiped his moustache with his forefinger. This grave tribesman did not seem to be lying. But it was incredible: *six* elephants! All in one place?

'Tell me about six elephants.'

'There are two bulls, two cows, one nurse' – here Mpengi indicated by standing up and holding out his hand a halfgrown calf, say about six years old – 'and a new calf. They all live inside the wire of The Man Who Runs With The Ball.'

The Englishman was silent for a long time, trying to contain his rage. He should shoot this stupid black. Lance Weber, the ex-rugger international, advertised his game reserve and his six elephants ('the last elephants in their natural surroundings anywhere in the world') with relentless persistence. He also protected them with an electrified fence that had cost, according to press reports, one million dollars and ran for several miles around his property.

Finally the Englishman recovered his composure enough to speak. 'Those elephants are not news that I would pay for. What would be news I would pay for would be a break in the fence.'

Mpengi nodded and waited.

It took the Englishman, who had seen the nod, a while to realize Mpengi was not going, slinking away into the night with his tail between his legs. Then hope and lust and greed flared in him and he signalled for a servant to bring the black man another beer.

'You know of a break in the fence?'

'I do, Bwana.'

'When I have seen it with my own eyes, when I stand on the other side of that fence, I shall give you one gold piece for each of those elephants.'

'That will be fair, Bwana.' Mpengi felt no elation. If this was not over quickly, the youngest of his children would die.

14

'Tomorrow we will fly in my aeroplane to inspect the fence.'

Mpengi shook his head. He was not going in that machine. He would return on foot.

'If they mend the fence before we get there, you get nothing.'

'Mpengi will go in the machine.'

Later, before the man obsessed with elephants went into his tent, he stirred Mpengi, sleeping beside the fire, with his foot. 'Tell me, Mpengi, how did you know of the break in the fence?'

'I saw the men who made it, Bwana.'

'Christ! Why didn't you tell me?'

Mpengi sat up. He hoped this would not put his gold coins, the food for his children, in jeopardy.

'Who were they?'

'I do not know. White men.'

'Christ!' Somebody else was after those six elephants. It was nearly five months since he had killed the tuskless bull. That goddamn Weber's six could well be the last elephants in the world outside a zoo. It was at least two months since he had even heard of another elephant – and each report since the tuskless bull had proved to be a mirage conjured up out of thin air and desperation by some hungry black man.

He had been thinking about going after Weber's elephants. The problem was not getting over the electrified fence – he could fly over it. But he would need labour to cut out the tusks and for that he would have to get a Landrover loaded with blacks through the fence.

Now somebody else was beating him to it. If they had not already come and gone.

'How did they do it?'

Mpengi recoiled from the snarl. This man had truly been bitten by a rabid dog. He was even foaming at the mouth. He was also gripping Mpengi fiercely by the shoulder. Mpengi told him quickly. 'They did it with a cutter, Bwana. And they left a dead zebra they had brought with them lying against the wire.'

'Goddamnit!' The elephants were probably dead now, the tusks gone. He noticed his fingers digging into Mpengi's shoulder and released the black man.

'Tomorrow we will go and look.' He turned and walked to his tent, calming himself. Telling himself it did not really matter who killed the last elephant outside a zoo, as long as it was killed. The plan, to be commercially successful, required only that the last elephant die, no matter who killed it. But he was not a plan; he was a person. For years he had looked forward to the day he would kill the last elephant. It was like when he felt the sap rising and his wife told him it was her time of the month.

He did not sleep.

The decapitated zebra against the fence enraged Lance Weber: did these people not know zebras were an endangered species? But then, he asked himself which species isn't, barring man and the insects?

No serious damage was done to the fence except that the open wire which carried the alarm and would give humans a mild shock of warning had snapped. They had run out of repair materials and Lance had sent to Nairobi for more. Then he had set out to track the poachers but lost them on the blacktop sixty miles away. Though he had never seen them, he knew a great deal about them: they drove a Toyota Landcruiser 4 WD, they drank Lion beer, smoked Gunston and Texan cigarettes (both unfiltered and very strong) and were neither familiar with the terrain nor comfortable in it. There were six of them, all in city shoes, none over size 7.

Lance, not really perturbed but careful all the same, had arranged for intermittent patrols round the perimeter of the fence. Nobody was taking them seriously. It was nearly Christmas; the last of the camera safaris from which they all made their living had returned to Sweden. Lance himself would be off to visit his parents in South Africa after the annual Christmas party. People kept dropping in by Landrover, car and light plane, bringing gifts, mostly of liquor. Lance drank with the rangers from the official government game reserves and made deals to swap animals with them; if any of them were envious of the luxury of his private game reserve, they did not show it, though many spoke wistfully of having, some day, a fence like his around their preserves. Hoteliers and charter aircraft operators and victuallers flew up from Nairobi to drink Lance's health: they did a lot of business with the camera safaris he brought from all points of the compass to photograph the game on his reserve, especially the last wild elephants in the world. A man from a zoo came, offering to swap any number of lions for an elephant. Lance laughed in his face. He had a firm policy of giving zoos absolutely nothing. Zoos were dangerous to the animals and to the ideal of conservation both. People thought that, because animals were preserved in zoos, the wild could be restocked; that was an impossible dream. 'You and I both know zoos have so many lions they can't give them away for free,' Lance said. He took a skull with a big hole in the cranium from a shelf. 'Female leopard. Paid twelve thousand for her in Germany, hoping against hope . . . The first day we let her free here, the male I wanted her to mate with did that. She didn't even know enough not to trespass on his territory. I can't take your lions even if I want to. Mine would kill them.' The zoo director left to try his luck on somebody less well informed – or without any lions at all.

When he had gone, Lance stood beside the landing strip and wondered if the man knew that zoo-bred lions, even when freed in a lion-less environment, would still have to be fed; they would not know how to hunt and fend for

17

themselves, nor how to teach their cubs to survive. He shrugged. The man ran a great zoo; presumably he knew. If he did not, whoever took his lions would probably know: or would find out.

Lance had long since lost his childhood belief that those in authority knew what was best – or even what they were doing.

On the porch he found Peter Brazenose, his chief ranger. Despite the physical spread of land, the whole operation was run by Lance himself, Peter, Peter's wife, and an acidulous ex-missionary of indeterminate age who was an excellent cook, with labour recruited from the villages on Lance's land.

'I wonder where that little so-and-so is, Mr Weber.' Brazenose at fifty-eight was thirty years older than his employer and insisted, despite repeated invitations to call him by his Christian name, on the formal mode of address. He was referring to the man they had sent in the Landrover to Nairobi to get the wire for fixing the fence.

'Don't worry about it,' Lance said. 'He's saying hello to all his cousins. He'll be here in a couple of days, hungover and shamefaced.'

'If he dents the Landrover I shall take it out on his skin,' Brazenose said darkly. His bark was worse than his bite.

They watched the small plane going over. Suddenly it dropped out of sight. 'I wonder what that fool thinks he's doing,' Brazenose said. 'I should think he landed pretty near our fence up there. Between the gates.'

'If he comes over again, Peter, we'll tell him he's frightening our animals and ask him to fly round.'

'All right: I'll keep an eye on it. Or mention it when he comes to pay his respects.'

Lance nodded. It was a colonial hangover: white people, few and far between, would call on each other if they happened to be in the neighbourhood. 'Here's one coming now.' They watched the twin-engined plane fly over the runway, repeat the process the other way, then land neatly.

'Professional pilot, never been here before, not local,' Brazenose said. 'Are we open for business?'

Very occasionally someone, usually Americans, would drop out of the sky unannounced and without reservations and expect to be received like royalty. 'Tell them this is a safari park, not a hotel. Send them on their way,' Lance said. It was only midday and his remote corner of Kenya was turning into the crossroads of the world: this must be the day's eighth or ninth plane. Sometimes weeks would pass without a single plane coming in, except their own, sent once a week to fetch the post and their guests.

Brazenose looked relieved. He and his wife were looking forward to the arrival of their daughter and son-in-law for Christmas, complete with first grandchild. They did not want their own holiday disturbed. 'You sure?'

Lance laughed. 'Don't worry, Peter. The banks aren't going to foreclose just because we turned down one party for a few days.' It was no secret from Peter that the fence had nearly broken him and that part of it had been financed by the bank. But, while the amount was large enough to impress a man on a salary, against the value of the game reserve it was miniscule. The operation had broken even two years running now and Lance was expecting a small profit in the coming year. Lance was still smiling when he saw the man climbing down from the plane. He stiffened: his face settled into straight lines and his eyes chilled over. Brazenose, who was of the opinion that young Mr Weber was at the best of times an awkward customer to cross, had seen this once before, when his employer had killed the two poachers who had shot at them. They had never referred to it since; Brazenose had not even told his wife.

'Who is he?'

'A ghost from the past,' Lance said, his voice level and controlled.

Brazenose studied the man as he walked towards them. He was just under middle height, middle aged, his wavy hair was thinning and greying, streaks of ginger still surviving. He looked fit and walked erect in his salt-and-pepper brown suit, cream silk shirt, brown knit tie and brown shoes. Even his sunglasses were tinted brown. He was a symphony in brown, thought Brazenose, who was given to reading in the long nights. He also thought the man looked inoffensive enough: except for the trim waistline and alert bearing, possibly, probably even, a contemptible city slicker. Then he saw the man's eyes, a sort of deeply colourless washed-out blue, very unlike the sky-blue of young Mr Weber's. The common factor was the chill that seemed to drag you in. Here was another who would kill two men with two shots, two single impossible shots, drive over to look at their bodies, and say, without the slightest trace of emotion. 'Get me the spade from the Landrover, will you?'

'Well, I'll be off then,' Brazenose said. He had the feeling he should fetch a shotgun and cover his employer's back. He felt irritably stupid, old and useless. It was a new experience for him.

The visitor moved faster than appearances would suggest. He was upon them before Brazenose could turn round.

Lance offered no greeting. 'Colonel Rocco Burger, Peter Brazenose,' he said automatically.

'Brigadier since we last met.'

A look of pain passed over Lance Weber's face. Brazenose wondered what catastrophe had occured at that last meeting. He shook the other man's hand and was surprised to find it warm and dry. 'How'd you do sir.'

Neither Lance nor Burger offered to shake hands with

the other. Lance stood aside so that Burger could enter the shade of the house. 'My pilot – 'Burger said.

'Get him out of that tin can before he fries,' Lance said to Brazenose, giving him a look which Brazenose interpreted as meaning And don't let him out of your sight.

Burger stood looking around the main block. The whole of the ground floor of the large building was open, except for a strip across the back that was the kitchen and stores. Dining-room, living-room and entrance area were differentiated by steps in the sapele floor. A wide gallery ran around the walls and from this led doors to what Burger guessed, correctly, were the guest bedrooms. The whole thing was pleasantly cool under the high shadowed thatch roof.

'You only take twenty guests at a time,' Burger said.

'Generally more like twelve.'

'Easier to control?'

'We like to give personal service. You can take a large party to see, say, lions or elephants. But to sit in a blind and view dik-dik, four's the most. Or to climb a cliff and photograph an eagle's egg, you can only take one person. Maybe two.'

'And it's the small touches like that you charge for?'

'We're expensive for a lot of reasons, Brigadier. The small touches is one. It creates another: repeat business, which in turn creates demand we don't really wish to fulfil. Would you like a drink?' Lance waved the older man to a cane chair.

'No thank you.' Burger sat, pulling at the creases in his trousers. 'This is very different, taking people on camera safaris, from being the world's biggest mass slaughterer of animals. How many crocodiles did you blow to kingdom come? A million?'

'Something like that. They were vermin, eating people.' Lance was in no hurry to hear whatever unpleasantness Burger had decided to visit upon him.

21

'And the proceeds bought this.' Burger watched as another spasm of pain crossed the younger man's face. He was probably remembering the lives it had cost to wrench his fortune from the river and the jungle and the greed of men. Good. 'As a matter of interest, is it true the going rate for taking someone to shoot a rhinoceros is twenty-five thousand pounds sterling?'

'That was about a year ago. It's probably higher now.'

'You must be doing well if, instead, you fence your rhino in.'

'Would you believe, Brigadier, my brother and Jacques Roux loved Africa.'

'I never doubted it for a minute.'

Lance remembered. Burger had been friendly with the Roux family. Jacques' death had been an accident of war caused by an over-eager young man under Burger's command. Lance had killed the young man without even paying conscious thought to the decision. His brother had died in the flames under an oil tanker only minutes before. It had been a very disturbed time.

'My brother was a conservationist. This place is in part in his memory and – '

'And to keep you away from the gambling lights of the cities.'

Lance ignored the vicious dig. He had not gambled for money for seven years. ' – and in part simply good business. In a radius of six hundred miles there are nine surviving rhino.'

Burger pursed his lips, a sign of surprise that there were so few.

'I have two, a pair, male and female. When people tell me, after I refuse their offer for shooting one, that they don't understand, do I want more money? – I tell them it's better business to let people shoot my rhino with cameras rather than rifles. After the camera safari they're still alive

22

for the next camera safari. You'd be surprised how quickly it mounts up.'

'Makes sense. Is it true the horn of the rhino is an aphrodisiac? I hear it now costs more by weight than pure heroin.'

Lance pulled a hair from the side of his head and held it up in forefinger and thumb. The light falling through the windows glinted golden on it. 'Is that an aphrodisiac?'

'No.'

'That's all rhinoceros horn is, hair.'

'I once knew some men who made a very good living taking rich men to shoot the biggest game in the world – a black man.'

'I never heard about that.'

'It was before your time.'

'What happened to them?'

'They fell out among themselves and killed each other before I could do it.'*

A black man wearing long white trousers and a white coat but barefoot padded up to near them and stood waiting patiently. 'Coffee please,' Lance said. 'Would you like something stronger, Brigadier?'

'Coffee will be fine.'

They sat silently until the servant brought the coffee and rusks. Burger took a rusk and inspected it. 'Homemade buttermilk rusks,' he said with approval and dunked it in his coffee.

Lance sat staring into his coffee, his thoughts seven years old, loaded with suppressed anguish of those years. Then another thought interrupted, a thought of the here and now. The plane that had flown over and landed near their fence. It was not the first time. He had heard it, whining low across the reserve and then suddenly dropping away, in the stillness of the dawn just before he had

* See ATROCITY WEEK, Panther Books, London, 1984.

23

been woken with his morning coffee. There was some significance to that but Burger was speaking again.

'I didn't come all this way to chew over the good old days with you.'

'You hardly could, considering that we only had one single bitter day together,' Lance snapped. Then he realized that Burger was acutely embarrassed. It gave him a delicious thrill of power to see the all-powerful boss of BOSS reduced to speechlessness. (The South African Bureau of State Security had, since Lance's soul-searing contact with them, been renamed the Department of National Security or DONS but Lance, who did not keep up with the news, was unaware of this.)

Burger tapped the file he had brought in with him with his forefinger. He was now sorry he had given in to the surge of compassion in bringing the news to this young man himself. He could have sent a subordinate. But he felt, irrationally, some responsiblity for the new anguish the young man would suffer. It was, he now realized, ridiculous to feel like that: Lance Weber was capable of looking after himself. Very capable indeed. Perhaps he saw in Lance the son he had never had, he thought, a son with all his own negative qualities but none the less a spiritual twin. Bury the psychology, Burger, he told himself. All you have in common with this boy is that you're both killers. The difference is that he's got six inches on you, not to mention twenty-five years, several million in the bank, and is besides as handsome as a film star.

Put like that, it was difficult to feel sorry for him.

Still, the Weber family had been close.

In the end, Burger said nothing. He simply took a photograph from his file and handed it to Lance. Burger was, as a superior had once noted on his file, never more brutal than he had to be.

Lance looked at the photograph. At first it did not register. Then he felt the breath escape him and the blood rush to his head. He half rose in his chair and then sank back.

Burger watched him closely. Considering the gory detail of the colour photo, Lance was taking it well. He was pale, true, but that was all.

'I know only one man who kills like this and he's dead,' Lance said. 'You know that. So why show me this?' He waved the photograph by one stiff corner. He only waved it once.

'Do you recognize her?'

'Hardly. But it's Briony Roux, widow of Colonel Jacques Roux.'

Burger leaned over to point. 'That's her boy, the bloody little bundle in the corner.'

Lance looked fleetingly at the photograph and made a sound like someone swallowing back vomit by force of will. He stared into the shadows of the ceiling.

Lance decided to let Burger get it off his chest. He could not guess what the man's game was. But there was no way he could help solve the murder by some deranged maniac of a woman he had not seen in seven years. He would ask no more questions. Boils burst in time even without prodding.

'You knew she had a little coloured boy after she was raped?'

Lance nodded.

'She was put in some kind of institution for a while but recovered her sanity before the child was born. She refused an abortion on religious grounds.' Burger paused to look at Lance. He wanted to know whether Lance was as surprised as he had been to find that the foul-mouthed Briony Roux had religious scruples. Nothing showed on Lance's face. 'Did you know?'

'About her religion? No. But I could have guessed. Jacques was quite a biblical scholar, my brother told me.'

Old Testament eye-for-an-eye scholar to be precise, Burger thought but said nothing. 'She claimed the child and left South Africa to live in Britain in a village near Brighton. She lived quietly, bringing up the child. Funny that, from such a racist.'

'Funny that, coming from the chief strongarm of the South African racist government,' Lance said.

Burger ignored the taunt. Lance knew better than to draw black-and-white lines; he was still disturbed. 'Motherhood. Than which there is nothing sweeter before the Lord . . . Then. Six days ago.' Burger tapped the photograph still in Lance's hand though Lance was no longer looking at it.

Burger waited but Lance said nothing.

Brigadier Rocco Burger sighed and took another photograph from his folio. He slid it on top of the other one in Lance's hand. 'I tried to prepare you,' he said but Lance was already halfway across the room, a strangled sound coming from him, his hand to his mouth. He crashed through a door at the back of the building. The door swung to hydraulically. Burger waited patiently. Patience is an essential for good policemen and counter-intelligence operatives; he was both.

He half-expected Lance to be trailing a rifle when he came back into the room. Many other men would have, men nowhere near as accomplished as Lance Weber with the rifle. Lance was the best shot with a rifle Burger had ever met or even heard of; he had seen for himself, on that fatal day seven years ago, how the firearm had sprouted fire in the young man's hand as if it were an extension of his limb. But Lance Weber had matured beyond that youth and beyond the kind of man who feels insecure unless he carries superior force in his hand, on his belt or slung over his back.

'Sorry,' Lance said. He was carrying two large brandy snifters, each with two inches of liquid in it. He gave one

26

to Burger and gargled with the other. Then he put the glass down and visibly steeled himself to pick up the photographs from where he had dropped them on the blue-stone floor. After a while, during which Burger sipped at his cognac, Lance spoke again.

'Why should anybody want to butcher my parents in their bed and then dismember their bodies with a meat-cleaver?' He drew a ragged breath. 'It doesn't make sense!'

'Not by itself. But read it with the similar murder of Briony Roux and it points straight to you.'

For a mad moment Lance thought Burger was accusing him. Then his mind cleared and he said, 'What do you want from me? I told you, I only ever knew one man who would kill like that and he's dead.'

'Is he? Think!'

Lance did not have to make any effort. He could see it through tears of grief now as on that day. A clearing between huts, the Congolese forest all round. Trucks loaded with crocodile skins worth a fortune for which many men had already paid with their lives. Including his brother, burnt to death under an exploded fuel tanker. They pass a circle of the tribeswomen sitting in a circle around Bruun, waiting to exact their own revenge. Bruun pleads with Burger to kill him. Burger says no, Africa takes its own revenge on tyrants.*

'Those women were going to skin Bruun alive.'

'Certainly. It is not unknown in that part of the world.'

'But you think he escaped.'

'You only know of one man who kills like that. I've heard of one or two others but they would have no reason to kill the widow of Jacques Roux *and* your parents. It's a warning: to you, Lance.'

Lance sat looking at Burger for a long time. The man

---

* See AFRICAN REVENGE, Panther Books, London, 1985.

had come to help him, perhaps even genuinely liked him. 'That would be particularly stupid of Bruun, giving me warning by killing them first. The last time he tangled with me he lost his balls. I don't think Bruun is stupid.'

'No. But he's vindictive. He wants to enjoy you running in fear.'

Lance looked at the older man, then down at the photographs in his hand. He put the photographs on the table beside him. He said nothing. He had no need to.

'All right. Bruun knows you're coming after him. *But what if you can't find him?* Then the roles are reversed. You become the hunted, he the hunter.'

Lance nodded. 'You're saying you don't know where he is.'

'I'm saying I don't think you'll find him.'

'Till three days ago you didn't even know he's alive. I'll have all the time in the world to find him.'

Burger shook his head. 'With my contacts and modern communications three days is all the time in the world. If I can't find him in three days, you'll never find him.'

'Then I'll sit tight and kill him when he comes for me, Brigadier. There are more ways than one to skin a cat.'

'He's not going to come himself. He'll send minions.'

Lance shrugged. He would catch a hireling and extract the whereabouts of his master from him. He could not let the murder of his parents and of Briony Roux, the widow of a friend, pass. 'You're a policeman. You find him for me.'

Burger refused to dignify the taunting suggestion with an answer. Instead he said what he had come to say: 'I can help you disappear. That'll break the links and in the end flush Bruun out.'

Lance knew Burger was sincere. 'Are you doing this officially, Brigadier?'

Burger spread his hands about two inches, a startling gesture from a man who sat absolutely still and spoke without gestures. 'You're a South African citizen. My charter is almost infinitely wide: what I say is official is official, unless the Prime Minister himself contradicts me.'

Burger would not have done this but for the fact that he had met Lance once before – and perhaps felt some guilt that the over-eagerness of one of his men had resulted in the death of Jacques Roux. 'Thank you, Brigadier, but no thanks. When I kill Bruun, I'll try not to cause any international embarrassments for you or the South African Government.'

'It's not only an offer, it's a warning, Lance.'

Lance stood. He knew that part of Burger's work was sweeping up, mopping up – burying – situations which could embarrass the South African Government; for this Burger had a paramilitary group that would go anywhere in the world regardless of national boundaries and do what was necessary. Mostly they operated up and down Africa.

'Stay for dinner and the night, Brigadier.'

Burger looked out of the window. Dusk was falling. 'Thank you. I'll go tell my pilot.'

Lance did not appear for dinner. He was out walking in the African darkness, crying for his dead parents and, later, for his dead brother and the dead Jacques and Briony Roux and the dead child of uncertain parentage. All the dead, tears from his cheeks into the dust. All these years he had thought the killing over. He did not like killing, though he understood that by genes and training he was very efficient at it, but he knew in his bones what his royal bearer Jimmy had once put into words, that some men need killing: Bruun was such a one. Jimmy had actually named Bruun. And now Bruun was here again in all his brutality, all his greed of other people's pain. Bruun, needing killing again. Towards

29

dawn, he wondered if Burger was right: would Bruun be so deep in hiding that nobody could find him? Is that, he asked himself, what Bruun has been doing all these years, digging a hole to hide in?

The Englishman who lusted to kill the last elephant did not sleep either. He sat up all night, cleaning his rifle again and again. He had flown over, establishing that there were still six elephants in the reserve. Then he had landed and found the break in the alarm wire still un-mended. He had paid Mpengi his six gold coins and sent him on his way because his own men would not work with one of Mpengi's tribe. Mpengi went away happy, unaware of the link he had built that would, in turn, fit into the chains of many other men's lives.

The Englishman considered the killing of the two bulls, the two cows, the nurse and the new calf. Funny how elephants were much like humans. The 'nurse' for in-stance. Just an older calf. The new calf would be trained to follow in the trail near its mother, the nurse always nearby. If the young calf tried to wander away, it would be gently nudged back. If it tried again, the mother or the nurse would spank it with the trunk or, if the disobedience was severe, with a stick.

He too had his doubts. He wondered whether it was worth the risk of sending in his men with the Landrover to cut out and bring back the tusks. After all, it was not the ivory he wanted but the exclusivity and commercial scarc-ity value of the tons of ivory he already owned when it became known that there would be no more ivory, ever, because there were no elephants left on earth to breed. That was why he had killed the tuskless bull, who would have died of hunger very shortly anyway – he had already worn down his sixth and last set of molars – but who could conceivably have impregnated a cow the Englishman and other hunters had inconceivably missed killing and, even more inconceivably, on heat just at that very moment out of the whole four years of her fertility cycle.

But leaving the ivory would be wasteful and that was against his nature.

Besides, he would be away in his plane. The risk would be entirely to the men on the Landrover. He would compensate them well if Weber beat them up, and look after their families in the unlikely event that Weber had them put in gaol. Weber was soft anyway for not handing poachers over to the law; the blacks had heads of rock, they could shrug off a beating just like that. It was marshmallow centres like Weber who had lost the Empire; sentimentality had never made anybody great.

He cleaned his rifle yet again. Tomorrow the last elephant in the world would be dead and he would be the owner of an uncountable fortune. The hard years of hunting and hoarding would have paid off. Handsomely.

He would be richer than Pan. His wife, waiting in England, was younger and more beautiful than Jennifer.

'Out of every twenty-four hours,' Peter Brazenose said to the policeman whom he now found excellent company, 'elephants must spend sixteen masticating the four or five hundred pounds of green fodder each one requires every day in order to survive.'

'A dentist's dream,' Burger said.

'Exactly. Each elephant grows six sets of upper and lower molars during its lifetime. They are pushed forward as the previous ones are ground down and fall out. The fourth comes at about twenty-five and the sixth usually not later than thirty-five. That makes nonsense of the myth of elephants growing to very advanced age. Forty is a good age for elephants. Ahmed lived to over sixty but he's the exception to the rule.'

'It is not good table-talk,' Burger said, 'but what does an animal with so few natural enemies die of?'

'Good God, Brigadier, when man is your enemy, you don't need any others,' Brazenose said. Then, recovering, he added: 'Young elephants often die of snakebite. Those who survive man's greed die of old age – in fact, of hunger after their last teeth are worn down.'

'Brrr,' said the pilot.

'In fact many of them commit suicide,' Brazenose said.

'Really? They're that intelligent?' the pilot asked. 'It's what I would do if I knew for certain I was going to die of hunger.'

'Anthropomorphism is dangerous,' Brazenose said, 'but yes, I believe in something like that. Have you heard of the elephant graveyard, now often scorned as a myth?'

'It is no myth,' Burger said quietly. 'My great-grandfather found one in what is now Tanzania. He bought the family farm in the Orange Free State with the proceeds.'

'Right,' Brazenose said. 'Well nobody in his right mind would believe in an animal "graveyard" in our sense of the word, a volitional, communal, final resting-place. But there is another sense in which the lives of living beings follow well-worn paths. Animals quite literally tread the path to the waterhole. Pass the port, please.'

The decanter was silently passed. They were hanging on his words.

'An elephant who can no longer chew fodder will try to fill up the awful hungry void with water. Some, weakened, will sink into the mud of the waterhole. I've seen this while on the track of an animal to put it out of its misery. What I've also seen is an elephant with all his teeth gone but still strong, walk calmly into the waterhole, right to the middle, and stand there sinking away without any sign of struggle. I could not believe that it was not planned.'

There was a long silence while they thought of this. Then Brazenose said, 'After man, dolphins and chimpanzees, the elephant is probably the most intelligent creature alive. So, after a few hundred years the waterhole dries up, the dust is blown away to expose a heap of bones: an elephants' graveyard. The early explorers, who fostered the myth by their secretiveness about the actual positions of these graveyards, would not of course know that once there had been a waterhole on the site.'

'These stories go back at least to Stanley and Livingstone,' his wife said. 'I think I believe them, given Peter's explanation, though we've never actually met anybody who's seen such a graveyard.'

'What about the domesticated Indian elephant?' Burger asked. 'Aren't they a bright spot in an otherwise gloomy conservation picture?'

Brazenose shook his head sombrely. 'Until quite recently, yes. Then ivory became more valuable than the four hours a day those elephants could be worked. Traders would give the mahout a truck or mechanical log-grabber in return for his elephant and then kill the elephant for its tusks.'

'What about the elephants in zoos?' the pilot asked.

'You can't put them back in the wild because they can't fend for themselves. I heard about one they tried to release that walked up to a poacher and nuzzled his hand, looking for peanuts. Then it drank from the tin can the poacher offered it. The can was full of battery acid.'

'People are not very nice,' Burger said.

'No.'

'Anyway, elephants do breed in captivity?' the pilot insisted.

Brazenose shook his head. 'They breed, sure. But the cow comes on heat only once in four years. If the bull misses, forget it. There's the famous long gestation period. After that the calf, two hundred pounds at birth, about three feet high, only reaches half its size after six years and often stays with its mother that long, especially if it is female, and sometimes longer. There is a long period of puberty and youth. No, the zoos, can hardly replace their own stock of elephants through captive breeding, never mind recreating the vast herds of elephants that once roamed Africa. And India for that matter.'

Brazenose poured more port before he continued. 'An elephant also continues growing until shortly before its death, say for forty years. While he grows, so do his tusks. It is these long timespans that have deterred people from breeding elephants for their tusks rather than just killing off the seedstock.'

'I have never found any hard, consistent evidence that people behave rationally,' Burger said.

'Quite. But this is more than irrational, this is stupid.'

'And it has made your six elephants very valuable,' the pilot said.

Brazenose looked at him with distaste. 'Certainly. They're insured for a million dollars each. But consider the enormous premiums and the million-dollar fence the insurance company insisted upon. In that light, you can see Mr Weber is never going to make a penny out of them. Without them, this place would long ago have made huge profits.'

'It is the fact that they have to be insured – and fenced, no matter how large the open space they enjoy inside the fence – for their own protection that is the irrational stupidity,' Burger said to the pilot. 'The actual amounts are irrelevant – newspaper flimflam to bring home to the general public the seriousness of the problem.'

They had all had a great deal to drink when they went to bed, except the pilot, who was flying the next day and, in the presence of his superior, observed the rules closely.

Fifteen minutes before dawn the Englishman stood watching as his men, using two cutters, removed a section of the fine-mesh fence large enough to drive a Landrover through. The bones of the zebra still had more than half its meat on them: even vultures, hyenas, jackals and other scavengers were becoming rare, the Englishman thought. When he had first come to Kenya, just after the war, there would have been nothing left of the zebra after a mere four or five hours. Not a hair. Just bones. Now . . .

He knew where the elephants were and he had his plan. He had noticed that they automatically ran away from the aeroplane sounds, as did almost all the surviving animals in Africa, even those not easily disturbed at their grazing. All had learnt that the sound meant death.

He explained his plan carefully to the men and drew a map in pencil on the aluminium bonnet of the Landrover so that they could not lose it. Then he saw them off through the hole in the fence. He waited five minutes by his watch and then took off into the sunrise. He spotted the Landrover and almost immediately came upon the elephants. They started their ambling run, front and rear legs on the same side moving simultaneously, their skins shaking, rippling over their backs. He had never seen an absolutely still elephant: as long as it was alive, there was movement, especially of the loose skin over the shoulders. He cut the power and glided down. It was not recommended procedure but he had scouted the ground the previous day and was a good pilot. He turned the plane under the last of the momentum to face into the wind and jumped down with his rifles. He placed one rifle on the wing of the aircraft and cocked the other one. He could not yet see the elephants but he could hear them and, behind them, the Landrover, the blacks screaming and laughing to drive the elephants before them.

The elephants broke through the trees, the two bulls leading. He dropped them with two easy shots. Then came the cows, huddling about the calves.

They saw him and stopped for a moment but the hated

roar and smell of petrol was approaching from behind them. They came forward, the cows flanking the calves protectively.

He dropped the left-hand cow with another easy shot. There were now three elephants left in the world, all females, he told himself. In his excitement he fluffed the next shot, missing at a hundred and fifty feet an animal that stood twice as high as he and weighed over six tons.

The cow took time to nudge the two calves behind the body of the dead cow, then turned and charged him.

He had been killing elephants for nearly a quarter of a century. The animal's trunk was stretched out towards him. He felt sorry for her. Even in extremity, she was enacting a charge of intimidation which would stop short of him. In the attacking charge, she would have lowered her head and rolled her trunk under her chin to bring the tusks into play.

He listened to the trumpeting and watched the elephant slow down in the sights of his rifle. When she had almost come to a hesitant standstill, he killed her with two shots to the brain.

He walked the fifteen paces to the dead cow, climbed on top of her and killed the nurse as it ambled pathetically towards him, trumpeting a thin rage.

The calf still had the hair with which it had been born. For a mad moment he thought of keeping it as a pet, but what if some interfering government somewhere were to take it from him, find a male, and repopulate the continents with new elephants? He fired all the remaining shots from the magazine into the little animal as it stood looking doubtfully at him with its soft brown eyes.

Lance, a thousand yards away, could see nothing through the long grass. He heard the plane, the elephants trumpeting, the shots, the Landrover engine racing. He scrambled up a tree to be able to see, skinning his knuckles in his haste.

36

Infuriatingly, he could see nothing. Other trees were in the way. But there was an ominous silence. His elephants were probably dead by now.

As he scrambled down the tree, he saw the cone of smoke rising straight up in the still dawn air. Bruun had killed his elephants and burnt his home.

So be it.

He ran through the long grass in the direction of the men who had killed his elephants. Bruun would wait at the house until Lance turned up; the elephant killers would go once their work was finished. He heard the aeroplane engine starte. Moments later it rose out of the grass in front of him, banking so that the wingtip parted the grass. Without raising his rifle from his hip, he raked it from stem to stern with a full clip. At less than two hundred feet, Lance Weber could not miss. The machine exploded. It was so low that the pieces fell below his eye level almost immediately. A largish piece whizzed past his head but he ignored it, running forward towards his elephants and the men he could hear shouting excitedly. The Landrover started up and he heard the engine race. They were going to try and run him over. He ran on, patting his pockets for a spare clip. There was none, of course. This was not a combat situation. Just a rifle he had automatically taken in passing, as they all did when they went out among the wild animals. A shot into the air would frighten off most attacks, he had heard. He had never been attacked, nor had Peter Brazenose, forty years a ranger. Peter had once seen a Landrover savaged by an elephant cow with a newborn calf whose security zone had been invaded by ignorant tourists; nobody had been hurt. The rifle was a formality, requiring no spare clips. He reversed the rifle, holding it by the warm barrel. He would use it as a club.

He burst into the clearing in time to see the Landrover disappear between the trees in the other direction.

He walked from elephant to elephant. He stood looking down for a long time at the still-hairy recent-born calf.

He decided to kill Bruun very slowly.

He went around stamping out the small fires the exploding aeroplane had caused. He found the body of the pilot, both arms gone but the face strangely untouched and serene, as if after sexual satisfaction. He was an elderly man, most definitely not Bruun. To be quite sure, Lance pulled up the trouser legs. There were no scars on the knees. There were no scars on the elbows either when he found the arms. When he was sure there would be no fire, he set off for the plume of smoke in the distance. He did not hurry. What had happened there had happened; hurrying would not undo it.

From a mile out, he circled the building-complex. He spotted the man by an irregular wave in the grass. He remembered the day he had first killed a man: it was the day Jimmy had instructed him in the mysteries of the grass by throwing stones into it. The rifle in his hand was the one he had used that day, given to him by Jacques Roux.

He walked forward quite upright but slowly. When he was behind the man, he jammed the muzzle of the rifle against his neck.

'Ech!' said the man.

Lance recognized the orange and purple striped pajamas as Peter Brazenose's and the thinning ginger and grey hair as Burger's. He sat down beside Burger.

'Any other survivors?'

'No.'

'Are they waiting for me?'

'That's the strange thing. I don't think so.'

Lance sat beside Burger, studying the scene through the telescope of the rifle. Buildings had been fired. He saw the servants first. Some had been shot, others attacked with the meat-cleavers the photographs Burger had shown him the day before had already led him to expect. They lay on the ground. It was like an abattoir.

Magda Brazenose's body had been nailed to a door. She was naked and upside down. The trunk of the ex-missionary cook stood in the doorway of a smouldering building. Her head, arms and legs had been severed and were artisitically arranged around her.

'What about Peter and your pilot?'

'They took them with them.'

'How'd you get away?'

'Out a window the back way the minute it started. I think the others might have opened their doors to see what was going on.'

'They would. Nobody was expecting an attack. Except you and – '

'I always expect the worse, Lance. It's my business.'

'And you didn't even manage to bring your pistol with you.'

'I don't have a pistol. I never carry firearms.'

'It happened just before dawn,' Lance said. A statement, not a question. It was the best time for an attack like that. 'Did you see Bruun?'

'You didn't seriously expect him to come himself?'

Lance shrugged. 'You were wrong. He isn't playing games, he's simple trying to kill me quickly.'

'Look at those buildings again. There's one unscathed.'

Almost automatically, Lance turned the telescope on his own *rondavel*, from this angle half-obscured by other buildings. Burger was right. It was the only building that had not been fired.

'He sent somebody to kill my elephants too.'

'You got that one?'

Lance nodded and rose. He walked to the smouldering buildings and inspected the dead. When he returned, he carried clothes for Burger. He was very pale. He had taken the bodies of the two women from the doors and laid them inside.

'These'll be too big but they're all there is,' he apologized as he gave Burger the clothes. He also had a shotgun, which he offered to Burger together with a box of cartridges. 'It's the only other firearm I kept. We didn't go in much for guns here.'

Burger handled the shotgun gingerly. It was nicely made, precise, expensive, functional. But Burger thought of himself as a man above and beyond firearms. He fought with his brain, directing the men who wielded the firearms.

Lance noticed his indecision. 'Shy of doing your own killing, Brigadier?'

Burger turned away and dressed. They walked to the village where Lance borrowed the headman's truck. An hour down the road they found the bodies of Peter Brazenose and the pilot. Both were still warm. Both had been tortured and then had their throats cut.

'Very crude work,' Burger said, referring to the torture.

'You should know.' Lance was looking at the tracks. 'Toyota Landcruiser. I've seen these tracks before. They shot a zebra after chasing into my fence – hey! That's why I heard that plane at dawn yesterday morning. He was spotting the position of the elephants and choosing his killing ground. Let's see if we can catch them.'

'No. They were going like blazes. They expect you to follow. Look at the position of the bodies. They didn't even stop to throw them out. They did – that to them on the move, then flung the bodies out. Let's chase those who went the other way, the elephant-killers.'

They did not have to chase the elephant-killers. They found them at the late Englishman's camp, getting drunk on his gin. Lance slapped one sober enough for Burger to question him. It took Burger only five minutes to ascertain

40

that their erstwhile employer wanted to kill elephants, nothing more, nothing less. Their presence on the reserve at the time of the attack on the homestead was a coincidence.

'Are you going to kill them?' Burger asked Lance.

'No. They were just earning a living. I've already dealt with the man who gave them their orders.'

'Let's take the Landrover anyway. It has to have a better ride than the truck.'

They left the black men drinking gin and returned the borrowed truck. They buried the dead, Brigadier Rocco Burger intoning the Lord's Prayer over their graves.

Then they drove off in the Landrover, Burger to find and charter a plane to speed him away from the possibility of scandal, Lance to explain to the generally sympathetic police that there had been a massacre of which he was the only survivor: he could offer no cause or explanation or motive. In the saloon bars they shook their heads and said it was just one of those things that sometimes happen in Africa, the price one has to pay for enjoying all its wealth and beauty.

Only foolish men ever claim to trace any of the mysteries that come out of Africa to an exact and exclusively definitive source. Bruun might be a source in his rivalry with Lance's late brother predating his first meeting with Lance. The gambling instinct that had sent Lance on that crocodile-hunting expedition in the Congo to cover his losses at the table could be another source. It is not now possible to say. For all anybody knows, Lance could have bumped into Esmeralda Ellimore in the street and so become involved – but that is speculation.

All that is certain is that Lance still did not know Mpengi, who, to quieten the hunger in the stomachs of his children, had sent the Englishman to kill Lance's elephants, which in turn drew Lance into the ivory hoards affair and Theodore Bruun after him, a congruence of events that was to prove fatal for a number of men in many parts of the world – though not for the taproot of involvement, Mpengi the Watusi.

Kent Widow

They found him in Sydney.

He was living in Kellett Street, just off the eight-way junction that gives King's Cross its name. He did not need an alarm-clock. Every morning at seven o'clock there was a motor-car accident to wake him. Once he had lost the habit of rising at dawn, he cursed this happenstance but chose not to move. It was an inconspicuous place to live. A woman on the plane, thinking him down on his luck from the cheap readymades he was wearing, offered him the use of her flat; she was flying on to Hawaii. From the number of different male voices who phoned her, Lance concluded she was a prostitute.

The Cross is a passing-place for all the world's adventurers. Other such places are Johannesburg and Brussels and San Francisco. Few actually live in these places but from time to time they pass through. The Cross had been added to the list when Sydney was widely used for R&R by the American Navy during the Vietnam war. Every night Lance would drink in the clubs, listening, managing to imply that he was available for slightly shady work, or even the near-legal. In three months he had not heard a single word about Bruun. Burger had been right. Bruun had either disappeared or, Lance (who had never before known how much one can learn merely by asking for the information you seek) was beginning to think, had been dead all along and the conjunction of killings inspired by some other cause. The problem with this line of thought, he would tell himself as he lay in bed digesting the information he had gathered, was that he could find no other motive but Bruun's. In the seven years since he had defended his property so effectively against Bruun's predations he could not remember anybody he had so offended that killing was called for. Or anybody he had offended at all. It was an impossible situation and he was beginning to see what Burger had meant by saying that, if Lance failed to find Bruun, he would himself then become the hunted rather than the hunter.

Sometimes he thought of just disappearing. He had a good deal of money and would have more when the insurance company paid for the six dead elephants. The buildings themselves had also been insured for nearly another million dollars against all risk, including arson. He had instructed his solicitors to sell the land, in itself a valuable property with its fence and established reputation as a game reserve. He would be rich beyond any man's dreams but he felt empty. He could not buy anonymous safety for himself while his parents, Briony Roux and her child, Peter and Magda Brazenose and the others lay dead and unrevenged. Nor, for that matter, even if there were no question of revenge involved, while scum like Bruun lived. The existence of Bruun was sufficient reason to squash him. Lance did not try to rationalize the urge to revenge by the secondary reason: a true son of Africa, he was perfectly happy with the concept of revenge.

All the same, it was nerve-wracking, having to wait for Bruun to take the initiative.

He was reading the paper, sitting in the sun on a bench under the fountain in front of the library when they found him.

'Mr Weber?'

He had been using the name Jackson. He waited till he had recovered from his surprise, then lowered the paper.

'If you know my name, you know what I look like.'

'May I sit down?'

There were two of them. The other one was burlier and less well tailored.

'It's a public bench.'

The man sank down on the bench with a sigh. 'I'm Anthony Brooke of Goldman, Pitt and Brooke.'

He gave Lance a card. It carried, beside the usual address and telephone number, the information that Anthony Brooke was a solicitor. Lance nodded.

'And that's Mr Carleton, an investigative agent retained by my office.'

Lance nodded at Carleton, who nodded back and smiled uncertainly. He was, Lance saw, weighing up his chances of taking the younger man and not rating them too highly. Lance turned back to Brooke. 'How can I help you, Mr Brooke?'

'I have a client in England who wishes to meet you, Mr Weber.'

Christ, yes, of course! He had been reading too many cheap paperbacks in which the villain is all-powerful, able to call at the touch of a button on subversive forces in all parts of the world. Of course Bruun would pay some perfectly respectable lawyer to find him and send him along on some pretext. Why the hell had he not thought of finding Bruun the same way? Like in the small advertisements: Theodore Bruun, last seen on the Congo (Zaire)/ CAR border being skinned alive by angry tribeswomen, write to Box xxx to get what is coming to you.

'Yes. I think you could say I'm keen to meet your client too.'

'Oh, I wasn't aware that you had already met Mrs Ellimore.'

'A woman?'

The lawyer stared at Lance for a moment. 'You *are* Lance Weber?'

'He's Weber all right,' Carleton said. 'You saw the photographs.'

Brooke ignored the interruption, waiting for Lance.

'I'm Lance Weber. I don't know any Mrs Ellimore. What does she want?'

'As far as I know, to offer you employment.'

'Thank you, but I don't need a job.'

'This is all highly irregular. I think – '

'Do you generally leave your office to deliver messages? If your sleuth can find me, he could find my address or phone number. You could write me a letter or phone me.'

Brooke was unperturbed. 'I've been given to understand that you are a special case.'

'Ah. So Mrs – '

'Ellimore.'

'Right . . . who knows more about me than I know about her, wants to offer me a job. Why?'

'I'm not privy to that information, Mr Weber. I have not met Mrs Ellimore either. I am simply acting on instructions from her attorneys in England, whose Sydney correspondent I am.'

'So all you know is she wants to offer me a job. Thanks, but no thanks.'

'Come on, Weber,' Carleton interrupted again, 'you've been hanging around the dives waiting for crumbs to fall off the tables of bigger men. How're you paying the rent?'

Lance looked at the burly man until Carleton coloured and looked away. Then he said, 'Mr Brooke, I should advise you to keep a tighter rein on your lackey.'

'I apologize. I do actually know something more. The nature of the employment. Mrs Ellimore wants you to recover some thirty tons of ivory that belongs to her. I've been instructed to tell you that, now the last elephant in the world is dead, this ivory is very valuable indeed and you will be paid for recovering it.'

Lance nodded and smiled. The lawyer flinched. He had never seen a smile so cold.

'All right. Tell me where I can got hold of her and I'll be in touch.'

Brooke brought an envelope out of his pocket and gave it to Lance. 'Air ticket. Cash for expenses. Can you make this afternoon's plane? My office will make the reservation for you.'

Bruun was even paying for his air ticket and giving him pocket-money! 'Sure. I suppose your instructions include having me seen onto the plane.'

'Er, yes, if you don't mind.'

'Why should I?' Lance hoped his tone was ingenuous.

'You'll be met at Heathrow.' Brooke rose and offered his hand. Lance shook it. The lawyer was an innocent messenger: he probably thought he had done Lance a good turn by bringing him news of a job. 'In case they miss you, the address and phone number is in there. Good luck.'

Carleton said not a word while Lance packed, nor in the taxi on the way to the airport, nor while they waited for the flight to be called. Lance hardly noticed. He was jubilant: Bruun had shown himself impatient. In another month of waiting Lance's nerve would have broken.

At Singapore he changed airlines and destinations, taking the first flight not going to Heathrow. He ended up in Copenhagen on a miserably cold and icy morning. He had to wait four hours before he could get a seat on a flight to Brussels. He sat, watching the other people. He could not spot anybody watching him; he admitted to himself that he would not know how to find out. Though he had grown up in a city, Cape Town, the city was no longer his milieu. In the bush he would have *known* if somebody was watching him: the hair on the back of his neck would have risen. It was, he decided, rationally unlikely that anybody would be watching him; Bruun could not possibly have a minion at every airport in the world.

He had never been to Copenhagen, nor to Brussels, where he saw more of the city than he did of Copenhagen. He was not impressed. To Lance a city was a city was undesirable. He pined for his reserve, except that he was selling it. He could not go back there, not with the shades of his murdered employees living there. But still he felt the loss acutely. It had turned him into a wanderer, a rootless man. He wondered fleetingly what he would do, what would become of him once he had satisfied his present driving purpose: killing Bruun.

He was still only half-persuaded that Bruun was alive. He would know soon enough.

The taxi deposited him in the driveway. There was about two acres, not very much land where he had come from, but he guessed that in this place, where there were so many people for so little land, so much area under established trees and well-tended shrubs, all behind a wall, signified wealth. A maid answered his ring. She did not understand English and Lance did not speak French. She closed the door in his face. Lance wondered why he had assumed that he would be welcome after all these years.

When the door was opened again, it was almost filled by the huge black man. Lance did not recognize him until he said: 'Mr Lance!' and swept Lance off his feet in a bearhug. He backed through the door with Lance still in his arms and kicked the door shut.

It was as well that he could not see Lance's face, which was a study of disappointment. Lance saw again, in his mind's eye, a picture that had been on front pages of newspapers across the world: this man and Lance's brother Ewart standing amid a scene of indescribable carnage; rebels in the Congo had raped and killed a number of nuns and Ewart and his men, too late to rescue the nuns, had fought the rebels, neither side taking prisoners. And yet not this man. He had been big, true, but not fat.

'Sergeant Sambo,' Lance said when he was put down,

shaking Sambo's hand. 'How are you!' Fat or not, it was good to see Sambo, almost a resurgence of that feeling of security he had had every time he saw Sambo in that month of troubles they had spent together seven years ago. 'You're looking well.' It was true. Sambo might no longer look like a fighting machine a man could shelter behind in a dangerous jungle but here, in his rich home, in his well-cut suit, his teeth gleaming whitely in a wide smile, he looked prosperous and content. And there was no disguising his glee in seeing Lance.

Later, when Lance was seated and the first rush of questions and answers and flash reminiscences had passed, Lance, drink in hand, asked, 'And your brothers? And Jimmy?

'Fat like me, many children like me, all except Jimmy. He's still strong and has no wife.' The smile went from Sambo's face. 'He runs our business but, in truth, it is not work for a grown man and he grows discontented with inaction.'

'Ah,' Lance said. 'It must be good to have a business that looks after itself.'

Sambo nodded. 'We were lucky. With the money that Major Weber paid us – and that you gave Jimmy – after the crocodile hunt,' he spread his hands to express once more his sorrow for those dead on that expedition, 'we came here and bought some land. Then the European Economic Community expanded very much and we sold the land. Now we have an investment company but almost everything is in blue chips. There is little for any of us to do.'

Sambo's wife came in, a statuesque blonde, with their five children, spaced at intervals of one year. Shortly afterwards Jimmy came, sweat dripping onto his track suit. He had been running. When Lance had first known him, he never needed to take conscious exercise. But he was still the same hard, trim, smiling Jimmy that Lance remembered so well. Except around the eyes. Lance would have been able to read the discontent in his erstwhile bearer's eyes even if Sambo had not told him.

'Lance! You bring news of new adventures? Something we can do?' He cast a guilty glance at his brother.

'Jimmy! I'm sorry, no adventures. I come only to seek information.' Lance glanced at the woman and the children and Jimmy immediately changed the subject. It was not mentioned again that day. They sat up late over the bottles and the old stories, drinking a maudlin wake.

In the morning Jimmy kitted Lance out for a run, saying it would clear the hangover from his head. In that the run failed but the raw egg broken into flaming Worcester sauce and doused with vodka that Sambo gave him on his return helped. Then the three of them sat in the sauna.

'You seek information,' Sambo said when there had been quiet for a while. It was permission from the head of the household for Lance to proceed to business, the amenities having been observed.

Lance kept his eyes closed. 'It is painful.'

Next to him he felt Sambo ripple as the big man shrugged.

'What I want to know is: What happened to Bruun after I left in the helicopter with Colonel Burger?'

There was a long silence. Lance opened his eyes. They were both looking at him. Lance remembered Jimmy once telling him that the man who likes killing will one day savour his enjoyment for a second too long before pulling the trigger and in that second a more workmanlike soldier will kill him.

Lance told them what had happened to Briony Roux and her child, to his parents, at his game reserve. He ended by saying, 'I can think of only one man who would order such things done.'

'Bruun,' Jimmy said flatly.

'You must be a lucky man, Mr Lance, if you can only think of one enemy,' Sambo said. He still insisted on the forms of address they had used in the bush. 'And him dead.'

A cold shiver ran down Lance's spine along with drops of sweat. Such things; so many of them, so pointed, did not happen by coincidence. He would go mad if some unknown enemy was out stalking him. For some unknown reason.

'Are you sure?'

Sambo shrugged again.

'Did you see his body buried?'

'Easy now, Lance,' Jimmy said, putting his hand briefly on Lance's knee.

Sambo shook his massive head. 'No, Mr Lance, I didn't see him buried. But when we left Lobengula's kraal, the women had already cut off his lips and staked him out on the ground. They were flaking his skin off in small pieces with their knives.'

'He wasn't even screaming any more,' Jimmy said. 'Lance, he was a dead man when we left there. He had maybe two, three days to live. If you could call what those women were doing to him living.'

Lance leaned back against the slatted wood. He was shivering again.

'No,' Lance said. 'It's impossible.'

'It was impossible for him to escape,' Sambo said with finality.

Later, as Lance toyed with his lunch, Jimmy said, 'Lance, if it's money, we'd be glad to – '

'No thanks, I have plenty. Who else?'

'But Bruun?'

'Yes. Did my brother or Jacques Roux have any enemies that would crawl out of the woodwork at this length of time and revenge themselves on pensioners, women and children?'

Sambo put his knife and fork down. The men were at table alone. 'A man like Major Weber had enemies of course. But I cannot think of any still alive. Unless he

53

made them before we knew him, in Algeria or Indochina perhaps. Your brother was not a talkative man.'

'That takes us back even further than the seven years,' Jimmy said.

Sambo nodded. 'I do not know about Colonel Roux's enemies but, like your brother, he was not a man to leave his back unprotected. Anyway, why should his enemies kill your family?'

'That,' said Lance, 'leaves Bruun.' He picked up a thinly-cut lamb chop and tore at it with his teeth. With food this delicious no wonder Sambo was fat.

'What about this woman you're going to see in England?' Sambo asked.

Lance shrugged. 'I thought she was a blind or a front for Bruun.'

'A trap,' Jimmy said.

'Sure. But you say Bruun is dead. In which case . . . I don't know.'

'I'll come with you,' Jimmy said. 'Watch your back. Just like the old days.'

'I'd love to have you, Jimmy. But I must refuse. This isn't your problem.'

'Don't worry about that, Lance. You're still Major Weber's brother.'

A look passed between the brothers.

Sambo said, 'We have a duty to look after you.'

'What about rebuilding the tribe?' Lance asked. There were very few men left of the tribe of which Sambo and Jimmy and the other brothers were the hereditary chiefs; seven years ago Sambo's aim had been to rebuild the tribe as quickly as possible.

'All the children are mine and the other brothers',' Sambo said. 'Jimmy has not done his duty yet.'

Ah. The source of the tension. 'Thank you, Sambo. But I don't think so.'

When the car came to take him to the airport Lance

recognized the driver as another of his late brother's men. He too seemed fat and prosperous. Sambo said goodbye in the driveway; Jimmy was coming to the airport with Lance. When they were underway and Lance had chatted to the driver, he eyed the shoulder bag on the seat between them. 'Going somewhere, Jimmy?'

'I'm coming with you.'

'The loyalty you owed my brother was buried with him.'

Jimmy shrugged. 'You don't understand. Sambo sends me. I obey. But even if he didn't, I'd come to get away from all this bourgeois shit.' He caught the vehemence in his own voice and clamped his teeth shut audibly. 'You don't know what it's like, you've been working out of doors in Africa. Some days, going to the office, adding up figures on my calculator, reading the analysts' reports, it becomes so unreal I want to beat my head against the wall till it cracks. I have to go running in a special suit to stop me looking like Sambo and the others.'

Lance burst out laughing.

Jimmy gave him a surly look. 'You should try it, see how long you last, before you laugh.'

'The unredeemed savage, eh?'

Jimmy smiled ever so slightly. 'Maybe not. I like good living occasionally. But I'm ever so grateful to be taken away from all that.' He jerked his thumb over his shoulder.

'You're welcome. If I'd known you were tired of the bright lights, I'd've had you out on the reserve in a flash.'

'Maybe when this is over . . .' Jimmy said. He was once more wearing the smile Lance remembered so well. Jimmy's trademark.

It was comforting to have Jimmy with him again. Jimmy had been his bearer on the crocodile hunt, always behind his right shoulder, always ready to guide Lance if his first steps into the unfamiliar heart of darkness faltered.

On the plane they napped. At Heathrow Jimmy said the

underground train was faster than a taxi. The Dorchester was expecting them; Jimmy's office had made the reservation. A rented car was waiting and they drove down to Lamberhurst in Kent.

Only one side of the property was approachable by road and that was walled. There was no higher ground from which the grounds could be overlooked.

'Mrs Ellimore, if she exists, certainly likes her privacy,' Lance said as they drove by for the second time. 'Stop in the village. We'll ask some questions, buy a couple of rifles and come back.'

Jimmy gave him a sharp look. 'Short of London, there'll be no gun shop you'll want anything from. And in London you'll still need a licence to buy a firearm.'

In the village, Lance found out by indirect questioning that Mrs Ellimore was beautiful and a recent widow. And that she was a foreigner but her husband's people had lived outside the village in the same house since his grandfather's time. He did not ask if she had any men living with her. Nor did he mention Bruun's name.

'There's a Mrs E.,' he told Jimmy on the way back to London. 'Mr E. died recently. Tomorrow we'll visit her.'

In the morning they went shopping for rifles; it was as Jimmy had said, they needed permits to take delivery of rifles in England. They bought what they could without a permit and drove down to Lamberhurst again. Along the way they stopped for target practice.

'Do you want lunch?' Jimmy asked.

'No. Let's get it over with.' Lance's palms were sweating. Jimmy parked the car on the verge and they walked into the wood next to the wall where it cut away at a right-angle from the road. When they could no longer be seen from the road, Jimmy formed a cradle with his hands and Lance climbed up to look over the wall.

'Nothing,' Lance said. 'No glass or wires on the wall.'

'Further along, on the ground?'

'No.' Lance climbed up on the wall and took the items Jimmy handed him. He dropped off on the other side of the wall and waited for Jimmy to climb over. 'I feel bloody foolish. Perhaps we should have driven through the gate.'

Jimmy grunted and they set off through the trees, Jimmy grunted again. Lance walked on alone. He climbed the steps to a terrace and found her sitting in a glassed-in porch beyond it. All that he could say with certainty about the house was that it was old, large, impressive, and had been built by many men over a very long period of time. It was also very ugly.

The woman was strikingly beautiful. Her hair was pulled back from a broad forehead and tied in a simple ponytail. It should have made her look severe. Instead it emphasized the olive smoothness of her skin and the flawless planes and curves of her features. She was sitting at a white-painted cast-iron table, eating a peeled gratefruit segment by segment. She was wearing a blouse open at the neck, riding-breeches and boots. A black jacket was hung over the back of her chair.

She looked up at Lance, surprise clear on her face. Then she did a double-take, as if she identified him from his photograph. She gestured for him to come in. With his hand on the door handle, he looked back across the lawns to the trees but he could not see Jimmy.

'Hello,' she said, indicated that he should sit. 'I'm Esmeralda Ellimore. You must be Mr Weber. We were expecting you the day before yesterday.'

'Yes. I'm here now.' Lance sat down opposite her. She was quite the most beautiful woman he had ever seen. He wondered what Bruun had bought her with. During the night he had made up his mind: it had to be Bruun simply because anything else was too incredible.

'So you are. Coffee?' She had a slight accent. From her name Lance guessed it to be Spanish.

Lance looked at the little man who slid the heavy tray

onto the table. If he was anything but a household servant, Lance Weber was a chimpanzee. 'Thank you.'

She said something to the little man in Spanish and he went away. She poured coffee. They made good coffee, Lance decided, black and strong.

When she seemed disinclined to say anything, Lance said, 'All right. You have a message for me. Let's hear it. Or is Bruun going to deliver it himself?'

She was either one hell of an actress or she knew nothing. A very slight frown appeared on her forehead. 'Message? Bruun?' She sighed. 'I do not understand. I sent you a message already, through the lawyers. You came.'

Lance smiled. 'Oh yes, about a job.'

'That is right. I wanted to see the man who killed my husband and to – '

'Are you nuts or am I?'

'Nuts?' Again the small sigh. Lance was beginning to identify it as her signal that she was not quite at ease with all the colloquialisms of English.

He made a circling motion with his finger at his temple.

She opened her hands and closed them again, a flashing motion of understanding. 'You do not even remember killing him?'

He was unaware that he had risen, the delicate coffee-cup shattering on the marble floor, or that he was raising her by the front of her silk shirt.

'You had my family and all those people killed because you think I killed your husband! You stupid bitch. I've never heard of anybody called Ellimore, never mind killed him.' He swung his free hand, crashing the back of it through her face. If he had not let her shirt go at the same time, he would have broken her neck. She crashed against a potted plant, upsetting its stand. Plant and woman crashed to the floor.

Lance became aware of the little man in the white coat sitting on his back, beating ineffectually at his head,

58

jabbering in some foreign language. He hauled the little man around to his front intending to take him into small pieces. The fear in the man's eyes stopped him. He dropped the servant to the floor, where he lay, staring fearfully at Lance.

There was something wrong here.

If there was a message from Bruun, it should simply have been delivered, a link in the chain.

If it was a trap, it should have been staffed with more spring in the backbone than the little man.

This husband he was supposed to have killed . . .

He walked outside and waved his arm to show Jimmy he was in no danger. Inside, he caught the little man just before he scurried through the door, presumably on his way to phone for the police.

The woman still lay where she had fallen. After plonking the servant in one chair, Lance pointed to the other. She rose, brushing herself, and sat down.

She was alert, perhaps apprehensive, but not overtly fearful. He had to admire her spirit, even though she was probably as mad as the proverbial hatter. She looked out of the window, trying to see who Lance had waved at.

'You do not trust me?'

Lance, his composure recovered, laughed aloud, derisively. After all the people she had had slaughtered upon a mistaken notion?

She shook her head sadly. 'I intended you no harm, even if you did kill a perfectly good husband.'

'Tell me about this perfectly good husband.'

'His name was Matthew Ellimore. He was sixty-three years old. He had been my husband for eight years, since I was sixteen, when you killed him. His hobby, his passion if you must, was killing elephants. You do not need to know any more about him.'

Lance felt his stomach contract. 'When am I supposed to have killed him?'

'You do not even remember killing him?' she asked the question again.

'The next time I have to repeat a question, the other side of your face will have a bruise as well. For the last time, when?'

She stared at him for some seconds, then said, 'Three months and eight days ago.'

'Aw, shit!' Lance said. He felt about three inches tall. He had come into this woman, this widow's home and beaten her up and slammed her servant about. All for nothing. It was a blind alley. Briony and his parents and even the people at the game reserve were all dead before he killed her husband. She had nothing to answer for. He was the one who had widowed her. He remembered now. The man who had shot his elephants, the plane coming out of the grass, the rifle in his hand, his thumb on the safety, not even raising the rifle from his hip to pump a full clip the length of the plane. The white-haired man with his old-fashioned moustache. He spread his hands. 'I'm sorry.' He rose and was already at the door when she spoke:

'You kill my husband, you come to my house and beat me up, then you say "sorry" and go. A very fine gentleman. Phuh!'

He turned to see her standing, rage flushing her face, pushing her fine breasts against the shirt, her whole body heaving. 'Why, yes,' he said. 'You invited me.'

'I invited you to listen to a proposition. You owe it to me! Sit!'

He looked at her for a moment. He had behaved very badly. He did owe her some courtesy. He sat down again. She snapped something at the little man in their common language. He scuttled out.

'If that one returns with a knife, it will be the worse for him,' Lance said. 'If he calls the police, it will be unfortunate for them.' Lance waved his hand at the trees across the lawn. Who knew, Jimmy might think the police a costume trick of Bruun's and shoot at their eyes with the air pellet gun which was all the strange laws of the country allowed them to buy: did the people who made the laws not know that, if used expertly accurately, a daisy gun could kill people? All you had to do was shoot through the eye into the brain, something Jimmy was perfectly capable of doing at any reasonable range. All Ewart's Baluba Butchers had been crack shots but, even among them, Jimmy had been outstanding. He was nearly as good as Lance himself.

'Your sense of hospitality is severely curtailed, Mr Weber.'

'I apologized. Now get on with it or let me go.'

'Nor do you have the right attitude for a man in search of employment. I suppose it is because you lack experience.'

'Oh yes, the job you wanted to offer me.'

'Please do not be sarcastic, Mr Weber. There is a . . . it's more of a task than a position, do I make myself clear?'

'No.' He had not considered the possibility that the job offer could be anything but a ruse. 'Do you mean it's a one-shot job?'

'Now I do not understand you.' She sighed briefly. 'What I mean is that this task must be performed. When it is finished, all will be over. You will be so well paid that you will not need to work again.'

Lance shrugged. He still felt uncomfortable. He had behaved boorishly. 'Go on. I understand now.' He wanted to get it over with so that he could absent himself from the presence of this disturbingly beautiful woman with the mark of his hand on her face. 'What is this task?'

'Do not be in such a hurry. First, I will explain about my husband and his elephants. Then I will explain about my reasons. Then I will tell you what I want you to do. That is a logical sequence.'

Lance sighed and settled back in his chair. 'All right. It's your story, tell it your own way.' He was mortally tired and there was fear growing in his stomach, a tight ball of it. Bruun was being patient. Lance had no threads, no leads, no lines, nothing. And in time Bruun would find him as simply as this woman had found him. When you are six-foot-two and blond, it is not easy to hide, especially not when the only places where you feel at home, jungles and savannahs, are also the places where news of your presence travels fastest.

Perhaps he should have taken Burger's offer of helping to hide him.

'My husband, when he was with the Colonial Office, a branch of the English Government, was very keen on conservation of animals. When the black states where he had worked were given independence and he saw the animals going, what he called an unstemmable tide of slaughter, he decided to turn what he could not stop into a good thing for himself.'

She was echoing her husband's very words, Lance knew. It was eerie, like hearing the dead man speak through the mouth of his wife.

'He started buying up ivory. In the nineteen-fifties and well into the sixties, he told me, ivory was incredibly cheap. About 1970 the elephants got scarcer and the prices rose.

'It was about this time that he quarrelled with his partner, a Chinese from Singapore. They split the ivory and each went his own way. They also divided the territory. The partner got India and China. Matthew got Africa.

'Into the eighties. You know the story from there.' She waited for Lance to nod. 'Matthew dreamed of shooting the very last elephant in the world. He used to tell me he had nothing against elephants, in fact rather admired them. It was only business, a commercial proposition.'

'Let me guess,' Lance interrupted her. 'He had built up this hoard of ivory over the decades. When the last elephant died, the price of ivory would rise phenomenally over a period of time and he would be a very rich man.'

'Yes. He used to say it was common-sense economics.'

'I hate to disappoint you, Madam, but that hoard of ivory is worth a lot less than you think. You see, other men have also had the same idea. For instance, Sir P. K. Pan has for years been buying ivory in Tokyo and Bangkok and Hong Kong and Singapore itself and he never sells any. The conclusion is obvious: he shares your late husband's vision.'

'P. K. Pan was my husband's partner, Mr Weber. His ivory and my husband's together constitute more than ninety per cent of all the raw ivory in the world today. Or on any future day.' She gave Lance a challenging look. He nodded; he had lost the point. 'So. To continue. It became an obsession with my husband. He had to kill the last elephant in the world. It consumed him.' She stared off into a private memory for a moment. 'You can understand why he had to kill your elephants.'

'And you can understand why I killed him.'

She gave him a long hard look. He met her gaze. 'Yes,' she said. 'I understand.'

'Good. I don't want you to get any cute notions of revenging his death. As you observed, I'm not much of a gentleman but, even if I were to hesitate, my friends would kill you.' Once more Lance waved his hand at the trees across the lawn. He felt slightly foolish making his little speech: he was, after all, himself embarked on a mission of revenge which would end only when either Bruun or he was dead. But if the hypocrisy removed a player from the board, it was worth it.

She stared at him as if he were a peculiarly revolting biological specimen, but also particularly fascinating. 'You, in your obsession with death, would have got on very well with Matthew. I assure you, revenge is the last thing in my mind. I doubt that Matthew would have wanted it. He was always going on about the law of the jungle. He could wax lyrical about what so-called civilized people could learn from Africa. Did you see him? He was buried by the time I got to Kenya.'

'I saw him. He looked like a man who's just inherited a whorehouse. His face was untouched.'

'I'm glad. He was a vain man.'

'This is macabre. Can we get on with the second part of your story.'

'We are dealing with it, Mr Weber. I sent for you because I think Matthew would have wanted it. You see, he believed that nothing was without its price. He wanted to kill your elephants and did; in return you killed him. He would have considered that fair.'

'Hardly,' Lance said sourly. 'If it hadn't been for the coincidence of the simultaneous attack on my property, I would've been on trial for my life on a charge of murder.'

She laughed. Her laughter was so genuine that after a moment he smiled gently with her. 'Matthew would've thought that ironic,' she gurgled.

'I bet.'

'Even in Africa they're – they're punctilious about such things?

'It's a large place. Standards vary. Kenya has rule of law. It was one of those things. I wouldn't have shot your husband, I don't think, if I hadn't mistaken him for one of the raiding party. I don't generally kill poachers out of hand, you know.' Suddenly he felt that her approval was tremendously important.

'Mmm. As I was saying, Matthew's compulsion to kill elephants robbed you of your livelihood, so – '

'How do you know that?'

'I asked when I was in Kenya. The barman at the hotel told me your game reserve was particularly well-known because of its elephants. So, without the elephants, no

64

game reserve and you drift off to Australia looking for work.'

Lance did not correct her misapprehension. He was still wearing cheap readymades he had bought in Nairobi and Sydney; he had not known where he would go from there and saw no point in wasting money on good quality but unsuitable clothing.

'So, it follows, that when there is a task to be performed relating to Matthew's ivory hoard, I should hire you. Matthew had a finely developed sense of natural justice. He would have wanted it.'

Lance had a sense of her husband, the man he had killed, being in the room with them. (Later, when he told Jimmy of this sensation Jimmy would nod wisely and say, But yes, of course, when you kill a man you gather his strength into yourself; every black savage knows that so why should it not apply to Lance, who was after all an honorary black savage and had a black tree-snake belt to prove it?) 'All right, so tell me what your late husband, with whom you are so miraculously in communication, wants me to do!'

'You are uneasy with the philosophy of life after death, Mr Weber?' She seemed surprised.

'Forgive me. But it is not every day I sit around a little cast-iron table with the widow of a man I killed and discuss what he would like – goddamn! – would have liked me to do.'

She opened her mouth as if to laugh, then caught the murderous look Lance threw her and decided against it. She clearly enjoyed having him at a psychological disadvantage but was not inclined to take it too far; she fingered the bruise on the side of her face.

'Very well. Matthew – *I* want you to find thirty tons of ivory that Matthew left me and bring it safely to market. For that I will pay you ten per cent of the value. Plus all necessary expenses of course. Do you know how much I'm offering you for an essentially simple task?'

'Sure. I can do simple arithmetic. Ivory is at present about fifty dollars a pound delivered in Venice or Bangkok. That's three dollars an ounce. If your husband's hoard represents, say, half of the world's total ivory stock and if a deal can be made with the man who owns the other half, your husband's onetime partner Sir P. K. Pan, to control the market, the price could well go up to, say, twenty-five dollars an ounce. That's twenty-four million dollars and my share would be two point four million dollars or something over one million pounds sterling.'

He saw her expression change.

He laughed aloud. 'Your precious Matthew told you the stuff would go as high or higher than gold by weight?'

'Yes.' She nodded to emphasize the affirmative.

'Forget it. Gold is that high because of psychological factors many centuries old. Ivory doesn't have that special charisma.'

'You cannot know that twenty-five dollars is the upper limit!'

'Greed turns even a beautiful woman ugly, Madam. And I do know. It is what your Matthew would have called a simple commerical matter, had he ever bothered to investigate it. At twenty-five dollars it becomes economically feasible to produce plastics that are totally indistinguishable from genuine ivory even by experts. So,' he mimicked her style of speech, 'when genuine ivory goes over twenty-five dollars an ounce, the commercial manufacturers step in and ruin the market with their ersatz goods.'

She gave him a look of reappraisal. It was not only the unexpected authority of knowledge, it was the rapidity with which he had turned the dominance tables on her. It was probably dangerous to take him at his face value of a handsome empty-headed hick down on his luck. Lance could see the wheels turning in her brain – though he suspected she would have phrased the results more elegantly.

'Twenty-four million dollars,' she finally said. 'About twelve million pounds.'

'After you make all the "ifs" come out right,' Lance said. 'If you find the ivory wherever your husband hid it. If you manage to transport it to market without the scum of the earth descending on you to take it for themselves. If you can make a deal with Pan to control the market. If you can survive the attempts Pan will undoubtedly make to pirate your share. If the artificial ivory manufacturers don't have a technical breakthrough that permits them to make the stuff for a couple of pennies a hundredweight.'

Her lips were compressed. They had been full and red, now they were a straight pink line. She was quivering. Lance thought she was about to burst into tears. But it was rage and he watched in fascination as the emotions fled across her face while she tried to control it. It took three minutes and he concluded that, if she could harness so much expression at will rather than in rage, she could be the greatest thing the theatre had ever seen. When it was over, he was almost disappointed. He felt a sense of loss that he would shortly leave this intriguing woman's presence forever; there was a great deal more of her to know than the bland, beautiful exterior.

'Will you do it?' she finally asked.

'No. Thank you for the offer but I'm already retired.' He rose. At the door her voice stopped him.

'One-fifth, Mr Weber. Five million dollars.'

He turned. 'I'll tell you something to make amends for slapping your face. You're not poor, you're young and beautiful. If you want to live to enjoy all of that, forget that ivory your husband buried somewhere in Africa. He already died for it. Unless you have a deathwish, leave it alone.'

He was at the edge of the terrace when she called him from the door. 'How did you know the ivory is buried in Africa, Mr Weber?'

He shook his head and ran down the steps, wondering how a man as transparent as Matthew Ellimore managed to find and win and hold a woman such as this one not only in matrimony but in respect and love and obedience – goddamnit! – even beyond the grave.

Jimmy effortlessly picked up a couple of Swedish tourists and they went on the town. Lance got roaring drunk but failed to drown the badger of fear gnawing away in his stomach. Soon Jimmy would go back to his calculator and his financial reports and then Lance would be alone again, waiting for Bruun to come for him. Waiting. In the morning Jimmy just as effortlessly got rid of the two Swedes while Lance nursed his hangover with raw eggs, Worcester sauce and vodka.

'What now?' Jimmy asked after the girls had left.

Lance shrugged. 'Very little. I find a lawyer and tell him to find me Bruun. Same way the widow Ellimore found me. You go on back to Brussels.'

Jimmy shook his head. 'I'm in no hurry. Where will you find a lawyer?'

'In the yellow pages.'

Jimmy snorted. 'Man, you need me! You'll get nothing but shysters that way.'

'So, how would you find a lawyer?' Lance snapped.

'Ask my London lawyer to recommend a colleague who specializes in that kind of work.'

'Okay,' Lance said dispiritedly. Then he had an idea. 'Hey! I'll ask my bank here to recommend somebody too and put them both to work.'

They made the telephone calls and made appointments for the next day with the specialists recommended. In the afternoon Jimmy took Lance shopping, insisting that he could not visit a top lawyer looking like a walking fire sale. In the evening they dined at the Dorchester and went to bed early.

The attorneys the next day disappointed Lance. Neither would be drawn into anything more positive than stating that they thought he was probably wasting his money: if the South African Police had failed to find Bruun, private efforts were unlikely to succeed. With both men Lance had to insist that he was desperate for even the smallest scrap of information before they would undertake the commission. One said outright that it was unprofessional to take on hopeless cases.

Lance, depressed, sat silently in the back of the taxi with Jimmy. They went back to the Dorchester to pack. Jimmy had spoken to Sambo on the phone and the head of the clan had insisted Lance stay with them in Brussels if he had no better plan of his own. Lance had no plan of his own at all. They had already checked in for their flight at Heathrow when the man with the moustache approached them and held out his leather-cased card to Lance. Jimmy stretched his hand past Lance and took the card, read it and then gave it back.

'Police,' Jimmy said. 'What can we do for you?'

'First, you can show identification.'

Lance did not like the man's tone, nor, for that matter, his prissy little moustache, but Jimmy pulled out his passport and Lance followed suit.

'You'll come with me.'

This was too much even for the courteous Jimmy. 'First, you'll give our passports back,' he said mildly. 'Then you'll explain what you want. Then we will decide.'

The policeman coloured and slapped the passports in Jimmy's outstretched hand. Jimmy gave one to Lance.

'Come into the office and I'll tell you what it's about.' The man strode off.

Lance and Jimmy stood looking at his back. After ten paces he sensed they were not following and turned around. He stared at them angrily for a moment, coloured again, then strode back. 'Two hard cases, huh?' he snapped.

Jimmy and Lance did not reply.

'It's about a murder. You are required to assist the police with their enquiries.'

'You mean requested,' Lance said. 'Go get a man in uniform, then we'll talk to you.' It was just possible this little snot was one of Bruun's.

The man stared at him for nearly half a minute before turning on his heel and marching away very quickly. He returned in five minutes with a uniformed constable who identified himself when Jimmy asked for his papers.

'All right,' Jimmy said, 'lead the way, squire.'

By now the other passengers were no longer staring at them and had opened a three-foot cordon sanitaire around them.

'You want to see British racialism at its finest, you only have to come through Heathrow,' Jimmy said to Lance, making no attempt to lower his voice.

'You know the plainclothes man personally?' Lance asked the uniformed policeman.

'Yes, sir.'

'Okay. Thanks. Then you can go.'

The plainclothes policeman led them into a glass-walled office that contained a desk and three chairs and absolutely nothing else except the bald man sitting behind the desk. He waved Lance and Jimmy to seats. The plainclothes man who had fetched them stood.

'Our plane leaves in ten minutes,' Jimmy said when he was seated. 'You can have five of those. Unless you've said something to interest us by then, you'll have to arrest us to keep us here.'

The man behind the desk looked at them for a long moment.

'Your abrupt subordinate offended my black friend,' Lance said.

'Yeah. We're ever so sorry. You're Mr Weber.'

'Right. How can we help you?'

70

'Do you know a Mrs Ellimore?'

'Yes, I met her once.'

'In what connection?'

'To offer me a job. Who's she murdered?'

The policeman ignored the question. 'What job?'

'To recover and market some ivory that belonged to her late husband.'

'Do you have any idea of its worth?'

'About ten, maybe twelve, million pounds of your money. If she . . .'

'If she what?'

'It's not like going down to the bank and drawing a deposit. A lot of other people are also going to be after that ivory.'

'There's your motive,' Moustache said behind Lance.

'Tough people?' the one behind the desk asked.

Lance nodded.

'Tougher than you, Mr Weber?

'Much.' Lance wondered how the hell the policeman knew who he was.

'I saw you play your last game,' the bald one said. 'My son was heartbroken when you stopped playing.'

'What happened to Mrs Ellimore?' Lance asked. It would be a pity if such a splendid specimen died for mere money.

'She's all right. Look, you seem to know something about it. Will you put off your flight and help us? That's a polite and courteous request,' he added, looking at Jimmy.

Lance looked at Jimmy, who shrugged.

'All right. But that is everything I know.' He had not expected the surge of relief he had felt when the policeman said Esmeralda Ellimore was unharmed.

Moustache drove them to Lamberhurst in an unmarked Rover. He was sullenly resentful. Lance refrained from questioning him. He would find out what had happened soon enough from the men on the spot. They were taken

71

to a police station in a town neither Jimmy nor Lance recognized and given coffee. A brisk man in a baggy suit introduced himself as Simps. Lance went through the Ellimore saga with him from the first contact in Sydney to the moment he left her, leaving out that he had killed her husband.

When there were no further questions, Simps said, 'She accused you, of course. Said you hit her through the face so hard she landed on the other side of the room.'

Jimmy said mildly, 'You have brought us here under false pretences. We shall answer no more questions until a lawyer is present.'

Simps looked startled. 'Oh no! You're not suspects. We know you were eating dinner at the Dorchester when it happened. I'm so sorry I haven't made that clear.'

'What happened?' Lance asked Simps.

'I hope you have a strong stomach.' Simps pushed some large photographs across the table.

Lance flipped through them and handed them to Jimmy. 'Bruun,' he said.

'Who?' asked the policeman.

'It was done with a meatcleaver, right?'

'Yes. You know who did it?'

'I think so. If you get in touch with the Brighton Police and with Brigadier Rocco Burger of the South African Police, you can compare notes. The common factor in these murders is me, my late brother, Ewart and the late Colonel Jacques Roux.' He explained about the murders of his parents and Briony Roux and ended by saying, 'I doubt the Ellimores ever had any contact with anybody but me.'

Simps looked bewildered. 'It's so . . . so . . .'

'There's an additional problem. Many people are convinced Theodore Bruun is dead. Even if he is alive, he is so horribly disfigured that he would be instantly recognizable if he ever appeared in public.'

'But you don't think he's dead?'

'No,' Lance said firmly.

'How did you ever get involved in this . . . this . . .' Again words failed the policeman. Such things were simply outside his experience. He looked anxiously at Lance and Jimmy, as if they were alien beings, likely to erupt violently at any moment.

'It's a long story,' said Lance.

'Excuse me.' Simps hurried out.

An hour later a uniformed constable told them the best pub if they wanted a meal was the second one along on the left. They ate and waited another hour at the police station before Simps returned to them. He again carried the photographs of the dismembered body of the little Spaniard who had been Esmeralda Ellimore's servant.

'How did she get away?' Lance asked.

'She had left her car at the front door. When the butler went to drive it round to the garage, they attacked him. She heard, saw, ran out the back and rode her horse bareback through them. One of the meatcleavers slashed her dress and broke one of the horse's ribs. She's some woman.' Simps shivered but not with admiration. He could have said: She's some black widow spider. 'I've spoken to Brigadier Burger and the man in charge of the Brighton murders.'

'Well?'

Simps shrugged. 'What they know is what you told me. Brigadier Burger says Bruun is dead.' Burger had also added the detail that Bruun had been crippled by Lance and Jimmy shooting him in the elbows and knees and emasculated by the late Briony Roux. Simps wished the table was wider. He had walked a beat in Brixton once and, in the Army, had had a tour in Ulster, but these two well-dressed, well-spoken young men terrified him. They sat so still! Like animals waiting to pounce.

'She saw them and survived,' Lance said tightly. 'Who

were they? What did they look like? Who sent them? Where are they now?'

'That's police business, Mr Weber.' They most certainly did not want these two applying rough-and-ready interrogation methods to whichever of the attackers they managed to catch. Burger had also given him Ewart Weber's background and the fact that Jimmy had been one of Ewart's Baluba Butchers. Simps shivered again.

'I think you'd better tell me,' Lance said.

They are both still sitting in their chairs, Simps thought. But it's the way they're looking at me! 'I can't tell you,' he said, 'but Mrs Ellmiore has a room at the place you ate lunch. Thank you for helping us. We'll reach you in Brussels if we think of any more questions.'

He hurried out without offering to shake hands.

'What a funny man,' Lance said, amazed.

Jimmy looked hard at him. Sometimes Lance could be very naïve. 'Burger told him more than he need have. He's frightened shitless.' Lance was still looking blank. 'Of us,' Jimmy added.

'Christ! She warned them while they were still murdering that poor little devil. You'd think they'd have caught at least one.'

'They wouldn't be so ignorant if they had one to beat the truth out of. Come on. Let's go have a word with your friend the widow.'

Outside, on the pavement, Lance said, 'You realize what's happened, of course?'

'No. I'm as confused as that policeman. Unless Matthew Ellimore was another of the multitude who made Bruun into an enemy.'

'Maybe,' Lance said. 'But there's another way of seeing it. Bruun's looking for me, maybe having an eye kept on me. Say he's heard the rumour of the ivory hoard being up for grabs from the widow – '

'Yes, go on! He always was a greedy bastard.'

'When I go see the widow, he puts the two together.'

'And?'

'I don't know.' Lance sounded deflated. 'That's the only explanation that accounts for him being able to act only a day and a half after I saw her.'

If you believe Bruun is alive, Jimmy thought. He said nothing. He had seen Bruun dying with his own eyes, he told himself. When Jimmy had last seen him, Bruun was as good as dead, the tribeswomen expending as much effort to keep him alive as on further tortures. Bruun was already out of his mind; it was possible that the ingenuity of the tribeswomen could have kept him alive another two or three days of agony. It was impossible to escape, impossible to survive if he escaped, and even if he survived he would be a vegetable kept chained under a table by some tyrant as a lesson to would-be supplanters.

'It's the only explanation,' Lance said fervently. 'Even if Matthew Ellimore spent half his long life making enemies, the odds against those also being the enemies of Briony Roux, my parents and me are . . .'

Jimmy touched his arm. They were passing through the lounge of the inn, a small room. Esmeralda Ellimore was rising at the far end of the narrow room, her fingers pointing.

'Murderers,' she said, her voice level and penetrating.

People stared at them. Jimmy smiled at them. 'Only on Thursdays and Saturdays,' he said. 'Other days we go in for grand larceny, a little arson and extortion with menaces.' People turned their eyes away.

'Sit down!' Lance told the woman.

'Murderers!' she hissed. 'You couldn't even do it yourself!'

So she had seen the killers!

'Relax and sit down,' Lance said.

'*Bolle de mendego!*' she hissed.

'Balls of butter,' Jimmy translated. 'She means we're cowards.'

'Those same people killed my parents and the widow of a friend and the employees on my farm,' Lance said. 'Please sit down.'

She stared at him for a long moment, then sank into her chair. All one side of her face was discoloured where he had struck her. Lance and Jimmy drew up chairs. There was an uncomfortable silence. Then Jimmy pushed his chair back and went to the bar, where the landlord was resting his elbows on the scarred oak while he considered interfering. Lance waited for Jimmy to come back with the drinks.

'Mrs Ellimore – '

'I think you'd better call me Esmeralda.'

'Lance. This is Jimmy.'

'After all, we're in the same danger.' She nodded at Jimmy.

'Did you see them?' Lance asked.

'Yes. They were Eastern.'

'And the police didn't catch one of them!' Jimmy said.

'Where in the East?' Lance asked. For all he knew, she could think of Arabs as Easterners.

'Chinese, Japanese, I don't know.'

'How many were there?'

'Four.'

'What did they carry beside cleavers?' Jimmy asked. 'Guns?'

'Nothing. That was enough. Oh, the police asked me what the . . . the murderers wanted to do with a pair of electric curling tongs they brought with them.'

Lance had another vision; a scout for highway bandits in the Congo, caught by Sambo and bent over with his trousers down, talking just before the lit firelighter reached his anus. 'As an aid in questioning you,' he said without thinking, looking significantly at Jimmy. That

76

they intended questioning her was proof that they were after the ivory.

She choked on her drink. Her hand flashed to her mouth and she ran out of the room. The landlord came to their table. 'Are you bothering the lady?'

Lance looked up at him. 'No.'

The landlord gave them each a hard stare and went away.

'Why is it that today everyone treats us like hooligans,' Jimmy asked rhetorically.

When she came back, she had repaired her make-up and changed her clothes. The bruise was emphasized by her paleness.

'Would you recognize any of them again?' Lance asked when she had another drink in her hand.

'No.'

'But you saw their faces? They weren't masked?'

'No. But the light was not good. They all look alike.' She looked apologetically at Jimmy.

'What kind of car did they use?' Jimmy asked. He was sensitive to racial slights, real or imagined, only when it profited him.

She shrugged. 'Common English sort of car. Not too big.'

'Did they speak?' Lance asked. 'Did you recognize the language?'

'Yes. Portuguese. That's why I swore at you in Portuguese just now. I apologize.'

'Macao,' Jimmy said. 'What do you think?'

Lance nodded thoughtfully. 'Thank you,' he said, rising. 'Take care they don't get you the second time round. Hire a bodyguard. Good luck.'

'Sit down!' she said, her voice cold. The landlord looked up.

Lance sat down. Jimmy had not risen; he smiled slightly.

'I've told you what I know. The very whole truth. Now you must tell me what you know.'

Lance shrugged. He told the story quickly. He was getting practised in it. He concluded: 'Bruun wants my life and your ivory. When our paths crossed, he acted. When I left Sydney, the news of the ivory hoard's owner being dead and leaving a widow had just started circulating. I guess it must have come to his ears. Perhaps before I heard it. Anyway, others will be looking for you right now and perhaps they'll get in Bruun's way. You're going to need that bodyguard.'

She had become even paler during his recital. Now she put a hand on his. 'I'm so sorry I accused you. Please believe me.'

'It's forgotten,' he said. Her hand was pleasantly warm. When she took it back, he rose again, noticing that Jimmy remained seated, smiling more broadly than ever.

'I shall come with you to Macao,' she said.

'What?'

'I shall come with you to Macao,' she said.

'Don't be ridiculous. I'm going to trace a man and kill him. All you should be interested in is keeping clear of people who want to ask you questions with the aid of electric curling tongs.'

She clenched her hands on the table but her voice was calm. 'You make a real way with words, don't you.'

'Have a real way with words,' Lance said automatically. 'Tagging around with us is like setting yourself up as a bull's-eye at Bisley.'

'Target shooting. Phuh!'

'You're the one with the dead butler,' Lance snapped.

'And your parents, your employees, your friend's widow!'

Lance very nearly slapped her face again.

'I have as good a reason for revenge,' she said. 'Good butlers are very hard to find and Spanish-speaking ones almost non-existent.'

Lance suppressed an urge to burst out laughing. She was in dead earnest. 'Vengeance is mine, saith the Lord,' he said instead, turning away. He was beginning to understand why Simps wanted to admire her from afar. She was likely to be too much for little men – and for many big men, too.

'Don't mock her,' Jimmy said. 'We may need her.'

Lance turned back to the table. 'How's that, Jimmy?'

'We get to Macao, we catch one or two of the killers. They were hired by a series of middle-men. You can hire any scum in Macao. We find Bruun took the precaution of killing one of the middle-men. The chain is broken. You're back right here in this overheated lounge bar of a provincial English public house, looking forward to nothing but fear and uncertainty.'

Lance shivered. 'That's a chance I have to take,' he almost snarled. 'I don't see how having a fifth wheel on the wagon changes that,' he nodded to Esmeralda, 'however decorative.'

'But it does,' Jimmy said. 'Sit down.'

Lance sat down. He had always trusted Jimmy with his life and he knew that Jimmy was more intelligent and more experienced in the ways of the world than he. Jimmy was also a volunteer in a dangerous business that he could have avoided without any loss of honour. Jimmy owed Lance no debts – indeed, the boot was on the other foot. Lance had never felt he was entitled to call on Sambo and the whole tribe's professed debt to his late brother and had set it aside firmly in Brussels when it had been mentioned by Sambo.

'Bruun, or whoever it is after you, has – '

'Bruun,' Lance said firmly. 'Bruun.'

'Okay. I believe you. He's demonstrated he wants that ivory. He'll play you along, enjoying your fear, after you hit the broken link in the chain out of Macao. Who knows how long? But if you cross him on the matter of the ivory he wants – which you can do simply by taking Mrs Ellimore under your protection – he has to act against you. Pride and greed will make him act. And the more often he has to act, the better the chance of some link in the chain remaining intact instead of being broken. We'll be waiting.'

'I don't like women in fire zones.'

'You don't mind beating up on them.'

'Beating them up.' Lance turned back to Jimmy. 'She's a bigger liability than you can imagine. She's going to get us looked at wherever we go.'

Esmeralda laughed aloud. 'Two men over six feet, one blond as a Viking, the other black as the Styx, you're not going to be noticed? Don't be ridiculous, you!'

Lance ignored her. This was childish. He wished Jimmy had not brought it up in front of her.

'She volunteered,' Jimmy said.

'If I'm to be your bait,' she said, 'I must have a reward.'

'I thought we'd come to the price,' Lance said. 'Get this straight: If we decide to take you – if – it'll be on our terms.'

'The price,' she said, 'is that you help me find my ivory and bring it to market after I help you kill this man.'

Jimmy and Lance both looked at her. Lance said, 'We're quite capable of killing one deranged cripple ourselves, thank you. Your help will be required, if required, only to find him.'

She sat back in her chair as if he had slapped her again. He could once more see the wheels revolving in her mind: she had again pushed him too far and was resolving not to do it again. But she could not restrain herself. 'Damn you! I have as much right as you to call this man to account for murdering my servant. My loyal servant!' A tear rolled from each eye and, heedless of her make-up, she smeared them away with alternate flicks of her hand, wincing when she flicked away the tear on the bruised cheek. 'Matthew would have gone after him.'

'Sure,' Lance said. 'We'll stand in for you just like you want to stand in for Matthew. We're old-fashioned. We let the men do the killing, including that done for their women. All right.' He turned to Jimmy. 'I don't like taking her. She could do something stupid. You've heard her.' Jimmy had started this discussion in front of the woman; if she did not like it she could lump it. 'I'll put up the bait myself.'

'Twenty-five million dollars or more?'

'No, not that much. But I have about eight and can raise another two or three against my signature alone.'

Jimmy looked at him with new respect. Then he shook his head. 'Forget it. Bruun will see right through it as a trap. He can always try for your money after he's got her ivory.'

Lance sat silently for a while. Jimmy had laid out the cases and now expected him to make a decision. 'You know, if Bruun catches up with me, he's not going to regard you as a supernumary and let you go.'

Jimmy nodded. His smile broadened. Lance remembered a day when Jimmy had arrived at the camp with the head of one of his brothers under his arm. He had found the head stuck on a pole beside the road. Bruun's work: Jimmy had a stake too.

'Okay,' Lance said. 'She can come.' He turned to her. 'Stay out from underfoot and do nothing on your own initiative, understand? I don't want your life on my conscience as well.'

She nodded. 'Thank you.'

'Let's rent a car and pack her up and go back to London,' Lance said.

'I have my car outside. I don't want anything from the house. I don't want to go back there. It's too . . . too . . .'

Lance looked at Jimmy, whose smiled flashed on and off: just now this woman had offered to help them kill Bruun.

Her car was a Rolls so old that Lance's medium-size suitcase and Jimmy's overnight bag filled the trunk completely. Esmeralda had her handbag and a vanity case which she kept with her. She held the keys out between the men and Lance took them.

'Drive carefully,' she said. 'Matthew bought this car the same year you were born.'

Jimmy held the rear door for her with exaggerated gestures, raising an eyebrow at Lance.

'Do you know what everything does?' she asked Lance when he settled behind the wheel.

'Sure. That switch panel's right out of a Landrover.'

Jimmy sniggered. Lance said, 'Shh! I'm listening for the clock.'

After that they drove in silence until Jimmy said, several miles up the A21, 'That car's following us.'

Lance looked in the mirror. 'There's a lot of traffic.'

'All going a steady fifty?'

'Maybe not. Let's find out.'

Lance kept driving steadily. At one of the villages that lined the road, he made a left turn, two rights and another left to bring him back on the A21. The lights of the other car stayed in his mirror. 'They don't care that we know they're there.'

'And now they know we know,' Jimmy said. 'Do you want them?'

'Yes. Hold on.' He ran the Rolls up to seventy-five. There seemed to be some power in reserve.

Jimmy turned the inside mirror so that he did not have to crane his neck to use it. Lance could still see the lights of the pursuit in the wing mirrors.

'They're closing up,' Jimmy said.

Lance accelerated a little. The old car was very near its

limit at eighty-five. He hoped new tyres had been fitted some time in its twenty-eight years, preferably recently.

'Fifteen feet,' Jimmy said. 'They're going to try their luck. Let's give them a surprise.'

Lance agreed. 'Hold on.' He stood up on the brake.

Esmeralda, anxious about the pursuit but misled by the lack of tension inside the car into thinking that no immediate action was contemplated, crashed into the picnic table on the back of the front passenger seat and fell to the floor.

Lance had not known a car that old would have vacuum-servo brakes. The following car crunched into the back of the Rolls. Lance let go of the brake momentarily. Esmeralda, rising between the seats, saw Lance's hands making small, slow, sure movements on the controls. He seemed to be in no hurry. Jimmy was holding onto the doorpull with one hand while with the other he returned the rearview mirror to its orignal position. Lance watched the wing mirrors as he braked again. The little car behind would have to go beside the Rolls. The driver chose to go left. Lance increased the pressure on the brake pedal, pulled on the handbrake, swung the wheel. The rear end of the heavy car slewed sideways and caught the small one just in front of its door. In the mirrors they could see its tail-lights twirling as it spun away. Lance brought the Rolls to a stop and reversed. Esmeralda was cursing steadily in Spanish. Lance brought the Rolls to a stop.

'What have you done to Matthew's car?' she asked in English in a strangled voice.

'We'll buy you another,' Jimmy said. 'It's only a car.'

'If I never hear Matthew's name again, it'll be too soon,' Lance said.

They climbed out and slammed their doors, cutting off her retort.

The small hatchback was on its side. They unceremoniously pushed it over on its wheels.

'Only one,' Lance said. 'He must have thought she was alone in the car. I'll deal with him. You make sure there's no metal cutting into the tyres on our car.'

Jimmy grunted and went back to the Rolls, where Esmeralda was standing, surveying the damage.

Lance opened the damaged door of the hatchback by the simple expedient of taking hold of it, putting his foot against the wheel and tearing the door off its hinges. He unfastened the seatbelt and pulled the unconscious driver clear. As he hauled his captive over his shoulder, he felt the resilient flesh where there should be hard muscle. 'We caught a woman,' he called to Jimmy.

Jimmy grunted. There was a tearing sound. The whole nearside rear wing of the Rolls came away. Jimmy looked at the piece of sculpted metal in his hands, then cast it beside the road.

'Matthew always – '

'You get in the front,' Lance said to Esmeralda. He threw the unconscious pursuer into the rear seat of the Rolls. 'You drive, Jimmy.'

'You fucking maniac!' His captive was awake and trying to scramble out of the Rolls. 'Do you want to kill us all? See what you've done to my car!'

Lance twisted her arm up and pushed her back into the Rolls. He pulled the door to behind him. Jimmy drove off just as the first car pulled off the road at the 'accident'. Esmeralda noted that it had all happened very quickly indeed though neither of the men had once made a hurried movement.

'You're hurting my arm, you bastard!'

'Be quiet while I think or I'll tear it out of your shoulder.' Lance gave an extra twist for emphasis.

'Ouch!' After a moment. 'What do you think with, you fucking – ' Another twist. 'Ouch!' Then there was silence.

'What are you going to do with her?' Esmeralda asked. 'She isn't one of those . . . she wasn't at . . .'

Lance ignored the questions. 'Okay. First, let me tell you chivalry is dead. If you want to play with the big boys, you take your licks like a big boy. I have two dead parents and a lot of dead friends. Believe me, being a woman gets you no consideration.'

'Let go my arm, you Neanderthal! You're tearing it – Aargh!'

'Who sent you?'

'Nobody! Aargh! Please!' She was sobbing, all the defiance gone.

'Bruun must have sunk pretty low if this is the best quality helper he can afford,' Jimmy said disgustedly.

'Please! I'll tell you anything!'

'If you don't, next time I'm going to put my foot against your chest and tear your arm off for real.'

'Sweet Jesus! Please! For God's sake, I'll tell you anything you want to know! Anything!'

'Who sent you?'

'Nobody. I – Aargh! Please, mister, please! I came on my own!'

In the front of the car Jimmy chuckled at this unlikely story. 'Give her back to Bruun and make it known she told us everything.'

Lance was in no mood for jokes. He put his new Church brogue on the woman's breast as he swung her body about, changed hands on her arm and started pulling steadily.

She screamed.

'In about twenty seconds your arm is going to come out of its socket,' Lance said. 'In forty seconds the flesh will tear, in a minute you'll be one-armed. Then I start on your other arm.'

She kept screaming.

'What kind of savage are you?' Esmeralda shouted.

'Be quiet, woman,' Jimmy told her. 'You wanted to come. You're here on Lance's terms.'

Lance stopped pulling but kept up the existing tension. 'Quiet!'

The screaming turned to sobbing. 'You should have thought of pain before you signed up with people who chop up old people and children in their beds with meatcleavers. Now, for the last time, who sent you?'

'Nobody-e-e-e-e!'

When there was only sobbing in the car, Jimmy said, 'Save it, Lance. We'll try something more subtle like electric curling tongs next.'

'Please! I came on my own! All I wanted to do was ask her to give the ivory to the World Wildlife Fund.'

Lance let her go and she slumped in the corner of the car. 'Who did you want to ask? What ivory?'

'Mrs Ellimore. I didn't know she kept gorillas as well as slaughtering defenceless – '

'Try not to get yourself into more trouble than you have already,' Lance said gently. 'Now answer my question, What ivory?'

'Do you live in the Dark Ages?'

'I'd pull her other arm this time,' Jimmy said with a fat chuckle.

'On television! It was on the news that the attack was connected with Matthew Ellimore's holdings of half the world's ivory.' The words were running over themselves. Despite the defiance she was frightened out of her wits. She sat hugging her throbbing arm, sobbing intermittently.

'And you wanted to ask her to give it to the conservationists?' Lance asked incredulously.

'Yes! I told you – Please don't start again!'

He had not made a move towards her.

'Christ!' Jimmy said. 'On the bloody television news. Now we'll really have to look smart.'

Lance too was thinking of every adventurer in the world who had not yet heard that the Ellimore ivory hoard was up for grabs, being apprised of the situation and descending on Esmeralda.

'Well, what about it?' their captive said aggressively.

'What about what?' Lance asked.

'The ivory, of course. Can I have it for the animals?'

Esmeralda said, 'No.'

Jimmy laughed and she cast him a dirty look.

Lance said, 'Forget that ivory, Miss. We're the nice guys. The baddies won't ask so politely if they think you know where it is. A lot of people are going to die for that ivory.'

'But –'

Jimmy stopped the car. 'If you don't need her any more, Lance?'

'No.'

Jimmy climbed out and held the door.

'Look here, you can't just drop me –'

Jimmy pulled her out. 'It's best if you don't know where we go. For your own safety.'

'What about my car that you –'

'That's the price of experience,' Esmeralda said sweetly. 'My husband is turning in his grave for what you did to his car.'

'What I did? Let him spin like a top! What you did!'

She ran after the car as they drove off. 'You haven't heard the last of me!' were the last words they heard.

'She recovered very quickly,' Jimmy said. 'Somehow I don't think you were cut out to be a torturer, Lance.'

'I don't think that's funny.' To his horror, Lance recalled that he had had every intention of pulling her arm right off her body. He had very nearly made a terrible mistake.

'Three first-class to Hong Kong,' Lance said. He gave their names and paid with his Amex card. He had always travelled economy before but had an idea Esmeralda

87

Ellimore was quite unaware that there was any but first class. Her extravagance when he had accompanied her on the shopping expedition had shocked him. He took the tickets. 'We'll make our onwards bookings there,' he answered the question. 'Excuse me, can you tell me just exactly where Macao is?' He had been too embarrassed to ask Jimmy or Esmeralda. He knew it was in the East and ivory and other smuggled goods, including drugs, passed through there. He also had a vague idea that Portuguese Jesuits were somehow connected with the place.

The attractive girl behind the counter looked up at him, studying his face for the first time. Perhaps he should have asked where the hell the place was before he bought three first-class tickets, one way only. She had a little map. 'Here, next to Hong Kong,' she said. 'Only forty miles away because this map is so small. Are you sure you want to go there?'

'Oh, another entrepot the Chinese allow as a shop window,' Lance said offhandedly. He had read in *National Geographic* that the Chinese consider Hong Kong a shop window on the world. The girl looked impressed. 'Sure I want to go there.' He moved away from the counter but stopped short when he heard the voice.

'I wanna go where he's going.'

The man was pointing at Lance. He must have heard Lance's conversation with the ticket clerk. Lance had been meant to notice. Lance stood and watched the girl write the man's ticket. He also watched the man. He was black, big, dressed in a well-cut lightweight suit. Over his arm he carried a tan lightweight raincoat. The tag on the briefcase in his hand indicated he had flown UTA from Dakar.

The strikingly blonde girl behind the black man kept staring at Lance. He wondered why she did not smile if she was trying to attract his attention, then dismissed her from his mind.

The black man paid for his ticket by credit card and headed past Lance for Jimmy and Esmeralda, walking by Lance without looking at him. Lance followed him. Lance did not hear the blonde girl saying to the ticket clerk, 'Me too. Same place they're all going.'

Four of the five suitcases on the trolley belonged to Esmeralda. 'Check the luggage, please.' Lance gave the porter the tickets. He wanted to hear what this purposeful-looking man had to say.

'Mrs Ellimore?'

'Yes.'

'I just missed you at the Dorchester. I should like a few words with you in private.'

'Who are you?' Lance asked.

'I'm not talking to you.'

Jimmy put down the overnight bag he was holding. 'Who are you?'

'Stay out of this, Brother.'

'Perhaps you'll tell me,' Esmeralda said, smiling brilliantly. She had been in a black mood all day, the events of the past few days catching up with her.

'Daniel Drang. I work for the Organization for African Unity and I'd –'

'Let's see some identification,' Jimmy said, holding out his hand. Drang looked at his hand as if contemplating spitting in it. 'Mrs Ellimore's unlikely to discuss anything with you until we're satisfied you intend her no harm.'

Drang took his passport and a card from his wallet and handed them to Jimmy, who studied both before handing them back.

'In private,' Drang said.

'Just get on with it,' Lance said.

'I told you before, I'm not talking to you.'

'I should think he's one of those who talk to white people only when it's absolutely unavoidable. Right, *Brother*?'

Drang nodded. 'I'd like to talk to you about the ivory your husband stole from Africa,' he said to Esmeralda.

Lance sighed and Jimmy chuckled. Esmeralda looked from the one to the other.

'And for which worthy cause do *you* want it?' Jimmy asked.

Esmeralda laughed.

'I want it returned to those it was taken from and who need it most, the Africans.'

'On behalf of the OAU?' Jimmy asked.

'I'm on holiday.'

'Ah, in your private parts,' Esmeralda said.

'Capacity,' Jimmy said offhandedly.

'Join the queue,' Lance told Drang. He took Esmeralda by the elbow and guided her around Daniel Drang. The porter came back with their tickets and Jimmy gave him a pound note.

'Uncle Tom!'

'Sure. And you did all your Uncle Tomming while you picked up that fine American accent,' Jimmy said.

'We'll talk again, Brother. I'll show you the pictures of the starving children – '

Jimmy shook his head. 'Try it on somebody else, Drang. If a big man like you is a personnel officer like it says on your papers, I'm a chimpanzee. And if you're on holiday, I'm with the CIA – the same people that trained you.'

Drang said nothing, standing quite still, staring at Jimmy. Jimmy shrugged and walked around him.

'That one's going to be trouble,' Jimmy told Lance, indicating with his head Drang on the far side of the departure lounge.

'One civil servant on holiday? You're getting paranoid.'

'He's OAU muscle and he's not on holiday. He's here semi-officially.'

'Oh dear,' Lance said. 'That means he can call up reinforcements'

'But I thought the OAU was like the United Nations,' Esmeralda said. 'They won't steal my ivory.'

Jimmy and Lance looked at her, Jimmy pityingly, Lance blankly. Then Lance said, 'Everything's different in Africa,' as if that settled the matter. He turned back to Jimmy.

She was not having it. 'How different?'

'Twenty-five million dollars is a lot of money in Africa,' Jimmy said. 'And the people who run the OAU haven't x centuries of Westminster tradition to fall back on. It's the quick and the hungry, you know.'

She did not, but could see Lance was impatient. She nodded.

'They're being stupid, sending the heavies,' Lance said. 'They should go to court about the ownership of the ivory.'

'No.' Jimmy shook his head. 'Then maybe it stays in the ground. She's the only one who knows where it is.' He looked at Esmeralda.

Drang was heading towards them. 'We can come to an arrangement,' he said to Esmeralda. 'We could let you keep some, say a quarter. For the other three-quarters we would provide legal export papers and, further, offer police protection until the ivory was shipped.'

She did not even shake her head. She looked at Lance. Lance looked at Jimmy.

Jimmy said, 'You already heard our names at the booking desk. Maybe you didn't make the connection. Lance is the brother of Ewart Weber, Major Ewart Weber. I'm the brother of Sambo, who was the major's sergeant.'

Drang's eyes widened for a moment. He looked closely at Lance, then at Jimmy. Finally he spoke. 'So? What am I supposed to do, melt away in fear before your big brother comes to beat me up?'

'Go home and catch your thrills reading the files,'

Jimmy said. 'I suppose the OAU has files, just like people,' he added tauntingly.

'Of course,' Drang said levelly, refusing to be angered. He turned on his heel and stalked away.

'That's funny,' Jimmy said. 'He and I both once worked for the same people.'

'Who's that?' Lance asked.

'The CIA.'

'Huh?'

'They trained every black security man in the world. And they paid your brother and us in the Congo.'

'I didn't know that,' Lance said.

'Drang's going to be a nuisance, following us everywhere,' Jimmy said.

Lance shook his head. 'Let him. He'll lose patience before long when he finds out we have no intention of going anywhere near the ivory.'

Esmeralda swallowed. She fingered the bruise on her face. She wanted the ivory but she wanted more to stay alive. And, more than anything, she wanted to be there when they killed the man who had her servant murdered. The servant had been under her protection. Murdering him had been a foul insult calling for revenge, whatever Lance Weber might think of the proper roles of men and women. He was not Spanish. It amused her to think that the years with Matthew Ellimore, that most English of Englishmen – belonging so much to a vanished past that he was almost a cariacature of himself, had only strengthened those facets of her character that were essentially Spanish.

Perhaps Lance was right. She had not much stomach for blood. But if she had to, she would steel herself to kill this man Bruun. It would be her duty. She had never failed in her duty.

And her final duty to Matthew was to bring his ivory out of Africa and sell it to the highest bidder.

Macao

At Karachi, Lance left the plane to breathe unprocessed air. The hot, humid blast struck his face like a blow. For a moment his senses reeled, then he straightened and smiled. The smell of the place was home. Perhaps not Africa, but near enough. He looked at Jimmy, who was walking on the other side of Esmeralda. Jimmy, too, had noticed. A current of understanding flowed between them. They were still inside a claustrophobic building but the oppression was different, lighter than that of London or Brussels. And different from the depressing formalism of the English countryside. Just out there, no further than a man could walk in half a morning, lay great open plains and sunlight unfiltered by man's excretions.

Esmeralda twitched her nose. To her the place simply smelt bad. But, to the surprise of the two men, she had noticed that they reacted differently. 'Well?' she said.

Lance shrugged helplessly and looked at Jimmy, who smiled and said nothing. They shrugged almost in unison.

'I hope no food is taken on board here,' Esmeralda said. 'This place is dirty.'

An hour before they landed at Kai Tak, Daniel Drang joined them. He sat across the aisle from Lance. He nodded politely, three times. 'What do you want in Hong Kong and Macao?' he asked. 'You can get a better price in Venice.'

Lance nodded. 'Or Paris or maybe Singapore. Since you ask politely, Mr Drang, I'll tell you. We have no interest whatsoever in that ivory. We are going to Hong Kong and Macao on private business of mine. Mrs Ellimore is with us for her own protection.'

'Against people like me?'

'Hey, the CIA left him with a sense of humour!' Jimmy said.

Drang shot Jimmy a sharp look but kept silent.

'Among others,' Lance said. 'You're wasting your time and your money following us around.'

'Is that so? Mrs Ellimore, if you have no interest in the ivory, why not let us have it? All you have to – '

'He's not interested in recovering the ivory. I am,' she said. 'But Mr Weber is right, it will be some time before I act on it. There is something I must do first.'

'If you need protection, I can offer – '

'No thank you, Mr Drang.'

Drang rose. 'You're all pretty good liars. But there ain't no way you can shake me. Right now, I'm offering a deal in which you get half. If you turn me down I'll just take everything for Africa.'

'Yesterday it was three-quarters,' Jimmy said.

'Yesterday I didn't know there was so much competition that Mrs E. here needs the protection of two big studs like you,' Drang said, smiling for the first time since they had met him. 'Think man. I'm offering official protection.'

Lance snorted. 'Official!' In Africa that meant the man with the biggest club; Drang could not be unaware of the irony.

'We can buy a whole African government for the price of a Mercedes,' Jimmy said, 'and, not to hide our talents under a bucket, we're not short of muscle. What do you offer for twelve million dollars – brains?'

Drang stood in the aisle, looking down at them, a tic at the corner of his mouth.

'Another thing,' Jimmy said, 'we'd be stupid if we believed you wouldn't cross us at the first opportunity. For Africa! Mother of God! Only an American could talk like that.'

'You just carry on Uncle Tomming to this mercenary white racialist colonial imperialist exploiter,' Drang said. 'We'll catch up with you.'

Lance let the accusation pass. He could not help the colour of his skin and the rest was untrue. 'Mr Drang, there is another consideration. The reason Mrs Ellimore is under our protection is that some very violent people are looking for her and for me. If you get in their way – '

Drang shook his head sadly. 'And your cardboard nigger cut-out don't like the way I talk. You can't frighten me with bogeymen.' He walked away.

'And that's his goodwill to all men for this year,' Jimmy said. 'People like that make me sick.'

'Save your emotions,' Lance said curtly. 'You can't change prejudiced minds. Especially the new Puritans.'

'Huh? I thought they were against sex.'

'Not really. They're against anything hidden, private. They want everything out in the open. They hate imagination.' Lance noticed that Esmeralda was staring at him but he could not stop. 'That's why the new Puritans are against the laws limiting the availability of pornography. But there's nothing permissive about it: it's a command. You shall look at pornography. The urban terrorist, who wants to simplify everything almost out of existence, he's the new Puritan.'

Esmeralda looked towards where Drang was just sinking into his seat. 'It makes sense. If you're white, you're evil. He said so much.'

'As much.'

'Well, it certainly cuts back on the amount of time spent choosing your friends,' Jimmy said but the joke failed to raise their depression. They were silent until they landed.

At the news-stand on the right after Immigration, Jimmy stopped dead. Lance bumped into him and cursed. Jimmy pointed. LONDON ZOO ELEPHANTS SLAUGHTERED.

'How could such a thing happen?' Esmeralda asked.

Lance bought a paper. The elephants had been shot, then dismembered inside their enclosure, behind their moat, by persons unknown. No meatcleavers had been left lying around but, for Lance, that had not been necessary. He pursed his lips at the further, irrelevant, information that the rhinoceri, behind the same moat but separated from the elephants by a wall, had not been harmed. Lance said, 'Bruun is sending us a message.'

After a brief, uncomfortable silence, Jimmy belatedly answered Esmeralda's question. 'A zoo isn't a bank. They have minimal security aimed mostly at making sure you pay to see the animals. Who the hell would want to steal an elephant?'

But we all know who would want to kill elephants, Lance thought: and why.

When the taxi deposited them at the Hilton, Esmeralda's nose rose visibly.

Jimmy noticed the disapproval on her face. 'At the Peninsula we'd stand out like a sore thumb,' he said.

She sniffed. Lance wondered if Matthew Ellimore had also sniffed to convey disapprobation.

'Actually,' Jimmy added, 'the Peninsula tried to put us in the annexe, so I said the hell with them.'

That seemed to satisfy her. She walked into the hotel. Jimmy winked at Lance, who had distinctly heard him tell the girl at the Dorchester 'Hilton' with nary a mention of the Peninsula.

'You've been here before,' Lance said to her as they went up in the lift. 'You didn't tell me.'

'You didn't ask.'

'And to Macao?' Goddamnit, could the woman not see it was relevant? If she or her precious dead husband had made enemies in Macao, there could just be a thousand to one chance that the death of her butler was totally unconnected with the other killings.

'Don't shout. I'm here.'

'Macao!'

'No!' She lowered her voice. 'Matthew never gambled.'

Not for money, Jimmy thought. But he shot Lance's elephants . . .

'You didn't go there. Did he? Matthew.'

'No. He said it was mostly churches and ruins.'

'So he did go there, but not with you.'

'No. He said he had never been there. What's this to go for?'

After a moment's thought, Lance derived the direction of her enquiry from her expression. 'You mean to-do.' His mother had used the word; no doubt Matthew Ellimore had too.

The lift doors opened and the bellboy led them to their suite. There were two bedrooms on either side of a sitting-room. Jimmy went immediately to the telephone, taking his notebook from his pocket. Lance tipped the bellboy who had wheeled Esmeralda's suitcases into her bedroom. Lance carried his own suitcase and Jimmy's overnight bag into the bedroom they would share. When he came out, Jimmy was putting the phone down.

'I have to go see a man who can maybe tell me how you hire a killer in Macao,' Jimmy said. 'You use the time to find out something about Matthew Ellimore.'

'I intend having a bath and recovering my lost sleep,' Esmeralda said through her door, which stood open.

'Later,' Lance walked through and picked his way across the open suitcases on the floor to stand in the bathroom door; it was the only clear space. 'Tell me about your husband.'

'That's a better attitude than the last time I tried to tell you about him.'

Lance nodded. 'Did you ever go to Africa with him?'

'No. The only time I was ever in Africa was for his funeral. And I arrived too late for that.'

'Why did he come to Hong Kong?'

'A man called Jardine had about a ton of ivory and Matthew wanted to buy it.'

'Did he succeed?'

'No. Sir P. K. Pan overbid him. He was furious.'

'What did he do?'

'About what?'

'When he was furious about losing the ivory.'

'Nothing. We went to dinner at the Marco Polo in the annexe at the Peninsula and in the morning flew on to Bangkok.'

'Did he make any threats?'

'No. That was not Matthew's way.'

'Can you think of any reason why someone should hire assassins to attack you?'

Again the slight hesitation. 'The curling tongs . . . the ivory.'

'Sure,' he said impatiently. 'What I'm getting at is this: did Matthew have any enemies in this part of the world?'

'Yes.'

'All right! Out with it!'

She looked at him over a hanger. 'Not Hong Kong. Singapore. Sir P. K. Pan. They were contenders for the same girl. Pan won.'

'Go on.'

'That's all I know.'

'Don't be stupid. If you know that much, you must know more.'

She shrugged. 'You're being offensive, Lance. Is it because you are afraid?'

'Goddamnit, Yes! And if you're not frightened out of your wits as well, you're either stupid or arrogant.'

'You don't know how!' She was pummelling his chest with her fists, the dress lying trampled on the floor behind her. 'The fear . . . not having to show it for Matthew's sake.'

He put his arms around her to pull her close, to imprison her arms between them so that the pummelling would stop. He heard himself say, 'There, there.' It sounded inane. She was warm against him. Then they were kissing, then rolling on the floor, then they were one. He remembered thinking, fragmentarily, explosively, that this particular escape from their fear was exactly the one that would render them helpless in any attack. Passion drove caution before it like a bucking stallion.

Afterwards he lay on her, in her, his nose in the fragrance of her hair. Of mingled sweat and semen – the line flashed into his mind. Had he read it somewhere? This was little better than hitting the widow of a man he had killed.

'I'm sorry,' he said and raised himself on his elbows.

With one arm around him she held him, with the other forcing his chin up so that she could look at him. 'Don't be. Matthew would've – '

He laid a finger across her lips. 'We don't need him here.'

But Matthew was there all the same.

'I needed to be loved,' she said a little defiantly. 'Come, you may share my bath.' She dropped the remnants of her clothes behind her as she walked into the bathroom. Lance was shamed by the realization that some were torn. A moment later he realized his own clothes were torn too and he smiled. He walked behind her into the bathroom, dropping clothes, watching her back. He burst out laughing.

'What are you laughing at?'

'I was thinking your haunches move sweetly, like that of a running leopardess.' He pulled his hand from the small of his back to show her the smear of blood on it. 'An appropriate image.'

She turned from running the bathwater and her deep

breasts brushed his chest. She was laughing as she took his now-limp member and gave it a shake. While he was still thinking he could easily be friends with this woman, it was not limp any more. He pulled her to him. Her arms went around his neck and she hiked her thighs up around his middle. They moved together gently until Lance said, 'You're a big girl,' and sank to the bathroom floor with her.

After she had washed him and he her, he stood, wrapped in a towel, and watched her clear up the clothes with her precise economic movements. 'I feel less frightened now,' she said.

'Don't.' He wished she had not brought it up. He wanted to savour the moment a little longer, just looking at her. To have possessed this woman, to have shared rapture with her, was something . . . he could not put words to it and decided he did not want to.

He stood for another moment, watching her body move under her dressing-gown.

'Just say what's on your mind, Lance. I'll understand.'

Suddenly, he knew she would. 'All right. First, you don't have to open your legs for me because you're under my protection.'

'You – ' The anger left her as abruptly as it had come. She stood looking down at the floor for a moment, then turned her gaze on his face, her eyes composed, her mouth relaxing. 'You're crude, but I understand. There's more.'

'Yes. It's dangerous to stop being afraid. Opium, sex . . . both make you less afraid. Both slow you down.'

She stood looking at him for a long while. He nearly apologized once more. But, what the hell, she was no cringing virgin and – if there was any question of it – she had used him as he had used her. He did not think the question would arise: he was becoming genuinely fond of her straightforwardness and her persistence.

She turned on her heel and went out through the bedroom door. She returned with his suitcase, throwing it on the bed and opening it. She talked as she hung his clothes next to hers. 'You're a primitive, Lance. So just think you won me the primitive way, by beating me up and raping me. Matthew would have approved enormously.'

'Jesus fell off the cross!' Primitives take the women of those they kill, he thought as he strode around the bed. He grabbed her elbow and pulled her around. 'You're the primitive!'

She shook her head. 'I'm Spanish in the same way you're a man. My second man. We can't just forget the first. I don't want to and it would be callous for you to do so.' Her eyes were untroubled as she looked up at him. 'But there's no need to mention his name between us, ever again.'

He nodded. He went into the bathroom to hang the towel and climbed between the sheets she had turned down. After a while she came and, still in her dressing-gown, curled up against him, a comforting warm presence.

'Do you want to leave her in a safe place?' Jimmy asked in an undertone. They were in the sitting-room, waiting for Esmeralda to finish dressing so that they could go to dinner.

Lance shrugged. 'It's not so easy.'

Jimmy spread his hands, indicating reluctance to comment on a delicate matter. 'If it's only *droit de seigneur* . . .' His hands moved up and down: 'On the other hand, if she's going to be your woman . . .'

Lance knew what Jimmy meant. If she was going to be his woman, he would not expose her to danger. He would deliver her to some safe place until he had dealt with Bruun. But Esmeralda was unlikely to behave like 'his woman'. Lance was looking at her bedroom door when it opened and she came through.

'You two were talking about me,' she said.

'Jimmy wants me to put you in a safe place until this business is over,' Lance said.

'No.'

'The situation is somewhat changed from when we decided to use you as bait. What – '

'I see. Then I was a chattel, a goat on a rope. Now I give you pleasure and you can't risk me.'

Jimmy headed for the door.

'You! Stay here,' she snapped at him. 'You expect women to be controlled by their men. And when their men fail, you shuffle your feet before their women.'

It was true. Jimmy was shuffling his feet! Lance burst out laughing. Jimmy gave him a venomous look but stilled his feet.

'Esmeralda, listen to me,' Lance said.

'I'm not going to – '

'Quiet!' Out of the corner of his eye he noticed Jimmy's smile returning as a sign of approval. 'What you say is true. I no longer want to risk you.'

'So, you are going to make orders to make me stay in a nunnery?'

'No. I'm going to ask you reasonably.'

'Then I say no. I still have certain duties to perform before I'll be entirely yours.'

'Your sense of responsibility could be the end of you,' Jimmy said, the smile no longer on his face.

'How much are you paying him?' she asked Lance, her voice sweet and reasonable.

'I'm not. He's here on his own account and that of his brothers and tribe.'

'I'm here on my own account and that of my late husband and butler,' she said with dignity. 'I will not be sent away like a child.'

104

Jimmy looked at Lance, but Lance had no further arguments. Jimmy walked to the door and held it open for Esmeralda.

Over dinner, Jimmy told them of his arrangements. He had talked to a man he knew who knew a man who would arrange for them to meet a man who could arrange for the hire of men of violence in Macao. The complex arrangements would be complete tomorrow by noon.

'How come you know a man who can hire killers ten thousand miles from where you live?' Esmeralda asked Jimmy.

'Old mercenaries never die,' Jimmy said. 'They become security advisers to multinational firms. About four or five times a year one of these people wants a job done somewhere in the world. They offer the job to my brother Sambo, who always turns them down. So we know who and where they are.'

'They keep offering?' Lance asked.

'Oh yes. Hiring mercenaries isn't as easy as people think. Hiring competent mercenaries is very difficult indeed. The good ones are grey and fat and ride to plush offices in chauffeur-driven cars and, four or five times a year, they call Sambo.'

'There must be next-best ones,' Esmeralda said.

'It's a profession where second-best is by definition short-lived,' Lance said. Sambo too was fat and given to chauffeur-driven cars; he was not grey yet. 'So you called one of these men. Who?'

'Lestronge. You don't know his name but he was with your brother in the Legion. Later he was in the OAS. In Biafra he was a company commander under your brother.'

'Did he explain why Bruun should want to hire people in Macao?'

'No. He thinks Bruun is dead and he's glad – he sends you congratulations for killing Bruun.' Jimmy drew his forefinger from his eye to his chin. 'Bruun cut him once with a broken beer-bottle. He says anybody who hires labour in Macao is either very stupid or very clever.'

'Why?'

'Because the communists count every pulsebeat there.'

'I still don't get it, Jimmy.'

'He doesn't think we're going to find anything. The reason the hiring was done in such an unlikely place is that it's a guaranteed dead-end.'

'If mercenaries are so hard to find, then murderers can't be easy,' Esmeralda said. 'It follows.'

'Lestronge says it's much easier,' Jimmy contradicted her. 'He offered to put me onto half a dozen men here in Hong Kong alone who would be happy to organize a little meatcleaver massacre for a most reasonable sum.' He saw Lance's lips tighten. 'Sorry Lance. The man's words, not mine. He added another thing we didn't know: he says Bruun's experience in the East was limited to a stint in Burma.' There was a long silence. 'He doesn't believe Bruun is alive.'

Esmeralda poured more green tea.

'But he's making a connection for us in Macao all the same?'

Jimmy shrugged. 'For the memory of your brother. To chalk up favours with you and with Sambo. He's a fat spider, sitting in the middle of a web of information, trading a piece here and there. He has a computer terminal beside his desk on which he called up my file and yours. Just, he says, two of the hundred thousand files of dangerous men he keeps. Dangerous, that's what he said.'

'Dangerous? All I ever did was get in trouble and run a safari farm. His files are worth nothing if he has my name on them.'

'You killed Theodore Bruun, and not by shooting him in the back. That puts you in Lestronge's highest category.'

'Category?' Esmeralda said.

Jimmy nodded. 'To hear him talk, you'd never think he was once a soldier for hire. He has three secretaries, all ugly as night; presumably a lot of work goes through his office.'

'What's the point, Jimmy? Another one who thinks Bruun's dead?'

'Yes. He's in a stronger position to judge than your Brigadier Burger because Burger is interested in revolutionaries while Lestronge is interested in men who for profit could organize and take over by violence an oil rig or other high-investment artifact. If Bruun were alive, he sure as hell would show on Lestronge's files. In fact, he does, labelled "deceased".'

'Sure. And he carries you and me too. A safari farm owner and an investment manager who has to put on a track suit and go running to keep the world from reading yesterday's menu around his middle.'

'Don't sneer, Lance. He sits on the main board of AP Oil Trusts and spends more than two million dollars every year just to keep the information in his files up to date.'

'The point remains, Jimmy, that neither you nor I are killers for hire.'

'But you are right now hunting a man with the intention of killing him,' Esmeralda said, 'and Jimmy accompanies you, if not for pay, out of loyalty to some past association. To men like Lestronge, I should imagine motives don't matter when they can read and interpret actions instead.'

Lance ordered cognac all round without consulting the other two. In the expectant silence, his mind turned the arguments over. And over. There was nothing to replace his belief in the evil presence of Bruun, even at their table now; nothing except the black void of despair. He felt they were waiting for him to say something.

'It's Bruun. Or it's some psychopath that kills anybody I come into contact with. I can't believe it.'

'Look at the world around you,' Jimmy said. 'It's run by psychopaths.'

'If it's a psychopath, his madness is his guarantee that we'll never catch him unless we come upon him while he's still red-handed . . .' Lance let it trail away while he waited for them to come to terms with the fact that you cannot catch red-handed a man who sends others to do his bloody work. 'That way lies madness for us. I don't want to hear any more about it.'

After another long silence, Lance added, 'All the same, Jimmy, call Sambo tonight and tell him he and all the brothers should look to the security of their homes and families.'

As they were leaving the restaurant, Daniel Drang stood up at his table as they passed. He said nothing, standing only to emphasize his continuing presence.

'Perhaps we should discourage him,' Jimmy said, making no attempt to lower his voice.

Lance, still in no mood for jokes, said, 'It's his own time he's wasting. He's irrelevant,' and walked on. Outside the restaurant the hustle and bustle of Hong Kong at night struck them at the same time as the humid air laden with smells of the East. Lance looked at the blonde girl standing to one side, rubbing her elbow, seemingly oblivious to the crowd on the pavement jostling her. Lance looked again. 'Mark Esmeralda,' he said to Jimmy and closed on the girl. She had been at Heathrow, climbed out of a taxi that had followed their own to the Hilton and been waiting downstairs when they came out tonight. And here she was again, staring at them. Waiting.

She yelped when he took her elbow. 'Hey, that's still sore!'

'Why are you following us?'

'I told you, for the – '

'For the animals,' Esmeralda said.

Lance groaned. He had not recognized the girl.

'Go home,' Lance said. 'You're wasting your time and your money following us around. We have no intention whatsoever of going anywhere near that ivory.'

'Yeah?'

'You're endangering your own life.'

For a moment she looked frightened, then the presence of so many people cheered her. 'You wouldn't dare!'

Lance dropped her arm and turned away.

'Hey, don't be such a killjoy. Let me come with you.'

When they arrived back at the Hilton, the blonde girl was in the taxi behind theirs, Daniel Drang in the one behind hers. They were barely in their suite when there was a knock on the door. Lance was nearest to the door. He opened it and sighed. He had seen the man around the Cross in Sydney. His name was Fitzmeikle and, with his brothers, he led the King's Cross Mob. He was tall and cadaverous and Lance thought he used oil in his hair. He walked past Lance into the room.

'You've come up in the world since you lived in a whore's flat right on the Cross,' he said to Lance. 'And this is the little lady who needs help fetching her ivory.' He offered Esmeralda his hand. She ignored it. His glance flicked across Jimmy as if he were invisible.

'I don't need any help of any kind,' Esmeralda said coldly.

'If you hire a guy that nobody's ever heard of as a bodyguard' – he waved the cigar in his hand at Lance – 'you most definitely need help. Never mind hiring a blackfella as well.'

'Who's he?' Jimmy asked Lance.

'Australian version of the Mafia. I think you'd better leave, Fitzmeikle. My friend doesn't like your racial slurs.'

'Mr Fitzmeikle. Your "friend" will speak when I speak to him.'

'He probably brought his own "friends",' Lance said.

'About the ivory,' Fitzmeikle said to Esmeralda, as if all other matters had been settled.

Jimmy reached out a long arm and snapped the cigar in two between his fingers. 'Next time, ask before you smoke in a lady's presence.' While Fitzmeikle was looking at the stump of his cigar with almost comic incredulity spreading across his face, Jimmy stepped up and kneed him smartly in the groin. Esmeralda gasped at the sudden, unexpected violence. Lance opened the door to their suite. Jimmy hustled the moaning Fitzmeikle out by his collar and the seat of his pants; they heard his head crack against the wall opposite. Lance and Jimmy stood on each side of the open door, waiting. Seconds passed. From being totally relaxed, Esmeralda noticed, they became tense as the seconds became half a minute. Fitzmeikle had long since slid to the floor; he was conscious, clutching his groin and rolling slightly on the plush carpet, moaning hoarsely.

After a full minute Lance cradled his hands. Jimmy climbed into the cradle and looked around the jamb of the door just under the lintel. He saw a white man on the floor, unconscious. Another white man was being held by an arm twisted up behind his back and by his long hair being used as a lever to force his head back so that his face became a grinning rictus, seemingly half bared teeth and gums. Over his shoulder, Daniel Drang grinned widely.

'I like doing my stalking alone,' Drang said.

Jimmy jumped down and Lance followed him out into the passage. Lance glanced at the blonde girl who stood down the passage before the lift doors, rubbing her elbow.

Fitzmeikle was raising himself painfully. 'You're all dead,' he said.

Lance ignored the groggy gangster. He raised the chin of the one Drang held. 'I want you to carry a message to whichever of the Fitzmeikle brothers doesn't have his brains addled by greed. Do you hear me?'

'Yes,' the man croaked.

'The message is simple. We don't have the ivory. We don't know where it is. Mrs Ellimore doesn't know where it is. Her husband died without telling her where he hid it.'

'Thargh – '

'Let him go, please, Mr Drang.'

Drang seemed reluctant but let the man go.

The gangster's bodyguard rubbed his scalp. 'They're not going to believe you.'

'Tell them to read the papers. The meatcleaver murders in England. We're just running for our own lives. From people much tougher than you. They chop up pensioners in their beds with meatcleavers.'

'I can only tell them what you said, Mister.'

'You do that.' The man's eyes told Lance his story had not been believed. 'And read the papers yourself, huh?'

Jimmy dragged Fitzmeikle fully erect, then bent down to take the still unconscious bodyguard by his collar. He dragged them both to the lift doors. The blonde girl scuttled away like a frightened crab.

'You're just going to let them go?' Drang said incredulously.

Lance shrugged. 'They're no use to me. Thank you for your help.'

'I wasn't helping you. I was removing an irritation in my own way. Don't get ideas beyond your station in life, Weber.'

And I bet you went to better schools than I did too, Lance thought but said only, to the bodyguard, 'Go on.'

The bodyguard was helped on his way by Drang's number eleven shoe planted firmly on his backside. Drang laughed aloud, a somehow sour sound. 'I'd have killed the bastards quietly and dropped them down the laundry chute. Does that buy me in?'

Lance shook his head and went into the suite. Esmeralda still stood in the middle of the room, looking a little dazed.

'How did they find us?' she demanded.

'Called your home, found you were at the Dorchester, called the Dorchester, found you were here,' Lance said shortly. 'They're not important. Guns are more their style than meatcleavers.'

'Not important? That man was threatening me!'

Lance took her in his arms but could think of nothing to say except, 'Jimmy's sending them down the lift.'

She broke free and ran to the bedroom, slamming the door behind her, just as Jimmy returned, dusting his hands and grinning broadly. 'I see the honeymoon's over,' Jimmy said.

'I think she's finally realized exactly what kind of people her ivory's attracting,' Lance said.

'Those poor specimens won't get ten miles in Africa before somebody eats their livers.'

'I know. But here, in a city, on their own ground, they're very frightening. She's not forgotten the electric curling tongs.'

Jimmy shuddered from top to bottom, a shimmering mass of revulsion. 'Scum!' he said.

Lance headed for the door Esmeralda had slammed. It was after midnight, though beyond the double-glazed windows cocooning them at a regulated 65°F the city still flashed neon and bustled people. He turned and said 'Tch!' at the tap on the door. Jimmy opened the door. The blonde girl stood there.

'You're not going to leave me out here all night with him, are you?' she said, indicating Daniel Drang who stood against the wall opposite their door, one large foot resting against the wall.

Jimmy's smile broadened and he opened the door wide. Lance went in to Esmeralda. The blonde was not bad but he preferred his women with a little more flesh on them.

In the morning, while they were still breakfasting, four Chinese turned up. They were the men Lestronge had sent to guard Esmeralda while Lance and Jimmy went to Macao. Their leader and the only man who spoke looked a bit like Elvis Presley with grey wings over his ears. All four wore plain dark suits, white shirts, plain dark ties. They would wait with Esmeralda until Jimmy and Lance returned, whenever that was.

Esmeralda seemed inclined to argue, but Jimmy whispered something in her ear and she remained sullenly silent.

'And her, she's not to leave until an hour after we've gone,' Lance instructed the guards, indicating the blonde girl, whose name was Christine Rawls.

'You bastard! Look, you make him – ' she appealed to Jimmy.

'Not me. He's in charge. I just follow orders.'

'But I – '

'Got a bed for the night in a fully booked town,' Jimmy said smoothly. 'We'll tell you all about it when we get back tonight.'

Drang came out of the lift, digging in his teeth with a toothpick, just as they reached it. He held the door for them.

'Four Chinese came and took Mrs Ellimore while you were having your breakfast,' Jimmy said to him, adding in Swahili, 'Fetch the axe so I can chop your head off, you halfwitted son of a hyena.'

Drang offered him a blank stare before he recovered his composure.

'I knew it!' Jimmy crowed. 'Son of the African soil and he can't speak the language.'

The lift stopped and the doors opened. Drang stalked out and they followed him. 'Hey,' Jimmy called after him,

113

'share our taxi and put it on your expenses. Earn yourself some pocket-money.'

Drang went through the doors and climbed into the first taxi. It pulled out into the traffic and dawdled until Lance and Jimmy's taxi passed it, then followed.

'What was that in aid of?' Lance asked.

'Just feeling my oats. That Christine is making a life's work of the animals. She also told me her father is a baronet *and* an Appeals Court Judge which, she claims, is a perfectly good reason for the two of us aristocrats to team up against a commoner like you.'

'She doesn't give up, does she?'

Jimmy nodded his head solemnly. 'No.'

'What did you whisper to Esmeralda?'

'That you would lose face if she argued.'

Macao was a disappointment. Lance had somehow, somewhere, gained a mental image of the Cradle of Oriental Sin, swashbucklers gambling their women's virtue before smoking a pipe of opium and visiting the Chinese girls with bound feet in their cribs lining the dark alleyways. After the glorious riot of Hong Kong, Macao struck him as so little and so drab that, inexplicably, he looked back at Daniel Drang leaving the hydrofoil behind them for the reassurance of the familiar.

Lance nudged Jimmy. 'Behind Drang.'

Jimmy smiled when he saw Fitzmeikle and one of his bodyguards. 'I suppose the other is in hospital. Do these people normally carry firearms?'

'I don't know. They won't use them on us until the ivory is in sight.'

'They could just be stupid enough to think they'd have a better chance at the widow if they did away with us first,' Jimmy said.

Lance shrugged. There was nothing he could do about it for now. He wished he was back in Africa, where he knew how to lose bothersome people.

'This place looks like nothing so much as a run-down general store,' Lance said. 'Is there anywhere else where Orientals speak Portuguese?'

Jimmy took the drift of Lance's doubt: Lance just did not see Macao as a likely place to hire killers. 'Timor.' He pointed vaguely in an easterly direction. 'But Lestronge says breeding assassins is one of the cottage industries of Macao. It's a hangover from the days before the Communist-leaning businessmen cleaned the place up. Timor's always been too poor to have crime but Macao wasn't always this seedy.' With that Lance had to be satisfied. He remembered what Lestronge had said: the man who hired killers in Macao was either very stupid or very clever.

Lance consulted the map. 'That's China,' he said, pointing.

'It's been China alongside the hydrofoil all the time,' Jimmy said, unimpressed. He took the map. 'It's not too far. Let's walk.'

The smell of the place reassured Lance a little. It was not quite like Africa but it did not have the metallic diesel-tang of Europe either. After a while, having walked far enough for the heat and humidity to turn his shirt limp, he asked, 'Where are we going?'

'There,' Jimmy said.

'In the middle of everything?'

'It's a burnt-out church,' Jimmy said.

'Somebody's got a sense of humour.'

'There are a lot of churches here,' Jimmy said. 'That one's St Paul's.'

They walked up the narrow alley, climbing the pairs of steps at intervals of thirteen or fourteen paces that led them gently up towards the façade still standing with sky showing through the empty windows. The food being cooked at the stalls set up under striped canopies smelt good. The steps broke their forward progress every time they got into their stride. Lance shortened his pace to that

115

of the Chinese in the alley with them and counted. There were twenty of the local inhabitants' paces between the pairs of steps. Fascinating.

They climbed some rubble and went through an arch. Beyond it Lance turned around a full circle. Through the arch he could see Fitzmeikle coming up the alley, looking uneasily behind him, presumably for Drang, who was nowhere to be seen. The cathedral had been built on a hill and Lance looked down into the balconies of flats, the railings as colourfully covered with laundry drying as the striped canopies in all the roads he could see. Cars could approach quite closely, though not from the alley he and Jimmy had come by; a taxi was just dropping its fare about a hundred yards away.

'Mr Weber?'

'Yes.'

'Who sent you?'

'Commandant Lestronge,' Jimmy said.

'Ah. You wish knowledge.'

Lance studied the old man. If he was an assassin, he was an assassin in retirement. He was grey and bowed and toothless and his English sounded as if he was trying to break into song.

Jimmy took some bills out of his pocket. He gave the old man a handful without looking at the denominations.

'We want to know if men from here have been travelling to Europe and Africa to murder people with meat-cleavers,' Lance said, his voice not completely under control, breaking momentarily.

'Yes,' said the old man without hesitation. 'Twice.'

Lance felt elation. 'Who hired them?'

'A Chinese. He was not from Hong Kong.'

'How do you know?'

'He did not speak like Hong Kong.'

'You heard him?'

'Yes.'

'Well, describe him, damnit!'

The old man took a step back. Jimmy peeled some more money from his roll.

'His picture in your very hand would be no good to you,' the old man said. 'He drowned in the harbour that same night.'

'Shit!' Jimmy said.

The old man looked longingly at the roll going back into Jimmy's pocket. 'I can tell you the names of the men he hired.'

'Who have not returned,' Jimmy said, giving the old man another handful of bills. The old man nodded sadly.

'Some never left,' the old man said as Jimmy and Lance were turning away.

Jimmy blew out his breath. Lance just turned back. He saw Fitzmeikle and his bodyguard on rubble above them, pointing pistols at them. Fitzmeikle, he noticed for the first time, had a bandage around his head. The Australian gangster was smiling tightly over the pistol he held in both hands. Lance pushed the old man towards an outcrop of wall and rolled backwards as Jimmy crashed into him. Once, as he rolled, he saw a spurt of dust in front of his face. Though he had not heard the shot, he knew what it was. Jimmy had been right about Fitzmeikle: the man was stupid. He crashed against a rail, Jimmy on top of him. They ran in opposite directions along the rail and around the corners of the building. Around the far side of the building they met, both breathing slightly faster.

'I want that old man,' Lance said. He picked up a child that had crawled out of the open door of one of the flats and put it over the threshold. He closed the door on its large eyes. 'Sorry,' he said when it began wailing. There was nobody else in sight.

'Let's see if we can come up on them from –'

Jimmy stopped talking as Lance raised his head to the single short scream and the ululation that followed it.

There were three shots and another scream. By the time silence fell – neither of them any longer listening to the frustrating howling of the baby behind the closed door – they were running around the building.

At first Lance thought Daniel Drang was dead, or nearly so, croaking his last. But the OAU man was merely on his knees, vomiting. Lance did not blame him. The ruins of St Paul's were a bloody mess. The old Chinese had had his head severed completely from the body. One of the bodyguard's hands had been likewise severed, and lay clutching his pistol in a curiously menacing manner; his head had been split open to the shoulders. Fitzmeikle seemed whole, merely unconscious, until Lance walked around him. The top of his skull had been taken away in a line an inch above the eyes by a very sharp instrument.

By contrast, the men who had made the bloody mess had died neatly. There were three of them, nondescript (to Lance) Chinese. He ran from one to the next to the last, feeling wrists, tearing shirts to listen to chests, hoping against hope one would be alive. One by one he flung the corpses from him. He turned on Drang and dragged him erect, not heeding the flow of thin gruel flowing over his hands from Drang's mouth.

'How many?' He shook Drang. 'Goddamnit, stop your puking. How many were there?'

Drang spluttered something.

Lance could not hear. He shook Drang again. Drang pushed a hand in Lance's face. Lance saw the thumb crossed across the palm, the four fingers standing upright. Drang's palm was curiously light coloured, cream with just the slightest dash of coffee.

Jimmy pulled at Lance. 'Four. He's holding up four fingers. One got away.'

Lance spun around. Which way? Only one direction could be discounted, the direction from which he and Jimmy had come.

Drang was on his knees again, hawking and spitting.

'You go that way, I'll go down here,' Lance said.

'Looking for what?' Drang croaked. He pointed to the four black-handled meatcleavers lying on the ground. 'I only saw his back. Chinese male. You know how many Chinese males there are on this fucking peninsula?'

'Never mind the sarcasm,' Jimmy snapped. 'We gotta get out of here before the police come.'

Lance listened to the raised voices approaching. 'We did nothing. I want to be here when they catch the other one.'

'They don't have *habeas corpus* and jury systems here,' Jimmy said. 'You'll be in gaol a year before they even question you.'

'Help me,' Drang said, obviously hating the words as he uttered them.

Lance grabbed his wrist and his elbow and heaved the big man erect. They stumbled down the rubble towards the flats. Faces were appearing in windows. Drang was pulling his tie free and stuffing it into his pocket; the tie was smeared with his breakfast, ham and eggs. On the far side of the block of flats they walked briskly down an alley. Some people here had heard the shots and the screams but not all, or perhaps the excitement had already passed. But enough noted their passing to be able to describe them to the police; there were not all that many Europeans about and none six-feet-two and accompanied by two equally large black men.

'I hope we're as indistinguishable from one another to these slanteyes as they are to me,' Drang said.

'Racist,' Jimmy said.

Drang grunted. 'God, I never saw such blood. Not even in 'Nam.' It was his apology and explanation. 'After this, they'll never be part of the human race again. Not for me. Never mind racialism.'

Lance stopped to consult his street map. Drang said, 'That way.'

119

They got to the hydrofoil with three minutes to spare. The next one would be in half an hour but the police would not need that much time to seal the whole place off. They went into the toilet and cleaned up as best they could. Lance had a tear in the shoulder of his jacket. It was straight and neat, as if made by a sharp knife. But it had been made by a high-velocity bullet he had not even noticed. He held onto the washbasin for a full five minutes to still the shivers, until Jimmy knocked on the door and asked if he was all right. There had also been an apparently innocuous puff of dirt only inches from his face. He sweated profusely in the air-conditioned hydrofoil for all the seventy-five minutes it took to reach Hong Kong.

'Which of the friends are after you?' Drang asked.

'I don't understand,' Lance said.

'Why is an intelligence service setting traps for you?'

Lance looked at Jimmy, who shrugged: he did not know if Bruun had ever worked in intelligence.

Lance told Drang the whole story as briefly as he could. Drang considered for a moment before he answered.

'Bruun's dead.'

Lance turned in his seat to stare resentfully at Drang. 'Maybe you know somebody else who's crazy enough to organize what we just saw.'

'Don't get your knickers in a knot, white boy. The meatcleaver is standard-issue sharp instrument, murderous, for the Chinese. But more likely in crimes of passion, I believe. For premeditated jobs they use the knife or the gun or poison.'

'So there's a special message for Lance,' Jimmy said.

Drang nodded. 'Sure. The whole thing is a message for him. Macao . . . Sheeet! If I wanted to make a white boy so shit-scared he pissed blood, I'd arrange everything just like that. He was meant to trace things back to Macao and then they – the ones left behind – would pick off any protection he brought with him. They'd let him go though – so the man could enjoy him peeing blood.'

'It might surprise you,' Lance said coldly, 'to know I've already worked out that much myself. You don't have to be a genius . . . What everybody who assures me Bruun is dead fails to do is to provide an alternative candidate.'

Drang ran his eyes over Lance's face in slow, insolent appraisal. 'You really are shit-scared, white boy.'

Lance nodded. 'Your candidate, Drang.'

'Hey, that's good, that you're scared. It changes my mind. I think maybe you're going to come out of this on top.'

'Your candidate.'

'I haven't got one. Who wants that ivory besides you'n'me and the meshuganah girl?'

'Let me put you straight. I don't want the ivory and I'm not heading for it. And this business with the meatcleavers started long before I got involved with Mrs Ellimore. The two things only meshed after I met her.'

'Come on, Weber! You're talking about heavy organization and heavy money. You gotta be a whole heap more megalomaniac than Nixon to think somebody's gonna spend that much dough and effort just to discommode you. Pull the other one.'

'I know one man who would go to any length for revenge on me: Theodore Bruun.'

'Then how come,' Drang said triumphantly, 'he hasn't yet attacked any of your brother's loyal Simbas, the family of your own personal Uncle Tom?' He looked at Jimmy briefly and then closed his eyes and leaned back against the headrest with its white doily.

Lance looked at Jimmy in dismay. Bruun had as much reason to hate Sambo's remaining tribesmen as to hate Lance. Drang had made a telling point.

They rode the rest of the way to Hong Kong in silence, Lance sweating, Jimmy unsmiling. As they left the hydrofoil, Drang said, 'Try not to look like suspicious persons.

We'll be long gone from Hong Kong before the request to apprehend us floats down through the bureaucratic layers.'

True enough, the two policemen they saw paid them not the slightest attention. In the taxi, Lance said, 'Why should we leave? I want to know what the Macao police find out from the fourth man first.'

Drang sighed. 'You're an innocent abroad. Get it through your head, they're not going to catch him. Even if I had been able to give a full description of him, including his fucking name and birthdate and address, he's protected, see?'

Lance nodded reluctantly. 'I still like thinking before I move suddenly.'

Jimmy said, 'When we got the visas for Macao, we gave the Hilton as our address.'

Lance sat deeper in his seat. He wondered if there was not some way they could remove the whole affair to the soil of Africa. At least he would not feel quite so naked then. Or quite so stupidly like a fish out of water.

In the lobby of the Hilton, Drang said, 'Whoever it is, Bruun's ghost, some other enemy, he knows you very well if he could put you in that ruined church in a place you didn't even know where it was until the day before yesterday. Believe me, boy, I'm sorry for you.' For once he did not sound vindictive. 'But I still mean to have that ivory for Africa.'

Lance stood looking after Drang as the black man walked towards the lifts, secure in the knowledge that Lance had to follow.

'What now?' Jimmy said.

'We cut the strings that pull the puppet,' Lance said. 'We do the unexpected.'

Jimmy smiled broadly and waved at the startled Drang just as the lift doors closed. Then he followed Lance out of the front door and into the taxi. 'Give him Lestronge's address,' Lance said.

Lestronge's office was in an onyx-coloured building of some composition stone and shaded glass. The uniformed receptionist sent them straight up and Lestronge did not keep them waiting.

'A younger, bigger edition of Ewart,' he said as he shook Lance's hand. He was tall enough to look Lance in the eye, but twice Lance's weight. His steel-grey hair was cut *en brosse* in an attempt to hide the thinning on the temples. 'But you aren't here for chitchat. Something happened.'

'They were waiting for us.'

Lestronge waved them to two of the huge leather armchairs in a circle about a coffee table and sank into one himself. 'That's a standard risk when one works through intermediaries. I hope it wasn't too wet extricating yourself. They're very self-conscious about their image over in Macao.'

'Wet?'

'Did you have to kill many?'

'There are six dead, but we didn't kill any of them. The Chinese killed some other people who were following us and the informant.'

'And Fitzmeikle killed some of the Chinese before he was himself killed?'

'Yes.'

There was a pause. Lestronge sighed. 'You wondered whether I had sold you out. No, don't protest. I'm too old, too fond of what remains of my life, to cross the Webers or their Simbas. Ewart had a pride that in another man one would have called vindictive. I remember it well.' Lestronge sighed again. 'He too had a talent for making enemies.'

'Major Weber's enemies are dead,' Jimmy said. 'Unless . . .'

'No. I haven't reconsidered since yesterday,' Lestronge said. 'Ewart was the most thorough man I ever met. His enemies are, as you say, dead.' Lestronge fingered the scar running the depth of his cheek. 'But I did give some consideration to Lance's lunatic delusion that Bruun might have escaped his just deserts.'

Lance gave Lestronge a sharp look at the gratuitous rudeness, but the man did not see; he had lumbered erect and was fetching a slip of paper from his desk. He sat down again and studied it. He said, pointing to a television terminal over a typewriter keyboard on a table beside his desk. 'Only the Pentagon has access to a bigger computer than mine. What the computer is is mainly an ultrafast filing clerk. You can ask the thing to reshuffle the files any number of ways and get an almost instantaneous answer. So I asked the machine to print out the names of people who are highly disfigured. Of this list, I assure you I am personally familiar with most and the rest are ruled out by age or race: none of them could be Bruun. In fact, I am left with only one name. I have no photograph to match the name and I think this man is a phantom, a myth.'

'Then why is he on your computer?' Lance asked.

'Because this phantom, this myth, is a creation of the CIA. Once they were, and perhaps are still, the main motivating force behind world trade in opium and heroin. They did it for two reasons. One was to raise money Congress could not call them to account for. The other was to prove to certain allies of theirs that they were serious people. It was a lunacy. The same lunatics not so long ago backed a group of revolutionaries to take over one of the offshore oilfields in my charge for reasons I'm still trying to fathom. So, I keep track of any phantoms the CIA create, especially in my own backyard. But I assure you, this man is a cipher – if he exists at all. He is simply a name in an account book, an entity incompetents can ascribe their evil misdeeds to when they are, inevitably, found out. No real man could possibly be so consistently yet so irrationally evil over so long a period of time. We're talking here about a period of six years since he first

124

showed up on my computers, this myth. In that time I have no first-hand report of a sighting, only third- and fourth-hand accounts of a scarred man living in seclusion in the centre of an impenetrable fortress in the jungles of Burma. The reason I tell you at such length about a man who does not exist, except as a bogeyman in my computer, is to impress on you the unlikelihood of Bruun escaping my net, were he alive.'

Lance saw Jimmy nodding attentively, respectfully, so he did the same. 'The problem, Mr Lestronge, is that your computer does not suggest an alternative enemy of such macabre imagination.'

'Why don't you tell me the whole story?'

Lance did. When he finished, Lestronge nodded his head twice, curtly. 'That must terrify you.'

Lance nodded.

'I can understand how you can suspect Bruun must be alive. But I knew him quite well and I cannot believe he would order torture unless he could himself be present to enjoy it. The man was the only genuine sadist I met in thirty years among the scum of the earth.' He held up his hand to stop Lance from challenging this. 'I will say this, however. The opportunism of including Mrs Ellimore in the cycle of murders – which must lead to an attempt to gain control of her ivory – sounds like Bruun. But, on the other hand, no old Africa hand would dare contest the ownership of that ivory with a Weber who, furthermore, has Sambo's backing.'

Lance was amazed: It was true – only outsiders (even Drang was an American) had so far thrown their hats into the ring.

Lestronge laughed, a deep rumbling sound. 'Don't be surprised, boy. Information and violence are only incidental to my job: what I deal in is men and their motivations.'

'All the same,' Lance said as politely as he could,

'Bruun did once try to take some crocodile skins from a Weber. And not from me, from Ewart. And from Jacques Roux. And from Sambo.'

'Certainly an irrational act,' Lestronge agreed. 'It got him skinned alive. Even if he survived . . . A man would have to be very stupid indeed to expose himself to such a terrible risk twice. And Bruun was never stupid.'

This was leading nowhere. Lance rose. 'Thank you for your help, sir. I apologize for my suspicions.'

Lestronge ignored the apology. 'I can offer you employment that would at the same time take you and Mrs Ellimore out of circulation for a year. We're starting to drill in the jungles of South America and – '

Lance held up his hands apologetically. Lestronge stopped his flow of words. 'What's the name of this myth in the jungles of Burma?' Lance asked.

'J. Arthur Rank.'

'Is that a joke?' Jimmy asked.

Lestronge nodded. 'A CIA joke.'

In the taxi on the way back to the Hilton, Jimmy explained that the Rank Organization was involved in the manufacture of photocopying machines in Britain and elsewhere. Lance shrugged. He failed to see either the joke or the relevance of it to his present unenviable situation. Lestronge had walked out through the office with them, impressing on them that they must leave Hong Kong that day if they did not wish to be questioned and perhaps detained by the police. He had also said that Lance's strategy of taking Esmeralda Ellimore, the owner of the ivory, into his protection was sound. He had emphasized again that he could keep both Lance and Jimmy occupied in parts of the world not easily accessible to Chinese with meatcleavers. 'Sometimes running may be the better part of discretion,' were Lestronge's last words to Lance.

'I thought you said Lestronge was French,' Lance said.

'I didn't say that. A lot of Germans served in the Foreign Legion,' Jimmy said, his voice betraying his lack of interest in small talk. 'He's from Alsace. Half-and-half.'

Lance was no wiser but did not press the point. The air conditioning in the car was freezing his despair into pointed icicles. He wound the window down to let in a blast of hot, humid air. The driver gave him a bewildered look over his shoulder. Jimmy snapped at the driver to keep his eyes on the traffic.

'This traffic is worse than Paris in the rush hour,' Jimmy said. 'Wind that bloody window up, will you?'

Lance had never been to Paris. He wound the window up. The driver smiled whitely at him in the mirror. Lance no longer had a sense of Asia as a place of familiar heats and humidities and smells and chattering people. Now it frightened him with its very alienness. He wondered where the driver kept his meatcleaver.

At the Hilton, Lance stood in the shower for fifteen minutes, thinking. When he came into the sitting-room, Esmeralda was just putting ice into a drink for him. Lestronge's four Chinese and Christine, who had been there when Lance and Jimmy returned, had all gone. Lance looked at the door. Drang, wearing clean clothes, had been standing in the passage outside when they arrived; he had not offered conversation.

'We've made a big mistake,' Lance said without introduction. The other two were obviously waiting for him to start. 'We've done what Bruun expected us to do. We went to Macao and we found a dead end. I think the intention was to kill Jimmy and whatever other people I had with me, but to let me go, in even greater fear.'

'I don't see what else we could have done,' Jimmy said.

'That only makes it worse.'

Jimmy nodded.

'So what can we do now?' Esmeralda asked. She had

hugged him very tightly when he had returned, holding him against her until he gently detached her fingers and hands and arms.

Lance looked at Jimmy. 'If you were Lestronge's computer, what would you forecast I would do?'

'Carry on the same way,' Jimmy said. 'Stay here and deal with the police. Go back to Macao and trace the one that got away. Try tracing the movements of the meat-cleaver Chinese to the murders and from there to wherever they are now.'

Lance nodded, giving himself time to assimilate all this. He had not carried it quite that far in his own head. 'In other words, do what we've been doing till now. Stand on the periphery of the action. Watch. Wait. Get shoved about. We can't even get near, never mind coming to grips with Bruun.'

'Bruun?' Jimmy said in a low voice. 'Bruun? You heard what Lestronge said. You're getting paranoid.'

Lance put his glass down on the coffee table. The glass cracked. He pulled his hand away from the broken pieces and the ice. He looked at his fingers; they were not cut. He waited until his voice was perfectly even. 'If you don't think Bruun's behind it, what are you doing here?'

Jimmy made no reply. Esmeralda found another glass and gave Lance a new drink.

'All right, it isn't a fair question. But you can't offer me an alternative candidate. So let's just call this evil intelligence that so dislikes us . . . Bruun. Like – what's the name for something, uh, by somebody else's brand name? Like "Coke" and "coke".'

'Generic,' Jimmy said.

'Yes. Well, "Bruun" is a generic name for anybody persecuting us.'

The phone rang. Esmeralda picked it up. It was for Jimmy. He listened and said something in his own language. Esmeralda looked up at him when she heard the series of clicks. Even Lance, who had heard it before, looked back at Jimmy.

Jimmy put the phone down. 'Sure enough, they attacked Sambo's home just before dawn. Sambo, sitting up after my warning, killed two with a shotgun and wounded another one. Unfortunately the police arrived before he could question the wounded man. The wounded man died on the way to the hospital.'

'Tch! Why the hell did he use a shotgun? Sambo's perfectly capable of disabling a man with a rifle.'

'He didn't have a gun in the house. The shotgun was the best he could borrow.'

Lance realized his manners were lacking. 'Did any of Sambo's family get hurt?'

'No. I congratulated him on your behalf.'

Lance felt himself blushing. He looked at the carpet. 'Do you want to go home in case there's another attempt?'

'Sambo's coping, wouldn't you say?'

'What about the fourth Chinese killer?'

'The police are looking for him.'

'Shit! Sorry, Esmeralda.'

'Bruun,' Jimmy said. 'There's nobody else that would attack both you and Sambo.'

'What happened in Macao today?' Esmeralda asked.

Nobody had told her! 'Sorry,' Lance said, and told her. He also recounted what Lestronge had said.

The corners of her mouth twitched. Lance asked her what she thought. She said, 'We have only two choices. We can try to hide, with or without Mr Lestronge's help. Or we can go over to the attack, though I don't know how.'

'But I do. That's what I was getting at earlier when I was interrupted. We were on the right track when we decided Bruun wants the ivory. We just handled it wrong. He knows the ivory isn't in Hong Kong or Macao, that we came following the string he was pulling. What we'll do next is to go for the ivory in earnest. We'll bring it out of Africa and sell it. Somewhere along the line Bruun will show his hand.'

Esmeralda was smiling brilliantly.

'Can we fly from here to Singapore?'

'Sure,' Jimmy said. 'Anywhere in the world.'

'The ivory's not in Singapore. It's in Africa,' Esmeralda said.

'I know. But first we want to make a deal with Sir P. K. Pan about marketing it. That's good economic sense. Also, we don't want him on our backs, trying to take it from us.'

'Why not just tell him where it is and let him get it out for himself?' Jimmy asked.

'Because he'll pay only one-third of the value and I don't think Esmeralda wants to give up sixteen million dollars,' Lance said, watching her rather than Jimmy. She squealed indignantly and flushed when he and Jimmy laughed. 'Anyway, one of the mistakes we've been making is fighting by somebody else's rules on somebody else's ground. In Africa, you and I will be on our home ground.'

'What about Drang and Christine?' Esmeralda asked. 'They're going to interfere.'

'In Africa we can choose to run circles about them or lose them altogether,' Jimmy said. 'It's a very big place and they're city people.'

'Well, Drang isn't quite irrelevant,' Lance said. 'He could make it more expensive for us to buy the necessary permits and non-interference from the civil authorities.'

'He means,' Jimmy explained to Esmeralda, 'that it could cost us more in bribes to government officials.'

'I don't think he's going to be so successful.' Esmeralda sounded quite definite. 'You see, the ivory's buried in Lake Kivu.'

'Mary, Mother of God,' Jimmy said.

'Save me from clever hiding-places,' Lance said.

They sat looking at her despondently. Lake Kivu lies between the Congo Kinshasa and Rwanda, a small country squeezed between Tanzania, Burundi and Uganda.

'The bloody exact middle of Africa,' Lance said disgustedly. 'How goddamn clever can you get?' he added bitterly. He was not being exact but for practical purposes a few hundred miles this way or that in Lake Kivu's position made no difference on the vast bosom of Africa.

Esmeralda, who had been triumphant, was now flustered. 'I thought you'd be pleased. I mean, Uganda's got a civil war going, so it should save the bribes and it's only a short distance to Kenya, which Lance knows.'

'Short distance?' Jimmy said incredulously.

She took a leatherbound Seven Star diary from her handbag. In the back was a fold-out map of the world. She showed it to Jimmy, who snorted disbelievingly.

'The scale's one centimetre to sixteen hundred miles!'

Lance said, 'I think metric. To get from Kenya to Lake Kivu we'd have to pass through Uganda. There's a civil war being fought in Uganda. It's also full of Tanzanian troops looking for somebody to shoot. There and back through Kenya to the sea, that's three thousand kilometres over mostly appalling and often non-existent roads.'

'Well, then go straight through Tanzania to Dar-es-Salaam,' Esmeralda snapped. 'It's more direct.' She held the map out to Lance, who noticed that Lake Kivu did not even show on that scale but was marked with a cross in ink. Lance did not take the book.

'I was just about to add that perhaps we'd better give Tanzanian soil a miss altogether and go north from Lake Kivu until we cross the border into Uganda before we head for Kenya. You see, the Tanzanians are very likely to confiscate your ivory without even waiting for Daniel

131

Drang to come tell them their duty. They're not only keen conservationists, they're socialists as well.'

'Then what about through the Congo to the sea?' Esmeralda tapped the map with her forefinger.

Jimmy inhaled sharply. Lance was speechless. When it was clear Jimmy was not going to explain, and after Esmeralda had pursed her lips impatiently, Lance said, as gently as he could, 'You don't know what you're talking about.'

'Then tell me!'

'There are no roads. There are bandits.' How could he explain to somebody who had never been? She could not possibly conceive of a place with no roads whatsoever and infested with people so desperate they will kill for small change. 'We'd have to go by road to Bangui in the Central African Republic and from there by riverboat to Kinshasa.'

Esmeralda was still not convinced. 'By road to Bangui . . . so there are roads.'

'Not that *you* would recognize.'

Jimmy said, 'We'd need an armoured division with air cover and we'd still lose half the ivory en route and most likely our lives as well. Believe us, we know. The Congo is where Lance and I made our money. For every one of your millions, a man will lose his life.'

'So you would prefer to fight the Tanzanian army and the Ugandan guerrillas instead of travelling through peaceful Congo?'

'I would prefer not to fight anybody,' Lance said firmly. 'You've left out the Rwandan police and the paramilitary forces of the local chieftains, as well as the various free-booters we might find it more convenient to pay tribute to than fight.'

'But you will get my ivory for me?'

'Yes,' Lance said. 'Unless I can think of another surefire way of getting Bruun out into the open.' He thought of another reason for not going through the Congo. 'The Congo's like a second home to Bruun. He lived and fought there for nearly ten years.'

'I'll give you still another reason,' Jimmy said. 'Congo Kinshasa politicians are the most venal in Africa. We'd have to pay them more than any others.'

'I'll call the desk and make reservations for Singapore,' Esmeralda said.

'Just a moment. You're giving me a fifth. What's Jimmy's cut?'

'But he works for you! You pay him.'

'Oh no. He's here on his own account. He could choose not to join us.'

Jimmy looked startled for a moment, then composed his face.

'All right,' Esmeralda said.

'All right what?'

'You're in charge; you decide.'

Lance looked at Jimmy, who said, 'You needn't fear being poor with that one, she'll make the household budget come out.'

Esmeralda turned her back and walked to the phone.

'You haven't seen her buying clothes without even asking the price. How much?'

'Ten per cent? That'll give you another tenth for smaller shares and bribes and expenses.'

'You'll be left with three-fifths,' Lance said to Esmeralda. She had her back to them but had been following every word. 'For my fifth, I'll also bankroll the expedition. Is that all right?'

Esmeralda turned around and smiled at him. 'You're the world's most expensive truck-driver. There's no need for you to pay the advance expenses. Matthew left me very well provided for without taking the ivory into account.'

'I'll ask Lestronge to provide protection for you

133

while Jimmy and I are in Africa bringing the ivory out.'

'Or you can stay with Sambo's family in Brussels,' Jimmy said.

'Please get us three tickets to Singapore on the first plane,' Esmeralda said into the phone. She listened, said 'Thank you,' and put the phone down. Her bosom rose as she turned to face them. 'I'm coming with you.'

'No,' Lance said. 'Don't be stupid.'

Jimmy nodded his agreement: it would be stupid to take her.

'Only I know where the ivory is,' she said.

Lance rose. He was hurt. He was disappointed in her. 'Have it your own way. Find somebody else to take your risks with you.'

'Lance!'

He turned in the bedroom door.

She spoke quickly for fear of losing his attention again. 'It's not a map reference or anything like that. The clue is a photograph of a place.'

'Then give me the photograph,' Lance said through clenched teeth.

'I can't. Matthew burned it after he was sure I would not forget the place.'

'Shit!' This time Lance did not apologize. He looked at Jimmy but Jimmy was staring at Esmeralda with a particular kind of horror, his mind already made up that they would have to take her along.

'What exactly do the directions consist of?' Lance asked, desperately seeking an escape.

'A map reference, a direction, the photograph, further instructions,' Esmeralda said.

'Can you describe the photograph?'

'Trees.'

Jimmy stood. 'I'm not risking my life for a description from a photograph. It's up to you whether you decide to call it off or bring her along.'

'You promised!' Esmeralda said, taking a quick step towards Lance.

Lance nodded. 'That was before I knew you'd most likely have to go along to disentangle idiotic schoolboy clues. We'll talk on the plane. We have to get away from here and Singapore is as good a place as any.'

Jimmy said, 'Maybe we can persuade Pan that he can find the ivory from verbal memories of a photograph.'

Singapore

Singapore is the frustrated housewife's ultra-neat version of Hong Kong, Lance thought. He sadly remembered the Capetown he had grown up in, slightly dingy, an ice-cream wrapper whirling in the south-easter; they had cleaned it up, widened the roads, built the freeways, made a charming city a sterile diamond glistening in a hard sea. Lance, who knew nothing of South-East Asian politics, thought that the people who ruled Singapore would surely have much in common with South Africa's coolly efficient masters.

He smiled at the immigration control officer. He had just remembered that the south-eastern wind was called the Cape Doctor. Now that his parents were dead he would probably never go back to South Africa. But Africa . . . he would go back to Africa, the moment he had dealt with Bruun. Or never, if Bruun dealt with him instead. He felt the sharp pain of loss when it struck him that, should Bruun decide right now to have him killed, he would not be buried in Africa.

'I'm hungry,' Esmeralda said as they waited for the driver to put their cases in the trunk of the Datsun.

'You refused all food on the plane,' Lance said.

'I was worried that perhaps they put it on board in India. I've never seen so dirty a place.' The driver climbed in and she told him, 'Raffles Hotel.'

'The Cockpit, Oxley Rise,' Jimmy contradicted her. 'They have a good restaurant – several, in fact,' he added. 'We can send our bags on to Raffles from there.'

'I was hoping to finish our business with Pan and take the first plane going to Africa,' Lance said, pressing the button on his watch to illuminate the dial. It was nine-thirty.

'If we're in too much of a hurry, he'll think we're at a disadvantage and try to force the price down,' Jimmy said.

'You seem to know a great deal about these parts and their people.'

'I got some of my own money – funds that don't belong to the tribe – in high-risk ventures out here,' Jimmy said.

'Does it pay?' Esmeralda asked with genuine interest.

'I started it mainly to have an excuse to get away from Brussels now and again,' Jimmy said. 'At first I lost my investments quite consistently but recently thirty thousand dollars I put into micro-chips paid off more than half a million.'

Lance whistled. 'It doesn't sound much different from gambling.'

Jimmy shrugged. 'Life's a gamble. Anyway, it takes me away for a while every year from Sambo and the brothers telling me ten times a day I should do my duty and start a family.'

All the same, Lance was immensely impressed with Jimmy. Lance saw his own rise to riches as something outside his control: he had joined the crocodile hunt only to escape his gambling debts. He had inherited from Ewart the crocodile skins that had cost so many lives. A buyer was waiting with cash. When he had stopped playing rugger, he found land cheap in Kenya and decided to have a game reserve; it had been the right time for such a venture, the exact moment of the explosion of public consciousness about conservation. He had wanted to build a fence to protect his elephants: the bank had lent him the money on condition that he insured his elephants each for the total value of the fence. When Matthew Ellimore had shot his six elephants, he had inadvertently – with some help from the bank, the insurance company, rising land values, and the hard work Lance had put into his game reserve – turned Lance into a multi-millionaire. Lance, who would have given half his soul to return to his previous status of a man rich in land and elephants and animals but totally devoid of cash, did not see this sequence as being his due or even good luck. Jimmy, on the other hand, had made *investments* that paid enormous returns.

At the Cockpit, Jimmy told the driver to book them in at Raffles and then return; he was hired for the duration of their stay. The food at the Cockpit was the best Lance could ever remember eating; he had toyed with the plastic food on the plane, his mind on Bruun and Africa, deciding, though he had not yet told the others, that the certainty that his proximity to the ivory would bring Bruun out into the open outweighed the dangers brought about by the overly clever hiding place and the civil war and banditry that had overtaken the area. The delicately prepared and imaginatively presented seafood was spicier and more piquant than any Chinese food he had ever had – Jimmy told him it was Thai food. Even Esmeralda indirectly made her approval known by asking, 'Is this place new?'

'Compared to Raffles, yes. About twenty years or so.'

Their taxi was waiting outside.

Daniel Drang said nothing as he passed them towards the taxi he had flagged down out of the bustling traffic. Christine Rawls said, 'You could at least have waited until I finished my coffee. I haven't got a room yet,' she added to Jimmy.

'Okay, get in,' he said.

'If you're going to follow us around, I'll give you some help with your clothes,' Esmeralda said. 'Don't you have anything but those workingman's pants?'

'Jeans,' Lance said automatically, trying to forestall unpleasantness. 'They're called jeans.'

141

'I'd be grateful,' Christine said. 'You got everything so together.'

Esmeralda sighed. Jimmy translated. 'She means you have excellent taste.' Esmeralda beamed.

Lance doubted that Christine with her almost non-existent hips and her small breasts would look good in the simple flowing clothes Esmeralda alternated with severely cut suits: the first would make Christine look sinewy rather than lissome, the latter prudish instead of elegant. Esmeralda was not fat or even plump but there was enough of her to give a severely cut skirt and jacket tri-dimensional curves in places it would simply hang straight and stiff on Christine. Lance looked forward to the results with malicious amusement. To Lance, women had always been divided into two classes: those who looked good with their clothes on and those who looked good with their clothes off. Esmeralda, by attitude, taste, bearing and exercise, managed to both.

In the morning, when Lance came out of his and Esmeralda's bedroom to have breakfast, Jimmy told him, 'Sir P. K. Pan says he's been expecting us.'

Lance involuntarily looked over his shoulder but all he saw was the palm tree outside the sitting-room window of their suite. It was conceivable that others beside Daniel Drang and Christine Rawls were following them: Bruun's people, Pan's men, who knew who else? Since he had decided to lead them all back to Africa the thought had almost ceased to haunt him. Never mind, he thought now, we're safe until we have the ivory. Almost immediately Jimmy shattered his confidence.

'What was that?' Lance asked Jimmy. 'I'm sorry, I was far away.'

'We aren't in Africa yet. We want to look out here, Lance. It would make good business for Pan to wipe us

142

out: then the Ellimore ivory hoard will be lost forever and his lot will be even more valuable.'

'I don't think so,' Esmeralda said as she came in. 'Good morning, Jimmy. Please don't rise. Pan won't touch us until he can see and touch my ivory. You see, like Matthew, he has long since passed the stage where he is collecting ivory for the money he'll get when he sells it. The ivory itself, the physical possession of it, has become a madness sufficient unto itself.' She helped herself to two poached eggs and some cold lean ham, pushing the toast-rack resolutely away from her. 'I wish this was all over. Until I have my horses again and can have proper exercise, I shall have to control my diet like some common office-girl.'

'A madness sufficient unto itself,' Lance said. 'Let's hope so. That's fine bravado, my girl, considering a spreading backside more important than your life.'

'I can't worry about my life all day long. But any woman can think about her appearance twenty-four hours a day.'

Lance knew what she meant. After a while the threat became commonplace: it could no longer be escalated. It had taken her less time to come to terms with it than it had taken him. 'Just don't get careless,' he said sharply. 'Where's Christine?' he asked Jimmy.

'Sleeping.'

'What time's Pan expecting us?'

'When we get there.'

'We'll leave when Esmeralda's finished her breakfast.'

'I'm not coming with you. I'll take Christine shopping. Don't look so surprised. You don't need me to come to an arrangement with Pan.'

Lance was flattered. 'Perhaps not. But we can't let you wander off unprotected.'

She made a moue of disappointment.

143

'When we've dealt with Bruun and sold the ivory,' Lance said, 'you can go shopping anywhere you want.'

Jimmy rolled his eyes to the high, patterned ceiling. Esmeralda, looking up and seeing only the whites, choked on her food. 'So much for domestic bliss,' he said and turned to Lance. 'What about Drang? You could ask Pan to keep him out of circulation as a demonstration of goodwill.'

'If we could buy Drang, he could help us.'

Jimmy made a scale with dynamic palms. 'I bet he crosses us.'

'I don't gamble,' Lance said stiffly.

'Maybe not with money,' Jimmy said. 'But don't bullshit yourself this ivory recovery is anything but a gamble for the highest stakes, your life and mine and Esmeralda's. Just going out to see Pan is a gamble and you know it.'

'Let's go see Pan,' Lance said, rising. Esmeralda hastily put her cup down. 'Seeing Pan is eliminating one unknown. Going to Africa after that ivory is a lesser evil than running in fear from Bruun, unseen and omnipotent.' He walked through the door and stood in front of Drang. The big black man had a toothpick between his teeth. 'Mr Drang, I'd like to hire . . . uh . . . a public relations officer for an African expedition. I'm paying one million dollars on completion. Out of that my man has to pay his own expenses. What's left over, probably well in excess of half, he keeps.'

'You mean you want me to be your bagman?'

Lance nodded.

'Well now,' Drang said, enjoying himself, 'it ain't that the pay is bad or that the conditions are worse than other jobs. It ain't even my moral objections to bribery'n'corruption. It's just that I don't like working for white mercenaries.'

Lance turned away.

144

'I'll make you an offer,' Drang said. 'Half for you, half for Africa.'

Jimmy had come out of the suite. 'And you put up the million or more dollars needed to finance the expedition?' he asked Drang. He waited ten seconds but no answer was forthcoming. 'I thought so.' He looked into Drang's red-veined eyes for a moment. 'You're a desk-pilot, Drang. Go back to your office before you get hurt.'

Pan's house in Tanglin stood in the middle of three acres of terraced gardens, looking vaguely Mediterranean with its white walls and orange-tiled roof and sea views. The whole made a hard-edged, artificial impact.

Around a curve in the driveway, hidden from the street, an iron gate stood open between two stone pillars. A man in khaki shorts and shirt asked for their names and passports politely. He was not armed but Lance judged from his confident bearing that he was not a man unused to arms. There was a telephone under a little sloping roof behind one of the pillars and the guard used it to confirm that they were expected. A second man they had not seen until then stepped out of the shrubbery to ride up to the house with them.

Sir P. K. Pan was waiting for them on a cool, shaded porch. 'Ah, Mr Weber, I've been expecting you. Mrs Ellimore, your beauty does your late husband great credit. My most sincere commiserations.' He did not offer to shake hands and, as Lance had noticed with the Chinese in Asia and Africa, he managed not to look at Jimmy; the Chinese, Lance had long since concluded, are natural racists. Pan was a middle-aged man, his hair still black, his face chubby, nearly as tall as Esmeralda's five-feet-eight – tall for a Chinese. He was dressed in a double-breasted dark blue suit with a pinstripe of barely perceptible lighter blue, white shirt and red tie. His shoes were highly polished. He spoke the same English Jimmy had picked up at an English public school.

Esmeralda sat in the chair he held for her and looked around curiously at the cane furniture with the piles of colourful cushions. Lance and Jimmy sat down in the chairs indicated. A servant immediately appeared with a tray. They were offered tea and cakes.

'You caused quite a stir in Macao,' Pan said.

Lance nodded.

'It would seem as if you have enemies. A regrettable circumstance.'

'Indeed,' Lance said, not wanting to nod again.

'And now you come to see me,' Pan said, turning to Esmeralda. 'About ivory, I presume?'

'Mr Weber will handle all the negotiations. I'm here strictly for decorative purposes.'

'How refreshing to meet a young woman who has not been infiltrated by the insidiously fashionable trend of the moment.' He turned his gaze on Lance once more. 'About the ivory then, Mr Weber. You wish to make a proposition.'

'Yes. It strikes me that a monopoly would be more profitable for the partners than a duopoly for the competitors.'

'Ah! You use economists' terms.'

'I was trained as one.' Lance was not going to explain that, on an athletics scholarship, he had naturally been a Phys. Ed. major, choosing filler subjects by letting the prospectus fall open at random pages; economics had been on one of these pages. 'If we combine to ration the amount of ivory coming onto the market at any one time, we'll be able to set our own price in absolute certainty of eventually getting it – something we could not do if we were offering ivory in competition.'

'An attractive idea. But there is a problem, is there not, Mr Weber? My ivory is in an easily accessible warehouse while yours has to be brought out of Africa before it can

146

be taken to market. I seem to remember some Latin from my schooldays – '

'Out of Africa always something new,' Jimmy interrupted him. He waited for a second to indicate he had seen the flicker of annoyance pass over the tycoon's face. 'If any or all of us should be eliminated, the newspapers in several countries will be informed of the location of the ivory, and you can be sure a poor African government, desperate for cash, will dig it up and put it all on the market at once – ruining the market for a decade or more.'

Lance saw Pan wince. It was only a small movement around his eyes and mouth but it was there. So much for the myth of the inscrutable Chinese. Entering into the spirit of Jimmy's fine invention, Lance said, 'In a taxi at your gate is a Mr Daniel Drang, a security officer of the Organization for African Unity. He too would like the ivory to raise cash immediately. He too will be told, a few days before the newspapers, where the ivory is . . . if we don't reappear.'

'I shall forgive your crudeness as expressions of your youthful exuberance,' Pan said. 'There is no cause to threaten me. But I should like to make you a counter-offer. You tell me where the ivory is and I pay you for the knowledge.'

'You will never get it out of Africa,' Lance said. 'I'm not being gratuitously offensive, sir, but I do know the difficulties involved.'

'*You* could bring it out, though?'

'I've had some experience.'

Pan nodded. 'So I've heard. But you misunderstand me. I have no intention of losing competent men of my own or paying large sums to adventurers to rescue that ivory from Africa. My sole intention is to destroy it in situ. That way my own holdings will quadruple in value.'

147

'Or better,' Lance said. Pan, like Matthew Ellimore, was ignorant of the abilities of the plastics-chemists and their threshold price! 'How much are you offering?'

'Five million dollars, American.'

'That's a ridiculous offer,' Lance said.

'Eight million.'

'It's worth twenty-five million delivered in Paris and sold as one lot to the highest bidder,' Lance said. 'Mimimum.'

'Ten million. That's my final offer. Think,' the Chinese knight said directly to Esmeralda. 'It will cost you at least ten million of your twenty-five to get the ivory out of Africa. I don't imagine men like Weber work cheaply. And he could fail. Then you will have nothing and even be out of pocket.'

She put her cup down and rose. 'Perhaps I may be allowed to look around your lovely garden while Mr Weber concludes the arrangements with you.'

However graciously put, it was a snub. 'Of course,' Pan said, rising. His voice lacked enthusiasm. He waved at one of the four men on the veranda, who trailed after Esmeralda.

'I'm willing to offer you another arrangement,' Lance said. 'I can, right now, offer you an option on the Ellimore ivory, delivered in Singapore or anywhere else you like, for a price of twenty-five million American dollars. You would then be the sole owner of ninety per cent of the world's ivory.'

Pan drew in his breath. He studied Lance's face closely. Lance fancied he could see the wheels turning, the tumblers clicking, behind the man's surprisingly soft eyes.

'And the price of the option?'

'Two million dollars.'

'Set off against the twenty-five million when you deliver?'

'Yes. But to be forfeited if there is any interference in our attempt at recovering the ivory.'

Pan once more looked at Lance. His face was stony and his brown eyes no longer doe-like

'I apologize for my barbarian friend,' Jimmy said. 'He lacks our advantage of an English public-school education. He is much given to saying things aloud. *Things.*'

'What about my two million dollars if you fail – if, for instance, some younger, larger, brasher predator takes the ivory from you?'

Lance hoped his consternation did not show on his face. Behind him, Jimmy yawned, distracting Pan.

'Do you know Lestronge in Hong Kong?' Jimmy asked.

'Yes,' Pan said. Lance thought he detected a note of apprehension in the man's voice.

'If you know him,' Jimmy said, 'it follows that you've already asked him about Lance and that you know nobody's going to take the ivory from us.'

Yes! Where else would Pan have acquired knowledge of Lance's 'experience'?

Lance had struck on the idea of making Pan pay something towards the cost of the expedition on the spur of the moment. He had been convinced, then, that the man's word alone would be worthless; an investment would speak louder than words. Lance rose. 'Of course, if you aren't interested . . .'

Pan stood too. 'I agree to your terms. Two million dollars for an option at twenty-five million dollars. I shall of course send a representative with you to watch over my interests.'

'Of course,' Lance said.

'That was just too bloody easy,' Lance said in the taxi.

'I was hoping to see his wife,' Esmeralda said. 'She is said to be the most beautiful woman in the East.'

'Are you listening to me? I don't trust that man.'

'Then go to the bank and see if his cheque is good.'

Lance and Jimmy both turned to look at Esmeralda between them in the back seat of the taxi.

'She sure cuts through bullshit,' Jimmy said. 'Driver, take us to the Ocean Building on Collyer Quay.'

Lance looked at the cheque. 'Actually, his bank is on Raffles Quay.'

'Sure. But you don't have an account at his bank, do you?'

'No.'

'Well, they know you from nowhere. They won't tell you anything about one of their clients unless you ask through your own bank. But I have an account with the Swiss Bank here. So let's ask them.'

The manager was, to Lance's surprise, an Englishman. He received Jimmy cordially. After some small talk, Jimmy passed the cheque across the desk to him. 'Is that good?'

The man studied the cheque. 'As gold.'

'Call them up and check, please.'

'If you insist.' He made the phone call. When he put the phone down, he said, 'I can send the cheque around by messenger to Raffles Quay.'

'Do that,' Jimmy said.

After it was arranged that the funds would be put into an account in Esmeralda's name that Lance could draw on for the expenses of their expedition, the bank manager said, 'If it's not indelicate, what did Pan pay you for . . .'

(Later Esmeralda would tell Lance that she had been tempted to reply, The usual services a woman provides.)

Jimmy said, 'To fetch some ivory out of Africa. It's a down-payment on twenty-five million. Is he good for the rest?'

The manager nodded. 'Not out of petty cash, like this

two million. But he can certainly raise twenty-three million. And I devoutly hope he raises some of it here.'

The whole episode left Lance vaguely dissatisfied. 'All we know is that he's an A-1 credit risk,' he said in the taxi. 'That doesn't tell us whether he keeps his word.'

Esmeralda squeezed his hand. 'You continue to amaze me. I didn't think you were such a brilliant businessman.'

'I couldn't have done it without Jimmy's help.'

'Don't hide your talent under a bucket,' Jimmy said. 'We went there to beg him not to kill us and you made him pay two million for the doubtful privilege of becoming in effect our guardian angel. Brilliant hardly describes it.'

Lance was not convinced. 'He played with us. The only times we saw the real man was when we overstepped the mark and he sat there and you could read on his face how much he would like to squash the barbarians on his veranda.'

'Sure,' Jimmy said. 'Be sensitive if you must. But be sensible too. He's not going to throw away an investment of two million dollars.'

Esmeralda nodded energetically.

'Rubbish,' Lance said with unaccustomed vehemence. 'A man that rich can drop two million on a whim the same way you risk thirty thousand just to get away from Sambo's domestic bliss.'

That stilled their arguments. They rode in uneasy silence to the hotel.

Just before they reached there, Lance said, 'We may have awakened the dragon quite gratuitously.'

Jimmy nodded. 'Funny how he didn't approach Esmeralda but waited for her to come to him.'

'What is the pertinence of that?' she asked.

'That he knew a woman would need his help. That he may not be pleased at Lance's intervention.'

151

Lance shivered. These bloody people had only two settings for the air-conditioning in their cars: off or freezing. 'Once we get to Africa, he becomes irrelevant. We leave as soon as we can pack.'

Sir P. K. Pan pressed a button and a section of the panelling slid aside; he did not consider the gimmick or, today, remember with his usual pleasure that his parents' whole home would have fitted twice into his study.

The woman had come at last, and accompanied by dangerous men. He had dealt with them well but now he had need of ivory in his hands. He picked up a piece of ivory and ran his hands over it, feeling the grain; he fixed it to the chuck of the Encomat lathe that was the centrepiece of the workshop revealed by the sliding panel.

His face had been well served by being forewarned. The temptation to take the overgrown Weber for the peasant he appeared to be could have led him into error. But Lestronge knew what he was talking about. And the black man was more than merely a loyal retainer; he was a difficult man in his own right, with dangerous relatives and interesting connections.

Pan studied the light glinting on the ivory in the lathe as it turned. He stopped the machine, caressed the ivory again, and trued it up in the lathe to gain the best advantage of its slightly conical shape for the least waste. He had always loved the soapy feel of ivory; he could not remember when he had first touched it. What distinguished genuine ivory from the finest plastic imitation was its warmth in the hand of an expert. Plastic would always feel like plastic but ivory would heat up in one's hand – but, and this made it truly exceptional to men of taste, not in everyone's hand: one had to know and appreciate ivory to feel that rare glow it exuded. Pan re-positioned the ivory; he did not consider it ridiculous for him, the owner of half the world's ivory, to take such care to save a few grammes. Some day, some day soon, those few grammes would be worth more than their weight in gold and few men would be able to afford a complete tusk such as the medium-sized five-footer resting in the corner of his study.

Weber carried more difficulties on his trail, the man Drang for instance. Lestronge had known about him too, from Vietnam. No doubt there were others, not as easily disposed of as the uncouth Australians Weber had lost so easily in Macao. There had been a sense, as always, that Lestronge was not telling all he knew.

Pan turned a fine chisel against the spinning ivory, took the blade away and bent close to study the effect. Perfect. Ivory is a natural product, a tooth pulled from a living creature. Without the stimulating flow of blood it will grow brittle with the years. It will also grow brittle with cold and with dry heat. Yet ivory seems to age gracefully on the slopes of Mount Kilimanjaro, Matthew had told him long, long ago, before they had split over a woman. It was the right temperature coupled with the correct level of humidity that would give properly seasoned ivory that soapy feeling that made it the only ivory worth having to the connoisseur. Pan had spent two million American dollars building a warehouse to duplicate the climatic conditions found on the northern slopes of an African mountain he had never seen; *all* his ivory was of the proper seasoned texture and colour. That was another thing: ivory, unless correctly aged, is not the colour most people would call 'ivory'; on the animal it is sand-coloured or dirty light grey, or sometimes a brownish red, especially on very old bulls, who, out of frustrated hunger, root in the ground with their tusks. Ivory that has been lying in the sun is dead white and very brittle. No, the deeply satisfying cream 'ivory' is, like the soapy 'feel' and

153

the warmth, the sign of properly preserved and aged ivory. *All* Pan's ivory . . .

He snapped the slender column he had turned with a blow from the side of a chisel blade – it was a small tap but in the context a gesture of consummate violence.

Matthew had known about the slopes of Kilimanjaro but the woman would not need men of the calibre of Weber to recover the ivory from there. But Matthew had also mentioned that ivory would age gracefully if stored in water of the correct temperature in direct sunlight. Pan picked up the pieces of his smashed Corinthian column and broke them unconsciously. Matthew had undoubtedly known other places, other methods. Matthew had known everything about ivory. The whole thing had been Matthew's idea; Pan's infatuation had followed. He had Matthew to thank for that great love of his life. And for his wife, Jennifer.

Matthew's ivory would almost certainly all be of the proper seasoned texture and colour as well. Pan placed the pieces in a row on his bench, then stared at them, horrified at having shown so much emotion even here in his inner sanctum.

It was not just a matter of competent men. Certainly, if anybody could bring Matthew's ivory out of Africa, Weber could. Lestronge had said so and Pan himself was an excellent judge of the potential of men. Nor was it a question of finding competent men of his own: young Henry Chew had a great deal of initiative and, like Weber, a misleading appearance.

But what to do? It would be delightful to have so much ivory. But . . . Yes. But would the *known* destruction of half the world's ivory not make the other half valuable out of all proportion?

He would sleep on it.

* * *

154

MORE ELEPHANTS KILLED
INTERNATIONAL OUTRAGE AS LAST KRUGER PARK
ELEPHANTS DISMEMBERED IN BLOODBATH

Lance picked up the *Straits Times*. He had visited the Kruger National Park with a school tour. Then there had been perhaps a hundred elephants, since drastically reduced by poachers from Macambique and Zimbabwe. But poachers do not dismember elephants.

Lance threw the paper back on the news-seller's stack without reading the report. There was no need to. He looked blankly at Jimmy and Esmeralda, then turned abruptly and headed for the plane that would take him back to Africa.

Blood Ivory

'The Washington Convention of 1973.'

Lance took the letter from Jimmy. 'And the resolution taken at the Delhi Convention of 1981,' he said, reading only a phrase. He read the whole letter while they waited in silence. 'What it comes down to is that we can't move the ivory through Kenya not matter what certificates of origin and export we have from other countries.' He passed the letter to Esmeralda but she did not read it.

'This one is from Rwanda,' Jimmy said. 'They've told our lawyer that, if we'll tell them where the ivory is, we can take half out if they get to keep the other half.'

'If we tell them where it is?' Lance said. He took the letter from Jimmy and read it for himself. 'Is this man stupid?'

Jimmy shrugged. 'He's a lawyer. He's passing a message from his Government to his client. He probably thinks that's a neutral activity.'

'Perhaps we can negotiate with them,' Esmeralda said.

Jimmy's tone was strained as he explained the obvious to her. 'That the man in charge of the permissions wants to know where the ivory is gives his game away. There'll be nothing left when we get there. So we negotiate to give him less and not to tell him where it is. Once we have the ivory he'll still take it all.'

'That's stealing from a widow!'

Lance laughed at her vehemence. 'What disturbs me more is the Kenyan attitude. The strict interpretation of the Washington Convention is that you can move the ivory once you have a certificate of origin. Now, because African officials are so corrupt that you can buy certificates of anything, some people are unilaterally deciding which certificates they accept and which they don't. That makes another layer of officials to bribe.'

'Then bribe the Kenyans as well.' Esmeralda relaxed visibly.

Lance shook his head. 'No, it's quite clear from this letter that there is no discretion: the Kenyans have a blanket ban on the transport of ivory through their country. Anyway, Kenya is probably the least corrupt of the black African states.'

'Well then, is the ivory Matthew died for lost?'

The anguish in her voice touched him. She firmly believed in her duty to recover and market Matthew Ellimore's ivory: her late husband had lived and died for that end.

'More important, since your husband is already dead,' Jimmy said, 'is what Bruun does to us when he finds out we're no longer going after the ivory.'

Lance shivered involuntarily. This last month in Africa, in a rented house at Thika, about forty kilometres north of Nairobi, he had almost forgotten about Bruun. Here he was on his home ground, no longer a stranger, a fish out of water. Once he had mentioned the strange discomfort he had felt in Europe and Asia to Jimmy, who retorted: 'What do you expect? You're a different sort of animal. Of course strange surroundings will make you uneasy. And of course city people look on you as a dangerous caged animal. The city is the cage and they have to share it with you.' Jimmy had remembered the policeman Simps and burst out laughing at the memory of the man's patent fear of them. Lance had not pursued the conversation. But he noticed that he and Jimmy – and Esmeralda, who had become part of him – bloomed in Africa while Daniel Drang and Christine Rawls and Henry Chew (Pan's representative) wilted even in the mild climate of Kenya's Highlands. Christine had called him a liar when he told her the temperature year-round was no higher than that of Zurich or Frankfurt or Vienna in summer. In that month Lance had flown to Port Elizabeth to buy heavy trucks from the General Motors plant there. When he had returned, Jimmy had gone to Brussels to select two of his tribesmen for the expedition; Sambo had reluctantly stayed to guard his family. Jimmy had also ordered equipment and supplies to be airfreighted to Nairobi. Putting together an expedition to the exact middle of Africa is not an overnight exercise, Lance had told Esmeralda when she became impatient. He was amazed at her: she had taken over the domestic affairs of their large household with a firm hand and a certain gusto that betrayed a genuine delight in her work; as soon as she learned all the ins and outs of Africa – and she was well on her way – she would be as good as the late Magda Brazenose. The memory of Magda's death brought Lance back to earth. Esmeralda could still go the same way.

Only almost. For Bruun had not forgotten them. The systematic extinction of the elephants in the zoos was continuing, a message as pointed as a finger. It had become a major international scandal, pushing several concurrent wars off the front pages. Zoos everywhere were stepping up security. Some had closed their gates to the public. In the more authoritarian regimes the army had been given responsibility for the security of the zoos; the Argentinians had caught one Chinese, the Detroit police another; in both cases the criminal had died under questioning before revealing more than that his orders had come through middlemen. Lance thought they knew nothing more to reveal. Both the captured Chinese had come from Macao. The more radical conservationists were mumbling about Chinese communist plots to upset the ecology of the West; that did not even raise a smile from Lance. He was doing his best to forget the whole business. It was not easy. There was nothing in the newspapers or on the radio but elephants. Dead elephants. Dismembered elephants. The price of ivory rising hourly on the ivory futures markets hurriedly instituted in Chicago and London, jumping several points at the news of yet another outrage at a zoo that no one had heard of until its elephants were found slaughtered.

'Who says we're no longer going after the ivory?' Lance asked.

'And there's Pan,' Esmeralda said to nobody in particular. 'He'll think we crossed him twice even if we give him back his two million dollars.'

'Doublecrossed,' Jimmy said. 'I don't fancy our chances through Zaire,' he added to Lance. 'I got this disease, see. A strip of yellow about two inches wide running from my head into my trousers all the way down my back.'

Lance nodded. He did not need to look at the map: from Goma on the northwestern corner of Lake Kivu to Bangui in the Central African Republic (from where the ivory could be floated down the Congo to Kinshasa or sent overland to a number of other ports) was about two thousand miles of atrocious roads through bandit-infested country. The owners of high-quality trucks like theirs, delivered from Mombasa yesterday, would have to fight to retain possession even when the trucks were empty. Loaded with valuable ivory . . . It was not an alternative even worth considering. He and Jimmy had been up that road before, eight years ago. Then the expedition had been led by Ewart and Colonel Jacques Roux, with Sambo and nearly twenty of his brothers and tribesmen. It had still been a hard, dangerous slog. Lance did not think he could do it with much more limited resources. Ewart had had a lifetime of experience. Not wanting to take the ivory overland across Zaire had nothing to do with cowardice.

'Even if it was a tarmacadam road all the way and safe

as houses, there'd be too many governments involved,' Lance said.

'We're going then,' Jimmy said flatly. He pulled the map on the table towards him but did not look down at it. 'Three choices,' he said. 'South through Tanzania, Zambia and Zimbabwe to South Africa. East through Tanzania. North through Uganda, Sudan, Ethiopia. On any of those routes we're going to be illegal. They won't give us licences, except as a pretence while they plot how to rob us blind.'

'Or through Uganda and Kenya,' Lance said, 'except I want to live in Kenya again and breaking the law would be stupid.'

'And you've given them advance warning by asking permission,' Esmeralda said. 'Can't we fly the ivory out from Lake Kivu or nearby? There's an airfield here at – '

'That's an airstrip,' Jimmy said. 'It takes light planes in the dry season. To airlift thirty tons of ivory, we want to go to an international airport – which means customs and the same men who want to take at least half your ivory.'

'What about a flying-boat that can land on the lake?'

'No,' Lance said. 'I know all about that. A couple of years ago I talked to a desert biologist with an institute up near Lake Rudolf. He had some large pieces of delicate equipment he wanted flown in and he didn't want to pay to lengthen the airstrips so he tried to rent a flying boat. Finally he found an old Sunderland he could buy for peanuts but it would've cost about a million pounds to put it in the air again.' There was a long silence before Lance added, 'Anyway, such a lumbering plane would be shot down within the first hundred miles by one of the air forces whose territory we'd be crossing.'

After another long silence, Esmeralda asked, 'What happened to his equipment?'

'He trucked it in and had about a million pounds' worth of breakages and then it got put together wrong and he

163

had to keep bringing out technicians from Europe and the States and in the end it cost about two million pounds more than it should have.'

'He shoulda' bought that flying boat,' Jimmy said.

'Yeah. Which route, Jimmy?'

'In via Tanzania with empty trucks, out via Uganda, Sudan and Ethiopia.'

Esmeralda turned her large liquid eyes on Jimmy. 'Through *three* countries with civil wars raging?'

Jimmy said nothing.

Lance considered the map. 'Actually, Jimmy's got a point about Tanzania. They can't object to the empty trucks going over their territory. They don't know about the ivory.'

Jimmy's smile broadened. 'Go on.'

'While the Kenyans do know about the ivory: they'll never let us come out across their territory. But they can have no objection to a solid citizen like me moving empty trucks across their land.'

'What are you getting at, Lance?' The excitement was rising in Esmeralda's voice.

'We go in via Kenya and Uganda, we come out straight across Tanzania to the sea,' Lance said. 'With any luck we'll meet no resistance.'

'You're as mad as Jimmy,' she said in a dull voice. 'There's a civil war in Uganda and Tanzania is still occupying Uganda as well. There are Tanzanian soldiers all over this area we'll have to cross with the ivory.'

'There's nowhere we can go that we won't have to fight,' Lance said gently. 'So I chose the shortest route that'll give no one warning of our intention.'

She looked from him to Jimmy, her face still but pain in her eyes. 'I didn't realize . . . We'll give Pan his money back . . .'

'Lance said, 'Well, uh, there's . . . uh, you see, there's –'

Jimmy helped him. 'If we don't bring out that ivory, it

won't be only Bruun and Pan after your blood, it'll be every cut-throat and second-class citizen in the world.'

'Why?'

'They'll think Lance's nerve failed him and that therefore he's vulnerable. In a way, it'll be worse than waiting for Bruun to make his next move because you'll never know when or from where the next attack will come. You can't guard against all eventualities.'

'Your life would be hell,' Lance said. 'You'd never be able to go shopping except with three or four body-guards.'

That convinced her that they had gone too far to retreat. For the rest of the day she was quiet and thoughtful; Lance wondered if she had only now realized the stakes they were playing for. He could not blame her. She had led a life sheltered from adventurers who would kill for far smaller fortunes than that involved here. And, like every outsider, she had failed to grasp the ruthless Darwinism Africa applied to the timid, the cowardly and the plain unlucky. Civilization is getting a second chance, Lance thought once when he woke in the middle of the night. Africa was not civilized; he suddenly realized that that was part of its charm for him, still the quintessential gambler despite the long absence of cards from his hands, that Africa was, is, *defined* by giving men only one chance in a game played only for the highest stakes.

But she had shown she was both willing and able to fit in . . . She was the first woman he had ever met he could spend the rest of his life with. He would ask her after the expedition, when he had dealt with Bruun. They could live in Kenya; the white establishment would ostracize them at first (It's not the done thing to shack up with the widow of the man you killed, old chap) but time and curiosity – and money – would overcome that problem.

Before he fell asleep, he thought that it was as well that Africa and Nature did not coincide exactly: whereas

Africa gave man the individual a solitary chance, Nature had given man-the-species control of the dice factory – to the glory of civilization and the detriment or annihilation of other species.

Lance did not think civilization much of a bargain. Conversely, he was aware that 'civilization' (or much of it anyway) could not by its own lights approve of him. The knowledge failed to disturb him. In the morning he told Esmeralda, 'The reason I'm fetching your ivory out, one reason apart from fear of Bruun and Pan and all the other unknown and unknowable predators out there, is that I don't believe people should change the rules after the event. There was no law against it when your husband gathered the ivory at the bottom of Lake Kivu. Coming now, years after the event, saying he shouldn't have done it and making a retro-active law – that's immoral.'

She put her arms around his chest from behind, careful not to jog his arms. He was shaving. 'You don't have to justify yourself to me, Lance.'

'I know. I'm thinking it out for myself. Aloud.'

'They're applying the law only so they can extract bribes from us.'

He rinsed the razor. 'That's not so bad. It's a tribute to power. The African way. Thanks.' He took the towel she handed him and wiped his face.

'They're also applying the laws very selectively.'

'Yes. I'm leaving for Mombasa after breakfast. I'll be back tonight or tomorrow.'

He drove to Nairobi and rented a plane. As he was walking out over the tarmac to it, a voice called, 'Hey, pal, they say you're going to Mombasa.'

Lance turned around. The other man was tall and well tanned with an abundance of tightly curled black hair. His teeth flashed white in a nervous smile. He wore the neatly pressed slacks and short-sleeved shirt, the wraparound dark glasses and crinkly lines at the corners of his eyes that marked him as a professional pilot. For confirmation he carried a scarred black bag that Lance thought probably held his spare shirt and underclothing as well as his logbook, maps and other pilot's impedimenta.

'Sure. You want a lift?'

'Please. If it's all the same to you.'

'Be glad of the company.' At the plane, he asked. 'You want to sit in the left-hand seat?' It was a courtesy; professional pilots like professional drivers prefer not to be passengers to amateurs.

Again the smile. 'Naw. It's okay. I asked about you in the met office. Sorry.'

Lance laughed. 'It's all right. I don't fly with just anybody either.'

Once in the air and on course, the pilot put out his hand. 'Tanner Chapman.'

Lance shook hands with him. 'From South Africa?' Chapman had the accent. 'I'm Lance Weber.'

'Yeah. I have a Chinese girlfriend, so I had to leave South Africa. Settled in Tanzania.'

Lance laughed. 'That wasn't too bright.'

Chapman flashed his smile. 'I should've asked. But it wasn't funny when they tried to force Ruby to marry a black man.'

'So you came to Kenya. Things will probably be better here.'

'For me and Ruby, sure. But there are too many pilots.' They talked of how the plane would replace the car eventually, of the Tanzanians' attempt forcibly to 'integrate' their Asians, of South Africa and of Africa. At Mombasa they parted. Lance rented a jeep and started his tour of the marinas. In the middle of the afternoon he found what he wanted. 'Twin Rolls-Royce engines with only two hundred hours since they were overhauled,' the agent said. 'Cost a fortune. I got the bills and receipts in the office.'

Lance studied the peeling paint. 'Why didn't they repaint her at the same time?'

'The hull's sound. Survey was done late last year. Halmatic built these things to last, the surveyor told me.'

'Why wasn't she repainted?' Lance repeated.

'Owner's in gaol.' The broker laughed. 'Occupational hazard for smugglers, you know.'

Lance nodded. 'Point me to the surveyor's office and if I'm still interested after I talk to him, I'll come back to you.'

The surveyor was happy to tell Lance that the boat was sound and had the range he specified. Lance went back to the broker. 'What's your best price?'

'It's worth upwards of half a million dollars in Nice.'

'This is Mombasa and you've had her on your books for nine months.'

'Four hundred thousand.'

'Two-fifty with full tanks and all transfer costs.'

'For that much I can let you have the fifty-two foot Hatteras.'

'It doesn't have my range.'

'Three hundred thousand.'

'Done. Can I hire a reliable crew here?'

The broker looked down at his desk. He put a hand above his desk and waggled it. 'For cruising with your wife, no. But I can point you to men who know all the coves and bays along the coast. You'll want to look bright sharply to your possessions and your life though.'

Lance smiled. It was clear the broker could not make up his mind whether Lance was a tourist or a smuggler.

'I can get you a good, honest, bonded crew from Nice here in forty-eight hours.'

'Let's talk about the men who know the coves and the bays. Will the promise of big money hold them to a schedule?'

The broker looked Lance in the face. 'Without supervision?' Lance nodded. 'It would have to be very big money indeed, Mr Weber. A broker in Nice would buy that boat for three hundred thousand for stock as long as the papers had no blood on them.'

'Forget I asked.' Lance rose. 'Here, Barclays will clear this cheque on the phone. The extra ten thousand is for provisioning the boat right to the limit of her range with a full complement of crew and guests.'

'I understand.'

'Today.'

'Come on, Mr Weber. This isn't Johannesburg, this is Mombasa. It will be done by tomorrow night.'

Lance nodded. 'As soon as I find him, I'll send my skipper to take charge. Meanwhile, you can find me care of my bank.'

The broker walked out with Lance. 'Tell me, Mr Weber, did you ever own a yacht before?'

'No.'

'Hmmm. You went unerringly for the only real ship around here. Compared to that one, the rest are toys. When you've finished with her, if she's whole, I'll take her back from you for two-fifty.'

Lance nodded. That man had finally decided Lance was not a tourist. That was good: his orders would be executed meticulously and quickly. It was too late to fly back to Nairobi, so he headed down the beach. After a few miles, he turned the jeep around and headed for the airport. He had had an idea. He found Tanner Chapman sitting on a bench in the met office.

'No luck?'

'They hired a pilot just before I walked in.'

'Know anything about boats?'

'Sure. I crewed in the Cape to Rio race once and I've sailed from Durban to Madagascar in my own boat. But that trade is a lot more competitive than flying and you need capital to buy the boat first.'

'I got a boat. You want a job?'

Chapman rose with alacricity. 'You bet I want a job.'

'Come with me.' Lance drove him back to the marina.

'What the hell do you want with an MTB?'

'What's that?'

'Motor Torpedo Boat. You don't know anything about ships?'

'No.'

'How much did you pay?'

'Three hundred thousand American.'

'Where's the survey?' Chapman held his hand out.

Lance gave him all the papers and waited for Chapman to find the xerox copy of the survey. Chapman went to the front of the jeep to read it in the headlights. Finally he came to where Lance stood on the quay.

'You bought a bargain, Mr Weber.'

'Lance will do.'

'What are you smuggling in? I don't want anything to do with the arms business.'

'I'm not smuggling anything in. I'm not in the arms business. But you're right, there could be trouble.'

'What kind of trouble.'

"Shooting trouble. I'll be taking something out. Other people also want it. But the trouble will be around me, not you.'

Chapman reached over to switch the jeep's headlights off. 'Better save the battery. I'm a Jew, you know. Tanner Chapman's English for Tannah Kirschmann. The Jews are pretty law-abiding people.'

'Okay. I'lls take you a night in a hotel and give you a lift back to Nairobi in the morning,' Lance said. 'Once there, I'll introduce you to some people I know who run air charters to the game reserves.'

After dinner they sat with a beer on the veranda and looked through the glass at the moon on the water.

'If you don't mind me asking,' Chapman said. 'You're

obviously a nice guy and well-connected, no crim. And you're not short of cash if you can splash out big round numbers for a boat. So why do you want to smuggle anything?'

Lance, taken unawares, said, 'Oh, it's not that I want to. I must.' After a moment of silence, he told Chapman most of the story. The man had a very comforting presence and, unlike most pilots, he was a good listener.

'You really got yourself in a twist, haven't you?' Chapman said when he finished.

Lance nodded and signalled for more beer.

'But surely you can hire some of the smugglers who live right here?'

'No. They're small men. Life is cheap to them. Including their own. I want somebody who values his life enough not to cross me or my friends.'

'Somebody with enough intelligence to enquire into the vengefulness of your friends?'

'I couldn't put it better myself.'

'Where are you going to find him?'

'We have connections in Europe and Asia that can find us such men. I don't know how they do it. One has a computer.'

'Jesus, this is almost like working for De Beers . . . What will you want me to do if I decide to take the job?'

'Lay off the coast every day at a certain time. Captain the boat to Madagascar or Durban once we have the ivory on board.'

'Okay. I'll do it.'

'You don't know how much I'm paying.'

'That's right, I don't. I also want a big policy on my life in favour of Ruby. She's my girl.'

'Sure. I'll pay you a hundred thousand American, a fifth now, two-fifths when we have the ivory on board, the balance on arrival in Durban.'

The next day, while they were flying back to Nairobi,

Chapman said, 'You're such a trusting guy. I'm surprised you're still alive.'

Lance laughed aloud. 'There's a myth about me that my enemies don't survive. The thing is, it appears to come true.'

'That doesn't matter, whether it comes true. It's enough to have people believe it. All the same, I won't cross you. Your friend Sergeant Sambo sounds like a keen enemy.'

Over dinner that evening, Lance told Esmeralda and Jimmy about the boat and its captain. Almost casually, he added, 'We leave the day after tomorrow at dawn.

'Nobody travels in the rainy season,' Esmeralda said.

Jimmy put his knife and fork down to give Lance his whole attention. 'She's right, you know,' he said.

'That's exactly why we will. Of all those who'll be contesting the ownership of the ivory with us, who has more experience of travelling in adverse conditions than us?'

'The army and the police and the bandits and guerrillas,' Jimmy said immediately.

'Sure. But we're better equpped than they are. And our most immediate enemies will sink into the mud and disappear.'

Jimmy groaned.

'You don't think losing Bruun's men and Drang is worth a little hard work?'

Jimmy groaned again.

'Well?'

'You're so crazy you could be right. It'll certainly sort out the men from the boys.'

'Okay. We won't tell anybody. We'll load the trucks tomorrow as if for practice and then just leave in the dawn.'

'What about Christine?' Esmeralda asked.

'What about her?' Jimmy wanted to know.

'Are you bringing her?'

Christine had tactfully absented herself for the evening when Lance had said he wanted to discuss business with Esmeralda and Jimmy. The blonde girl was now almost part of them, eating all her meals at their table, sharing a bedroom with Jimmy. Drang, keeping his distance, had rented a house down the road; he had called up reinforcements: two young black men who could not speak any of the native languages and seemed ill at ease even in the relative civilization of Thika. Of Bruun's men there had been no trace and there were no other suspicious persons in the district. This did not mean, however, that there were no watchers and waiters; they could sit in Nairobi and listen to gossip and be as well informed as Drang watching Lance's compound with his binoculars.

'No. I've told her to go back to England when we leave here.'

'She'll follow us.'

'I can't stop her.'

'She'll get killed behind us.'

Jimmy nodded. 'I've told her. But she's a free agent.'

'Then why not bring her with us?'

Lance entered the discussion. 'We're taking you because we cannot avoid it. Taking women is not generally recommended in some of the parts we'll be passing through.'

'But she's coming anyway.'

'She won't get far.'

'Before she gets killed . . .'

'What's this, Esmeralda?' Jimmy asked irritably. 'She's not on our side, you know.'

'Then what's she doing in your bed?'

'Spying,' Jimmy said, and burst out laughing.

Esmeralda blushed and hissed something furious. Lance diplomatically turned his own laughter into a cough. Esmeralda got hold of her anger and waited icily for Jimmy to finish laughing. She was gathering what

Lance thought of as her 'Spanish dignity' about her. 'When you finish cackling like a drunken hyena,' she said when she had their attention, 'consider how you would feel if she was raped and killed while following us.'

'We'll lose her as soon as we can,' Lance said. 'It's not going to be a drive through the home counties, you know.'

'I say we take her with us. She's very useful around the house.'

'We have enough servants,' Lance said.

'She'll cross us,' Jimmy said. 'Why invite a viper into your bosom?'

'Because I don't want her killed for love of you. Don't you see, the animals are now only an excuse?'

Jimmy put his knife and fork down again. 'We're not going on a honeymoon cruise, Esmeralda. But I wouldn't want her on my conscience or yours. Equally, I don't want you to lose your ivory because of her. Because she *will* cross us.' Jimmy sipped wine from the Waterford crystal Esmeralda had miraculously conjured up in Nairobi. 'For her, conservation will always come before anything else.'

'I want to take her,' Esmeralda said to Lance, who turned his eyes from Jimmy to her. 'Otherwise you must leave her here with a guard to see she doesn't follow us.'

'That's kidnapping,' Lance said flatly. 'Let her come. If she does decide to cross us, there will be nobody for her to team up with. I don't see what she can do by herself.'

'Mr Weber, I expected you go give me fair warning of your departure so that I could warn my principal,' Henry Chew said sternly. The top of his head was level with Lance's shortribs but Chew resolutely refused to look up when he addressed anybody taller than himself. Jimmy had a theory that Pan's representative believed himself the norm and that everybody else, especially freaks over six feet, should bend down to him. Maybe Chew is right, Lance had thought at the time: there are more Chinese in the world than anybody else.

'You can send a telegram from the first stop.'

Somewhere in the darkness Jimmy sniggered; Lance wished he would restrain himself. Chew was difficult enough without making fun of him.

'My guidebook says Kenya is one of the more efficient countries in Africa,' Chew said precisely. 'Since it takes half a day to post a registered letter here, I can only surmise that from anywhere else it is totally impossible. You must do better, Mr Weber.'

Jimmy sniggered again. Chew was right. From Kampala, the next city on their route, it was faster even in peacetime to drive to Nairobi than to telephone (if the telephones were working, on average one day in the month) or to send a letter (which, four times out of five, would not arrive). But it would not do to let Chew think he was in charge. 'Phone him now, Mr Chew. You have fifteen minutes, then we leave.'

'Sir P. K. Pan may be otherwise engaged!'

'Then leave a message!' Lance snapped. 'The phone's through there. We leave in fifteen minutes, with or without you.' He turned to test the ropes holding the inflatable dinghies in their orange drums on the truck. Out of the corner of his eye he saw the Chinese walking quickly into the house. 'Don't ride him, Jimmy,' he said in a low tone.

'He loves me as little as I love him.'

'He conceals his feelings better. Try, will you. We're going to have him in our camp for a long time.'

'Considering that he watches you for a guy with two million at stake, he's pretty inoffensive,' Christine said. She put the hamper in the back of the Range Rover and walked back inside the house.

Lance and Jimmy had discussed this before and concluded that Pan perhaps had no gangster types to send.

'What did you tell her?' Lance asked, nodding his head at the door through which Christine had disappeared.

'If she behaves, I'll make a contribution of a quarter million to the animals when this is over.'

'The expedition will carry it.'

'Thanks.'

'You could try to sound more grateful, Jimmy. It's a lot of money.'

'You're starting to sound like Sambo in his old-woman moods. When there's twenty-five million in sight, we're not going to buy her for a quarter million.'

'We'll face it when we have to,' Lance said. He wondered how Jimmy could tolerate her in his bed if he was so sure she would betray him. 'Today we're going to root out some bigger threats,' he added with satisfaction.

'Yeah.' Jimmy turned away from the trucks and he and Lance stood looking at the custom-made gun racks inside the two Range Rovers. The guns were already racked.

'I don't really like guns,' Lance said before he could stop himself.

Jimmy shrugged. 'They're tools. I don't like trucks but they're tools too. I've lived in the city too long to go bush with a loinskin and a spear.'

'Which are tools too,' Lance said.

'Why, so they are!'

For no reason they burst out laughing. They were standing there holding their sides when Esmeralda and Christine came out of the house. Esmeralda stood waiting at the front door until Chew came through, then locked the door and gave the key to the messenger who would return it to the owner of the house. She made a tour of the outbuildings to see that they were all locked.

'I trust Pan was not discommoded by being informed that we are about to set out on the expedition he has invested in,' Jimmy said to Chew, aping the speech patterns of the Chinese.

Chew looked steadily at the middle button of Jimmy's safari jacket for thirty seconds, then turned on his heel and went around the back of the Range Rover to make sure his large satchel was firmly wedged in.

Lance grunted warningly. Jimmy smiled brilliantly at him. Esmeralda returned from her tour of inspection. The household servants – cook, peeler, washer-up, water boy, fire boy, waiter, laundryman – sighed with relief that she had found nothing amiss and climbed on the back of their truck. None of them could drive to Lance and Jimmy's satisfaction and one of Jimmy's brothers had therefore been assigned to drive the chow truck, which carried its own refrigeration unit. There were fifteen vehicles altogether: two Range Rovers and thirteen trucks, of which nine would be required to carry the ivory once they recovered it. None of the trucks were going empty; they were loaded with provisions and camping and diving equipment; the provisions would be consumed and the equipment abandoned once it had served its purpose. Two of the thirteen trucks were fuel tankers because, Lance had explained, once out of Kenya, filling stations were non-existent and anyway diesel was unobtainable even at the point of a gun – which was how other parties would try to obtain their fuel and the reason they needed two tankers even if they required only enough fuel to fill one. Even with new trucks, chances were they would lose one through natural causes – getting irrecoverably stuck in mud or a ravine or irreparably bent in recovery – or through what Jimmy laughingly called 'local causes': somebody taking it from them by stealth or superior force. Jimmy's crack enraged Christine, all the more so when he asked, 'So you think people, because they're poor, should be allowed to steal our trucks?' Even Esmeralda, who never asked what

177

something cost before she bought it, queried the lavish scale on which Lance bought equipment, especially expensive trucks to the tune of very nearly a million dollars. Lance stopped her cold by asking her if she would like to lose three million dollars' worth of ivory for lack of a truck; Jimmy said it was Pan's money they were spending anyway and Henry Chew made what sounded like a sob and said he was at a loss to understand how anyone could (*a*) lose something as large as a truck and (*b*), worse, contemplate the prospect in advance with equanimity. 'You want to explain to Pan we left a few million dollars of ivory behind because we were short a truck?' Lance asked Chew. 'No? Then don't kibbitz.' If Chew could use fancy words, he knew a few too. Chew had proved to have a genius for checking that the thousands of items of spare parts for the trucks – enough to build complete drivetrains for two trucks plus large margins of all the consumable parts for thirteen trucks and two 4WDs – had been delivered and properly sorted and packed and distributed among the trucks; it was the kind of finicky work he rejoiced in and he did it well though Lance doubted the little Chinese believed how deadly serious it could be for them if they ran out of, for instance, something as simple as air-filter replacements after they had crossed the Kenyan border. 'Darkest Africa,' Jimmy had explained to Christine, 'is a place where people kill for the light globe from a truck headlamp.' She refused to believe him. Once, when a radio was on to the BBC World Service, Lance saw Christine look suddenly thoughtful and stare at the set. Lance listened to the item: more than thirty diplomatic vehicles had been taken from their owners at gunpoint in Kampala over the last month; the reason was that cars and spare parts commanded astronomical prices and diplomats owned the only near-new, well-kept cars.

'It would have been better to let me go ahead and grease our way,' Nasheer said, tapping the breast pocket of his safari jacket. Lance had hired him to deal with officaldom if it should become necessary. Nasheer was an Arab, the youngest son of a cadet branch of an important Zanzibar trading family. He had been recommended to Lance by his bank manager. Nasheer worked for what Jimmy called 'Dutch commission': he could spend as much as a hundred thousand on bribes but was paid a percentage of the unspent balance at the end of the expedition; the system had an inbuilt incentive for him not to spend wildly.

'It would have been a sign for the watchers that we were near to departure,' Lance said, wondering why Nasheer always tapped his breast pocket as if it contained something – which Lance knew it did not since Nasheer carried their 'float' of high-denomination dollar bills, gold coins and small diamonds in a belt around his middle. Smaller notes Nasheer kept in a tin box with a brass padlock and a chain that bound it to the gun rack in Lance's Range Rover on the assumption that if anybody got to the guns the expedition was doomed anyway.

'They can see us go anyway.'

'But without time to prepare their own departure in an organized manner,' Lance said patiently. Nasheer was twenty-five, three years younger than Lance, but as touchy as a teenager. 'I doubt they really know what it's like out there.' Lance pointed west. 'That's an advantage well worth having.'

Nasheer nodded. 'Even before the trouble in Uganda, when we had a branch there, things were always difficult there.'

Jimmy said, 'You have a talent for understatement, Nasheer. Cultivate it.'

Lance raised his voice. 'Fall in. Arms inspection. You too, Nasheer.'

'For so much money, I can buy you the Cabinet of Uganda, Mr Weber. I doubt we'll have to fight.'

'I hope so,' Lance said without smiling. 'All the same let's be prepared.'

This time Jimmy did not chuckle until Nasheer was out of earshot. 'You sound more and more like your brother. Arms inspections when there is not the faintest possibility of attack. Being kind to the vanity of children.'

'Let's hope I don't blot the Weber record,' Lance said. 'Make sure those Watusi drivers have clean and loaded weapons.'

Lance started at one end of the line, Jimmy at the other. They had hired thirteen Watusi drivers, simply because they were the best drivers to be had. The problem was that the Watusi, who virtually own and run Kenya – they have so many Mercedes Benz cars that they are derisively but enviously known as the Wabenzi – consider themselves mentally superior to their fellows to the extent that it is almost an hereditary article of faith with them that they can outwit everybody else without fighting. All the same, Lance had kitted them out with the latest Kalashnikovs as issued by the Russians to insurrectionist groups on South Africa's borders; Lance had been offered any number of these rifles in Dar-es-Salaam, straight off the ship, wrapped in greasepaper, in crates with Cyrillic markings, complete with attachments to turn them into machine pistols, grenade-throwers, sniping rifles, with as much ammunition as he cared to order. It seemed the revolutionaries were shorter of money than arms. Lance had thought it an effective weapon, perhaps not as nicely made as the FNs his brother and Jimmy's people preferred, but more versatile and absolutely foolproof. The Watusi treated the weapons with such contempt that one actually shot himself in the foot and had to be replaced. Even Jimmy lost his temper with them. 'Your brother would have shot a couple of them as an example,' he said. When Lance refused to oblige, Jimmy knocked one down and systematically kicked him unconscious. It worked a treat. Suddenly the Watusi were keen on their firearms: they could be used against barbarians like Jimmy. But they were keen on firing their guns, not on looking after them.

By contrast, Jimmy's two brothers and the thirteen Swahili warriors Lance had hired to protect the convoy were serious fighting men. Neither Lance nor Jimmy had seen them march or asked them to do so. But their arms were clean, oiled and loaded and they were alert and ready to use them. The youngest of the Swahili was a breathtaking shot; with practice he would come into the class of Jimmy, the two brothers and, with a little luck thrown in, into Lance's own elevated level of skill.

Lance had originally armed the domestic staff as well. On the second day he had disarmed them because they made up in enthusiasm what they lacked in skill: they were more likely to kill themselves or their comrades than any of the enemy.

When Lance came to the middle of the line, Jimmy had one of the Watusi by his shirt and was snarling quietly into his face that he would kill him instantly if he ever again found an empty clip in the man's rifle. The Watusi had a faintly bored half-smile on his face as if he was unsure whether this was a threat or a joke; he looked around at the trees and the sun peeking shyly over the black horizon as if to say, What can threaten me here so that I have to go armed?

Jimmy flung the man from him in disgust. 'We should take some spare drivers,' he said to Lance. 'These fucking Watusi are so slap-happy, they'll be the first to get it in any attack.'

Lance gave Nasheer back his rifle, which was spotlessly clean and which Nasheer could use with skill surprising in a banker. 'It's too late now, Jimmy. Any more of them are just going to get underfoot.'

'We could train some Swahili to drive.'

Lance considered it. 'That'll take till the dry season. Then we lose the advantage of our superior experience in wet-weather travel.'

Jimmy stood staring malevolently at the Watusi, who smiled at him in their superior manner. 'It's a pity these bastards are such natural drivers,' he said. It was true. Put a Watusi behind the wheel and he was magic; Jimmy's tribe had their own skills and magic with automatic rifles – the difference was that they could drive *as well*. Lance could read the unspoken thought in Jimmy's eyes: But there aren't enough of us.

'Let's get the show on the road,' Lance said, embarrassed at another unspoken thought, this time in his own mind: If it were not for the Webers, more of Jimmy's tribe would now be alive. Even as the thought was in his mind, he knew it was false: If it had not been for Ewart Weber, even these few men of Jimmy's tribe now alive would also have been massacred by their tribal enemies.

The big diesels roared into life. The cacophony was painful.

'So much for leaving quietly,' Esmeralda shouted in Lance's ear. She was beaming: they were starting out to recover her ivory.

Lance started the Range Rover and waited five minutes until all the truck engines were properly warmed through. Then he pulled out into the road and drove half a mile at walking pace. He stopped the Range Rover and waited five minutes. He watched the mirror as one by one the trucks ground to a halt behind him. He turned the Range Rover and drove down the other side of the road. The two fuel trucks and the refrigerated truck were in the middle of the convoy, the refrigerated truck separating the two tankers. Lance had not told the cook, but he intended to use the bulk of the refrigerated truck to shield one of the tankers should anything happen to the other. Jimmy's brother, who was called Boo because nobody else could pronounce the series of clicks that made up his name in his own language, had his instructions about pulling the refrigerated truck between the tankers and any attack. The other brother, a sleek man called Pierre for the same reason, rode in the leading tanker; Lance thought it likely they would lose the rearmost tanker first and he wanted a quick thinker in the remaining tanker. He had explained the risks to Pierre, who had smiled and said he would rather have the tanker detail than riding in the refrigerated truck, ordered to block bullets, bazooka rockets and grenades fired at the tanker. Lance wished he had a few more like Boo and Pierre but had felt unable to ask Sambo for any more men: he had not even asked for these two – they had been volunteered by Sambo. And, like Jimmy, they seemed to be hugely relieved to be out of Brussels and with action in prospect.

At the back of the convoy he had a few words with Jimmy, bringing up the rear in the other Range Rover. He and Jimmy laboriously spaced the trucks out so that there was fifty metres between vehicles. The Watusi had been taught to keep the fifty metres. Under attack, they had been told, they should close up to ten metres; they had practised this manoeuvre. Lance hoped they remembered. The sun was two hands above the horizon when they were ready to move off. Jimmy stopped his Range Rover next to Lance's. He shouted out of the window:

'Bruun was beaten as much by bad drivers as by anything else.' He drove on without waiting for an answer.

Lance looked at the blue sky ahead. Why did people conspire to remind him of that unhappy time? Perhaps because it was relevant, he thought; perhaps he needed reminding. In all this time, no sign of Bruun's minions. But still, he would not be setting out today to recover Esmeralda's ivory from the heart of war-torn Africa if the tentacles of his and Bruun's shared past had not reached out from the darkness to drag him out of his sheltered, ordered, safe existence. Perhaps they were reminding him because, on his home ground, he had been getting cocksure. Africa was also Bruun's happy hunting ground – he should not forget that.

All the same, he was almost lightheaded for joy to be in action at last. Even at Thika he and Esmeralda and his friends had been vulnerable to attack by Bruun. Now they were on the road, a moving armed camp, ready – as soon as the Watusi realized it was not a game – to pull into a defensive laager at the first shot. That they were not alone on the road was a minor consideration. He would be very surprised if any of the other parties who desired the ivory lasted the course: Drang or the others he did not know of but would find out about before this day was out. He was absolutely certain there would be more. It was impossible to mount this kind of expedition in secrecy; he had been told that it was said openly in the bars and clubrooms in Nairobi that he had murdered Matthew Ellimore for his beautiful young wife and his thousand tons of ivory and that he was going to fetch the first instalment of ivory. (Esmeralda had been very angry at this slander but Lance had laughed and said, 'Let them think I've already killed for that ivory, it'll keep the small fry at home and out from under our feet.')

Those in his own camp who wanted the ivory, Chew and Christine, would do nothing until the ivory had actually been sighted. He put them out of his mind.

Lance glanced sideways at Esmeralda. She was studying the surrounding countryside. Lance returned her smile. In the mirror he saw Chew in the back seat, studying a leatherbound notebook. Lance punched Bach's *Aria mit Veränderungs* into the cassette deck and wondered, as the first clear notes rang out, if the admittedly mathematical but nevertheless wondrously imaginative variations really were intended to put Herr Goldberg to sleep. His love of good music was something else he had inherited from his brother.

Lance kept a steady 60kmh. The good blacktop was capable of much more but he wanted the drivers to get used to the crawling discipline. Later they would be lucky to make a hundred kilometres in a day and then the discipline would be everything. All the same, at a steady 60kmh, leaving Thika with the sun two hands high, by 1000 hours they were at Nakuru where Lance had planned their first stop.

Over brunch, Christine said, 'We've come better than a hundred miles even at snail's crawl. You guys have been bullshitting me.' She tapped the map in her shirt pocket.

Nasheer snapped his head up at her but decided she was not mocking his gesture and stuck into his kedgeree again.

'Wait and I'll show you every tomboy's dream,' Jimmy said. 'Mud you can sink in right over your head. We'll be there in four or five days.'

'Three,' Lance said. 'We're staying on the road until darkness falls.'

Jimmy, Esmeralda and Nasheer stared at him; Christine had chosen that moment to attend to her food. The other three knew the almost invariable pattern of travel in Africa: a light breakfast of coffee and rusks and the convoy sets off a little before dawn and travels until 1000 hours when a stop of an hour, at most two, is made to prepare and eat brunch; travel from 1100 or 1200 until 1530 when the travellers start looking out for a campsite; stop by 1600 to make camp, look after the vehicles and equipment, make the camp secure, alas no longer against animals but only against thieves and cut-throats, prepare and eat the main meal of the day.

Lance shrugged. 'We can camp after dark. Our pursuers are not likely to be as well organized or protected as we are. I'd like to lose them today. If we let them follow

185

us across the Ugandan border, their lives are going to be on our conscience.'

Nasheer pursed his lips. 'We've seen nobody, not even Drang.'

'True. But he will come. And others. Within the next few hours.'

Jimmy nodded.

Christine asked Lance, 'How do you know?'

Jimmy laughed. 'Black man's magic.'

'Aw shit, not him too. He isn't black.'

Jimmy stuck out a long arm, grabbed Lance's belt buckle and onehandedly raised Lance's 205 pounds above the table for a moment. 'See that black tree-snake belt. Lance is an honorary black man.' The chair creaked as he lowered Lance into it.

'It's logical that people will follow us to find out where the ivory is,' Henry Chew said. 'Security has not been very tight.'

'The warehouse where Pan's ivory is stored belongs to a public company quoted on the stock market,' Jimmy said. 'You can find out the address by calling up and asking. Now that's what I call security.'

Okay, okay,' Lance said, his high spirits evaporated by the bickering. 'Somebody's coming and the sooner we lose him, her, them or it, the better.'

Esmeralda said, 'Then why don't we travel through the night?'

Lance shook his head. 'No, then they'll be in Uganda before they find out exactly how hopeless it is to try and follow us.'

'Yeah,' Jimmy said reflectively. 'For the first time I'm sorry the good road goes so far. If the bad road started sooner, we'd be certain of losing them that much quicker.'

'Esmeralda, hurry them up over the dish-washing and clearing up,' Lance said.

All the same, when everything was loaded, he took five minutes to make sure they were leaving the campsite spotlessly clean. It was yet another thing he had learnt from Ewart.

Less then half an hour later Daniel Drang's convoy caught up with them, in such a hurry that the leading open jeep had to brake sharply to avoid ploughing into the back of Jimmy's Range Rover.

'Drang didn't even have time to wash the sleep out of his eyes,' Jimmy told Lance on the radio. 'If looks could kill, there'd be daggers in my back.'

'I think he's surprised to see us travelling so slowly,' Christine added. 'One of his sidekicks is munching a half loaf of white bread. Imagine coming all the way to Africa to eat white bread!'

'They're Americans, they don't know any better,' Lance told her. There was a moment of silence on the radio link. 'Jimmy, cut up to the front of the convoy, then disappear into the side of the road and wait for whoever is behind Drang.'

'Okay. Drang doesn't have a fuel truck. Just a jeep and two trucks.'

'Maybe he's got drums on the backs of the trucks.'

Jimmy snorted. 'Or maybe he thinks he's going to fuel up at the friendly local filling stations lining the roads and vying for his trade with free give-away offers.'

In his side mirror, Lance could see Jimmy's Range Rover overtaking the trucks. 'Nobody who works for the OAU could be quite that ignorant,' Lance said.

'You wanna bet?'

There was a moment of uncomfortable silence, then Lance said, 'No.'

'Sorry. I keep forgetting.'

'Don't worry about it.' Lance switched the sound system back to music; any signal from Jimmy would override the music. He saw a puff of dust in the mirror.

187

Jimmy had driven off the road and disappeared into the tall grass and stunted trees.

Six minutes later Jimmy cut into the music. 'What was the name of that man who got meatcleavered in Macao? The Australian.'

'Fitzmeikle.'

'Somebody that looks remarkably like him just came by in a Datsun Patrol, white with a fancy red flash along the side. A real travelling brothel. Two younger men with him, both white. Loose canvas flapping from their roof-rack cover.'

'The Fitzmeikle brothers do look remarkably alike.'

'Do you want me to take care of them?'

'Good God, no. We'll just lose them.'

'Okay.' Jimmy sounded disappointed.

A minute later Jimmy cut in again. 'Ask young Henry if he's brought some friends with him.'

Lance turned to look into the back of the Range Rover. 'We'd consider that very unfriendly.'

Chew's mouth curled down at the corners and he looked Lance full in the face. 'If your friend's referring to Chinese sharing the road with us, there are eight hundred million of us. But tell him no, I have not brought any "friends". Sir P. K. Pan has full confidence in my ability to look after his interests without help or supervision.'

'You hear that, Jimmy?' Lance looked briefly at Esmeralda. She looked thoughtful. The implication had not escaped her: Bruun had sent somebody.

'I heard him. Unfortunately their Landcruiser isn't wearing Macao number plates. And the Chinese got their own mafia, called Tongs.'

'Those that visited my game reservation twice each time drove a Toyota Landcruiser.'

'Which are very common vehicles,' Nasheer said.

'Thank you,' Lance said. It was of course possible that the Chinese in the Landcruiser had nothing to do with

Bruun. They could, for instance, be gangsters from the Tongs, intent on grabbing the ivory before Pan could take delivery. Or Chew could be lying, they could be his back-up team. Lance preferred to think they were Bruun's emissaries. 'How many of them are there, Jimmy?'

'Five.' Jimmy waited for a reply but Lance only grunted. Jimmy said, 'They're travelling even lighter than the Australians. Nothing on the roof-racks and only two spares that I can see. Shall I take care of *this* lot?'

Suddenly Lance did not find the suggestion that Jimmy 'take care' of other travellers on thc highway quite so bizarre as only minutes before. If they were indeed more of Bruun's meatcleaver men . . . 'No, but thanks for the thought, Jimmy. I've changed my mind. We're not going to lose anybody. They're all adults. I'll stop and tell Drang and Fitzmeikle to go back.'

Jimmy laughed raucously. 'Forget it. They won't listen and you'll make a fool of yourself. Like you said, they're adults.'

Lance clicked the transceiver to standby and the music started again.

'Then we can camp in comfort while there's still light?' Esmeralda asked. Now that they were on the way to recovering her ivory, she was perfectly content to leave the strategy to Lance while her thoughts turned naturally to their housekeeping arrangements.

Lance's mind was on Bruun. 'What?'

'If we follow normal travel procedure now, we don't risk losing them through their own inefficiency.'

Lance nodded. 'Right. We'll camp at 1600. That'll also make it easier for you and Christine.'

'You got my brother killed.'

'Your brother's greed and stupidity got your brother killed,' Lance retorted. 'As your greed and obstinacy will get you killed.'

Fitzmeikle looked up at Lance over his glass. 'Are you threatening me, you young snot?'

Lance shook his head unhappily. 'No.' This was the eldest of the Fitzmeikle brothers and the most intelligent, the leader. 'I'm telling you to turn back for your own good, because I don't want your life on my conscience.'

Fitzmeikle drank before he answered. He also smiled. He had a long, horselike face; Lance wondered how a man with any pride at all could let his teeth go without attention so long. 'That's a threat in any language, boy. The only reason I don't take serious offence is because you come alone and unarmed.'

Lance shifted his feet. Fitzmeikle, sitting under the awning stretched from the side of his 4WD, had not invited his visitor to sit even though the two men with him had vacated their chairs to stand well apart to each side of him. 'You're out of your depth. You have neither the experience nor the equipment even to reach the ivory, never mind bringing it back.'

'Another threat but I'll let it pass. You have the equipment. When the time comes, I shall take it from you.'

Lance ignored the threat. 'Goddamnit, Fitzmeikle, are you stupid? There's a civil war on in Uganda and the rains are upon us. You don't speak the language – '

'Don't raise your voice to me, boy,' Fitzmeikle said. His voice had sunk to a whisper. 'I might be forced to get my boys to teach you some manners. I don't want to have to do that to a future partner.'

Lance snorted. 'You can offer me nothing I haven't got already. I don't go into partnership with snakes.' Losing his temper was going to get him nowhere with the Australian gangster. 'Go back to the city, man.'

'For a guy with thirty armed men to back him up, you talk awfully polite,' Fitzmeikle said thoughtfully. He had

190

not missed the pleading note in Lance's voice. Then he spoilt it: 'Or are you worried your niggers will fold up when they have to face three white men?'

Lance turned on his heel and walked away. After ten paces, he looked back. 'Don't forget to take your Paludrine.'

'What?'

'Malaria tablets.' Lance walked away in the direction of Drang's camp. The health of King's Cross gangsters was the least of his concerns but that single telling precaution not taken hinted at all the other ways in which the Fitzmeikle expedition was inviting disaster. 'It's their lives,' he said aloud to himself.

Drang had recruited some experienced local black men and his camp had a semblance of order and purpose. His two lieutenants spotted Lance first. 'What do you want?' one asked. 'Whitey pays social calls out here in darkest Barbary, don't you know,' the other one said. They both had American accents. Jimmy was of the opinion they had been recruited the same place as Drang: the CIA. They were young and tough-looking and kept their jackets on at all times; each had sweat-marks in the right armpit of their jackets but none in the left armpit which, Jimmy said, proved they were right-handed and carried their shoulder holsters in the left armpit.

'Can the comedy,' Drang said sourly. Unlike his two aides, he was not sweating. 'What do you want, Weber?'

'For you to turn back, Daniel.'

'I've heard that tune before.' Drang smiled briefly. 'I want that ivory for its rightful owner, Africa. And don't try to give me the same shit you've been giving me since London, that you aren't going after it.'

'I'm fetching it all right,' Lance said. 'It's on the Congo side of Lake Kivu.'

'Let's beat the exact location out of him and then terminate him,' one of the lieutenants said, rising.

'Sit down,' Drang said, his voice mild, his head nodding thoughtfully.

Lance felt a flash of hope. If Drang understood that directions to natural features of a multi-featured landscape would not be enough, he might also understand the futility and danger of following Lance.

'You sit down too,' Drang added to Lance. Lance drew up a chair and sat. Drang poured bourbon into a glass and pushed the glass across the folding table to Lance. The younger black man sat down resentfully, his red-rimmed eyes turned on Lance. His charcoal-grey suit had a reddish sheen of dust on it – and they were still on the blacktop.

Lance knew that, when he blew his nose tonight, a small market garden of the same coarse red dust would settle on his handkerchief. He hoped Drang's two sidekicks both had serious sinus conditions. Lance drank. Drang had excellent taste in bourbon, which had been Ewart's favourite drink.

'I'll make you a new deal,' Drang said. 'Since you already laid out the money to finance the expedition, I'll throw in my services and OAU cooperation for a quarter of the ivory to Africa.'

Lance suppressed a laugh. Once over the Ugandan border, the writ of the OAU ran only intermittently – and, west of Lake Kivu, not at all. Drang and his expedition would only be a drag in that they would have to be protected and a drain in that they would have to share the provisions and fuel. Perhaps, on the way out, in Tanzania, Drang could smooth the way but even that was doubtful since Tanzania confiscated all ivory on principle.

'I'm sorry, Daniel. It's too little, too late.'

'Then we'll dog your footsteps every inch of the way and throw a spanner in the works the minute you have the ivory. And then, *then* we'll take it all for Africa.' Drang smiled broadly and Lance realized the OAU man was drunk. 'You can't hide from me.'

'Not with an expedition the size of yours,' one of Drang's men said, 'not with a white woman with tits out to here.' He held his hands cupped in front of his chest.

Lance threw half a glass of bourbon in the other gunman's face and, by the time this one had his gun out of his left armpit and into his right hand, Lance had the one with the offensive mouth by the upper lip and forced on to his knees.

'Shoot,' Lance said. 'My muscles will tighten up and I'll tear his face off.'

Drang laughed aloud. 'You puppies think they train you so tough at Langley! And then you fall for a sucker-split play like that. Put your gun away, Frank. You Turner, you apologize to Mr Weber for insulting his woman,' he ordered the other one, who was emitting a high-pitched whine.

The man mumbled something and Lance let go. Immediately two splayed fingers were heading for his eyes as the man surged upwards. Lance swayed his head, watching the other hand travelling to his midriff. He kneed the rising man in the face and, as the man staggered back, the stiffened fingers flying an inch past Lance's chest, he kicked the man in the stomach, his boot rising upwards under the shortribs.

'Jesus fucking Christ!' Frank said. 'He was a Karate nine point five.' Covering Lance with the pistol that had appeared in his hand again, he bent over to feel the wrist of his companion. 'Dead.' He rose. 'Now what?' he asked Drang.

'What would have happened if his hands connected?' Lance asked.

'He woulda popped both your eyes,' Frank said.

'And his other hand?'

'Same as you did to him. Straight into the heart. Massive coronary occlusion.' He looked quickly at Drang before turning his eyes back to Lance. 'What shall we do with him?'

Lance felt sick at the stomach. It had happened so quickly, the killing starting again.

Drang tore his eyes away from the corpse. He poured some more bourbon and looked into the glass. 'I told you two smartass kids to read the file carefully but you – '

'What the fuck are we going to do with this killing animal?!' Frank shouted.

'Don't piss yourself, Frank. You got the drop on him, ain't you?' Drang laughed.

'Shit, he's drunk,' Frank said to Lance. 'What now?'

'First you apologize for calling me an animal. However true it may be; I have at least pride left.' Lance stepped across the body at his feet and advanced on Frank, his hand outstretched towards the pistol.

Frank took a step backwards. 'No, you don't!' His knuckle tightened over the trigger.

'Hold it right there,' Drang said sharply. 'You Frank and you too Weber.' He waited for both men to be still. 'Put away the gun, Frank.'

'But – '

'Put it away! You saw what happened. Even a white mercenary shit like Weber has the right to defend himself against attack. And if that stupid bastard had killed Weber, I would have terminated him myself. We're better off without undisciplined hotheads.'

'What . . . what're we gonna tell the cops?'

'What cops?' Lance asked. They still did not understand.

'The cops at Webuye. That's the little town – '

'Put your gun away and go home,' Lance said wearily. He turned around and walked away.

'Hey! You can't just – '

'Bury him and forget you ever knew his name,' Lance heard Drang order behind him.

Lance walked slowly, wishing they would shoot him in

194

the back. Then it would all be over. But it would not be fair to Esmeralda or Jimmy or all the others. He had known, of course, that in going after the ivory he would set himself up as a target to be shot at. And then he would have to shoot back, to kill or be killed. But that the killing should start so early, because he had lost his temper like some knight out of a children's fairy tale defending a lady's honour . . . He had not meant to kill the man, only to distance himself from those lethal-appearing fingers with their ridges of bone-like hardened skin. Karate. The man had voluntarily deformed himself all the better to kill. He had heard of such things happening in the East but in America, in Africa?

'What are you shaking your head for?'

Lance started. It was Jimmy, coming up on him through the soft dusk.

'And talking to yourself,' Jimmy added. 'Are you okay?'

'No.' Lance told Jimmy what had happened.

Jimmy was less concerned. 'He was an ill-mannered dog. You kicked him like a dog. He died like a dog. Drang will bury him like a dog, in an unmarked grave.'

Sometimes Lance despaired of ever understanding Jimmy. Or anybody but himself. 'I didn't mean to kill him. I panicked and misjudged.'

Jimmy shrugged. 'No. *He* misjudged. He paid for it. Forget it.' Jimmy paused. 'Look, it's none of my business. But Esmeralda is going to notice you're down in the mouth and ask why. Just tell her the truth, not some cock and bull story. You're a bad liar.'

'Shut up, will you.' Lance had been wondering what he would tell Esmeralda. He did feel like saying: This man made a rude reference to your anatomy so I killed him. 'It was just a mistake.'

Jimmy chuckled. 'Oh my Lance, you've been living with the animals on your reserve for too long. That spook was

195

going to stick his fingers through your eyes into your brain and wiggle them around to scramble your life like eggs in a pan. And if that failed, he already had his other hand on its way to your heart. And he wasn't making fine judgements, he was going for the whole of your life.'

Lance spat the foul taste in his mouth into the dust at his feet. Even if Jimmy was right, he wished Jimmy would save it for another day.

'The only mistake you could have made was to let him kill you. These martial-arts experts all make the same mistake of thinking they're the only athletes in the world.'

To live only by my reflexes, Lance thought, that would make me an animal. Exactly what they called me.

As if he could read Lance's mind, Jimmy said, 'Your brother used to say it wasn't enough to be a good soldier, to be quick and smart. There would be other good soldiers, maybe even quicker and smarter. Major Weber was convinced that the man who believed he was doing right would always win.'

Lance nodded in the darkness. He had heard his brother say so.

'You don't want to forget that, Lance.'

'Yes, all right!'

'A lot of people depend on you.'

'Jimmy, I'm not stupid. I can work that out for myself. But I don't have to like killing. And that, back there, it wouldn't have happened if I had kept my temper and not twisted his lip.'

'He would have found some other way to measure himself against you,' Jimmy said with absolute conviction. 'A man like that, with his training, doesn't attack in anger. Only in cold calculation. He wanted you dead.'

'Why?'

'You got a white skin, haven't you. Don't agonize over it. Africa doesn't need racists, of either colour.'

'Talking of colour,' Lance said, 'Aren't we forgetting the yellow peril?'

'I've taken a look at their camp,' Jimmy said. 'They're going to sleep in the Landcruiser and under it. One of them came to take a look at our camp. I don't think they know we know they're there.' Jimmy stopped to shine his torch on the ground. 'That's their Landcruiser track. Recognize it?'

'Who do you think I am, Tonto the Indian?'

'I think Tonto was the horse.'

It was worth a small smile. Lance studied the tyre tracks but, as he had expected, they told him nothing. He rose and Jimmy put the torch out. They stood still while recovering their night vision. 'Probably rented,' Lance said.

'Yeah.'

'They smoked Gunston and Texan cigarettes, drank Lion beer, and none of them wore shoes over size seven.'

'It fits. But Lance, it fits all the Chinese in East Africa.'

They came to their camp. Everything had been tidied up after dinner in readiness for instant departure in the morning. Outside the ring of light cast by the Coleman lamps, Lance touched Jimmy's elbow and they stopped.

'Those Chinese. Pan's or Bruun's?' Lance insisted.

Jimmy shrugged. In the dark Lance felt rather than saw the movement.

'Guess.'

Jimmy shook his head. 'What do you think?'

'I don't know. If they're Pan's we've nothing to fear from them until we have the ivory. If they're Bruun's, I think they'll harry us to the ivory and all the way to the coast.'

'And beyond.'

'We have to take precautions as if they're Bruun's. I'll take the first guard shift with three of the Swahili and you and Pierre and Boo divide up the rest of the night between you. Okay?'

Before Jimmy could answer, Lance felt the pressure of a hard object in the back of his neck. There is only one hard object that makes that kind of steady circular pressure. A gun. Lance felt Jimmy stiffen beside him and glanced at him out of the corner of his eye, careful not to turn his head.

'I'm going to cut Pierre's balls off if I get out of this alive,' Jimmy said softly.

'You set out a guard?'

'Yes.'

Behind them, there was soft laughter. 'You have to catch me before you can cut me,' Pierre said.

Lance whipped around. Pierre and the youngest of the Swahili, the marksman, were standing behind them, smiling hugely. Lance took the young Swahili's rifle and checked the safety. It was on. He gave the rifle back. 'Very funny.'

'For being such a fucking comic,' Jimmy said to Pierre, 'you can stand guard all night.' He followed Lance into the camp.

Lance surveyed the camp. It looked almost domestic. Henry Chew was reading his little notebook, Esmeralda was making an entry in her household journal, Christine was brushing water-colour on to a sketchpad, Nasheer had his scales out to weigh small nuggets of gold he cut from a three-foot rod with the pliers from the toolkit; from the Watusi fire came laughter, from the servants' the sound of a banjo expertly strummed, from the Swahili a plaintive song. Jimmy went straight to the liquor cabinet. He held up a bottle of scotch and a bottle of bourbon, waving them at the rest of the bottles to indicate Lance could choose something else if he liked. Lance pointed at the bourbon; he had started on bourbon tonight and might as well finish on it. He took two glasses and an ice bucket from the serving table in front of the mess tent and put them on a card table away from the others. Jimmy sat down across the table from him, unscrewed the top of the bottle and crumpled the piece of tin in his huge hand before putting it with exaggerated care on one corner of the table.

When the bottle was empty, Esmeralda was asleep and in the morning she did not ask why Lance had felt the need to get drunk.

The roar of the many diesel trucks of Lance's expedition woke the followers from their uncomfortable rest. Dawn was just breaking as they rolled stiffly off car seats or crawled resentfully out of sleeping-bags that seemed all lumps. By the time they had missed breakfast in their hurry to pack their gear, Lance was, even after his usual leisurely campsite inspection, twenty kilometres down the road. The question in the minds of those tracking him was, Which road? Even Drang, whom Lance had told his destination, was not keen to let his quarry get too far ahead. He kicked Frank awake and got their convoy on the road in twenty-five minutes, thanks to the experienced camp-boys he had hired in Nairobi. Even so, the Chinese and Fitzmeikle, with less to pack, beat him to it.'

'We're not the only guys on Weber's ass,' Frank said, looking up from the map.

For the time being Drang was not interested in the other hunters. 'You just keep your nose in that map.'

'I thought you said Weber's too stupid to lie.'

'Yeah. But he's got that woman of his to do his thinking for him. And that Uncle Tom of his plus two Tom-Tom brothers, all three of them a whole lot cleverer than you.'

'There's no call to be offensive.'

'They each made a fortune in Brussels. A tough town. I know, I was there for four years with the Company. That makes them cleverer than you'n'me.'

'And Weber faster on the mat than Turner. Send me

back to 'Nam!' Frank laughed shortly. 'What am I looking in this map for?'

'Where else they could go. I mean, turning left at Eldoret and camping at Webuye and then telling us he's headed for Uganda . . . I tell you, he knows he's got company, so why signal his moves? Why not camp at Eldoret or stay at the hotel there in comfort, for chrissake, and let everybody stew where he turns from there?'

'Yeah,' Frank said. 'Only, he could still turn for Kitale and then he's got six hundred kilometres of the Rift Valley in front of him and beyond that the Sudan and Ethiopia and they go off the fucking map, man. No fucking wonder he's got two fuel tankers. Or he can double back and then he's got all of North and East Kenya in front of him to lose us in.'

'What if he goes north and then west?'

'Six official border crossings into Uganda in the next three hundred klicks, then nothing. If I were him, I'd head for Lodwar, flat out, then hit the tracks for the border somewhere near Kaabong. If he's such an expert in rough travel as his file says, he could lose us in these Murua Nigithigerr Hills.' Frank stumbled over the pronunciation. 'Which road are we on now?'

'To Malaba on the Ugandan border.'

'And if he's going to cross illegally?'

'Don't be such a fuckhead, Frank. What do you think he's got that Arab banker for if he's going to cross illegally?'

'So we're headed the same place we were headed yesterday?'

'Sure. It'll only take us a couple hours to get there, check whether he's passed through and then double back. With a convoy that size, a two-hour lead isn't much, not once you go off the main road.'

'Yeah,' Frank said. 'And he can't give us a miss without going off the main road, can he?'

200

All the same, they raced ahead of their provision trucks and repeatedly risked their lives passing the trucks in a convoy carting cement from Mombasa.

They need not have bothered. Lance's convoy was sitting on the road at Malaba, waiting for Nasheer to conclude arrangements with the border guard. Nasheer was in no hurry. The convoy had transit papers to the Congo and permits for all its armament. Lance had told Nasheer not to draw attention to them, so the Arab offered a small baksheesh and then threatened to wait while he sent to Kampala for a senior official who could release the border-post commander from duty. The post commander retaliated by demanding to inspect all the papers and every item loaded aboard the trucks. Nasheer offered a little 'convenience money'. Fitzmeikle and the Chinese arrived, followed by Drang, the cement convoy and Drang's trucks. Esmeralda had lunch prepared and served. Nasheer mentioned that a spare bottle of the liquor the party could be seen drinking might be found. The post commander would like a bottle of scotch but would find a rotor for a truck distributor much more valuable. Nasheer had his lunch and then consulted Lance, who told him sharply to give away money, gold, diamonds, liquor and promises but no spare parts for the trucks.

With the sun at two hours past noon, Lance nodded at Jimmy, who went up to the post with his rifle hanging loosely in his hand. Pierre climbed down from a truck, his own rifle in plain view. 'Mr Weber is getting impatient,' Jimmy said to Nasheer. 'Our papers are in order and time is valuable.'

'Just a moment, Your Highness, please,' Nasheer said. To the border commander, he said, 'Soon there will be no baksheesh and no convenience money and no liquor. Just trouble. These people are very powerful trouble.'

'I vebby powaful trubble too,' the border commander said.

'I got a gold nugget I could let you have in place of the money,' Nasheer said, rolling it between his fingers.

The man waved the gold away disdainfully. 'Rota for Gennul Mota distributa.'

'Don't you listen,' Jimmy said. 'We only want to pass into your country, not buy the fucking place.'

Nasheer watched Jimmy's broad back through the door, then picked up the money and the bottle from the scarred desktop. 'You know, you just made a bad enemy there. Your brother-in-law in Kampala is going to be very angry with you when our messenger reaches him. And you're going to be out of pocket.'

'Okay, I taka de money, de bottle, de gold.'

Nasheer put it all back on the desk, and, without a further word, walked out. To Lance, he said, 'This convoy is too big and too rich. It's no use telling me not to splash out and attract attention, Mr Weber. It's going to waste a lot of your time.'

'We're only crossing two more borders legally,' Lance said. 'I have time for that. But we start splashing money, we look like shady characters in a hurry about their illegal business.'

'Round these parts you won't find any but shady characters, and nothing but illegal business,' Jimmy said. 'Amin corrupted this place but good.'

Nasheer nodded. 'An economist from the Sorbonne visited Uganda right after the Tanzanians ousted Amin. He told my father half the national income was in bribes and the Ugandan inflation wasn't in goods but only the greed of the officials.'

On the far side of the border, Nasheer burst out laughing. Lance turned around to look into the back of the Range Rover. The young Arab had never struck him as the merry type.

'Sorry Mr Weber, Mrs Ellimore.' He ignored Chew. 'I just can't help it. That border post thief, he sees this rich convoy but it's got too many guns and too many powerful connections in Kampala – or so he thinks – so he has to let it pass for a few trifles, not even one spare part for a truck. So who's he going to take it out on?'

After a moment, Lance started laughing. Then Esmeralda joined him and Nasheer renewed his crowing. Henry Chew stared blankly at the incomprehensible antics of the Occidentals.

The Chinese drove rudely past Fitzmeikle. Fitzmeikle swore at them but the slot in front of the barrier was wide enough for only one vehicle at a time. The border commander disposed of the Chinese in short order. 'No cool-lies,' he said, pulling at the corners of his eyes to emphasize his point. When they seemed inclined to argue, he drew his revolver and aimed it at them. They left. He saw them sitting in their Landcruiser, talking excitedly and waving maps. He had helped Idi Amin massacre the Ugandan Asians – several times – and would dearly have loved to order his men to open fire on these but the Kenyan border post was in clear sight and they had the nasty habit of reporting shooting incidents to Uganda's new Tanzanian overlords.

'All right, just stamp there and lift the barrier.' Fitzmeikle did not climb out, he simply held the papers through the window. The post commander turned his back. He was going to enjoy this. He crooked his finger over his shoulder and walked into his office.

Two hours later, when Daniel Drang walked through the door, Fitzmeikle was holding a pistol on the border commander and walking backwards out of the office. 'Out of my way, nigger,' he said to Drang.

Drang sighed. 'It's people like you that give the Big Country a bad name,' he said.

For a moment the pistol wavered between Drang and the border commander, then Fitzmeikle was gone. The border commander ran around screaming and a jeep was sent after Fitzmeikle. The jeep broke down half a mile along the road. It cost Drang a thousand American dollars to calm the commander down and be let through.

'And I came out here to save people like him from white imperialism,' Frank said. The OAU paid him two thousand a month.

Drang said nothing. After another year or so Frank would learn to save that kind of talk for public consumption or addressing white people.

Lance, concerned about losing the Chinese, possibly his only link to Bruun, considered turning back but only briefly. While he was heading for the ivory, Bruun and his Chinese had to come to him. For once, he held the commanding position.

Instead of going after the Chinese, he turned his angry concern at losing them into a malicious choice of campsite. He kept the convoy on the road at a steady 60 kmh until they made camp between Kakira and Bugembe an hour before sunset. Camping there was an invitation not only to the thieves of these two towns but to the gangsters of Jinja, possibly the most dangerous city in all of Africa. If any of the others caught up with them tonight they were going to find out that his warning was not hot air.

At table, Christine said, 'They're not doing so badly.' She pointed at the children who had gathered at the edge of the camp. 'Look at all those potbellies. All those stories of food shortages and even famine must be exaggerated.'

'Maybe,' Jimmy said. 'But they don't have potbellies because they over-indulge. When people become really hungry, when their stomachs are absolutely empty, gasses form and blow up their bellies.'

Christine pushed her plate away. 'We must feed them!'

Lance shook his head. 'I'd like to. But we can't. We

don't have enough to feed the populace every place we camp. They know that.'

'Then what are they doing here?'

'Waiting to steal what they can,' Nasheer said.

'You unfeeling savage!'

Nasheer's nostrils flared, then he smiled. 'Even if you did give them food, they would never get to eat it, Miss Rawls. You see, there are others, stronger, waiting in the darkness behind them to take their food or whatever they steal.'

Christine's eye fell on a tin of sweets on the table. 'But we can give them some of our luxuries. Nobody can take a boiled sweet out of their mouths once it's in.'

Jimmy took her wrist. 'Put those sweets down, Christine.'

'How I could ever . . . A man so mean and insensitive – '

'Christine, listen to me,' Esmeralda said. 'Those children haven't ever been to a dentist. Their teeth are rotten. These boiled sweets will cause them nothing but agony.' She gently took the tin from Christine's hand and put it back on the table.

'I told you about giving the children sweets back at Thika,' Jimmy said. 'Remember?'

She flung his hand from her wrist and ran to her tent.

'These people are just under-nourished, not even starving. I wonder what Miss Rawls would say if she saw a real famine,' Nasheer said.

'Oh, shut up, Nasheer,' Esmeralda said without force.

'It would be more pertinent to ask who profited by the millions the international relief agencies poured into Uganda over the last few years,' Henry Chew said precisely.

Lance and Jimmy simultaneously looked at the liquor cabinet. Lance shook his head; he had had a hangover all day and did not want one again tomorrow.

'This kind of talk I can hear in Brussels cocktail bars any

night of the week,' Jimmy said. He bowed to Esmeralda and went after Christine.

'The Westerners improved the health of the savages,' Nasheer said seriously to the Chinese, 'without increasing the agricultural output in proportion to the greater infancy survival rate and longer life expectancy. When you have a population explosion without a food explosion, famine results. It is so simple, many of my friends at the university thought it was an American plot. But of course it happened from good intentions.'

'Good Christian intentions,' Chew corrected him. 'Christianity is the curse of history.' He looked challenging at Lance.

Lance noticed Nasheer was also looking at him, though perhaps apologetically.

Esmeralda said, 'Religions have their sole justification as unifying forces. Whether they unite for good or evil depends on the men who originate and preach them.' She rose. 'Apportioning the blame will not feed the hungry.'

'I must inspect the guard,' Lance said. He rose. He could not resist the temptation. 'For the record, I am not a Christian. My religion is laissez faire: every man shall be entitled to do whatever he pleases as long as it harms no other man.' He was gone into the shadows before they could debate this with him.

Later, when they were in bed, Esmeralda said. 'That was a brilliant summary of your essence, darling. I had not suspected you knew yourself all that well.'

'I had a lot of time on my game reserve with nothing to do but think,' Lance said.

'Hmm. Sometimes you frighten me. Hold me close.'

Wong, the leader of the Chinese, hated everybody, even sometimes, on bad days, other Chinese. He had an order of the undesirability of non-Chinese: Japanese were most

206

undesirable of all, then Indians, then Portuguese, then all other Whites, then Negroes.

Today was a very bad day. Wong was not a very intelligent man. He preferred action to cerebration. It never occurred to him that he was now on the receiving end of the same racism he practised. All that he saw and understood was that at two border posts he had been turned down before being given even the opportunity of offering a bribe – simply because he was Chinese. He resented being called a coolie.

More, if he lost the white man's very visible convoy, his employers would kill him. Wong had no objection to dying in action. He had spent all his life preparing to die in action. But to be killed as punishment for failure, that would be a humiliation that would preclude him forever from his peculiar conception of a martial heaven.

At the third border crossing, near Bukwa, he held a thousand American dollars in his hand in plain sight. The border commander also called him a coolie but, on production of another five hundred dollars, let him and his men through. Wong decided that, when his present assignment was finished, he would come back and kill the three border-post commanders for insulting him. Meanwhile he would savour the insults while they nourished his hatred. If there was time, he would kill them slowly.

By the time they reached Mbale, they had used up both their spare tyres. Wong was torn between pressing on and having the tyres repaired. He decided to have the tyres repaired while he made enquiries. The white man could have turned north from Tororo, in which case he would have had to come through Mbale. Or he could have headed west towards Kampala, in which case Wong would catch up with him sooner rather than later. But not if his transport had a flat wheel without a spare.

Getting the wheels fixed took six hours. The people had no conception of time or pride in their work. Wong spoke

to them sharply only once: they stopped work and it took
him an hour to buy off their resentment. It was after
midnight when they set out for Bugembe, Jinja and
Kampala. Beyond Kibuku, the driver hauled the jeep up
sharply.

'What is it?' Wong wiped the sleep from his eyes. One
of the things wrong with the human race, he had once
thought after having a woman, is that even men of iron
will like himself sometimes have to sleep.

'Ferry.' Wong's associates too were men of few words.

They roused the ferry operator from his hut. He came
out carrying a shotgun that could do double duty as a
blunderbuss. They promised him money and paid half of
it. They ran the Landcruiser up on the ferry. The ferryman put his shotgun down against the wheel of the vehicle
and pointed to a snake's nest of bare wires hanging from
the motor.

'Battery,' he said.

There were no tools in the Landcruiser. Wong undid
the nuts holding the terminals to the battery posts with his
fingers. When he had finished lifting the battery out, the
ferryman held up two fingers.

'Two battery,' he said.

Wong very nearly swore but that would lose him face in
front of his underlings and, worse, to the black man.

They tried the single battery but it would not turn the
sludged-up old engine of the ferry. When it was nearly
flat, Wong put it back in the Landcruiser and ran the
engine to charge the battery. Then they settled down to
wait until someone with another battery should come
along. The ferryman crawled back into his hut, cradling
his shotgun.

While they waited, none of the Chinese spoke.

Lance took the time to put on a pair of shorts and lace up
his boots and tie a double knot in the laces. He was the

208

leader and had to look one; he also had competent men under him who would take care of the situation meanwhile. 'Lie down and stay down,' he told Esmeralda. He pulled the tent loose from its pegs at the back and rolled out, cradling his rifle. The shooting and the screaming continued. Lance rolled under the refrigerator truck and out the other side. He was not disoriented. The fighting was a fair way off. But better faintly ridiculous than dead. He rose.

Pierre and Boo had both stopped to put on their boots but were otherwise naked. The Swahili, with harder feet, were totally naked.

'You're bloody disgusting,' Jimmy said. 'Go put your clothes on.' He was fully dressed. It was his turn to command the guard. That made it, Lance thought, some time between two-thirty and five in the morning. 'Get your goddamn head down and keep it down until I tell you to raise it,' Jimmy snapped at Christine, who was peering round the flap of their tent.

'But there's nothing – '

'Do what I tell you!'

Christine disappeared. Everybody got dressed. The fighting a few hundred yards away continued. Lance told Esmeralda and Christine they could come out. Esmeralda persuaded the cook nobody was shooting at him. Coffee and rusks were served. Lance noticed Christine's bare feet.

'Put on some shoes,' he told her.

'Christ, not you too. I've just about had enough of this shit of being ordered around. The last memsahib retired to a rose garden in Kent in 1922 or maybe you haven't heard.'

'On damp ground near villages, there's hookworm. The hookworm larvae crawl into your body through the skin of your feet.' Lance shrugged. 'It's pretty painful and incurable. But if you're so smart . . .'

Christine looked at the bare feet of the Swahili. 'But they – '

'Put on shoes, then come and apologize,' Jimmy said. 'Their feet are harder than yours.'

'Now listen here – '

Jimmy took her by the arm and led her away. Ten minutes later she came from their tent, wearing shoes. She did not apologize but Lance had already forgotten the incident.

A truck started somewhere in the night. There was a renewed burst of firing, the truck engine raced, then the firing died as if cut off with a knife.

'Probably Drang's lot,' Jimmy said.

Lance nodded. 'Or the Chinese,' he said. They did not know which of their pursuers had caught up with them last night. Lance had decided it was dangerous to go scouting in the dark with all the predators waiting just beyond the ring of light cast by the Colemans. Whatever Christine wanted to believe, here it was easy to be killed for the shirt on your back. 'We'll take a look at dawn,' he decided.

'You're not going to help them,' Christine said flatly.

Lance ignored her. Jimmy gave her a sharp look but said nothing.

'Well?' she insisted.

'In this light, they'll kill us too before we can get to them,' Pierre said gently.

'Besides which,' Esmeralda added drily, 'none of them are exactly our friends.'

Jimmy laughed aloud. Christine threw her head back and stalked off.

'Maybe,' Jimmy said loudly, 'we should go help the local bad guys wipe them out.'

'Except the Chinese,' Lance said. He sat down at a table to wait for dawn.

At first light, Lance went with Jimmy, Boo and the

Swahili marksman in the direction of the fighting. The attack had been on Drang's camp. He had lost one of his trucks with all it contained. His camp servants had straightened everything out by dawn. Drang was sitting at a folding table with Frank, eating a hearty breakfast of eggs, sausages, bacon and grilled tomatoes.

'As usual, the white mercenaries and their tame niggers arrive after it is all over,' Drang said in greeting.

'Gracious as ever,' Jimmy said. 'When the sun rises, that heavy breakfast is going to sit like a stone in your stomach, friend.'

'You wouldn't have paid somebody to attack us?' Frank asked. He had a large square of Elastoplast on each cheek and talked thickly.

'You'll excuse his suspicion,' Drang said. 'A bullet went through his mouth from side to side. He was inches from death.'

'No,' Lance said. 'If it was necessary, I wouldn't hire incompetent help. I'd do it myself.'

Frank picked up the pistol lying on the table. 'I shoulda killed you yesterday. In the States a smartass like you wouldn't live a week.'

'This is my country,' Lance said mildly. 'And if you point that thing at me one more time, I'm going to lose my temper.'

Drang put his fork down, reached over and took the pistol from Frank. 'Until we find out where the ivory is, you got insurance, Weber. Until then, stay out of my camp.'

Lance walked away without another word. On the way to his own camp, he saw Fitzmeikle's Datsun Patrol pulling up beside the road. It was cool but Fitzmeikle looked hot and bothered. He and his two sidekicks all had red-rimmed eyes. They looked like they had been on the road all night. And, judging by the dents in what only yesterday had been a shiny new 4WD, inadvertently off the road more than once. Of the Chinese there was no sign. Lance was tempted to wait for them to catch up but decided against giving in to the temptation.

'Let's hit the road before Fitzmeikle can wash up and have breakfast,' he ordered when they got back to their own camp.

On about every tenth shop the steel shutters were being taken down as they passed through the wide main drive of Kampala. The rest, Nasheer told Esmeralda, had been 'protected' by Amin's soldiers, robbed by criminals, or looted by mobs so often that they would never open again. In the half-hour it took them to drive through Kampala, the few sidewalk 'mammies' they saw with food to sell came and went, their meagre stock sold at the first asking price. 'Once there were mammy-wagons,' Nasheer said. 'Before my time. When the British were here and for a time afterwards. They brought meat and fruit and vegetables to every door. Now the mammies walk and have a few yams, soon gone.'

'Hundred American dollars for a pound of sugar,' Esmeralda said, reading a sign outside a shop. 'That's a funny bargain. What happened to the wagons? What about the horses that pulled them?'

'They were minitrucks,' Nasheer said. 'The soldiers took them. Spare parts were unavailable. There was no petrol.'

A sleepy soldier at a roadblock waved them through. A sign indicating a hospital nearby hung at a crazy angle and was riddled with bullet holes. One of its support poles had been chopped off with an axe. Across the road, the sign to Entebbe International Airport still stood, though also bullet riddled and decorated with the graffiti 'Kil Bib Astilss'. On the far side of Kampala a roadblock delayed them for an hour while the Tanzanian soldiers manning it sent for an officer who could read. The officer accepted a bottle of vodka and a hundred dollars from Nasheer after less than five minutes' haggling. 'His heart wasn't in it,' Nasheer said. 'He's gone back to sleep.' Drang, Fitzmeikle, and the Chinese, who had caught up in Kampala, drove through on the bribe Lance paid: the officer having gone, the soldier took the easy way out and assumed they were all part of the same large convoy with papers that were perfectly in order.

'All present and accounted for,' Jimmy said when he spotted the Landcruiser. 'They don't look any more rested than Fitzmonkey.'

'The Chinese?'

'Yes. Did you doubt they would catch up?'

'Never.'

'Bullshit. You were pale and wan like some lovelorn teenager.'

'Let's aggravate everybody by keeping on the road till we hit Goma,' Lance said. He felt like singing. He *had* been worried about losing the Chinese, his link to Bruun. 'You need a permit to camp there.' In the back of the Range Rover, Nasheer waved their permit, cackling softly to himself.

'That's going to be after dark even if everything goes right,' Jimmy said.

'The road really breaks up from here onwards,' Nasheer added.

Lance chuckled. 'Sure'n'all, me hearties. But on their maps it shows blacktop all the way to Goma, right? Now they're going to find out the hard way.' He heard Jimmy chuckle, then switched the music back in.

Later, while he stood hip-deep in a pothole to repair a broken suspension member on the Range Rover, Lance questioned the wisdom of this decision. It was only two hours after they had left Kampala but already they had lost the others. Between the Kenyan border and Kampala the road had been bad, deteriorating steadily the further it left Kenya behind. During the Amin years the roads had

213

received no maintenance at all and after the Tanzanian takeover and the installation of a puppet government there had been no money to repair roads. This side of Kampala it was probably a case of replacing the road altogether rather than mere repair. For long stretches the tarmac was so broken up that a new road had been cut in the dirt beside it by the many vehicles preferring to drive beside the road rather than on it. And when that new road became too rutted, another new road beside it. And so on. In some places the current road was a kilometre or more from the original good blacktop designed by Scottish engineers. Sometimes Lance felt like leaving the road altogether and simply cutting through the derelict plantations of the once-prosperous Uganda. Once this road had been described as 'Africa's finest freeway' . . .

Christine looked doubtfully at her map, then at the road. She checked the key, then turned the map over to find the maker's name. 'This man should be prosecuted for false representation,' she said.

'This is a first-class road,' Pierre reassured her jovially. 'It's going to get much worse.'

Christine looked doubtful, but for once decided not to argue.

At Mbarara, 283 kilometres from Kampala, Lance decided to call it a day. It was after five in the afternoon and Goma was at least that far again and the road was still becoming progressively worse. They had already put in a very hard day.

And the last thing he wanted was to lose their pursuers altogether.

Drang's party arrived, surprisingly, before midnight. Their jeep had lost its windscreen to rifle fire; they had been attacked yet again.

In the dawn, Lance stood looking eastwards into the sun, waiting for the Chinese to come. While he waited, Fitzmeikle and his two hooligans arrived, red-eyed and bloody. Their recently shiny Datsun Patrol had travelled some of the way on its roof. Lance burst out laughing when they stopped next to him.

'We want some petrol,' Fitzmeikle said without greeting.

'Over there in the town,' Lance said, immediately regretting giving them even that much aid and assistance. Where were the goddamn Chinese? 'Go home before it gets worse,' he said but they were already driving off to Mbarara, a smoky haze three klicks up the road.

Boo reported that during his stint at guard duty, there had been a commotion at Drang's camp, probably local thieves. Esmeralda thought they might have stolen food.

'By now Drang and Frank are so tired they won't care much about food,' Lance said.

'I feel a bit that way myself,' Christine said. 'I wish you'd had those Range Rovers air conditioned. The heat . . .,

The Chinese caught up with them just as they were finishing brunch. Fifteen minutes later, when they were on the road again, Jimmy reported that the Chinese 'don't look too good but a hell of a lot better than Fitzmeikle. Give them another night without sleep and they'll just fade away.'

'You don't want that to happen,' Esmeralda said.

'Chinese are very persistent,' Henry Chew said. 'But these are starting to concern me, they are *so* very persistent.'

'Well, I don't want them to kill themselves on the road from fatigue,' Lance said more sharply than Chew's remark warranted. Pan's representative grated on his nerves.

'It may be best,' Chew said. 'The ivory is our main concern. Sir P. K. Pan – '

' – can wait for his ivory until I give it to him,' Lance said. 'Those Chinese are a personal concern of mine.'

'So many concerns,' Jimmy said mockingly on the radio. 'You should start a cooperative. What do you want to do, Lance?'

'We'll camp at the usual time tonight. Let me know if we lose anybody.'

'If you let them know you want them to keep up, they might start playing clever games.'

'Then we'll just have to be cleverer,' Lance snapped in exasperation. 'This is our only chance. Let's try not to fuck it up.'

Esmeralda shivered. 'I wouldn't like Bruun on my neck for the rest of my life.'

It took them three more days of sweat and bruised knuckles to cover the 340 kilometres to Goma, travelling from dawn to four o'clock every day. In fairness, this was not all the fault of the road: a total of six hours was spent with police, customs and immigration on crossing from Uganda into Rwanda and from Rwanda into Zaire.

'Thank God it didn't rain,' Pierre said when they stopped at Gisenyi on the Rwanda/Zaire border, at the bottom of the last of the mountains. 'Going down those hills riding a fuel tanker is going to feature in my nightmares for a long time to come.'

Lance did not tell him that, coming out, probably pursued by people shooting off guns at them, he was considering turning south from Gisenyi into the even higher mountains.

They had lost all their pursuers but Lance was not worried. He was prepared to sit at Goma until the Chinese turned up. As he explained to Esmeralda: 'Your ivory is only about a 130 klicks down that earth road there, a day's drive. We don't want to drive right up to it without being sure we're alone.'

He meant, With only those we *want* to see us, but did not say so. Esmeralda understood him perfectly.

In Uganda, Daniel Drang was starting to wonder if

there was something wrong with having a black skin, even in Africa. He was attacked again and lost his jeep and his truck, this time to a platoon of men whose sergeant claimed to be commandeering the vehicles to fight rebels. Drang knew he was lucky to escape with his life, the clothes on his back, and the American dollars taped to his instep. He also still had Frank. Because there was nothing else he could do, he headed for the nearest Tanzanian command post to complain that a representative of the OAU had been robbed on the public highway, in broad daylight, by soldiers.

Also in Uganda, Fitzmeikle was sitting beside a road, waiting for a suitable vehicle to stop so he could take its tyres – or perhaps the whole vehicle. They had used up their spares and then driven on until all four tyres were in shreds. He intended having that ivory, not because he needed the money (Fitzmeikle was a very rich man, richer even than Jimmy) but because he wanted it. He rationalized this desire to himself and his hirelings by saying his brother had died for that ivory and therefore the Fitzmeikles should have it.

At the Uganda/Rwanda border, Wong and his men, who had averaged three hours sleep for five nights now, and looked like it, were having more trouble leaving the country than they had entering it. They were 'coolies' and not supposed to be in the country at all, 'regardless of stamps in your passports obtained with bribes from corrupt officials'. This was the border commander's way of saying he wanted a very big bribe. He wanted a very big bribe because he was smarting from the cavalier way in which Nasheer had treated him and the humiliation of letting himself be intimidated by the seeming swarm of purposeful men who all appeared to have a modern automatic weapon grafted to their hands. Wong took a while to catch on. Then he paid and added this border commander to his list of border commanders. When

Wong turned up at Goma, Lance, having serviced all the vehicles, checked all the equipment and given his men a rest, was ready to move out instantly.

The lookout reported that the Chinese were at the border post. Fifteen minutes later, Lance turned the Range Rover out of the campsite onto the road. From Goma there are only two roads westwards, one of which splits into three a few kilometres west of Goma; four roads altogether. Lance was under no delusion that the others – Drang and Fitzmeikle – when they caught up would fail to find them again. But it would waste their time finding out which road he chose, and that might be enough time for him to be gone with Esmeralda's ivory without having to fight the latecomers for it. It could take them days to check out the other roads, hours even to find the road some places.

They were all first-class earth roads, meaning that most years they could be used year-round by 4WDs. But, as Jimmy explained to Christine, some years one would need an amphibian or at least a canoe. And in the rainy season, a road marked *Passable* meant exactly that: there was no guarantee of speed.

After an hour in which, without accident or breakage, they did thirty kilometres, they had lost the Chinese again. In the second hour they did twenty, in the third sixteen. Then Lance called a halt for the day.

'That was pretty good going,' Jimmy said over a drink. 'We didn't even have to get the PSPs out once.'

Lance nodded. Manhandling the Pierced Steel Planks from the rear to the front of a truck in heavy mud was slow, exasperating work. Sixty-six klicks in three hours was marvellous going, even in the dry season.

'Remember how, working from dawn till dusk like pigs, we used to think we'd done well if we did fifty a day in the Congo?' Jimmy asked.

Lance nodded again. That time was not one to become nostalgic about. But Christine and even Esmeralda, having seen for themselves what 'first-class road' could mean, wanted to hear more. While Jimmy told them, Lance set out guards against thieves.

When they set out in the morning, the Chinese had still not arrived. Lance was tempted to drive back to Goma to look for them, but that would let them know he was concerned about losing them – and that could cause them to behave unpredictably. Until now they had had the Chinese off-guard by the speed of their going. They had surged halfway across the continent of Africa in one smooth motion, keeping the pursuers one step behind them all the way. But soon they would be a stationary target and then, surely, the Chinese would execute their orders to harass them. Bruun would never do anything as simple and straightforward as telling his men only to take the ivory once it was found. No, he would tell them to unbalance the other party unremittingly: to terrorize them with surprise attacks in the middle of the night, the day, anytime, anywhere.

Unless they were Pan's Chinese . . . In which case Lance's grand ploy had failed and he would be back in the nightmare, never knowing when and where Bruun would strike next . . . Such an existence, especially now that he had Esmeralda, did not even bear thinking about.

Between Bobandana and Mukwima, Esmeralda scrutinized every clump of trees intently. There was a Haydn symphony in the tape player and Lance led the convoy at the same pace as the day before, as fast as the road would allow. The first Henry Chew and Nasheer knew of their arrival at the approximate location of the ivory was when Lance turned the convoy around at Mukwima and started retracing the ground they had just covered.

'What are you doing?' Henry Chew asked. 'Your private vendettas are of no interest to – '

'The ivory is here somewhere,' Lance said. 'Now shut up so Esmeralda can concentrate on finding the landmark.'

At Bobandana, late in the afternoon, Esmeralda shook her head in defeat.

Lance picked up the microphone and pressed the button. 'Jimmy. Camp where you can find enough water. It might be a permanent camp, so look to your lines of defence. Okay?'

'Okay. You're going to have another look?'

'Yes. That overgrown section about three klicks back looked like an older part of the road.'

Lance found the overgrown section and set the Range Rover over it, losing what little paint was still left below its waistline after the pounding of stones and gravel it had taken since they crossed the border from Kenya less than a week ago.

'A different angle perhaps,' he said when they rejoined the 'new' road. He turned the Range Rover around and started back across the overgrown section.

Once more back on the 'main' road, Esmeralda said nothing. She did not have to. Her failure was in her air of total dejection.

'Tomorrow's another day,' Lance said.

Dinner was a subdued affair. Afterwards, Henry Chew said, 'I shall have to report to Sir P. K. Pan that you took his two million dollars without knowing the exact location of the ivory you were purporting to sell for it.'

'You don't have to sound as if you're enjoying it,' Nasheer said. 'Poeple will laugh at me when we get back, coming all this way for nothing.'

'Sir P. K. Pan will lose face *and* two million dollars,' Chew said. 'He will not be able to let such a thing pass.'

Jimmy reached one brawny hand across the table and raised the Chinese by the front of his shirt. 'This is the wrong place to threaten us, Chew.'

'Put him down, Jimmy,' Lance said wearily.

'I'd be happy to arrange a little accident for him,' Boo said from where he leaned against the refrigerated truck with a bottle of beer in his hand. 'The drivers think he's bad luck.'

'Put him down, Jimmy. He's only doing his job – or thinks he's doing it.' Lance put his hand on Jimmy's wrist and forced it down.

Chew, finding his breath now that Jimmy's huge knuckle was no longer pressed to his windpipe, spluttered something. Jimmy leant across the table and bared his teeth at the Chinese. 'Snarl!' he said. Chew fell over backwards. He picked himself up, dusted himself down while looking at Jimmy, then turned and walked away, his back straight.

'Now you'll *have* to kill him,' Pierre said. 'It was stupid to damage his pride like that, Jimmy. He's not going to forget.'

'He was getting on my tits,' Jimmy said shortly.

Lance turned the map on the table over. 'What instructions exactly did your husband give you to find the ivory?' he asked Esmeralda.

'Between Bobandana and Mukwima I would see, if I looked hard enough, three trees in a certain formation. He showed me a photograph which he destroyed after I memorized it.'

'And then?'

'A line through the tree at the sharpest point of the triangle bisecting its base will lead straight to the ivory.'

'How far along the line is the ivory?'

'I don't know.'

Jimmy said, 'Huh?'

Christine said, 'Oh dear.'

Nasheer said, 'It could be miles.'

Henry Chew sat down at the table again. He said nothing.

Lance said, 'He must have told you something.'

'Yes, Matthew said to follow the line and it would be so obvious that anyone not knowing he was looking for ivory would stumble over it and stumble on. He quoted some poetry about hiding in plain sight. Then he told me to be prepared to dive for pearls, which is why I told you to bring scuba equipment.'

'So the base of the triangle, its shortest side, lies nearest the lake,' Lance said. He slid the map to her. 'You got a pen or pencil or something? Draw the trees Matthew showed you a photograph of.'

'I'll get a sketchpad and charcoal,' Christine said, jumping up.

They waited silently until Christine brought the drawing materials and while Esmeralda drew, rubbing out many times as she marshalled her memory. When she finished, she slid the drawing pad across the table to Lance. The others crowded around behind him, Jimmy holding a Coleman high overhead to light the drawing.

'Three trees looking like three trees, that's all,' Jimmy said.

'Were there no distinguishing features you could remember?' Lance asked.

Esmeralda shook her head numbly. 'No. The clue is not the three trees, really. It's what Matthew said. "If you look hard enough," he said.'

Lance remembered the first day he had met her: then too she had sounded as if she talked with her husband's voice. He shivered. He pushed his chair back. 'Tomorrow we'll look hard enough.'

After driving to Mukwima and back twice, with no result, Lance had an idea. 'Of course. "If you look hard enough . . ." Don't look towards the lake, look away from it and – '

'Yes! And reverse the image of the trees so that we're

222

looking for two trees closest to us with the third visible between the other two.'

At quarter past four, on the overgrown piece of disused road, they found it.

'There's nothing but lake out there!' Esmeralda was dismayed. She stood with her back to the trees at the apex of the triangle and looked out across the lake.

'There wouldn't be.' Lance was more confident. 'After going to all this trouble, he wasn't going to put up a sign saying Here lies the ivory of Matthew Ellimore, was he? Come on, we'll shift camp tomorrow. By tomorrow evening you'll be the proud owner of half the world's ivory.'

'Shouldn't we mark this place?'

Lance laughed. 'No, now that I know where it is, I could find it blindfold in a hurricane.'

'Is the lake safe to swim in?'

Lance waggled his hand. 'A little bilharzia, a few crocodiles, an electric eel or two . . .' he said judiciously. He started unbuttoning his shirt but she was out of her clothes and in the water before he had it off. Later they made love on the warm sand and Lance forgot all about the ivory until Nasheer asked plaintively, when they arrived back at the camp, whether they had found it.

There was no jubilation about finding the ivory. The Chinese had arrived in the early afternoon and spent the rest of the day simply sitting in their Landcruiser staring at the other camp. 'They're taking turns to sleep,' Boo said. 'Funny, I'd never seen a Chinese sweat before.'

Across a hundred metres, Lance needed no binoculars to see the Chinese now had eight spare wheels and that their Landcruiser was festooned with innumerable fuel tanks.

'They sure learn fast,' Pierre said and everybody laughed.

Lance laughed with them but he was uneasy. He could

223

not forget the photographs Burger had brought him. His parents, Briony and her child. The butchery at his game reserve. More butchery on Esmeralda's Spanish major-domo. The bloody mess in the ruined church in Macao.

'Boo, I want you to do nothing but watch those Chinese all the time. When you eat, pee or sleep, let Mwanzo spell you.' Mwanzo was the Swahili sharpshooter, an alert boy with twenty-twenty vision. After dinner, Lance doub-led the guard and went around himself to position the men. He took the first shift. When Jimmy took over from him, Lance said, 'I wonder why they haven't done any-thing yet.'

'They have. They made you double the guard and look like a shivering old woman. It's called psychological warfare.'

Lance laughed. 'Better ridiculous than dead, Jimmy. Wake me if they move, Boo.'

Nobody woke him up and in the morning, despite a protest from Henry Chew, Lance took only Esmeralda with him to find the location of the ivory. 'We don't want to attract attention by mounting a major expedition.' Lance said. 'Those Chinese probably think you're the most important man here; if you come, they'll follow us.'

'Crude flattery does not influence me, Mr Weber.'

'All the same, you can't come.'

Lance and Esmeralda left the oxygen tanks in the Range Rover, first swimming out wearing only flippers and goggles. Esmeralda was a strong swimmer and Lance a competent one. After half an hour they had seen nothing. They lay floating on their backs.

'There's an island a way out there,' Esmeralda said.

'No. It has to be within plain sight of those trees.'

'Why?'

'Because, the further you go from the trees, the greater the multiplication of error in such rough-and-ready measuring methods. At a hundred metres, a couple of degrees isn't a large error. But at ten kilometres, even a fraction of a degree of error would cover an area impossible to search. No, the trick of those trees on the side of the road most people wouldn't look to, that was all the protection your ivory needed. We're probably right over it now.'

Esmeralda turned face down in the water. Lance knew what she would see. Clear water on top, then a murky layer, then weeds and mud.

'Another thing,' he said when she turned around again to face the sky. 'That ivory isn't any more than ten metres deep.'

'How do you know that?'

'"Be prepared to dive for pearls." Pearl divers work in about ten metres of water, I think.'

'You think?'

'It doesn't matter if people can work up to, say, thirty metres without breathing apparatus. This whole stretch from here to the shore is between ten and thirty metres deep according to the map.'

They went back for the scuba gear, seeing nothing on the way back.

'We should put up a buoy with a balloon out there in a straight line from the tree,' Esmeralda said. 'It's very tiring on the neck muscles pulling yourself out of the water to align yourself every so often.'

Lance shook his head. 'That'll be the same as signposting the ivory. For the moment we're two young lovers having a picnic and doing some scuba diving.'

'Nobody's going to believe that, Lance. Not after we came all this way.'

'I don't care if they believe it, that's what we'll try to make it appear like. Nobody but Drang knows the ivory is on Lake Kivu and we've lost him.'

They swam out underwater, twenty metres apart. When they decided to turn back, they had found nothing. Lance took a spear gun and went after a catfish he had seen.

Esmeralda built a fire over which they grilled the fish for their lunch.

'It tastes rather good for such a great big ugly blunt fish,' Esmeralda said, wiping her mouth with the back of her hand.

'For a great big ugly blunt fish it moved damned fast around these pointed rocky outcrops on the lakebed,' Lance said, reaching for her. 'Come here and let's make like young lovers.'

He stopped pulling her towards him. Their eyes met. Then they were grabbing for the scuba gear.

'There shouldn't be any rocky outcrops on the lake bottom — not here,' Lance called to her as they ran towards the water.

She got there first, but only by a length. The ivory was less than a hundred metres from the shore and, as Lance had forecast, in water about ten metres deep. Lance scraped at one of the curved points with his knife. The algae floated away. Behind it was the smooth cream of good rich ivory, gleaming mellowly even in water ten metres from sunlight. Lance turned around. As far as the eye could see, curved algae-covered points stuck out of the bottom of the lake. He shot to the top.

'Incredible,' he shouted at Esmeralda as she too came up and pushed her goggles back. 'Hidden in plain sight. Probably planted by native labour with no breathing equipment.'

Lance dived again. He swam around the periphery of the pointed 'rocks'. It was a long swim. After a while he sensed someone with him. He looked around. It was Esmeralda, her hair streaming out behind her. She pointed to the ivory and hugged her arms to her chest, then pointed upwards. She wanted to take one tusk with her. Lance shook his head.

'Why not?' she asked when they were on the beach again.

'Because we don't want anybody outside our own camp to know we've found it. When we're ready, we'll come here and get it all out and on the trucks and be on our way in the minimum possible time. Meanwhile, we don't want anybody else to muddy the waters.'

She looked disappointed. Lance laughed and drew her towards him. 'It's probably those fields of phallic symbols all sticking up, ready to serve.' He peeled her out of her bathing costume. Only after they had made love and she lay with her head in the crook of his shoulder, did it occur to him that there was a superior motive to lust. 'That ivory,' he told her, 'that was an altar your husband built, a terrible sort of a pagan altar. And we've just celebrated a pagan feast on it in the only possible way.'

'she smiled serenely. 'I'll turn you into a Spaniard yet. You have the beginnings, the understanding of life in death and death in life.'

Though she did not say it, Lance knew she was glad he had at last come to terms with the presence and grand scheme of the man he had killed.

When they were sitting in the Range Rover, Esmeralda taking one last lingering look at the water that covered her ivory, he selected the March of the Valkyries to push into the tape player. When the music started, she looked at him, surprised.

'That's what it's going to be like, getting that much ivory to the Coast.' Lance turned the volume up.

'Drang's here.'

'I can see that.'

'He's brought half the fucking Tanzanian army with him,' Jimmy added.

'This is Zaire territory,' Lance said. Immediately he felt stupid. Still, for clarity, he asked, 'How did they cross Rwanda?'

227

'I don't know. You don't have to cross Rwanda to get into Zaire from Uganda.'

Lance looked through the window of the Range Rover at Drang's bustling camp. There were four vehicles and about twenty men. They wore khaki shorts and shirts without insignia but that they were soldiers was obvious: the material was darker where the insignia had been taken off.

'Son of a bitch,' Lance said. 'It's obvious what he's done.'

'What?' Esmeralda asked.

'He used his authority as an OAU official to involve the Tanzanians. It should be obvious even to a blind man that only a maniac will take the ivory west into Zaire. Therefore we will take it through Tanzania which, logically enough, the Tanzanians control, or through Uganda which, as it happens, the Tanzanians control by right of conquest. I'm only surprised Drang didn't do it earlier.'

'Are you all right, Lance?' Jimmy asked. 'You sound lightheaded. A touch of the sun.'

'We found the ivory. Get in. There's no sense in watching them. They have no authority here.'

Before getting into the Range Rover, Jimmy looked into Lance's face. 'Are you sure you're all right? They got trained and armed men, they're here, camped in good order. And we're talking about a great deal of money.'

Lance drove on towards his own camp. Drang and his Tanzanians had chosen to camp about half a kilometre away. 'I like the way Drang and Frank sat there staring at us,' Lance said. 'I mean, he's probably learnt more about Africa in these last few days travelling on my tail than in however many years he spent with the OAU. He should be grateful for the opportunity.'

'Shit! Can you be serious for a minute? Those guys mean to fight for the ivory.'

'Sure, Jimmy. But not here. Not till we're either in

228

Tanzania or Uganda. They want us to make it easy for them by finding it, bringing it up, taking it to where they have jurisdiction.'

'I wouldn't bet on it, Lance. Sorry. It's nice and quiet and remote here and they're only two days' hard driving from Uganda. They might chance it.'

'Jimmy, Drang knows the ivory is in Lake Kivu. Since we've camped here for three days now after running like hell halfway across Africa, he can only conclude we've arrived and that the ivory is not too far away. But he knows it won't be in plain sight. He needs us at least until we've pinpointed the location for him. And at that point we'll be ready. Okay?'

'Okay.' Jimmy did not sound very enthusiastic. 'At least this time, when we go out on the open water, we won't be sitting on a boatload of nitroglycerine. Remember how you brought up your lunch that day? Twice.'

'My hero,' Esmeralda said. 'Or perhaps just plain stupid. Was it necessary?'

'Yes,' Jimmy said categorically.

'As necessary as fetching your ivory,' Lance said. 'It seemed like the thing to do at the time.'

Lance could feel Esmeralda's eyes on him. He refused to meet hers. He knew what she was thinking. He had had the experience once before and here he was again. Why? If he had the answer to that question, he would be the wisest man in the world. Jimmy and Boo and Pierre were here and prepared to take on the Tanzanian Army out of a sense of loyalty to Lance's dead brother. Esmeralda was here, sent by a sense of duty and obedience to a dead husband. He tried to tell himself he had been guided here by his fear of Bruun but Lestronge had offered him a job where he would be inaccessible to Bruun and he had turned it down; he could not claim to have any overpowering reason for being here except that he had brought himself – because he wanted to. The hell with them all: it was enough reason for him and should be enough for them.

In their camp they drank a toast to success.

'Tomorrow morning, an hour before dawn, we're shifting camp three klicks down the road,' Lance said, 'At first light we start diving for ivory. We'll dive till nightfall and during the daylight hours of each succeeding day until we have brought all the ivory up. When it is all aboard our trucks, we will immediately set off.'

'We have a generator. We could floodlight the lake at night,' Nasheer said.

Lance shook his head. 'That's an invitation to snipers.'

No more toasts were drunk.

Lance bumped against Esmeralda as he turned over. It was pitch dark. They were almost in the exact centre of Africa. It is not a place people drive around in the middle of the night.

Quietly, so as not to disturb Esmeralda, he put on his boots and shorts and took his rifle out into the night.

'Woodat?' The click of a small precision switch. The safety on a firearm. The engine in the night had also disturbed the guards.

'Me. Lance Weber.'

'Good evening, Massa.'

'What happened?'

'Somebody leave camp in your Range Rover.'

'Uh-huh.' The sound that had woken him had started further away. But sleep can be deceptive. 'Who?'

'I don't know, Massa.'

'And then?'

'The yellow ones go too, Massa.'

'Boo, where the hell are you?' Lance called.

Boo came out of the darkness just as Jimmy came out of his tent. Pierre also materialised out of the thick night.

'Christine's in bed,' Jimmy said.

'But Henry Chew isn't,' Pierre said. 'I just looked.'

'He went off in Lance's Range Rover and the other Chinese followed him,' Boo said. 'In the direction of our ivory.'

Lance had a sinking feeling but it was nothing to do with the ivory. The ivory had suddenly become totally irrelevant. The Chinese in the Landcruiser were Pan's! Not Bruun's. He was back where he had started, in the nightmare of not knowing when Bruun would come for him and those he held dear.

'Lance?' It was Jimmy. 'Are you just going to let them go?'

'No! That's Esmeralda's ivory and she shall have it. You come with me, Jimmy, and Boo and Mwanzo. In Jimmy's Range Rover. Let's go!' Before he slammed the door Lance told Pierre, 'Wake up everybody and prepare to move camp immediately you receive my order. And watch your back. Drang might think this is his big chance.'

Pierre chuckled roundly. 'Then he's in for a fat surprise. I'll be waiting for him.'

Jimmy dropped the clutch and they roared off into the night as Pierre turned to go about his preparations. Lance felt the warm glow of having competent help. And of impending action. 'Pass me some ammo,' he told Boo. He checked that his rifle was fully loaded, then stuffed the boxes into the pockets of his shorts. He threw two boxes into Jimmy's lap. Jimmy kept both hands on the wheel.

'Ouch! Chrstine still wants those, you know. We're just going out to deal with a few treacherous slanteyes, not starting a war.'

'Well, don't get over-confident,' Lance said. 'Put the lights off, Jimmy. We're nearly there.' The Chinese would of course hear the racing engine and Jimmy's snatched gearchanges as he fought to keep the Range

Rover on that terrible parody of a road at over a 140kmh. But keeping the lights on would provide them with an easy target.

The Range Rover thrust through the little dip, all four wheels off the ground as Jimmy flung it over the following small rise. Then he spun at the wheel and snatched at the gear lever as the moonlight suddenly revealed the Land-cruiser of the Chinese in front of them. Jimmy swore as the Range Rover swung sideways with all four wheels scrabbling for purchase.

None of the other three paid attention to Jimmy's problems: Jimmy was driving and beyond that it was in the hands of the gods. Lance swung his rifle up and over and then had it peaking out of the window to rake the Chinese. He noted that Boo was also covering the Chinese and Mwanzo, on the other side, had his rifle out to cover Chew and, in case they should spin around again, the Chinese from the other side. Lance liked that; it showed the young Swahili not only did not panic but could also think beyond the immediate danger.

The Chinese did not shoot. Perhaps it happened all too quickly for them too. Lance had not even seen them, just their Landcruiser. Lance unlatched his door but kept his hand on the pull to hold the door from swinging open. At the apex of one of the Range Rover's swings he let the door go. It swung away from him. As the Range Rover jerked in another direction, in that moment of almost no motion between two phases of acceleration, Lance propelled himself out of the 4WD. The heavy door slammed shut over his head but Lance paid it and the swinging Range Rover no attention. He searched the night with his rifle. Nobody fired at him though the slamming door must have marked his approximate position. He heard the Range Rover door slam again as it swung once more. That was Boo dropping out. They now had any would-be attackers in a crossfire. Lance relaxed long enough to glance at the lake. There was something on it but he could not keep his eyes on it for long enough to make out what. He had to pay attention to the landward side. He hoped Mwanzo, who lacked his and Boo's experience with mechanical contrivances, would not be tempted to emulate them: if Mwanzo misjudged either the speed or the impending direction of the Range Rover, he could be seriously hurt or even killed.

The Range Rover was slowing down. Lance heard Jimmy shout something at Mwanzo and almost immediately there was the slam of a door as the Swahili rolled out. The Range Rover came to a stop not too far from where Lance lay on the ground. The driver's door hung open. Jimmy was no longer in it.

'Cover me,' Lance called softly, immediately rolling away in case his voice had marked his position. He undid his boots and kicked them off. Then he ran into the water and started swimming towards the moving dark mark on it. It was remarkably careless of Chew and his Chinese not to leave someone on the shore to guard their retreat.

The dark blotch was stationary. It was difficult to judge its position from water-level and in the dark but Lance was certain it would be right over the ivory. He kept swimming steadily. When he was still the length of a good swimming-pool away, he stopped – in pure surprise. There was only one man in the inflatable dinghy. Where were the rest of the Chinese? If they were ashore, there would surely have been some shooting by now. Lance cursed. There was something here that he did not understand and therefore dangerous.

'Stay away from me.'

It was Chew's voice. He was standing up in the inflatable, his hands twisting together. Lance kept swimming. Chew put whatever it was he had in his hands down to reach into the bottom of the inflatable. Lance, suspecting a firearm, dived. He came up near the inflatable. Chew hit out at him with the paddle, hitting Lance on the shoulder.

Lance, gauging the rhythm and speed of the blow from the numb pain in his shoulder, on the next blow caught the paddle with his other hand. He started hauling himself hand over hand up the shaft. After a moment Chew realized what Lance was doing and let go the paddle but Lance was near enough to grab the side of the inflatable. Chew stomped on Lance's fingers but the air cushion gave and Lance laughed as he swung himself over the side. Chew aimed stiff fingers at his head but Lance, the memory of Drang's man still fresh, reacted no more than to turn his head aside as his momentum carried him rolling into the inflatable. The violent motion of the little raft upset Chew's balance and, before the Chinese could recover, Lance had pushed him over and then fallen on top of him, pinioning him in the bottom of the flimsy, unstable craft. Lance turned both the hands of the Chinese up behind his back, holding him well clear so that he could not use his feet.

'Now, what's this all about?'

'You'll be well paid to let me proceed,' Chew said. There was nothing in his voice except the words.

Lance noticed the absence of fear in the little man's voice. He scanned the waters but nobody was coming. He returned his eyes to the bottom of the inflatable. Wires. Detonators. All too familiar. But how could Chew by himself possibly hope to mine the extensive ivory field? Lance looked apprehensively at the water. If the Chinese were down there with scuba gear, they could come up on him from any direction. But where would they get diving equipment? Answer: there were two sets on his own Range Rover for a start and more in his camp. He was going to have something to say to the guard when he returned to camp. If he returned to camp.

Lance heaved mightily and threw the Chinese his own length. The splashing water was still falling when Lance started rowing the inflatable inshore, ignoring Chew's cursing and spluttering.

'Jimmy?' Lance said softly, knowing how far a normal voice will travel across water. 'It's me. Don't shoot.'

Somewhere a long way off he heard Jimmy chuckle. 'Row the boat, Michael.'

Lance was not feeling religious or even charitable. He was making himself a target from either the shore or the water. His bottom itched. I don't really fancy a spear up my backside, he thought, remembering how the catfish he had speared for his and Esmeralda's lunch had wriggled. He slipped over the side and pushed the inflatable the last fifty metres inshore.

Goddamnit! he thought. Now that I know those Chinese aren't Bruun's, why am I doing this? Because it's there to be done, his brother's voice mocked him in his mind, you choose to do it. Don't blame the world. You're a free adult individual. You don't even need the money. Nor does Esmeralda.

'Bullshit!' Lance said aloud, adding in his mind. You would be here too, Ewart. It runs in the blood. You may as well blame lions for hunting zebra.

'What?' Boo called.

'Bullshit!' Lance shouted. 'I said, Bullshit!' Still nobody shot at him. He dragged the inflatable up on the coarse grass. Jimmy rose like a wraith from the darkness and put the lights of the Range Rover on. He came into the light with Lance to study the equipment lying in the bottom of the inflatable. Boo and Mwanzo stayed out of the light.

'Detonators, timers, batteries, wiring. Where the fuck's the dynamite?' Lance asked, angry at himself for having made such an exhibition of his fear. 'That can't be nitro in those canisters, can it?' he asked, taking an involuntary step backwards, remembering how he had fallen on the tins out in the lake.

Jimmy laughed and hefted one of the canisters in his hand. 'No. War-surplus napalm.'

'Huh?'

'Huh is right. Very clever. You see, it burns under water. They weren't going to take our ivory, just burn it in place. So that makes them Pan's, that's for sure.'

'Yeah,' Lance said. 'He destroys our ivory, he owns all the world's ivory and there's less of it so the price will more than double. For paying us two million to show him where the ivory is, so Chew could destroy it in situ, Pan would have made thirty, perhaps forty million.'

'Neat,' Jimmy said reflectively.

Chew came stumbling out of the water not far from them.

'What are you going to do about him?'

'I'll decide in the morning,' Lance said. 'I'm too angry now.'

'Let him walk back,' Jimmy said. 'Maybe he doesn't make it and we save a bullet.'

Chew shuffled off into the darkness.

'His friends are still out there, wearing our diving gear,' Lance said after a moment. 'We need it back. Any ideas?'

Jimmy put the lights of the Range Rover out. 'You don't think they're planting the napalm right now?'

'No. Chew had only just arrived when I got there.'

'Then why aren't there any lights in the water?'

'I wondered about that. I think they're waiting till we leave so they can come out to their vehicle and their firearms. Let's go grab their weapons. You take the left-hand side, I'll take the right. Cover us Boo, Mwanzo.'

Lance and Jimmy were halfway to the Landcruiser when they heard the single scream, immediately cut off. There were some muffled thunking sounds, like an axe biting into a wet log, and some piggish grunts.

Lance and Jimmy fell to the ground. It was all over in seconds. Lance listened for a minute, then rose and started walking softly in the direction the sounds had come from. Off to one side he caught a glimpse of Jimmy, then on the other side he thought he saw a man pass the other way. He swung his rifle but the shadow seemed to offer him no threat and passed into the night. Had young Mwanzo lost his bearings in the dark?

An engine started behind them. They fell to the ground. The lights swivelled over them, then the vehicle roared off into the night. For a moment all was silence, the night reverberating only with fear. Then Lance rose, walked to the Range Rover and put its lights on.

The scene was at the very edge of the cone of light but the dull dust glinted brightly red around the trunk of Henry Chew. His head, arms and legs were artistically arranged around his trunk: his arms and legs as a swastika, his head as an exclamation point. For a small man he had bled a lot, Lance thought.

'Madre de Dios!' Boo said, reverting to the language he spoke most commonly.

After revulsion, Lance felt relief. So they were Bruun's Chinese after all. Or at least not Pan's Chinese, his sober mind corrected him immediately: they could still be Tong Chinese, ethnic mafia.

'Bury him and cover the blood,' Lance said. 'We have to camp here tomorrow.'

'There was a message for us back there,' Jimmy said as he drove back to their camp with Lance. Boo and Mwanzo were bringing the other Range Rover.

'What?'

'If Bruun gave them instructions not to interfere with us, he's going to be even more difficult to deal with than we thought.'

Lance shivered, though the night was warm. He knew what Jimmy meant. Before, Bruun had defeated himself through his own hot-headedness. If Bruun had turned calculating as well as cunning, patient as well as persistent, cool as well as cruel . . .

In their camp, Esmeralda said, 'You took only three men to deal with six Chinese?'

'Look to your house, woman,' Lance snapped and turned his back.

'You are my house!'

He turned in the entrance to their tent and held her in his arms for a long time, neither saying anything.

'The Wabenzi say they didn't know they signed on to drive illegal cargo,' Pierre said. 'I say we shoot the ringleader as an example.'

'I agree,' Jimmy said. 'I've had them up to here.'

Lance walked out of the water towards Pierre. He and Jimmy each carried an ivory tusk. The disc of the sun was half over the horizon. 'What exactly are they going to do?'

'Strike.'

Lance laughed. 'Pierre, use your head. Without our transport, they're dead. How do they think they're going to get home?'

'I doubt they've thought that far.'

'They're not stupid. They're trying to blackmail us. Tell them any who wish may leave now. For those who stay there will be a bonus at the end of the expedition. You will of course refuse to discuss the amount of the bonus.'

Pierre nodded thoughtfully. Lance called to him after he had walked ten paces:

'Oh, Pierre. I think the Watusi are good swimmers. Tell them any who want to help us dive will be on double wages.'

'Okay. Several of my Swahili can swim, you know.'

Lance had noticed that Jimmy, Pierre and Boo automatically identified with the warrior Swahili rather than the trader Watusi. 'Thanks but no thanks. We need them to protect our backs.'

All of them looked towards the sound of Drang and his Tanzanians setting up camp. The Chinese were sitting in the Landcruiser in plain sight, staring balefully at Lance's party.

Lance threw the tusk of ivory on the ground and accepted a cup of coffee from Esmeralda.

Jimmy also accepted a cup of coffee. Then he moved his tusk of ivory aside with his foot and followed it one pace sideways. Lance realized it was the spot on which Henry Chew had been killed by the Chinese. He too hastily stood aside. Esmeralda looked at them strangely. Before she could frame a question, Lance started making his dispositions:

'Esmeralda, your staff must help with the loading. Boo, take six men and watch the Chinese. If – '

'Six men, Lance?'

' – six. If they try to split up, don't follow. Just kill all but the leader and one of the others. You mark the leader yourself, understand? I want him alive.'

'Six men? I don't nee – '

'Do as I say, Boo. It's very important. Pierre, you're in charge of the rest of the operation ashore. What did the Watusi say?'

'Four will swim if nobody shoots at them. The rest will graciously accept a bonus.'

'All right. Let the others load. Use your Swahili to guard against attack by Drang and the Tanzanians. Organize the inflatables to run backwards and forwards out to Jimmy and me. Okay, everybody?'

'I can dive,' Christine said.

'Maybe later, when we've seen what everybody is going to do once they realize we're bringing up the ivory.'

'There's going to be a lot of work keeping everybody fed if our kitchen staff is side-railed into manual labour,' Esmeralda said.

'Side-tracked,' Christine said. 'Haven't you ever heard of woman's lib?'

'What's that to do with detours?'

'Oh, I give up! Please, Lance.'

'No.'

'Jimmy!'

'You heard the boss. Maybe later. And maybe later you won't be so keen to be out there in the open.'

At ten o'clock Lance and Jimmy came ashore for brunch bringing their diving crew with them. The hard part in diving for the ivory was not getting it to the surface but pulling it from the suction of mud in which it had been planted. Once loose, it was only a matter of a good hard shove and the diver could follow it to the surface to be sure the men in the inflatable grabbed it. Pulling the ivory out also disturbed the mud on the bottom and the churned-up silt clouded the water to make it difficult to see what they were doing. They stood looking for a moment at the pile of ivory already ashore. Pierre had decided to unload all the trucks before loading any of the tusks. It was an impressive heap of ivory.

'But,' Lance voiced the thought also in Jimmy's mind, 'there's many times that much still down there.'

Their eyes turned first to the Chinese, now outside their Landcruiser and leaning against it, then to Drang and Frank and their tame Tanzanian officer who had taken up position a hundred paces away on a convenient log.

'I hope they're sitting comfortably,' Jimmy said. 'They could be there a long time.'

In the afternoon, Lance let Christine dive for ivory but the Watusi refused to work with a woman and Lance sent her ashore again.

Late in the afternoon, the first rains fell.

'Good,' Lance said, surveying the closing horizon with great satisfaction. 'Now they can't watch us without coming threateningly close. Mwanzo, come here. I want you to sit here and look in that direction. If you see anything move, shoot at it.'

'Anything, Massa?'

'Anything. One warning shot and then you shoot to kill.'

'Yes, Massa Lance.' Mwanzo sat himself down and checked his rifle.

Once, an hour later, there was a shot. Mwanzo had not recognized the scout though he described him as 'Black man, Monkey-from-the-South': a Tanzanian. Boo reported that the Chinese were still there, sitting on the little humpback that was the only access to the road for the heavy trucks.

Lance revelled in the frustration of the Tanzanians. He had been watched too long and had hated every minute of it. He was sorry when the rain stopped as suddenly as it had come; the rain had not stopped work.

At sunset Lance and Jimmy stood before the pile of ivory, stretching tired muscles.

'Another two days to bring it all up,' Lance said. 'We'll leave on the morning of the third day from now.'

That night there was a commotion in the Tanzanian camp. Christine was restless but Lance resisted the temptation of curiosity and would not allow her out of the camp either. In truth, his curiosity was sated by a kind of sick certainty: Bruun had become so subtle that not only had he told his minions to do nothing to hinder Lance, he had even given them instructions to aid him by molesting his enemies. At least until Lance had brought the ivory to an accessible place. That Bruun had tempered his hot hatred so well by greed did not bode well for the prospect of finding him, especially since Lance had always considered Bruun to be far more intelligent than himself.

As Lance stood with Jimmy, having a drink before going back to bed, Bruun was on both their minds.

'You know,' Lance said softly, 'it's ironic. Bruun's hatred is directed at you and me but it was really Colonel Burger who gave him into the hands of the tribeswomen by refusing to take him away. I was just supernumary cargo.'

'If hatred was rational, there'd be none of it left in the world,' Jimmy said.

In the morning, Boo reported that the Tanzanians were burying two of the their soldiers who had mysteriously been chopped up and killed in the night. Drang and the Tanzanian officer were facing a mutiny from their superstitious and frightened men.

Lance stopped laughing about this when the OAU man and the Tanzanian officer decided to boost morale by letting their men take potshots at the divers. He first found out when he saw the bubbles streaming forcefully overhead as he came up with another tusk. There had been two Watusi in the inflatable. One was halfway to the shore, swimming for his life. The other lay in the bottom of the inflatable, gibbering. Lance rolled over the side and grabbed the rifle the Watusi on the way to the shore had left behind. Shots were ringing out but it took him a moment to spot anything to shoot at. He adjusted the sights and clicked the safety off. He fired two shots and, knowing he had hit his target by the scream echoing faintly over the water, turned the rifle away to find a new target. From his right came two quick shots. Lance saw a hand with blood on it rise above the shrubbery. He put a shot low down into some notional human anatomy and was rewarded by a man rising, clutching his stomach. A single shot from his left plus a fusillade of shots from the shore. The Tanzanian was held up by the bullets for a second, then slowly crumpled into the bush he had been hiding behind.

Lance waited for it. The Tanzanian half rose and shot the Watusi in the water. At less than fifty metres he could not miss a head-on shot, even in water. Both Lance's shots hit the Tanzanian in the chest. Jimmy's two shots blew his head off.

'Thank you, but I already had him,' Lance called drily.

'Don't mention it,' Jimmy replied.

Lance waited to shoot any of the retreating Tanzanians

ill-trained enough to expose himself. There were none that he could see. Jimmy fired one shot and snorted disgustedly as the Tanzanians retreated quickly. There were also two quick shots from the camp but Lance could not make out what they were shooting at. He shot at the radiator of one of the Tanzanian trucks but got the tyre instead as the inflatable sank underneath him. He surfaced and smacked the Watusi, still gibbering and swallowing water, through the face. The man grabbed at him. Lance knocked him out with a forearm jab against the chin and dragged him towards the other inflatable. Jimmy hauled the man aboard.

'Lotta help, these Wabenzi,' Jimmy said. He pointed. The two that had been manning his inflatable were both in the water. One was floating in that particularly disorganized way only dead men can achieve. The other one was swimming strongly for the centre of the lake. 'Hey you, son of a hyena, it's all over. You can come back now.'

Lance looked at the two black faces peering cautiously over the side of the inflatable. It was the two Watusi who had been diving with them; they had been hiding behind the inflatable.

'Boo!' Lance said to them, putting his face close. Lance watched them fall back into the water. He was too weary to laugh. 'I suppose we're going to have to teach Drang a lesson,' he said to Jimmy.

Jimmy smiled evilly. 'I've been waiting to teach that insolent *American* a lesson for a long time.' He hauled the two Watusi over the side. 'Mr Weber is inclined to shoot you for your cowardice. But I have pleaded with him for your lives. Paddle, you woodlice, like your lives depend on it, and he may yet let you live.'

They avoided Lance's eye but they paddled well. Lance jumped out while the inflatable was still knee-deep in water. Pierre threw him his own rifle, the custom Mannlicher that had belonged to the legendary Colonel

Jacques Roux. 'What happened?' Lance asked him. Pierre was a competent man so these Tanzanians were probably well trained and well led. And Drang was nobody's fool.

'They split their party and sent some of their soldiers around us to the far side while keeping up normal activity in their camp. By the time I caught on, they had us boxed in.'

Lance nodded. 'Okay. You lose any men?'

'No. Only the two Watusi out on the water.'

'We'll worry about getting the corpses back later. Right now we're going to warn Drang and his Tanzanians off.'

'Permanently, I hope,' Pierre said.

'They were shooting at us to kill,' Lance said.

'The law of the jungle,' Christine said.

'You're welcome to walk over there and try reasoning with them,' Lance said shortly. 'Just let us know first whether you want a religious burial. Boo, you stay to watch the Chinese and take care of the women. Arm the kitchen servants again, Esmeralda.'

'Come on, Lance,' Boo said angrily. 'Esmeralda can look after things here. I have a right to go with you.'

'Then Pierre has to stay,' Lance said. 'Or Jimmy or me. After that disgraceful display out there, do you think we can leave the women and the vehicles to the Watusi?'

'You'll get your turn to fight,' Pierre said.

'Sure, but by then that sneering son of a bitch Drang might be dead.'

'We're wasting time. Pierre, take Mwanzo up into those trees on the little rise there. They probably got a watcher there. See if you can eliminate him without attracting attention. Then set up a diversionary fire. Keep your positions until we're back here and no longer need covering fire. Understand?'

Pierre looked disappointed but said nothing. He was a famed close-quarter fighter and this was punishment for having failed to protect the diving team. He gestured at Mwanzo and set off at a lope.

'Jimmy, take four men and go round the landward side. You four go with him,' Lance added to the waiting Swahili. 'You four come with me. You three stay with Boo.'

'I'll come with you,' Nasheer said.

'I hired you for your brains, not your muscle, Nasheer. While I'm gone, I want you to explain to the Watusi that either they're part of this expedition or they can start walking back – before I return to camp. We start diving again the minute we get back. Make sure the Watusi understand I'll shoot any of them who cause holdups.'

Without waiting for a reply, Lance walked away, calling over his shoulder to Jimmy, 'Make sure you get all their vehicles. That could give us a small edge.'

'It would just make them desperate,' Jimmy said.

Lance stopped to think for a moment. 'All right. Leave their vehicles. Concentrate on getting the leaders.'

Lance had not looked at Esmeralda or waved to her. He just disappeared with his men into the shrubbery. One moment he was there, the next gone.

Christine noticed the single tear on Esmeralda's cheek. She also saw Esmeralda cross herself. 'I didn't know you were religious, Esmeralda.'

'A reflex from my childhood faith,' Esmeralda said. *'What have I done?'*

'It's not too late to give that ivory to me. I could still make a deal with Daniel Drang,' Christine said quickly.

'Don't be stupid, Christine. Lance would never "make a deal" with men who kill his retainers from ambush.'

'You know, you live in another age,' Christine said.

But Esmeralda was no longer listening. She kicked a plump bottom sticking out under a Range Rover. 'The fighting's over,' she told the cook. 'Get the others from their hiding places. We're fetching the bodies from the

245

water.' She had no intention of following Lance's order to arm the kitchen staff; they would start firing at noonday shadows and kill each other and, like every housewife, she did not want to lose well-trained staff. If Lance lost the battle with the Tanzanians, the kitchen servants would run whether they were armed or not.

Before she pushed the inflatable into the water, Esmeralda looked up the little rise to the trees. She saw nothing.

Pierre, among the trees on the rise, also saw nothing. He was not looking. He was listening. After three minutes he heard it, the small crunch of a twig as a foot was resettled more comfortably. He looked up at Mwanzo, twenty paces away. The young Swahili too had heard the sound, selected it from all the other sounds of the African landscape as the unique indicator of human presence. Pierre pointed. Mwanzo nodded and pointed in the same direction. Pierre pointed to his own eyes and then motioned Mwanzo out and away from him. The Swahili moved in almost imperceptible stages but three minutes later he had gone twelve paces and had the watcher in sight. Mwanzo signalled to Pierre, who walked forward, whistling.

The Tanzanian swung around, his rifle rising, as Pierre came up to him. 'Sprechen sie Deutsch?' Pierre said to him.

Mwanzo came up behind the man, making a relatively large amount of noise. But the Tanzanian was mesmerized by Pierre's steady progress towards him. Mwanzo hit him in the back of the head with the butt of his Kalashnikov.

'Very efficient, these Russian weapons,' Pierre said as he stepped aside to avoid getting the falling man's blood and brains on his trousers. 'But no finesse whatsoever.'

They stood watching the Tanzanian camp. They could not see Lance or his party. It was not a hill, just a little rise. In their own camp there was nothing to be seen except Esmeralda taking the inflatable out with two of the kitchen staff paddling to fetch the bodies. The Watusi who had been heading for the deep water was now swimming back shorewards. Pierre made a bet with himself that, as soon as the shooting started again, the man would reverse course once more. 'Wait for Mr Lance to start shooting,' he told Mwanzo, who was searching the Tanzanian camp over his sights.

Jimmy was also waiting for Lance to start shooting. He had his men spread out. They would have to advance twenty paces or more to be able to see the Tanzanians. They could hear them, laughing and shouting, celebrating a famous victory. I wonder if they really are stupid enough to think we'll fold like Ugandan soldiers, Jimmy thought. He ignored the fly settling on the tip of his nose.

Jimmy started when the truck engine roared into life. 'What now?' he asked himself aloud when two more engines started up and then a fourth. The trucks warmed up briefly, then moved off at a smart pace. Jimmy walked into the middle of the Tanzanian's deserted camp. Lance was standing there, waiting for him.

'That Drang sure is a lot smarter than we've given him credit for,' Jimmy said.

Lance nodded. 'He knew I was coming after him.'

'We can still pin them in a crossfire between us and Pierre.'

'No. As long as they're out of our hair while we bring up the ivory, we'll let them be. They won't go far. Later we can punish them for attacking us. For now we have work to do.' Lance waved at the trees. Pierre stepped out into the open and waved back. Lance gestured for him to come down. The Battle of the Lake, as the Watusi would start calling it around their campfire that very evening, was over.

That evening Fitzmeikle arrived. He chose the abandoned Tanzanian campsite to park his stolen truck. He and his

247

two lieutenants bathed in the lake and watched Lance's camp from afar through binoculars. 'A very resourceful man, if he came by a new truck in Uganda,' Nasheer said, setting Lance and Jimmy nodding their heads thoughtfully. Fitzmeikle seemed also to have learnt from his experiences that patience was a virtue since he made no move towards the pile of ivory on the ground.

The next morning Fitzmeikle was dead. So were his two sidekicks. All had been dismembered by meatcleavers. The mess turned Lance's stomach. Nothing had been heard all night from the Fitzmeikle camp except a single pistol shot. That presumably had accounted for the missing Chinese, as there were now only four Chinese left in the Landcruiser. Lance had the Fitzmeikle party buried, then went back to his work of diving for the ivory.

'When are you going to do something about those fucking murderous Chinks?' Christine shouted at him halfway through a brunch which had thus far been unrelievedly silent.

'Chinese,' Lance said flatly. 'This is not the place to cast racial slurs.'

'What are you going to do about them?!'

'Nothing.'

'They're the enemies of our enemies,' Jimmy said, his smile for once in abeyance. 'That doesn't make them our friends. But we're in too much serious trouble to question the hand that offers us help.'

'Help? Killing those poor Australians in their beds, you call that helping us?'

'It saved the bullets we would have used for the same purpose,' Lance said bluntly. 'Are you deaf, girl? Fitzmeikle as much as told us he intended to take our ivory at gunpoint.'

'You know what you are? You're an animal. You're no better than – '

Her chair fell over backwards as Jimmy struck her

248

through the face with the back of his hand. He did not hit her very hard and she fell more from her own evasive action than the force of the blow. She made no effort to get up.

'You know, Christine,' Esmeralda said conversationally, 'I distinctly remember Lance telling you exactly what it was going to be like, the very first time we met you. Remember? You chose to come. So did Daniel Drang and this Fitzmeikle man. Lance even had the courtesy to warn them, after they had threatened him. Your own motives for being here are not pure either. But you chose to come. If you wilt in the heat, get out of the cook's way.'

This time nobody corrected Esmeralda's quaint version of English idiom.

'How do you think you're going to take the ivory from us when it gets to be your turn?' Jimmy asked. 'And don't tell me you don't think about it. You talk in your sleep about taking the ivory "for the animals". For the animals . . .'

'I'll only be giving back to the animals what belongs to them. And not by violence.'

'And Fitzmeikle thought the ivory belonged to him. By the same logic. He saw it, he wanted it, he said it belonged to him, therefore it was his. Never mind the megalomania. Tell me, Christine, how are you going to take anything from Lance and the rest of us except by violence?'

'Aw, let her be, Jimmy,' Lance said, pushing his plate away.

'No. I lose face by having such a birdbrain for a woman.'

'I'm not your goddamn woman! And I'm not a birdbrain!'

'Then try learning from experience,' Jimmy said, pushing his chair back. He bent over to pick Christine up and put her on her feet. 'If you want to screw for the animals somewhere else, you don't need to give me any notice.'

'Jimmy, we got work to do.'

'Yeah, I'm coming.'

They were in the water before Christine recovered her breath.

Lance said, 'I'm not surprised you can't find a wife.'

'Doesn't it bother you when she attacks you so wrongly?'

'Why should it? She's just one of the many who come to Africa with little venetian blinds drawn over their eyes. They see a small piece through a thin slit and then interpret it according to presumptions recorded on the backs of slats that block out the real view. How can the opinions of someone so misinformed matter?'

'Man, she's part of a majority. That's what makes me angry.'

'Thanks for the concern,' Lance said. 'But I don't think it's worth the energy.' He dived. They came up beside the inflatable together.

'Maybe you're right,' Jimmy said. 'They don't see, they don't listen, they don't learn. Let's fetch some ivory.'

Late on the afternoon of their second day of diving for ivory, Lance took a survey. Then he sent Jimmy down to check his observations. They hung side by side on one of the inflatables.

'What do you reckon?'

'Half a day's work,' Jimmy said.

'That's what I thought. Tomorrow we'd better slow down a bit so we can finish at sunset. I don't want Drang and his Tanzanians to know we've finished here until we're on our way. We'll pack up after dark tomorrow and leave an hour before dawn the next day.'

'Since they're sitting on the only road between us and Goma, we're going to have to deal with them first. If there's going to be a pitched battle, we'll lose fewer of our men to our own fire if we attack at dawn rather than an hour before.'

'Oh, we're going to attack them all right. We owe them for killing our drivers. But there will be no pitched battle. Just a surprise attack from cover and a holding action in the rear.'

'Huh?'

'We're not going north Jimmy. I'm taking the southern route around the lake, through Bukavu and then east to the coast.'

Jimmy whistled. 'It's daring all right. Drang might even lose his Tanzanians if it looks like we're heading even further away from their base in Uganda.'

'Exactly. And if things get too hot for us in Rwanda, we can slip over the border into Burundi before heading through Tanzania. Not that we're going to have much time for ducking and weaving, not at the speed I intend going.'

Jimmy hitched his elbows up on the inflatable and formed a square with his fingers within which to visualize the map. 'I'll command the rearguard, of course.'

Lance shook his head. 'I'll do it myself. I don't like people taking potshots at my men.'

'We'll both stay then, hm?' Jimmy laughed a little self-consciously. 'I don't like people taking potshots at me.'

They dropped off the inflatable and started swimming inshore.

'You know,' Pierre said that evening, 'we can't find the grave for the missing Chinese anywhere. I wonder what they did with the body.'

'I've been studying their food supplies through Lance's binoculars,' Esmeralda said. 'They don't have much. Perhaps they ate him.'

'Aargh!' said Christine and snuggled closer to Jimmy on the grass, her earlier anger at him forgotten or suppressed.

'You wouldn't eat cats, dogs or horses, would you?' Esmeralda said reasonably. 'But the Koreans, Chinese and

French do. So, maybe there are some people who consider other people protein.' After a moment, she added into the silence, 'You never know.'

'Go on, Christine, call her a savage,' Jimmy said gently. Christine bit her lip.

Lance said, 'But you do know, Esmeralda. About four hundred kilometres that way – ' he pointed west ' – there's a tribe of cannibals that still practice on their mothers-in-law. My brother told me.'

'Did he also tell you he and Colonel Hoare, the Mad Mike of legend, once dined with their chief?' Pierre asked.

'Good God, no. Did they?'

'They had roast suckling pig. The Chief assured them it tasted just like his mother-in-law,' Pierre said.

'It's true,' Boo said. 'I was there.'

'Funny how I know nothing of it,' Jimmy said.

'You were too young to fight then. You were at school still in England and then in Belgium.'

'Your brother, Major Weber, was under normal circumstances a man who tailored his manners to his company,' Pierre added. 'From the humblest to the highest, everyone considered the Major a prince among men. In addition, he had a stomach of steel – once for a fortnight we lived on nothing but raw grubs and a few grasshoppers a storm had blown in from the Sudan.'

'I remember that,' Jimmy said. 'I couldn't wait to get the vile taste out of my mouth and have a proper steak. Not your brother. First he had a bath and a shave, then a few drinks, *then* dinner.'

'Well,' Pierre continued his story, 'with this cannibal Chief your brother absolutely insisted on having the meat carved at table right in front of his own eyes. The "table" was a paw-paw leaf set on the ground in front of the Chief's hut. Your brother, having guessed that it would not be changed too often, brought a sheaf of fresh paw-paw leaves with him.'

After a silence, Christine asked, 'Is that it? The whole story?'

Pierre shrugged in the darkness. 'Yes. Except that, after that, if a man wanted to get out of cooking chores, all he had to do was cut his finger. The Major would immediately put him on latrine duty instead.'

'I don't see the point in a story about a man who went to eat with a cannibal and then ate pork carved on a fresh paw-paw leaf,' Christine persisted.

'The point is that there actually are cannibals,' Lance said. 'They're not a figment of someone's imagination. Real live people, people you could run into just going about your everyday affairs, people like Pierre and Boo have in fact dined with them.'

Christine drew a sharp breath. 'Your daring stuns me. One doesn't meet people like you "just going about one's everyday affairs", Lance.'

'Here you do,' Lance said obstinately. 'The proof of the pudding etcetera.'

'Sure you do,' Jimmy said. 'If you saw Pierre in Brussels, wearing a blue suit and a maroon tie, sitting behind his chauffeur in his Rolls, he'd look exactly what he is, an overweight stock speculator approaching middle age.'

'With an insolent younger brother,' Pierre added, kicking Jimmy sharply in the ribs. 'I'm big, not fat. And I'm barely forty. I'm an investment banker, not a speculator.'

'Middle age is thirty-five,' Jimmy retorted.

'Technically,' Pierre said dismissively.

'When all this is over, I'm going to need some investment advice,' Lance said.

Christine drew another sharp breath but said nothing.

In the morning, while they were swimming out to the inflatable, Jimmy said it for her. 'I say Lance, one does not, going about one's everyday affairs, meet people with

253

quite your monumental self-assurance.' He mimicked Christine's voice perfectly.

Lance smiled. 'She'd probably call it arrogance. Maybe you should keep her on after all this is over.'

'I've given it some thought. But with that mouth, she'll make her life and mine hell with the family.' Jimmy laughed wryly. 'One of the reasons I'm not married is because my brothers all married such straitlaced women. Haven't you wondered what Pierre and Boo are doing here?'

'I thought Sambo told them to come, same as he told you.'

'Sambo asked for two volunteers and those two and several others jumped at it. Pierre married into a banking family and he's doing well in the business. But his wife turned into a real frump. Kinder, Kirche, Kuche.'

'Children, Church, Kitchen.'

'Right. Pierre's got a mistress. Now Sambo's wife, she's real attached to her Catholicism.'

'Whom God hath joined together let no man – '

' – let no woman put asunder. She makes Sambo's life hell about it and Sambo dumps on Pierre.'

'What about Boo? I thought he had a happy family.'

'Yeah, sure. But, like I told you, things get a little stifling in Brussels. I get out to the East, Boo bought himself a couple of fighters in Paris.'

'What fighters? I thought you'd given up soldiering.'

'Boxers.'

'Oh. Fist-fighters.'

'You meet a lot of semi- and minor criminal types around the boxing ring.'

'I didn't know that.'

'The upper classes breed race-horses, the middle classes race motor cars, the lower classes hooligan at the soccer, the criminal classes back boxers. Unfortunately for Boo, there was a big police investigation into exactly who is who in boxing and some of his friends went to jail. Sambo feels that, after we fought so many years for law and order in our own country, we shouldn't encourage lawlessness in someone else's.'

'Hell, that's a bit narrow. I mean, I'm sure Boo had nothing to do with them as criminals, if you see what I mean.'

'I know. I think Boo's such a never-mind he didn't ask who his associates were and what they did away from the ring. Sambo's wife has been at Boo's wife and now the whole lot have been in his hair for a year or more. Boo just refuses to sell his fighters. He says he's not doing anything wrong and his investment is making a lot of money.'

'How the mighty have fallen,' Lance said sadly, thinking of how once these men were revered or feared wherever soldiers met.

'The Baluba Butchers harried by their womenfolk?' Jimmy said. 'Shit, I think it's funny.' He went under laughing and came up choking. Fortunately they were near the inflatable and Lance towed him to it.

'You didn't think it was so funny back in Brussels.'

Jimmy stopped choking. 'It isn't only that. Everybody volunteered. They all like you but it's more than that. Africa gets into your blood . . . and then it keeps calling you like some first love.'

They looked at each other for a moment, then Jimmy adjusted his goggles and dived.

Late in the afternoon, while they were trying to make raising the last few tusks last until sundown, a light floatplane came low over the lake, rose a little to give itself room to turn, then settled onto the water and taxied up to them. It was the Bukavu lawyer Lance had retained to smooth their way, the one who – probably with the help of some official associate – had tried to cut himself in. The lawyer stayed in his plane. Lance sat on the rolled edge of the inflatable to talk to the man.

'I see you started recovering the ivory without my counsel, Mr Weber. I don't know whether that's wise.'

Lance said nothing.

Behind Lance, Jimmy said, 'The bush telegraph's been working.'

'I think I can still arrange things for you in Bukavu,' the lawyer said. 'Against guarantees, of course. It will not be cheap.'

Lance had an inspiration. 'We already have guarantors, thank you. They're securing the road northwards to the Ugandan border. We shan't be requiring your services after all but thank you for coming.'

Behind Lance, Jimmy sniggered.

The lawyer's forehead creased above his bloodshot eyes. He lowered his sunglasses from his hair to his nose. Lance's duplicated mirror-image turned as the lawyer looked ashore to estimate the amount of ivory. With his eyes still on the loaded trucks, the lawyer said, 'You will need services all the same. It would, for instance, be inconvenient for you if the authorities at Ruthsura were to attempt to interfere.'

'I volunteer to shoot him,' Jimmy said.

Lance shook his head. He called out to the lawyer, 'They won't, unless you tell them.'

The lawyer opened his mouth as if to protest, then closed it again. He pulled the door of the plane to and snapped something at the pilot. The plane taxied, then took off. Jimmy followed it into the air over the sights of his rifle.

'I have a nasty feeling we're going to hear from him again,' Lance said. He watched the small plane make a complete circle over their camp. Next it circled the Tanzanian camp. The Tanzanians took potshots at it but hit nothing. After a while the plane flew back southwards. They watched it until it disappeared, then had to hurry to bring the last of the ivory up before darkness fell.

* * *

256

The Tanzanians had chosen their campsite too well for Lance even to consider a frontal attack on it. They also, Pierre had reported, set out six guards every night. Lance simply did not have the manpower to take out six guards all at once – not if he wanted to do it quietly. So Lance planned to make his main stand at the road rather than the Tanzanian camp. Once in position, they had five minutes before Pierre would order the first engines started up. Lance, Jimmy and Mwanzo spent the five minutes creeping forward. When the trucks tore the tender fabric of the night, Lance picked off one of the guards he had spotted. Mwanzo got the other one. That left four guards. Lance heard a rustling to his left and fired at it. The guard fired at his muzzle flash but Lance had already rolled. Jimmy got him.

'We can't wait to spot the others,' Lance said. 'Let's go.'

'And hope they're round the other side,' Jimmy said.

They ran forward until they were within sight of the Tanzanian camp. Some men were taking cover. Others had not heard the shots and were standing around wiping the sleep from their eyes and looking in the direction of the noise. They too took cover the moment their three attackers started firing. Predictably, Drang, Frank and the Tanzanian commander had heard the shots and taken cover. They were shouting at the men to take cover and fight back.

Mwanzo killed one of the guards as he ran into the camp. The other two guards slunk back into the trees.

'Mwanzo, watch our back. Those two might try to circle round.'

Mwanzo melted away into the night.

'Once I could move like that too,' Jimmy said.

'You'll have to, just before first light,' Lance said. 'Otherwise we're going to find out what if feels like to be caught naked in a cactus plantation.'

Across the still landscape – the birds had settled again –

came the growl of a laden truck churning away in low gear, then another and another. By the time that first bass sound had rumbled into infinity, the higher-pitched whine of trucks speeding up had almost passed beyond hearing. The Tanzanians prepared frantically to defend the road next to their camp. It was ten minutes before they realized the ivory was travelling in the other direction.

Lance pushed Jimmy, who was shaking with laughter and had his handkerchief stuffed in his mouth to prevent the sound getting out, in the ribs with the barrel of his rifle. He gave Jimmy the night glasses.

'Get the vehicles,' Lance said. 'Just one tyre on each to start with. You start on the right, I'll start on the left.'

'Okay. Say when.'

'Now.' Lance shot, rolled, aimed, fired, rolled, aimed, fired. He ignored the fusillade of bullets that rained into the ground all round him but mostly where he had been a moment ago. He hit three tyres with three shots, then lay panting, wiping the earth from his eyes. One of the bullets had come very close, kicking up dirt into his face.

Jimmy came up and took the night glasses. 'You all right?'

'Yes. Just dirt in my eyes. How'd we do?'

'Six tyres between four trucks. We could do another two, so that they have to change two tyres on each truck before they can use them.'

'No. They're waiting for us now. Let it rest.' Lance held his stainless-steel Rolex up close to his face but could see nothing (it had belonged to Ewart, who had ordered it without phosphor on the hands). He looked up through the leaves at the stars. 'We have another ten minutes or so here. Maybe just before we go.'

They sat with their backs against trees, facing away from the Tanzanian camp. After ten minutes, Lance looked at the stars again, then rolled over on his stomach and studied the Tanzanian camp through the night glasses.

All the fires were now totally out, not a coal gleaming. Nothing moved. The Tanzanian commander was willing to wait the few minutes until dawn when his attackers would find themselves in an untenable position. Lance studied the trucks.

'Okay. One more tyre each. You do the rear wheel of the truck near the table, I'll do the other one.'

'Right, call it,' Jimmy said when he too had studied the target through the night glasses.

'Three, two, one.' Now, Lance said silently to himself as he squeezed the trigger and withdrew immediately behind his tree. He listened to the bullets crunching into the trunk on the other side.

When the Tanzanians stopped firing, Lance and Jimmy rose and slipped away through the trees without talking. Halfway back to their positions beside the road, they found Mwanzo sitting against a tree. He had seen nothing.

The eastern sky turned purple, then orange, then yellow. After that it turned a blinding white, too painful to look at. Lance watched the sunrise with great pleasure. For the moment there was nothing to fear from the Tanzanians. They would first have to ensure that their immediate surroundings were safe and then have to change the wheels on their trucks before they could give pursuit.

An hour and twenty minutes after sunrise, the Tanzanians came. They had repaired only two trucks and crowded all their men on them. They had left most of their camping equipment behind in their hurry. Lance could understand that: whatever Drang might do, the Tanzanian commander would be keen to catch up with the ivory before it was taken over the Rwandan border, especially at such a densely populated point as Bukavu.

Lance shot out the two front tyres of the leading truck, then tried for the radiator. As he had expected, it was armoured and the bullet whined away after ricocheting from the protection. Lance methodically put a shot into each of the rear tyres of the truck as well. Mwanzo killed two of the Tanzanians as they jumped from the truck.

Lance watched as the second truck settled on flat tyres. Jimmy also tried for the radiator next and with the same result. The Tanzanians from this truck all made it into the bush alive, though Jimmy winged one in the arm.

Lance had given instructions that Mwanzo was to kill two of the Tanzanians in retribution for the two Watusi killed and had forgotten to retract the order after accounting for three guards. For the rest, they were to fire to keep the heads of the Tanzanians down.

Drang came out of the second truck and Lance, in a mischievous mood, shot the heels off both his boots. Jimmy disappointed with his results at radiator-shooting, did the same for Frank. Lance could hear Jimmy roaring his amusement on the other side of the road.

After that they settled down to the dull grind of keeping the Tanzanians pinned to their position.

Lance woke up with a start. Mwanzo was shaking him, pointing to the sun. God, he had fallen asleep! Mwanzo was looking at him strangely. 'What's happened?'

'Nothing, Massa. They in no hurry to die.'

Lance looked at his watch. Ten o'clock. Time to go. 'Let's go quietly,' he told the Swahili.

Jimmy was waiting at the Range Rovers. 'Where were you when I needed you?'

'Sorry, I fell asleep.'

'Christine will love that. Your common, everyday sort of fellow. Falls asleep while people are shooting at him, he's so used to it.'

'Okay, okay! I said I'm sorry. Let's go.'

'I'll have to tell Boo we have another champion never-mind in the family.'

'Get stuffed, Jimmy.' Lance slammed the Range Rover's

door. 'Anyway,' he said out of the window, 'you used to tell me old soldiers sleep every chance they get.'

'It was obviously a mistake to tell you,' Jimmy said, chuckling loudly.

Lance let the clutch in fiercely enough to leave Jimmy standing in a cloud of dust. He could understand how Jimmy's sense of humour would sometimes drive his family up the wall. On the other hand, it had been irresponsible to fall asleep in the circumstances. But he and Esmeralda had made love fiercely until only a couple of hours before he had to get up again to deal with the Tanzanians. And, anyway, the bloody Tanzanians were keeping their heads well down like the good little well-trained soldiers they were, he thought savagely.

Three hours down the road, at Kabare, they found Pierre standing beside the road, wiping his mouth and looking anxious.

'You'll have to hurry your brunch,' Pierre said. 'I want to get the convoy back on the road. That crooked lawyer's plane has been snooping around.'

'There wasn't enough excitement for Lance, so he fell asleep,' Jimmy said.

'We'll eat on the move,' Lance said.

'What are you going to do? There's a good blacktop road that runs this side of the border all the way to where you can cross into Burundi at Bujumbura.'

'How long since you saw the lawyer?'

'Fifteen minutes.'

'Then we'll take our chances he hasn't had time to organize a reception party at Bukavu. The Tanzanians are only an hour and a bit behind us and the longer we stay in Zaire, the better their chances of catching up with us. They won't follow us into Rwanda.'

'I wouldn't bet on it,' Pierre said.

'I'm not,' Lance snapped. 'But as long as we're on the Zaire side of the border they're certain to follow us. Get

261

the convoy on the road. Jimmy, you drive on and find us a place to cross the border without attracting attention.'

'What about my lunch?'

'Your sense of humour will nourish you. Get on with it.'

An hour later they found Jimmy waiting for them in the outskirts of Bukavu, munching a Keller melon. He led them through the market gardens lining the shores of the lakes.

'This is going to be the difficult part,' Lance told Esmeralda. 'I'm reluctant to do violence to the police here. They're only doing their job. On the other hand, if Nasheer can't buy them quickly, that lawyer and his high-up, greedy friends are going to catch up with us. They don't want a small bribe, they want the lot. The police will have to take their side, which will put us in an unenviable position.'

'Can't we just outrun them?'

'That's what I'm hoping to do. You see that watertower? Beyond it lies the city limits of Bukavu.'

'That's good, then.'

'It's not barely-populated open country. They practice intensive agriculture over large parts of Rwanda and Burundi.' Lance swung the Range Rover around a slow-moving, decrepit old light truck, then braked sharply to avoid striking a mule being led down the middle of the road. Cyangugu, Butare said the sign. Lance drove back onto the tarmac road and checked the mirror to make sure all the trucks were still with them. The ivory was covered with tarpaulins Lance had bought used in Nairobi mainly for the faded legend on them: Basil Herman's Agricultural Equipment & Machinery. It was not much, but it might get them past a lazy policeman or customs inspector.

The 19 kilometres to Cyangugu took almost an hour because the road was clogged. 'It's worse on market days,' Nasheer offered.

'We'll come back for the tourist attractions another day,' Lance said. He picked up the microphone. 'Jimmy?'

'No sign of them. I reckon, even if they have the devil's own luck, they're still half an hour behind us.'

Just before Gikongaro, Lance stopped the Range Rover ten paces short of the light plane parked in the middle of the road. 'I see you have a new partner,' he said to Daniel Drang.

Drang smiled sourly but let the lawyer do the talking.

'Your "guarantors" are only an hour behind you, Mr Weber. I think we should talk urgently.'

'Very urgently, before I push your plane off the road,' Lance said, putting the Range Rover in gear.

'The Chief of Police at Butare is a very close friend.'

By way of reply, Lance let the Range Rover roll forward.

'I warn you, Mr Weber, if you won't be reasonable, I shall have to make a citizen's arrest.'

'Pass me my rifle, if you please, Nasheer.'

Lance knocked the safety off with his thumb as he pushed the barrel out of the window. The bull bars across the front of the Range Rover were touching the propellor of the plane. Lance heard the pilot shout something at the lawyer but kept his eyes and his rifle on the lawyer and Drang.

'Smartass,' Drang said to the lawyer, who was foaming at the mouth.

Lance let the clutch in and the light plane was pushed backwards into the rough ground beside the road. One of the propellor blades was bent in the process. The lawyer ran beside the Range Rover, shouting at Lance and trying to strike him in the face. Lance kept him at a distance with the barrel of his rifle. When the road was clear, Lance pulled the 4WD off the road and got out, pushing the lawyer aside. He waved his trucks by. Then, not raising the rifle from his hip, he shot off the aerial over the plane's cabin. The pilot scrambled out but Lance was already back in the Range Rover and passing the trucks in the dust storm they threw up.

'Now we're going to have to go like a bat out of hell,' Lance said as they regained the head of the column. 'That lawyer wasn't bullshitting. He probably does know the head cop at Butare. Get that map, Esmeralda. What's the shortest way out of Rwanda?'

'To where?'

'Anywhere, just out.'

'Through Butare to Ngozi in Burundi.'

'Anything else?'

'Not that I can see. The border is only about twenty kilometres beyond Butare. That lawyer and Drang and their friends and even the Tanzanians will catch up with us before we've cleared the customs.'

Lance laughed aloud. 'No, they won't. There's nothing there except, only sometimes, a single policeman.'

'He won't be any trouble,' Nasheer said. 'It's the regular smuggling route.'

'How far from there to the Tanzanian border?' Lance asked.

'Something over a hundred and twenty kilometres,' Esmeralda said.

Lance kept both his hands on the bucking wheel. He led the convoy across the rough gravel road at a hundred kilometres an hour. 'What time is it now?'

'Nearly three o'clock.'

'We're going to have to drive into the night. I don't want to camp until I'm well into Tanzania.'

'Why don't we camp in Burundi? Nobody will know we're there.'

Lance just shook his head.

Nasheer said, 'The men who keep the border open for smuggling no doubt include the police chief at Butare. When he finds we slipped the net, he'll call his opposite number in Burundi and then – '

'Yes, I see,' Esmeralda said. 'It is part of the pattern.'

'Exactly, Mrs Ellimore.'

The radio crackled. Lance realized suddenly that music had been playing all along, unheard and unheeded, drowned by the sounds the speeding Range Rover made.

'Guess who just caught up with us?' Jimmy asked.

'The Monkeys-from-the-South.'

'No, not them. Our yellow friends.'

'I'd been wondering when they would show.'

'Well, they're here now. What's the hurry? That plane back there is out of commission with a bent prop and missing its radio mast.'

'I want to be in Tanzania tonight.'

'Groan! Are you serious?'

'We don't have any other choices.'

'We could lose a truckload or two of valuables.'

'I know.'

There did not seem to be anything more to say. Lance put the mike back on its hook.

As they thundered through Butare, Lance saw a man rolling a white-painted drum in the road. The man jumped aside and the bull bars on the Range Rover cast the concrete-filled drum off the road. Lance saw a rifle swing at him from beside the road, then he was past it. Beyond Butare he pulled onto the track for Ngozi and waved the trucks down it. He counted the trucks. They were all there.

Lance reached for the mike. 'Jimmy, where are you?'

Just then Jimmy's Range Rover came roaring around the bend.

'They'll take a while to get organized and follow us,' Jimmy said. The rear side window of his Range Rover was missing, presumably shot out. 'They meant business but we caught them unprepared, I'd say.'

Lance saw Jimmy give him a cheery wave as Lance brought his own Range Rover past Jimmy's on the narrow track. Christine looked pinched and frightened. Lance felt sorry for her: until a few minutes ago she had probably not believed anybody would ever maliciously direct a rifle against anyone as well-meaning as her. 'Where are the Chinese?'

'Playing cowboys and sheriffs back there,' Jimmy laughed. 'The local robber baron wasn't quick enough for us but he caught the Chinese in his net.'

Lance laughed too. 'Useful friends, those Chinese.' He could see nothing but dust. He would surge the Range Rover forward in it until he saw some glint of metal, then swing out and pass the truck in front. He did not envy Jimmy his backmarker position, having to drive in that dust all day long. At night it would throw up a lethal fog-like barrier against the lights.

'You're going to get us killed!' Christine shouted at him over the radio link. 'And you laugh, you bastard!'

Lance clicked the switch off and put the mike back on its rest. In the mirror he saw Nasheer smiling broadly. The Arab was too intelligent not to be frightened but he had more experience of dangerous situations and came from a culture where showing fear was deplored. His ethos prescribed that women were unworthy and Christine had just proved it. Lance took a moment to glance at Esmeralda. Her face was relaxed, her body swayed easily with the movement of the vehicle, her hand rested on the grab handle only tightly enough not to lose her hold on it. Her eyes were open and she was studying the dust, ready to warn him if she should see the dangerous rear of a truck before he did. Nasheer, for all his superior smile, was also watching the dust in front of them carefully.

Without warning, passing a truck, they came out in the open. Lance sighed his relief. He throttled back to ninety kilometres an hour which was, in truth, too fast on that road for the heavy trucks. It was a miracle none of the trucks had broken down or crashed yet. The Watusi were wonderful drivers.

'It is almost enough to forgive the Watusi their cowardice,' Lance told Esmeralda. 'Whoo-pee!' The biggish stream could only be the Akanyaru. It was the border between Rwanda and Burundi. 'Ready with your money, Nasheer?'

'Just drive straight through, Mr Weber. I'll throw a bundle out of the window. By the time he's finished counting it, we'll be long gone.

The Range Rover hit the water at such speed that it aquaplaned almost all the way across the stream, at the end of the dry season narrower than usual and with only eighteen inches of water flowing sluggishly, before ploughing in to send up a spray of water. Lance in fact had the wipers on before the spray hit the screen and for a moment he could see nothing as the wipers smeared the dust. Then the water hit and the whole screen was covered by a muddy paste. He also got a faceful of water through the open window beside him. By the time he could see again, he was two hundred metres past the hut he knew was there.

'Was there anybody there?'

'I don't know, Mr Weber. I threw out a thousand dollars anyway.'

'A thousand? He doesn't make that much in a year.'

'So he'll be counting all year. And if his bosses don't come in person to read the sign on the ground, he'll try to keep it all by denying we passed this way.' Nasheer sounded hurt.

'I wasn't criticizing, Nasheer. Only admiring the exact fitness of the figure you chose.' Out of the corner of his eye, Lance saw Esmeralda wink at him, without turning her head. 'Give Nasheer the map, Esmeralda. How far to the Tanzanian border, Nasheer?'

'Hundred and twenty kilometres, Mr Weber.'

'We have to pass through Ngozi,' Lance said after a moment's reflection. 'But the next big town . . .'

'Muyinga,' Nasheer said. 'There's a big police and army installation there – '

' – where our Rwandan friends will have done business before, splitting the border takings between them,' Lance said.

Nasheer got the point immediately. 'Turn at Ngozi for Muyinga, left after Muyinga for Mukenke, back down to Kobere which is on the Tanzanian border. It adds about thirty klicks but it gives us a choice of roads once into Tanzania.'

'All right.'

'It's mostly earth roads, not gravel.'

Esmeralda groaned.

'It'll be worth the detour not to have to fight the Burundi Army,' Lance said.

'The BOSS paramils,' Nasheer said.

Lance looked at Esmeralda. 'It's that Brigadier Burger I told you about.'

'But he's a South African.'

'The South Africans have set themselves up as the policemen of Africa,' Nasheer said. 'They have some paratroop police they send anywhere in Africa where there is some disturbance that will not reflect well upon them. They make no arrests and take no prisoners.'

'I still don't see why that should concern us.'

'What Nasheer means is that I'm a South African. If we make too many waves, Brigadier Burger will come drop on us like a ton of bricks. Most likely he'll kill all of us. He warned me when Bruun first reappeared.'

'Mr Weber bears a name that is very famous in Africa and, with the South Africans, if you'll forgive me, Mr Weber, perhaps infamous. His late brother's exploits up and down Africa were widely reported.'

'That'll do, Naheer. We don't want to do anything that can be misinterpreted as some kind of mercenary activity. If a group led by me, by Jimmy, Pierre and Boo, had a shooting disagreement with the army of some black state, that's bound to be misinterpreted as an attempted coup.'

'Then what about Drang's Tanzanians?' Esmeralda asked.

'I think that's a private venture by the officer. He would never get official sanction to invade Zaire. And, having invaded Zaire and, if the lawyer wasn't lying, Rwanda as well, he can't now very well go to his superiors and make it an official matter.' They passed through Ngozi. Lance glanced at the odometer and the clock. Twenty-seven kilometres in just under twenty minutes was very good going. 'At least I hope not,' he said when the convoy was through Ngozi. 'One consolation is that Drang will probably insist on bringing in the Tanzanian Army. In self-protection, the Tanzanian officer will have to kill him.'

'If I'd known about these appalling risks . . .' Esmeralda said.

'Forget it,' Lance said. 'I knew the risks before we set out. Remember, we're running these risks to trap Bruun and avoid a bigger risk.'

They were silent, thinking about this, until Lance led the convoy off the gravel onto the dirt and then he had no further time for cerebration as he fought to keep the Range Rover heading straight down the ruts. In four hours Lance spoke only twice to his companions, once to thank Esmeralda for giving him some water, once to explain the teeth-clattering vibration set up in the Range Rover by the corrugated surface of a section of the road: 'Sympathetic vibration between the road and the car's body at this speed. We don't want the trucks to shake to pieces but it's extremely unlikely they'll vibrate at the same frequency, so we'll just keep going at this speed.'

Between Mukenke and Kobere, tantalizingly within sight of the border, one of the trucks broke down.

'What now?' Jimmy asked.

The sun was about to set. A light plane was flying at them and at the sun. The plane circled the convoy.

'Lance?'

'Two million dollars of ivory,' Nasheer said.

'What's wrong with it, Jimmy?'

'Spring hanger broken. Half an hour's work.'

'All right. I'll come fix it. You get to the head of the column and lead it into Tanzania.'

'I'm perfectly – '

'Do as I tell you, Jimmy.' Lance pulled the Range Rover off the road and waved the trucks by. 'Jimmy'll pick you up here,' he said to Esmeralda and Nasheer.

Nasheer climbed out, his hands busy shuffling notes into small packages.

Esmeralda said, 'I'm staying with you.'

'This is no time for heroics. Go on, Esmeralda.'

'Leave that ivory.'

'No. There is not threat to it.'

'Except the reinforcements that plane is calling up.'

Lance walked around the Range Rover. He opened Esmeralda's door, unclipped her safety belt, lifted her out bodily. She kissed him on the mouth. He ran around the 4WD and turned it around by gunning the engine and sliding the rear wheels on the loose dirt. The last trucks were still thundering by. Jimmy's Range Rover appeared through the dust. Lance saw him stop to pick up Esmeralda and Nasheer.

Mwanzo was riding shotgun on the broken truck. The Watusi driver was standing against the front of it, smoking. His eyes belied his poise: they were rolling up to the plane, back along the road, forward along the road.

Lance hit the Watusi through the face with the back of his hand. The cigarette went flying. The driver looked as if he had just woken up and saw Lance bending over him. 'Now get the jack under the truck,' Lance said. Jimmy would have told the Watusi to start the repair. When the Watusi hesitated, Lance hit him through the face again, from the other side. The man put a finger to his lip and looked at the blood on the finger. The colour seemed to electrify him. He sobbed and crawled under the truck to get the jack from its clip on the main cross-brace. Every truck carried its own jack, tools and spare parts, including two pairs of spring hangers. The spring hanger had already been taken out of the box by Jimmy. Lance threw away the greaseproof wrapping with its Chinese character to show it had passed inspection by the late Henry Chew. He took the one-and-fifteen-sixteenths spanners he knew from experience fitted the hanger bolts on this American design. Jimmy had already laid these out with a greasecan. By this time the Watusi was under the truck, positioning the jack while Mwanzo stood by the handle, ready to pump it. The Watusi was jabbering with fear, not looking what he was doing. Lance hauled him out by his feet. He crawled under the truck himself and positioned the jack.

'Now,' he told Mwanzo. When the weight was just off the hanger,' he said, 'Stop.' Behind Mwanzo he could see the Watusi studying the Range Rover. Lance crawled out from under the truck and fetched the keys from the Range Rover and put them in his pocket. He went back to the truck and undid the bolts. There were four of them and it was not difficult to do, only slow. He went to look in the toolbox but the speed brace was missing. He fitted the new spring hanger. Now he needed another jack and fetched the one from the Range Rover to press the spring back into the new hanger. Lance tightened up all the bolts and squirted grease from the can.

The Watusi was climbing into the cab and had the engine running before Mwanzo had fully lowered the truck. Lance threw the tools into the cab through the open door. Mwanzo flung the heavy jack through the door. The Watusi took off before Mwanzo could scramble aboard. 'Come with me in the Range Rover,' Lance said, grabbing the Swahili's arm to prevent him running after the truck and perhaps getting sideswiped by it as it slewed this way and that on the excess of power the Watusi was feeding the wheels.

Overhead, the plane stopped making circles and changed heading to follow the road to the border.

Mwanzo picked up his rifle from the dust. He inspected it carefully. The tyre marks of the truck were clear on the barrel. Lance took the rifle from him, held it by the barrel, swung and threw it far into the scraggly bushes beside the road.

Mwanzo looked at him curiously. 'It was a rifle, Massa.'

'But not good enough for you, Mwanzo. The barrel could be bent or squeezed out of shape. It would blow your head off the first time you fired it.'

Mwanzo looked so forlorn that Lance nearly laughed. There was a spare Kalashnikov on the rack in the Range Rover and Lance gave it to Mwanzo. Lance's own rifle still stood in the front passenger footwell. They set off after the truck and the plane.

Try as he might, Lance could not get past the truck. The Watusi was driving along that dirt road at a 110 kmh. He was driving as if his life depended on it. Which, Lance allowed after a moment's thought, it did. The presence of the plane was evidence that by now the police or the army were on their way from Muyinga to Kobere. The police and the army had to cover only twenty-six klicks of good gravel road while he had to cover less than half that distance on this terrible dirt road. Who got to Kobere first depended on when the others had left Muyinga . . .

Mwanzo finished inspecting and loading his new rifle and stuck the barrel out of the window. Lance hoped there would be no shooting. He had seen Burger's men in action; he did most emphatically not want them to drop on him out of that guileless sky inhabited only by those who retain their innocence by being judge, jury and executioner all at once, those who never hear any answers but their own because they make no arrests and take no prisoners.

But neither did he relish the idea of being a hostage for the ivory. There had been no need to give Jimmy, Pierre and Boo instruction on that possibility. They might make an armed attempt to rescue him but they would never allow Esmeralda to succumb to blackmail and exchange the ivory for him.

The Watusi in the truck was laughing and crying. Tears rolled down his cheeks. He could barely see the road but that hardly mattered. He had first driven a truck when eight years old. To him this hellish rutted surface was just another road like all the others he had driven over; gravel roads were a luxury for white men with bad prostate glands and ill consciences. Soon he would be across the border into Tanzania where the monkeys who inhabited the place were at least amenable to reason or money. But this mad white man – it was obvious, despite the fear the mere mention of his name inspired in the elders of the tribe, that this mad white man knew nothing of the Burundi. The Burundi were not reasonable. They shot first and talked afterwards. An upside-down world. Men who talk first, especially to Watusi, never get around to shooting: it becomes unnecessary. There was a village in sight, and some green trucks coming up the road, led by a green jeep. The Watusi put his foot down hard and headed straight for the jeep. The jeep went bush and the trucks after it. The Watusi laughed and cried and new tears rolled down the dust on his cheeks.

'Hey! Whoopee!' Lance shouted as he pushed the Range Rover through the scattered vehicles of the Burundi. As far as he could make out, it had happened too fast for the Burundi to fire even a single shot at them. Soon the Burundi would be hard on their heels. Lance hoped the village was Kobere. He pressed the horn and flashed the lights. The Watusi either saw or turned left by

273

instinct. Lance knew that, if it was not Kobere, they were lost in Burundi. That would be unfortunate.

Chickens scattered from the road like fat from a pan. People too, amazingly few. Of course. A detachment of the Burundi were setting up the ubiquitous white drums filled with concrete, a lethal road block once in position.

The Watusi never saw the drums or the Burundi diving for their lives.

'Don't shoot, Mwanzo,' Lance said.

'Massa?' Mwanzo looked surprised. He knew little of politics and cared less. If people were your enemies, they shot at you. Then you shot back or, better, you killed them before they could start shooting at you.

'Don't fire.'

The bull bars on the truck scoooped up the drums and cast them aside, one, two, three. The fourth drum – forty-four gallons of scrap metal and concrete – rocked in the draught set up by the passage of the truck. The Range Rover slid sideways as Lance flung it into a tight turn to avoid the flying drums. One hit the Range Rover behind the rear wheel, ringing the whole structure like a bell. Mwanzo braced his feet on the dash and pumped his ears with one hand, with his other holding onto his rifle.

Lance had no time to pump the ringing out of his ears. The Range Rover swung completely around, three full circles. When it stopped, Lance was looking straight into the face of a bewildered Burundi policeman.

'Smile,' Lance said to him and the policeman automatically touched his stick to his forehead. Lance put the Range Rover in gear and drove out of the village square. Only two shots hit the rear of the Range Rover before he was gone. He arrived at a deserted lifting-plank barrier while the pieces were still falling to the ground after being snapped by the truck.

'That Wabenzi, he in very big hurry go home,' Mwanzo laughed.

'Even cowards sometimes have their good points,' Lance agreed, laughing aloud with the young sharp-shooter.

'Lance, are you all right?' It was Esmeralda on the radio.

'Yes, I'm all right. Where are you?'

'Then why are you laughing?'

'I'm laughing at the crazy Wabenzi who singlehandedly beat out the Burundi Army.'

Jimmy came on the radio. 'We're at the crossroads beyond Kabanga. The Wabenzi just shot up the road to Kanazi. I'll go get him. There's nothing up there except the Tanzanian police.'

'Okay.'

'I've sent the trucks on to Mbuba but they have to cross the Ruvubu by ferry before they get there. Got the picture?'

'Yes,' Lance said slowly. 'If the Burundi cross the border, they can squash us against the river or against the Tanzanian police. The crossroads are the key. I'll try to hold them.'

'If you can't, I'll cut crosscountry with the Range Rover and join you at the ferry. But the truck won't make it.'

'Let the truck go, Jimmy.'

'No, I'm right behind it already. He's slowing down.'

Lance slowed right down as he went through Kabanga. He watched the mirror closely. As they came to the crossroads, he saw the dust storm behind him. The Burundi had decided to cross the border.

The crossroads were not a good defensive position. There was not much cover and nowhere to hide the Range Rover. It would be obvious to the Burundi that an attempt at ambush was being made and, from its being made at such an unpromising position, that the crossroads were for some reason important to the fugitives. Human nature being what it is, Lance thought, that would make the

275

Burundi all that much keener to take the crossroads. Without cover he and Mwanzo by themselves were never going to hold several truckloads of Burundi for long.

Lance climbed on top of the Range Rover. 'Climb up here. Don't shoot until I tell you.'

The twilight was deceptive. Lance rubbed his eyes. He had not had much sleep last night and he had been working since an hour before dawn, near enough to sixteen hours. His hands were disgustingly grimy and he could imagine what his face would look like, muddy with dust and sweat, smeared with oil. He brought his rifle up and sighted through it, trying to find some mark a thousand metres away in the almost featureless landscape. If he could keep the Burundi at that distance long enough, he would not have to kill many of them and he and Mwanzo would be relatively safe, even exposed on top of the Range Rover. He doubted the Burundi would have the weapons or the expertise for accurate shooting at that range. Unless the Burundi commander had found his own equivalent of Mwanzo, a natural marksman . . .

Lance raised the rifle to watch the Burundi approach through the scope. Then he burst out laughing.

In the lead vehicle he had looked straight into the face of Wong the Chinese, grimly set and cut about the forehead from glass escaping the shattered windscreen of his transport. Behind Wong came the Burundi. Lance looked the other way. No sign of Jimmy and the Watusi. He could hold the Burundi only until dark: under cover of night they would surround him and storm him.

Lance had an idea. He studied Wong's vehicle through his scope. It would be easy to put a shot in his tyres and then he would fight the Burundi while Lance escaped. But the Burundi were many and Wong seemed to have only two men left out of the original four. With a shock Lance realized the Chinese were holding handguns. They had no rifles! For the briefest moment sorrow for them surged in

276

him, then his rational being mocked him for the ridiculous extreme of sympathy for men who live only to kill. But he still needed them . . . Jimmy was his friend.

Lance aimed at the front left tyre of the Landcruiser. If they reached the pattern of shade on the ground he had decided was a thousand metres away before Jimmy came, he would knock them out. At that range he could help them deal with the Burundi. Perhaps they would survive. Hell, as long as one of the Chinese lived, his main plan was safe. Or did only the leader know how and to whom to report back?

Lance cursed, waited for his breathing to recover steadiness, then started squeezing the trigger. On a custom-made precision instrument there was no slack. His first shot missed as the speeding Landcruiser hit a bump and rose into the air. Lance refocused the electronic zoom. He took his finger off the trigger and turned around to look. The Wabenzi was driving his truck down the road, being shepherded by Jimmy in the Range Rover.

Lance waved them by. He turned his rifle on the first of the Burundi vehicles and blew both its front tyres with three shots. 'Get their tyres, Mwanzo. Try not to hit people. Don't shoot the leading Landcruiser – they're with us.'

It was not easy in the gathering dark but it took only minutes to reduce the Burundi column to a chaotic mass of twisted metal and men running hither and thither, seeking cover, thinking their lives were in danger.

Wong pulled his Landcruiser up beside the Range Rover. He stared balefully at Lance. Today had confirmed his worst suspicions. This occidental and all the blacks were in a conspiracy against him. Today he had already been forced to fight in four countries, two of which he had never heard of before (and the other two strangers to his lexicon until twelve weeks ago, but he had already forgotten that). He had lost a good man to people without honour, people who never came close enough to come to grips with, people so cowardly they invariably fought with rifles from a distance. And black, at that. Barbarians. Not that this white barbarian was much better, but at least he had killed one of the black men with his bare hands back in Kenya. Still, Wong wanted to kill him where he stood beside his Range Rover, smiling coldly but politely at Wong and – insult of insults! – asking if he could be of any assistance.

' – a first-aid kit? I wouldn't want to lose you after you've followed me so far.'

Wong considered spitting on the ground at the barbarian's feet but only killing was strong enough to express his disgust. He put the Landcruiser in gear and drove off.

'Little yellow man not like you,' Mwanzo said. He thought it a great joke, chuckling all the way to the ferry.

Daniel Drang was being consumed by his own rage. The Tanzanian Army captain worried, first, about explaining to his superiors how he had lost two trucks in Zaire when he was supposed to be on police duties in Uganda and, two, about invading Rwanda. Drang was uncomfortably aware that they were behaving much like the detestable white mercenaries, like Colonel Black Jack Schramme who with Moise Tsombe's Katangese secession forces had captured Bukavu and Rwanda and held it for four months in 1967 against the Congolese National Army. The Tanzanian captain knew nothing of this but, illogically, after breaching the sovereignty of two countries, refused to follow the Weber party across the border into Burundi. Drang was worried about his ivory – about Africa's ivory. He did not trust the Bahutu, who had been running Burundi ever since disposing of their Batutsi rulers in a gory bloodbath shortly after independence. They were crooked and greedy. They would try to keep all the ivory for themselves. It would all go into Swiss bank accounts. Nothing for Africa.

And the idiotic Rwandan lawyer, thinking Weber would fold before nothing more than verbal threats! The man had been defeated by his own greed. If he had gone to the police at Butare, they could have held Weber until the Tanzanians arrived. But no, the lawyer wanted everything for himself.

The lawyer had gone to Butare to telephone his friends in Burundi. The Tanzanian captain had turned north so as not to have to cross into Burundi. Drang had decided to stick with the Tanzanians. The captain was stupid and greedy and in this only for his own pocket, but he was also a man of small imagination. He would be satisfied with a few hundred thousand and think he had received the major part of the loot; a million was outside the scope even of his greed.

If the Burundi took the ivory from Weber, all was lost, Drang knew. But, having seen the speed at which Weber could move a heavily loaded convoy over almost non-existent roads under adverse conditions, including armed attack, Drang thought the Burundi would have to look very lively even to catch sight of Weber before he disappeared into the vast spaces of Tanzania.

'Now if only the Burundi will hold Weber up long enough for us to get to Rulenge before Weber makes it, we got him,' Drang said, stabbing the map.

'Weber could cross further south.' Frank was massaging his bruised heel, bracing himself in the back of the jolting truck by his elbows and knees.

'No. He'll want to stay in Burundi as briefly as possible and then head the shortest, quickest way back into Kenya.'

'So. Then we should forget this thick-skulled soldier and let Weber go. Once he's in Kenya, we tell the government and the ivory falls into our laps.'

'I told you before, Frank. Weber only looks like a dumb jock. Do you think a stupid man would have come so far?'

'Sure, I remember. You also said he had his woman and his Uncle Toms to do his thinking for him if he slips. I still say we give our feet a rest and wait till he gets to Kenya – '

'Where the first thing he'll do will be to hide the ivory in another safe place until the hue and cry dies down. He's not some broken-down minor-leaguer who's gotta make a score immediately or starve. He's rich. He can wait.'

'Then why's he doing this?'

'Shit! Why are you and I doing this instead of running security for Multinational Ripoffs Incorporated?'

'Yeah, I suppose so.'

At the next stop, Drang persuaded the Tanzanian to keep driving through the night. There was a good 160-kilometre stretch of blacktop all the way from Kigali to the Rusumu Falls on the Tanzanian border. From there to the crossroads at Rulenge . . .

The Tanzanian was swaying on his feet from fatigue. Drang told him of all the women much money could buy: blonde white women, honey-coloured Asian women, full-breasted black women. The Tanzanian gave orders to keep on driving for Kigali. When the men seemed mutinous, Drang distributed American dollar notes. They crossed the border by the simple expedient of driving around the posts. They saw nobody. Two hours before dawn they reached Rulenge and settled down to wait for Lance Weber, his party and his ivory.

The one around Wasini Island, south of Shimoni, is the smallest of Kenya's famed Marine National Parks. Tanner had never seen the other two, but if they were even half as good as this one, Kenya had a fabulous resource. If not quite in the class of Australia's Great Barrier Reef, it had the attraction of being almost deserted. For their morning swim he and Ruby never bothered with swimsuits and their evening dip was usually after dark.

The other great advantage was that an interest in

Marine Park allowed Tanner to anchor the converted MTB right on the Kenya/Tanzania border. From there he had a clear run down the Pemba Channel along the Tanzanian coast and another good run out into the Indian Ocean. It was an ideal position, though even the man who pumped the gas in Shimoni (two pumps, one petrol, one diesel) knew that the MTB belonged to Lance Weber, that Tanner and Ruby worked for Lance and that Lance had gone to fetch the ivory for which he had killed the beautiful Spanish lady's English husband. A thousand tons of ivory, it was said.

Tanner worried about the authorities but Ruby told him to laugh it off and, even if it were to be mentioned to him directly, not to start a fight for Esmeralda's honour or his employer's. *That* would really start the tongues wagging.

A customs launch paid a social call. The commander mentioned in passing that the previous owner of the MTB was serving a sentence for smuggling. Tanner laughed easily. His employer was a very rich man: the story would no doubt amuse him. The customs man suggested Mr Weber was also a man of action and he was at present travelling with some very famous men of action in his retinue, not to mention having hired Swahili warriors and armed them with the latest automatic rifles. There had been stories of ivory . . . Tanner nodded and said he had heard them. Of course there was not a thousand tons of ivory in all the world but idle tongues would wag. The customs official nodded gravely. There was a law against removing even one ivory tusk from Kenya and he had to enforce it. From Kenya . . . A drink would be very pleasant indeed. It would be very bad medicine to have to fight Mr Weber and his Belgian Congolese officers and his Swahili, but the Tanzanian coast was not far away, it was possible the Tanzanians had not heard and, anyway, the Tanzanians were not as efficient as their northern neighbours.

Besides which, Tanner said, Mr Weber had assured him he wished to live the rest of his life in Kenya – as a good citizen.

When the customs launch had gone, Tanner told Ruby, 'I nearly made the most godawful mistake and offered that man a bribe. But he doesn't want money, he wants peace and quiet.'

'Yes,' she said reflectively. 'And with this man Weber's reputation and friends, I don't blame him for not wanting to fight. I just hope the Tanzanians haven't heard the same story. It could get very uncomfortable for us if they're waiting ashore for that ivory.'

'Or offshore,' Tanner said. 'These people are no respecters of twelve-mile limits.'

'I wish the rains would come,' Lance said, dunking his rusk in his coffee. For the second night he had not slept well. Esmeralda, after a day of being shot at – yet more fearful for him than for herself, had needed the reassurance of his body. He had had to take a turn at guard duty. And they had camped late.

The reason for camping late was that Lance could read a map as well as Drang. He could see the importance of the crossroads at Rulenge. But, Lance reasoned, if the positions were reversed and he was chasing Drang, he would not have headed for Rulenge at all. Instead he would have cut across the track from Sekeseke to Nyakahura forty-five klicks *beyond* Rulenge. Therefore he, Lance, had to camp the night beyond Nyakahura.

It had taken three hours to get the trucks over the Ruvubu on the ferry and another two and a half hours to reach Nyakahura. Of the Burundi there had been no further sign; presumably, once they had put their vehicles and men in order, cooler heads had prevailed and called them back from their armed invasion of a much larger country. All the same, it had been a tense three hours with

282

their backs against the river, every passing second expecting the Burundi to open fire at their exposed position out of the darkness.

Now, if it had rained, that track would definitely have been impossible and impassable, even for him and Jimmy, never mind a rookie like Drang. He could have camped just beyond Rulenge and had a couple of hours more sleep.

'Well, I don't wish the rain would come,' Jimmy said. 'I'd rather fight than dig.'

'Can't we simply outrun them?' Christine asked. 'We have so far.'

'That's true,' Esmeralda said. 'We have outrun them.'

'This is their own country,' Lance said patiently. 'They possibly know it better than we do. They do not have to make detours to avoid invading other people's countries. They can call up reinforcements. Every man's hand won't be turned against them.'

'So?' Jimmy said. 'The faster we get away, the less chance they have to bring their advantages into play.'

'And the more clearly they can see the ivory slipping from their grasp.' Lance's patience was finished. 'Therefore the more tempted they will be to call in help even if it means they have to share the loot. If it rains, they will not be so far behind us. We will always be temptingly in reach, until the very last moment, when it will be too late for them to call up reinforcements.'

'The donkey with the carrot on a stick,' Pierre said.

Lance finished his rusk, drank some coffee and threw the grounds out on the earth. 'I want to be on the road at first light.'

'Road,' Christine said flatly, rubbing her bottom. 'Sometimes I wish I was fat.'

Lance walked over to where the Chinese were sitting in plain sight. In the light from his own camp he could see what a sad state their Landcruiser was in, scratched, dented, bullet holes and broken glass. Their flat black eyes radiated hatred at him. Still, they were going to be his salvation.

'You'd better fill all your containers with water and fuel at Nyakanazi,' he said to the leader who sat behind the steering wheel.

The man spat out of the window and Lance stepped back to avoid the spittle splashing on his boots.

'Fill up with water and fuel every chance you get. We're going to go long stretches where you will get neither.'

The Chinese simply stared at him. He might not have existed. He turned around. Christine was standing ten paces behind him.

'How does it feel to help murderers?' she asked.

Lance laughed. For once there was no antagonism in her voice. 'I could say you should give them the benefit of justice and wait until a court condemns them. But I won't. It burns me up inside to need such people.' He saw her flinch from the chill of his voice but that was her problem: she had asked. 'If I did not need them, I would kill them.'

There was a silence. Perhaps because she thought she was expected to comment, Christine said, in a small voice, 'I see.'

'And when I no longer need them,' Lance said almost casually now, 'I shall kill them.'

Christine walked on in silence. She no longer doubted that Lance would do exactly what he said. In London, I would of course not believe him, she told herself. But here, here he had yesterday travelled illegally in four countries, taken on the armies of two and the police of another. Any man who would stay behind with one young tribesman to take on the army of an independent nation *and come away unscathed* was either mad or frighteningly competent. The awesome thing about Lance Weber was that, in this time and place, he was the sanest man in the world.

Christine sublimated her fear in speculation on how she could turn Lance's very competence against him when the time came to take his ivory. She shivered in the warm morning. If need be, she would die to put twenty-five million dollars to work for the animals. She was quite as determined as Lance Weber.

Once they were underway, Nasheer asked, 'Where will we camp tonight, Mr Weber?'

'Between Sekenke and Shelui.'

Nasheer sighed.

Esmeralda looked at the map, adding the figures. 'But that's nearly five hundred kilometres of that gravel *road*!' She pointed, then grabbed at the handle as they went through a pothole. 'That is murderous, Lance.'

Lance shrugged. 'It is the next place we can camp where they cannot get between us and the sea. Everywhere else they could sneak around and block our route.'

'But they're far behind us.'

'They could catch up. Never under-estimate your enemies.'

When they camped that night, Lance was wondering whether he had not over-estimated their enemies. Drang would never give up but he was not in command, the Tanzanian was. Africans do not, generally, have the persistence Henry Chew had so prided himself on in the Chinese. And soldiers are apt to want their food and rest.

They had been travelling for fourteen hours, making an average speed of 35 kmh, including all stops for food, to take on water, to relieve themselves – and to repair broken trucks. Once again they had to camp after dark. But it was worth it, Lance thought, another day nearer the sea, another day on which he did not have to fight the Tanzanian army, another day on which he did not invite the likes of Brigadier Burger to drop out of the sky and attempt to exterminate him like some pest. They had lost the Chinese before they stopped for brunch but Lance had no doubt they would catch up again. Of Drang and his Tanzanians there was no sign.

But Lance knew, because the police at Ugisha and Nzega had not attempted to stop them, that Drang and the Tanzanians were still on their trail. Once they despaired of catching up, they would call in the local authorities.

The Chinese arrived two hours before dawn, Boo reported at breakfast. 'They do not look like they love us, Lance. It worries me that they have done nothing yet.'

'They'll wait till we reach the water,' Lance said.

'Then why not kill them where they sit?'

'Because I want to question them first and we haven't time.'

Jimmy looked at Christine, waiting for the outburst. For once she said nothing.

That day they did less than half the distance covered on the previous day.

Beyond Singida, Lance led the convoy off onto an earth track. I hope you know what you're doing, one half of his mind told him. I hope so too, the other half replied. Till then, they had covered one hundred and twenty-five kilometres in less than four hours. The next ninety-one took ten hours. Late in the afternoon the rain came, slowing them down even further. When the first truck got stuck in the mud, Lance stood beside it, his dusty face raised to let the large drops turn it muddy, then wash it clean.

Jimmy looked up from hooking the stuck truck to the back of the one in front and the two Range Rovers. He too was smiling broadly. 'This sure is going to sort out the men from the boys,' he said, ducking as one of the Watusi swung a pierced steel plank perilously close to his head. 'Do you want to die painfully, Watusi?'

The sun had set when they camped. Esmeralda performed a miracle and had a hot meal ready in forty minutes. Lance gave all the servants an issue of whisky.

After the meal, Jimmy explained to Esmeralda how clever Lance had been. He spread the map and made a cross on it.

'We're here, just beyond Kwa Mtoro. Now, Drang's not going to believe Lance took a million dollars of trucks and twenty-five millions of ivory across that track. Nor, since the rain, can he come look.' Jimmy winked broadly.

'But won't the dry out the road?' Christine asked.

'Some of the water, yes. But some will turn to mud. And tomorrow it will rain again. Drang's Tanzanian pals won't dare take their trucks in there for fear of being stuck till the end of the rainy season. So Drang has to go the long way round. And the beauty of it is, there are two long ways round. See here, at Kwa Mtoro, we can choose to turn either north or south.'

'He'll turn south, because the road is better and he now knows we're not heading back to Kenya,' Lance said quietly.

'Which,' Pierre said, 'will be a mistake as we have already turned north from Kwa Mtoro. We can be at Arusha tomorrow night – not too much after dark,' he added apologetically to Esmeralda, 'if the next stretch isn't too badly muddied. From Arusha to the sea is blacktop all the way.'

'In two days, three at the most, your ivory will be on board ship,' Jimmy said, also to Esmeralda.

'Three days,' Lance said firmly. 'We don't want Drang's tame Tanzanian to get the idea we're too near the Kenyan border while he's too far from us.'

'And you don't want to lose your Chinese,' Christine said. 'If we were heading for Arusha all along, why the fuck did we have to bust our gut on these terrible roads when we could have travelled these good roads here?' Her finger traced a line across north-western Tanzania.

'Because those roads are often as bad as the ones we've

been travelling on, though not, I grant you, as bad as today's. But they lead through game reserves. You don't want to take thirty tons of ivory into a game reserve and try to bring it out again. A lot of game rangers think like you, that they should have the benefit of all the ivory in the world. Okay, let's get some sleep. We still have to do seventy klicks of mud tomorrow and then nearly three hundred of wet gravel. This is likely to be your last early night for a while.'

Even Esmeralda joined the chorus of groans.

'You know,' Jimmy confided to Lance in the morning, 'for a moment there I thought you were crazy enough to try and cross the Kitwei Plain in the rainy season with a million dollars' worth of trucks loaded with twenty-five million in ivory.'

'I thought about it,' Lance said. 'But it wasn't worth the hassle after we already bluffed Drang out and sent him south when we're heading north.'

Daniel Drang's problem was not stupidity, nor even prejudice against the colour of his skin. He was intelligent and talented enough to overcome both the colour of his skin and the lack of opportunity that he had been born to. Daniel Drang's problem, through school, college and the CIA, had been his own prejudices, his unreasoning hatred of a world that had created him disadvantaged. And when his Africa, the unsullied place of his dreams where every man would be born free and equal, had disappointed him, his hatred had nowhere to turn but inward. Until Lance Weber and the black men he had inherited from his brother came along.

Daniel Drang let his hatred of Weber and his Tom-Toms simmer on the back boiler while he explained the facts to the Tanzanian captain. The facts were simple. The rain had conspired with Weber against the rightful owners of the ivory. There was no way they could follow Weber

288

along that track of muddy earth, though his tracks were plain for anyone to see. It would be suicide. So, Drang had told the Tanzanian to come south on the good road to Dodoma, where Weber would surely head next – unless *he* intended to commit suicide by attempting the Kitwei Plain in the wet season.

'That man do anything,' the Tanzanian captain told Drang when this was mentioned. 'I once hear man cross Kipwei wet season on donkey.'

'Okay,' Drang said at dawn in Dodoma. He had not slept all night. 'Okay. Now Weber must come to us.'

'Unless he turn north. Arusha,' the Tanzanian captain said blackly. 'Arusha, then Kenya. Nothing for me.'

'Then why didn't he head for Kenya the shortest route from Burundi? Try using your head for something besides bashing brick walls.'

'Okay, you very clever. But I kill you I get no money.' The Tanzanian captain traced a road on the map. 'This man with our ivory, he turn Mele-Mele, come out Buigiri, shortcut Dodoma.'

'That's a dry-weather road.'

'Yesterday he travel dry-weather road.'

That was true. Drang traced a line on the map. 'Son of a bitch! That bastard Weber has finally outsmarted himself. See here. Segera! He can't go any fucking place except through Segera. Through Dodoma, around via Arusha, across the Kitwei, he can't go any fucking place except through Segera. We'll wait for him at Segera.'

'Hims go Arusha, hims go Kenya.'

'I told you no. He's a law-abiding citizen up there. Let's move like a dose of castor oil to Buigiri, then we can loaf to Segera. He can't beat us to it.'

They already knew the Weber convoy had not passed through Dodoma before their own arrival.

At last I got you, you white mercenary bastard, Drang thought.

On the third day, in the morning, he woke up less certain of it. In the Company they had always covered all their bets. Here he did not have the budgets . . . This was his last chance at that ivory. If he lost it now, the biggest allocation of money and manpower and equipment in the world would never recover it. He sent Frank the seventy kilometres across the good blacktop to Tanga to rent a plane and try to spot on which of the possible roads Weber was approaching.

While Frank was gone, Drang sat in the truck, staring at the rain and at the map, torturing himself with the many possibilities. Weber could have followed him to Dodoma, then instead of turning northeast for Segera, turned southeast for Dar-es-Salaam. How did he think he was going to get the ivory out through that busy port, crawling with police and customs? What had made Weber think he could cross half of Africa with thirty tons of contraband ivory? And he had done it. Almost. No, Weber had to be heading for somewhere on the coast between Dar and the Kenyan border, where a ship would be meeting him. And, if he wanted to use any of the good, fast roads, he had to come through Segera. The problem with that argument was that Weber had already demonstrated that he was willing to take on any road under any conditions. He could still turn onto one of the many seasonal roads that intersect the main road both north and south of Segera. There was no way Drang, even with the help of a plane, could cover all these possible routes. But why should Weber, such a smartass, go off into the discomforting crawling mud if he thought he had rid himself of his pursuers? Pure cussedness?

No, Segera was a good place, even if it did make the Tanzanian captain uncomfortable to be so near what he called 'cibilization' with hospitals and police posts within hailing distance.

The shadows were already long when Frank's plane

290

landed on the highway and was immediately pulled off to let the backed-up traffic pass; it was a busy road.

'Where the fuck have you been?' Drang greeted him.

'Dar-es-Salaam. Dodoma. All the way across the fucking Kitwei Plain, which isn't a plain at all when you gotta fly under the clouds. All the way up nearly to the Kenyan border.'

'Never mind the travelogue! Did you find him?'

'Yeah. I found him.'

'Come on, goddamnit!'

'Heading straight for us.'

Daniel Drang did a little war dance in the mud, stomping ankle deep in it. 'Where?'

Frank turned to the pilot, who said, 'Between Hedaru and Mkomazi.' He had an exaggerated British accent. 'They're doing a steady hundred klicks an hour.' When Drang scrabbled for his soggy map, the pilot added. 'That's an hour and perhaps a bit away, the way they're going.'

Drang looked at Frank. He could see Frank was thinking the same thing. They would have to move like lightning to set their ambush. 'What's Frank paying you?' Drang asked the pilot.

'Usual hourly rates. Plus a little bonus. I was the only black pilot he could see but I was just going off duty.'

'Okay. Can you use a rifle? Do you know the ground around these parts really well?'

'Yes and yes. What do you want to hide?'

'One hundred thousand dollars for you. It's a flat fee.'

'All right, I'm in, if it isn't suicide.'

'It's not even criminal, my friend.' Frank showed the man his OAU idenitification. 'We want to take thirty tons of ivory from a mercenary – a white mercenary – who's trying to smuggle it out. We want to give the Tanzanian Army their share and then disappear with ours, probably into Kenya. Clear?'

The pilot looked at the Tanzanian captain, who had been listening to all this impassively. He looked at the armed men. Then he looked at Drang and Frank. These two could outsmart the Tanzanians any day. Besides, the captain was not from his own tribe; the man was *ipso facto* treacherous. A hundred thousand dollars . . . He would resist the temptation to try and take more from these two with their American accents. They were waiting for his answer. 'I already said I'm in.'

Drang started pushing the Tanzanians on the trucks. He wanted to get a couple of kilometres between him and Segera. There was no point in letting its inhabitants know there was cargo valuable enough to fight for on the road.

On that road, an ambush was easy to set. Drang was not overly concerned with the possibility of pinning Weber down and taking his ivory from him. Time was against Weber. What bothered him was that others, third parties, would come along and interfere. It was a busy road and full darkness was yet two hours away.

An hour later Weber had not come. Another half an hour passed. Drang looked at Frank. 'He's made a habit of camping only after dark.'

'Yeah,' Frank said. 'Maybe he thinks he's got nothing to fear so he's making it easy for the women to get his dinner. I could do with a decently cooked meal myself.'

'Get in the plane and go find him.'

'Now?' asked the pilot.

'Now. That's what I'm paying you for.'

'It's bloody nearly dark, man. Those mountains up there are real killers.'

'I'll give you something on deposit, say ten thousand.'

'Well – '

'It's more than you make in a year jockeying tourists around.'

'Okay.'

They were back inside twenty minutes.

'Son of a bitch!' Frank shouted as Drang came running up to the plane. 'The bastard's outsmarted us again.'

'Or maybe just outsmarted himself,' the pilot said. 'Nobody takes a convoy of heavy trucks into the Usambaras in the wet season. Not even in the dry season, if he's got any sense.'

'What's happened?' Drang shouted frantically though the pilot had switched off before speaking.

'They came as far as Korogwe, then turned east,' Frank said. '

'So they could be aiming to rejoin the blacktop at Moyusi for Tanga or behind our backs while we stand here talking for Dar via Segera?'

'No,' the pilot said. 'They're past that turnoff and there's no place he can turn those big trucks.'

'You don't know this man,' Frank said to the pilot. 'When he wanted to kill the crocodiles in the River Congo, it would have taken too long to shoot them one by one. So he mined the river with nitroglycerine and blew it up a mile at a time by throwing in a log.'

Drang hit his fist into the aluminium skin of the aeroplane. The pilot looked at the dent and then at Drang. 'Keep your panties on, Mister. You won't have to fight this guy for his ivory. You'll be able to pick it out of his crashed trucks. He's picked the best road through the mountains but it still ain't much of a road. He can't turn, there's almost nowhere to camp, he can't go on in the dark. He's still be there tomorrow.'

Drang ignored him. Without asking permission, he reached into the cockpit of the plane and fetched the map the pilot and Frank had been using. That bastard Weber had come within twelve kilometres of the trap Drang had laid for him, before turning away as if he had second sight.

'You didn't scare him off by letting him see you?'

'Christ, what else? We were flying right up the road at

him. There's nowhere else to fly in these mountains if you want to see what's below the cloud.'

'And scary too,' Frank said, shivering.

'No, no, no! The first time, on the main road.'

Frank shook his head. 'No man, we were just a plane going over and disappearing. We made a detour coming back so as not to roust him.'

'You didn't linger for any time, to check it really was him?'

'Shit, Daniel, I'm not stupid. Anyway, who has a convoy that runs with such precision, the trucks all exactly spaced, a Range Rover front and back, a refrigerator truck and two fuel tankers?'

'Weber.'

'Nobody else.'

'You sure?'

'Of course I'm sure. He's got those same tarps too. Basil Herman Agricultural Machinery.'

'No, not that. Are you sure he didn't make you?'

Frank shrugged. 'As sure as I can be. If he had, he would just have taken the shortest route that would put him behind us, he wouldn't have headed into the mountains, would he?'

Drang showed him the map. 'Then why did he come all the way south to Korogwe only to turn north again?'

Frank took a pace back. 'Look, distributing the blame isn't – '

The pilot interrupted him. 'He came all the way south to Korogwe and then turned north again because it's the best road through the mountains. It's also the shortest, because the others wind so. By staying an additional hour or less on the tarred road, he saved himself fifteen, perhaps twenty hours in the mud.'

Drang was still studying the map. 'He can still turn a lot of places in an area the size of Connecticut. The question is, will he?'

'I hate to contradict a guy who's already given me ten grand and promised me more, but I think the question is: Will he make it through the mountains?'

'He will,' Frank said.

'Okay, if you say so. Then the question is not Where? but When? He can't turn off before Mkujane. All we have to do is get there before him. We can go through Tanga and approach Mkujane from the other side. We don't have to go through the mountains and through very little mud.' The pilot lent emphasis to his words by squashing an imaginary mosquito with his thumb on the wing of the plane.

Drang shook his head. 'We've fallen into that trap once before. When do you think we'll get to Mkujane?'

'If we start at dawn – '

'Weber will be at Mkujane before us. Now that he knows we're on his tail, he'll travel through the night.'

'He can't.'

'Tell him that.'

'Nobody can.'

Drang shook his head. He was not going to argue. 'We will travel on the blacktop to Tango now. Tomorrow at dawn, you will fly out and find out which way Weber turned at Mkujane and then we'll intercept him, on the road that runs up the beach, when he reaches it. It's obvious he's going to put the ivory on a boat there somewhere.'

'Why not duck into Kenya with it, old chap?'

Drang sighed, not just at the form of address. 'He lives there. He's had lots of chances to "duck into Kenya". What's the coastline like north of Tanga?'

'Rough in places. Mostly deserted. Ideal for smugglers.'

The Tanzanian captain said, 'I have cousin in Navy.'

'Do you really want to share with him?'

At the first false dawn of that morning, they had covered sixty kilometres in fourteen hours. All of them were covered from head to toe in mud. They had lost one of the fuel tankers and a truck down the mountainside. Lance had had the ivory on the truck laboriously winched up the slippery slope and put on a spare truck that had been carrying their camping equipment, which was then thrown into the ravine. One of the Watusi had a broken arm, received when a jack he had positioned sloppily slid out from under a truck; he was lucky not to have had his ribcage crushed. Miraculously, there were no other injuries or losses. Jimmy had a scratch down his face, made by Christine's fingernails when he had joked that she was in her tomboy's heaven, mud over her head; nobody sympathized with him.

It was not dawn yet when they passed Mkujane and turned almost directly north to Mkameni from where they would sweep back to the coast.

Esmeralda held the thermos upside down over the mug. Not a drop rolled out.

'My soul for a cup of coffee,' Nasheer said.

'Don't sell yourself cheaply,' Esmeralda said. 'My virtue for a hot bath.'

'In three hours you can have a dip in the sea while we load the ivory,' Lance said. 'Maybe less if nothing goes wrong.'

'What about that plane we saw yesterday?' she asked.

'What about it? He thinks we're sleeping and maybe by tonight we'll reach Mkujane. By the time he gets there, we'll be fishing in the middle of the Indian Ocean.'

In the rear Range Rover, Christine said, 'I could almost become fond of this mudbath.' She pointed to the earth road, a streak of mud through the vegetation, churned up to sill height on the Range Rover by the trucks in front of them. 'At least it's safer than that goddamn mountain we drove through last night. I've never been so frightened in all my life. All those bottomless black holes.'

'It's very beautiful in the day,' Jimmy said. 'Sometime I'll bring you back to see it.'

'Thank you, but no thank you, Jimmy. I'd just see more things I should have been frightened of last night. Africa has for me sort of lost it's . . . you know . . . mystique, I suppose.'

'Then you're no longer going to try and take our ivory?'

'Don't be silly. The poor dumb animals still deserve to be saved. But I don't think I'll come back. And Oxfam will knock at my door in vain.'

A little later, she asked. 'Why do you keep looking in the mirror? What could possibly be behind us here?'

'The Chinese. We lost them last night and they still haven't caught up.'

'Maybe they had more sense than to attempt that mountain in the dark.'

'Maybe. But this whole expedition was about two things. Esmeralda's duty to her late husband's wishes. And Lance and Esmeralda and I catching up on a man called Bruun. Those Chinese are our only link to him.'

'Yes, I've put that together from what I've been over-hearing. Funny how you don't mention twenty-five million dollars of ivory.'

'The ivory's not important.'

'Men have been killed for it!'

'Their greed killed them. Going after the ivory was stupid and under normal circumstances Lance wouldn't even have considered it. But none of us could live for the rest of our lives not knowing when Bruun would strike. We have to get him first. As you've seen, twenty-five million in ivory proved an irresistible attraction to half the scum and fortune-hunters in the world – and Bruun bit too.'

'So this isn't over?'

'No.'

She thought he was going to say something else but he

was distracted by the sound of an aeroplane coming at them from behind.

'My last day in Africa,' Christine said, 'and I missed the dawn because I was discussing the insignificance of twenty-five million dollars with you.'

Jimmy reported the plane on the radio but Lance had already seen it. Lance watched it go. Almost immediately they came to a village and the good gravel road. Lance sped up.

The music stopped and Esmeralda punched a new tape into the cassette. It was Chopin's First Piano Concerto, Ashkenazy playing. The sudden burst of music delighted and invigorated her. 'How delightfully apt,' she said. Almost at once the music was cut as Lance picked up the microphone. It was an hour after dawn. Time.

'Where are you, Tanner?'

'My ETA is fifteen minutes.'

'Mine's about twenty. Are you clear?'

'No. I have friends standing off to the north. They won't interfere as long as I stay in my pool.'

Lance thought about this for a moment and concluded correctly that Tanner was referring to the Kenyan authorities, lying north of the border in a boat, watching him. He hoped Tanner was right about their not interfering. When he had spoken to Tanner about an hour before dawn, nothing had been said about any trouble.

'We might have a spot of bother ashore.'

After a pause, Tanner said, 'See you in twenty minutes then.'

Ashkenazy played on.

'Please pass me Mr Weber's rifle so I can check it's loaded, Mrs Ellimore,' Nasheer said.

'That's the sea,' Lance said. 'We've arrived. That's our ship.' He took the rifle from Nasheer and jumped out, waving the trucks on to the rocky outcrop. He wondered how long they had till Drang or whoever had sent the spotter plane caught up with them. 'Where are my Chinese?' he asked Jimmy as the backmarker stopped next to him.

'Haven't seen them all night. Are you sure there's enough depth in that little bay for such a big boat?'

'That's Tanner's problem. Ours is that plane.'

'Drang's sidekick, the one you say is called Frank, was riding passenger in it.'

'Pierre, you and Boo get the ivory on board. Mwanzo, you come with me. And you and you,' Lance indicated two more of the Swahili. 'The rest of you help with the loading. Jimmy, fill up all the trucks, then bring the fuel tanker down the road. Before you come, block the track there with the refrigerator truck. Move!'

Fifteen minutes later Jimmy brought the tanker to a halt beside the road where Lance was standing, waving him down. Of the Range Rover in which Lance had come there was no sight.

'It's still half full,' Jimmy said.

'Leave it standing there.' Lance gave Jimmy the binoculars. 'Watch the road. Let me know when Drang comes.'

'What's that village there?'

'Mabza.'

'What makes you so sure he'll come from the south? He could have followed us.'

'Could he?' Lance smiled. 'No. He's not stupid. He worked out we're heading for the coast between Tanga and the Kenyan border. He'll be waiting for us on the good road, not taking a chance on losing everything by getting stuck in the mud.'

'The same chance you took.'

Lance walked away to the Range Rover to ask on the radio how the loading of their thirty tons of ivory was going. Esmeralda reported it was going well. 'You've been very clever, my darling. Please don't risk your life now.'

'I won't,' he said, fully intending to keep his promise.

Esmeralda's admiration was directed at the method Lance had devised to get the ivory off the trucks onto the ship. Back beside the Lake Kivu, the ivory had been split up in five-hundred pound lots and each lot packed on an uninflated inflatable. Eight men could manhandle the package with the greatest of ease, rolling it off the truck and carrying or dragging it to the water's edge on the rush mats they had carried to the middle of Africa and back again for exactly that purpose. Each truck had its own electric and mechanical pumps so that inflating the rafts was quick and easy. A line was paddled out to the ship, it was tied to the first ivory-raft, the second tied to that, and so on. Then Tanner started the winch and some men went aboard to drag the ivory away once it came over the side. They were winching aboard a quarter-ton of ivory every minute but even so it would take two hours to get all the ivory off the beach and onto the ship.

Lance wandered back to Jimmy. He left one of the Swahili at the Range Rover to call him if Tanner or Esmeralda wanted to speak to him on the radio.

On the road south, still nothing moved. Lance knew it would not be long. Even if Drang had no radio communication with the plane, the plane would long since have reached him even as far away as Segera – but it was far more likely that Drang was at Tanga or even this side of Tanga. In that case he would be here in under an hour.

As if to confirm Lance's logic, the little plane came on them from the south and started circling them. Lance looked at it through his scope. It was staying out of reach but he had no intention of shooting at it: it could belong to the Tanzanian army.

'Here come Drang and his tame Tanzanians,' Jimmy told Lance forty minutes later. He pointed to the small plume of dust in the distance, across the village of Mabza. 'They'll be here in ten minutes.'

300

Lance took the glasses and studied the convoy. It was Drang and his Tanzanians all right. He could even make out Drang sitting next to the driver in the second truck. The Tanzanian captain was next to the driver in the leading truck. He gave the glasses back to Jimmy.

'Shall we turn the tanker into a *big* Molotov cocktail?' Jimmy asked with relish, unbuttoning his shirt.

Lance had to laugh. 'Button up your shirt. It's too muddy to burn. A Molotov's too uncertain and too sudden, over too quickly. Just run the fuel out on the road.'

'Hey! Where are you going? You're not going to sleep on me again, are you?'

'I knew that was going to arise sooner rather than later. I'm just going to find out how much time they need to finish loading the ivory.'

After a moment's delay, Lance got Esmeralda. 'How long before we can sail into the sunset?'

'Drang?'

'Down the road and closing fast. I don't want to have to kill any of his men. Even about their private affairs of brigandage, like now, they're still Tanzanian soldiers.'

'Don't let your scruples put you in harm's way.'

'Nicely put.'

'Pierre says, can you hold them an hour?'

'Tell him, perhaps. Tell him, hurry it up. And I want you and Christine to go out to the ship now. Immediately. Understand?'

'Yes. Do you want Pierre to send you some men?'

'No. If he has spare men, tell him to let them turn the empty trucks around to face the road. We don't need any help here, only time.'

'You few against the many.'

'It's like the pass in that Greek play.'

'Thermopylae.'

'Something like it.' He wanted to tell her he loved her but he could hardly say the words face to face, never mind

301

on the air waves. 'I'll see you soon,' he said lamely and put the mike back on the hook. 'You,' he said to the Swahili tending the Range Rover, 'call me if anybody calls on the radio. You are to leave here for no other reason. Understand?'

'Yes Massa!'

'If you see anything move, shoot to kill.'

The Swahili smiled broadly. He, and the others, had been fretting under the general restrictions put on their natural inclination to shoot first and never to ask questions, as well as what they considered Lance and his lieutenants' undesirable habit of doing most of the shooting themselves. What good was a fine weapon if one was never allowed to use it? 'Yes please Massa!'

'We'll call out to you first. The call of the kiekewiet. Understand?'

'There are no kiekewiet here, Massa. Monkey-from-South eat dem in soup.'

'Yes, that's why I chose it,' Lance said, though it was untrue. It was a shock to realize he would never hear the kiekewiet again here, in its natural setting; would there be any migrants left in Kenya? 'Don't shoot at us when we make the sound of the kiekewiet.'

'Yes Massa!'

Lance went around the other two men at their positions to tell them not to shoot at people but only at vehicles. He could now hear Drang's trucks. As he walked, he pumped up the blowtorch he had brought from the Range Rover. He borrowed a box of matches from one of the Swahili. Funny, he could not even remember if Jimmy smoked. Yes, cigars, sometimes. He doubted Jimmy would carry matches.

Jimmy was hopping up and down anxiously. 'Goddamn-it, were you sleeping again? Give me that.' He grabbed at the blowtorch.

'What about the tanker?'

'We can't take her with us. Let her blow.'

'No. It's a waste. Let's save it. I'll move it. Don't for chrissake light the lot before I get it clear.' Ewart had died in the flames. Lance wondered fleetingly if he should ask Jimmy to shoot him in case he burned. No, he would not have to ask Jimmy. Jimmy would know, as Lance had not with Ewart; Sambo had had to put Ewart out of his misery while Lance stood frozen, straining against Jimmy's arms, trying to run to his burning brother.

'Here, take this. I'll move the truck,' Jimmy said, thrusting the blowtorch at Lance.

Drang's trucks were just over the hill.

'No. I'll do it.' Lance swung up into the tanker and started the engine. He put her in gear and let the clutch in slowly. It would not do to stall her now. In the mirror on the door he saw the prow of a truck crest the hill behind him. Jimmy shouted something. Lance could not hear what. He let the truck roll up close to the rock of the cutting. Something clanged against the back and a ricochet whined away, a sound somewhere between a busy bee and an angry wasp. Lance turned the engine off and let the tanker stall against the clutch. He grabbed his rifle from the seat next to him and flung the door open. He jumped, rolling immediately. Somebody was shooting, but not at him. He looked over a rock. Jimmy was sitting out in the open, pumping the blowtorch, trying to light the diesel.

'Just put it down and get the hell out!' Lance shouted at him.

Jimmy hesitated a moment, looking at Drang's two charging trucks now less than a hundred paces away. The Tanzanians were hanging on the sides and over the roof, shooting at Jimmy. If they had the sense to stop, they could have picked him off like a clay pigeon. Jimmy put the blowtorch down, pumped it a couple more times, then picked up his rifle and ran. Almost immediately the blowtorch superheated some of the diesel.

303

To Lance it seemed as if the diesel was taking for ever to light. 'Hurry,' he shouted at it, his eyes twisting from Drang's trucks to the diesel. The flame spread slowly, slowly, slowing down in one of the ruts where the diesel lay deep and therefore took a long time for the flame to heat to ignition point.

'Don't hurry me, I'm here,' Jimmy said beside him.

When the leading truck was fifteen paces from the diesel, Lance took out its front tyres. He heard Jimmy firing as well, presumably at the same target. In that moment the diesel flamed and they could see nothing. The heat was searing and they had to move back.

'I wonder if Mwanzo got the tyres of the second truck,' Lance shouted as they climbed the rocky outcrops of the cutting, Lance and Jimmy each to one side of the road.

Lance came out on top and saw the flames reaching nearly as high as he was standing. Above the flames was a dense pall of evil-smelling smoke.

'Mwanzo?'

'Yes Massa, here, Massa.'

'Did you get their tyres?' Lance's eyes were streaming and he wiped them while Mwanzo pulled him down behind a rock.

'No Massa, sorry. They came round corner just when His Highness fire de big bang.'

Now Lance could see for himself. Infuriatingly, the second truck stood behind the first where he could not see the tyres. And from the line of sight he had given Jimmy and the other Swahili, it was not on for them either. Of the Tanzanians he could see nothing.

'De Monkey captain and Mr Drang push dem behind de bush and rock,' Mwanzo said helpfully. 'I shoot at dem head to keep dem behind de bush and rock.'

'Try not to kill anyone. We only want to delay them a while.'

Mwanzo lowered his head in shame at such weakness. These white people were touched by the sun. The Monkeys-from-the-South would shoot to kill.

Lance was not unaware of Mwanzo's sentiments. But for the moment the Tanzanians were keeping their heads down, sorting themselves out. He was in no hurry; he had already gained twenty minutes.

'Lance, can you get a shot?' Jimmy's voice.

'No.'

There was a fusillade of shots. Lance and Mwanzo kept their heads down. When the shots died down a little, they looked up. The Tanzanians were trying to rush forward. Lance wounded one in the arm. Mwanzo, remembering Lance's trick at Lake Kivu, shot the heel from one man's boot.

There was a howl of outrage, then silence.

'Next time I get other boot,' Mwanzo said apologetically. 'He not in the open long.'

'You're doing fine.'

'Weber!' Drang's voice.

Lance kept his head down and did not reply. There was no point in giving direction to a grenade launcher.

'Weber, we got you cornered. You can't go into Kenya and you won't have time to rebury the ivory. Fifty-fifty before more people die for that stuff.'

Lance could not resist the temptation. 'And you guarantee your Tanzanian friends don't kill me for my share?' He rolled as he called softly to Mwanzo, 'Get him.'

Lance raised his trunk from behind another rock just as the Tanzanian with the grenade launcher attachment to his rifle tumbled over backwards, blood spurting from his throat, the top half of his head above the eyes suddenly blurred and squishy.

'I only shoot him in arm,' Mwanzo said defensively.

'It's all right. I saw.' Lance raised his voice. 'Jimmy!'

305

'I got taken by surprise,' Jimmy shouted. 'Sorry!'

There was another fusillade of shots. When Lance stopped rolling, he dinged one Tanzanian's rifle barrel and saw Mwanzo shoot the other heel from an unfortunate Tanzanian's boots. Mwanzo cackled like a madman at this feat, lying on his back behind a rock and roaring at the sky.

Lance looked at his watch. There was a broad bloody furrow across the middle finger. A blood blister. That bullet had come awfully close. That blister was going to hurt like hell when he had to burst it.

He had to look at his watch again. Only twenty-five minutes more. Just about now the Tanzanians would be preparing their big rush. He looked to his left and down. The diesel was still burning but very low. There was more smoke than fire. He considered the second truck below him. It must have occurred to Drang by now that the reason they did not immobilize this other truck was because they had no line of fire on it. If Drang could get his men aboard the truck, they could rush through the flames and smoke and they would be invisible to the men holding them.

They would also be between Lance and his ivory.

'Half of them are going to come for us or provide covering fire while the other half are going to try for the truck,' Lance told Mwanzo. 'Concentrate on discouraging those heading for the truck.'

Across the crevasse cut in the hill for the road, Jimmy told his Swahili. 'Soon, they're going to make their big effort. Keep your mind on those running for the truck. We don't want them to get to it.'

'About now,' Lance said and less than a second later a fusillade of shots rang out.

He and Mwanzo lay on their backs. Mwanzo was looking expectantly at Lance. Lance counted aloud. 'One, two, three, four, five. Now!' He rolled and as he rolled put six shots into the windscreen of the second truck, high up, hoping not to kill anybody but to spray them with broken glass. He came to rest behind a rock and inspected the tears at the elbows of his shirt. There were going to be scabs on his elbows for quite a while. Mwanzo was having huge fun shooting off the clasps that held the tarpaulin to the frame on the back of the truck. The tarp was now flapping in the rising air caused by the fire and Lance could see there was no one in the back of the truck. Nor in the cab, though there was a bloody handprint where the driver had put his hand through the broken glass in his hurry to get out.

Mwanzo was bleeding at the back of his shoulder. Lance crawled over and pushed the young Swahili down while he had a look. It was a clean wound in the fleshy part of the upper arm. Lance looked doubtfully at his handkerchief, then tore the tails from his shirt to make two pads to stem the flow of blood, which was not large. Until he had drawn the Swahili's attention to the wound, Mwanzo had apparently not known he had been hit.

'Tomorrow,' Lance said to Mwanzo's big eyes, 'that arm is going to be sore and stiff. But you won't die.'

For an answer Mwanzo looked over the top of his rock and squeezed off a couple of shots that must have chipped rock into some Tanzanian's face from the sound of it.

Lance looked at his watch again. It was time to go. But there was a problem: they could not arrive at the boarding site with Drang hot on their heels. They would be sitting on the water like ducks in the closed season. Drang and his Tanzanians would not shoot to wound. Hell, they were not shooting to wound now.

'I'll be back shortly,' Lance told Mwanzo and crawled away. Near the Range Rover he made the sound of the kiekewiet and was surprised to find his call being answered from a tree: perhaps the kiekewiet was not extinct after all! But it was only his Swahili, waiting in a tree for something to move so he could kill it. He grinned down at Lance over his rifle. Pierre said the last load was going out on the water at that very moment. Lance gave his instruction and ran back to Mwanzo, attracting only two shots before Jimmy from the other side laid down a fusillade that caused the Tanzanians to pull in their heads once more.

Lance searched for and found Jimmy on the other side of the cutting. Jimmy was not looking at him. Lance found a pebble and threw it. He hit Jimmy on the side of the knee. Jimmy inspected his knee and seemed surprised to find no blood.

'Psst!'

When Jimmy looked up, Lance looked at his watch and pointed backwards. Jimmy pointed in the direction of the Tanzanians and spread his hands: What about them? Lance gestured to Jimmy to come to him. Jimmy and the Swahili laid down a barrage of shots first, then scampered down the cutting, across the smoking road, up the cutting and to Lance and Mwanzo, who were firing at nothing as the Tanzanians were not showing even the whites of their eyes.

'What a noise,' Jimmy said, and, when Lance had explained his plan, 'Even if it works, it won't gain us much time.'

'Got a better plan?'

'No.'

'Let's go then.'

Lance had to grab Mwanzo by the wrist and drag him a little way; he was not keen to leave. 'I stay, Massa. Rearguard action,' he added, pronouncing the words with extreme care.

'Move your ass, you murderous black bastard,' Jimmy said in Swahili. Mwanzo smiled broadly, then came. 'He surely likes shooting at Tanzanians,' Jimmy said to Lance.

'You've helped him acquire a taste he could have a hard time breaking.'

Lance, behind the wheel of the Range Rover, asked, 'If you were Drang – '

'God forbid I should be such a sourpuss!'

' – what would you think if you heard our engine start up?'

'You're attacking or trying to encircle him. He's bound to put the worst interpretation on it.'

'Let's hope so. It could be worth an extra minute.' Privately, Lance doubted it. True, Drang was not exactly the soul of cheer but he was intelligent enough to learn from experience. He *must* by now have noticed that Lance had not used his many opportunities to wipe out the Tanzanians and Drang himself. Unless, of course, Drang ascribed that to incompetence on Lance's part . . . In which case it was going to be tricky. Lance started the Range Rover and set off at speed.

The tricky part was where they came down the incline of the hill and were for a moment outlined against the abandoned tanker for the Tanzanians. If that tanker blew while they were anywhere near it . . . Mwanzo and the other Swahili were firing out of the windows with great gusto. Lance doubted that they would hit anything – the Range Rover was bouncing violently – but it kept a few Tanzanian heads down and every little bit helped. Jimmy was calmly occupied in cutting a cross on a bullet. He loaded it into his rifle just as Lance guided the Range Rover through the narrow gap between the tanker and the rocks. He pushed the rifle barrel out of the window.

'Now,' said Lance. The mirror beside him shattered. 'Now,' he said again, not raising his voice.

'I don't fancy blowing myself up,' Jimmy said.

'I don't fancy being shot!'

'Then go faster!'

Lance had his foot in the corner. He looked into the inside mirror. There were at least four bullet holes in the rear window. It was a miracle none of them – or the fuel tank – had yet been hit.

After what seemed a century, Jimmy seemed to think they were far enough. 'Hold her steady. We only get one chance.'

Lance straightened the Range Rover. Goddamnit, Jimmy was taking his time aiming. He hoped it would work. Just as diesel does not burn easily, so too it does not explode easily and for the same reason, its low volatility. One way of exploding diesel is to compress it to the extent that it ignites spontaneously. This is essentially what is done in a diesel engine and why it is called a compression combustion engine. Sometimes, by a freak such as had killed his brother Ewart, a common hardnosed bullet will be enough to explode a diesel tanker if it hits it just right. But most hardnosed bullets will pass in and out of the tank too quickly and with too little force, cutting a small hole on entry and exit for the gas and pressure to escape through, in effect doing exactly the opposite of what is desired. Lance wondered, in that long moment of fearful, still eternity, whether the bullet of the Armalite M16, a light plastic concoction designed by the ballisticians to tumble so that it could do maximum damage to the Viet Cong, would serve the same purpose as Jimmy's dum-dum. Perhaps, perhaps not. Even Jimmy's dum-dum would have to hit as square-on as possible to avoid ricocheting harmlessly from the rounded metal of the tanker.

Jimmy let his breath out audibly and Lance, out of the corner of his eye, could see him squeeze the trigger. Immediately – perhaps a pause of one-tenth of a second – Jimmy squeezed the trigger again, this time to fracture the tanker with a hard-nosed bullet to give the explosion a start in ripping it apart.

In the mirror still intact inside the car, Lance saw the tanker split open like a dropped watermelon. There was not much smoke or fire but the concussion wave funnelled out of the cutting rocked the Range Rover so that Lance hit his head on the steering wheel. Jimmy fell into the footwell, so missing the spectacular after-effect of his act of mayhem.

Lance was busy trying to straighten the Range Rover before it crashed into the jagged part of the tanker's chassis that had been thrown into the road in front of them; even after Jimmy's delay that could have cost them their lives, they were still too near the explosion. He nearly missed the two sides of the hill caving in spectacularly on the wreck of the tanker – a wondrously destructive vision even in the narrow confines of the inside driving mirror. He was too busy fighting the wheel, the gear lever, the brake and accelerator pedals and the list imparted by a flat rear tyre to look around.

'Wonder-Jimmy strikes again,' Jimmy said as he climbed from the footwell. He looked over the back of the seat. 'You three hyenas can now stop hiding.'

Mwanzo and the other Swahili came up loading their rifles. There was nothing to shoot at. Mwanzo chuckled but the other Swahili looked outraged. Jimmy smiled at them and after a moment the men realized it was a joke and started laughing too.

'We have maybe a five-minute lead,' Jimmy said. 'There's no reason they shouldn't drive their four-wheel-drive truck cross-country around the obstruction. Or even across the rubble.'

'We're not stopping to fix the flat,' Lance said. They could go no faster either. 'Jimmy, there's a chequebook in the cubby. Give each of these three a big bonus.'

Jimmy found the chequebook and a ballpoint which he licked. 'Five thousand each?'

'Make it ten each.'

Jimmy wrote the cheques.

'Anything behind us?' Lance asked.

'No, Massa.'

They were nearly there. Lance swung the Range Rover towards the sea around the refrigerated truck. The Range Rover lurched sideways on its flat tyre. Lance signed the cheques on the steering-wheel boss and held them out to the black men. 'Barclays Bank in Nairobi. Do you know it?'

'Yes Massa, thank you Massa.'

'I come with you, Massa,' Mwanzo said, not taking the slip of paper.

Lance folded the cheque and put it in Mwanzo's shirt pocket. The young Swahili winced as the shirt pulled against his wounded shoulder. 'Sorry. I know where to find you. I will come for you when I return to Kenya. Now get in one of the trucks.'

Lance had to shout over the roaring engines. Pierre was waving his arms and shouting at the Watusi to get a move on. The Watusi were laughing and shouting in their excitement at their bonus.

'You gave them the trucks?' Jimmy asked. He still disliked the drivers intensely.

'Sure. Waste not, want not.' Lance raised his voice even higher. 'The Monkeys-from-the-South are coming,' he shouted. Almost immediately the trucks started pulling out. Lance watched one go, its tarpaulin flapping, displaying its load: inflated inflatable rafts, last used to move the ivory to the ship.

'What did you tell Nasheer to give the Swahili?' Jimmy asked.

'Five thousand each.'

Jimmy nodded. 'You'll spoil the market for fighting men forever.'

Nasheer paid the last of the Swahili and the man jumped up on a truck. Nasheer rolled up some notes left in his hand and put them into his shirt pocket. His work done, he stood dancing from foot to foot at the edge of the water, near the dinghy. Lance waved to Mwanzo, passing in the very last truck to go out on the road and turn north. Then he ran after Pierre and Jimmy. Nasheer was in the dinghy with a Chinese woman.

'You must be Ruby. Hello. I'm Lance.'

'We can make introductions later, Mr Weber.' Ruby pointed upwards at the circling plane.

Lance did not hear her. He was standing ashore, his rifle slackly in his hand. 'Where are Bruun's Chinese?'

Pierre took his eyes from the plane long enough to look at Lance and say, 'For God's sake, Lance, we – '

'I'm not leaving without at least the leader. All this was to attract Bru – '

That was when Jimmy hit Lance a short, sharp uppercut to the chin.

Pierre caught Lance's tumbling body and lowered him into the dinghy. There was little space left for the rest of them.

'I wouldn't like to be in Your Highness's shoes when he wakes up,' Nasheer said.

Ruby looked at them with large eyes and jumped into the water to push the dinghy adrift. The roar of engines had faded to the north and been replaced by the whine of a single racing engine approaching quickly from the south.

Bruun

Jennifer Pan, rising forty, was still the most beautiful woman in the East. She remained so by the simple expedient of designating her body a temple and dedicating her life to it as its high priestess. Nothing was allowed to interfere with the beautification and preservation of the temple, neither time (and let us be clear that Lady Pan would not consider this a pun) nor household nor social duties, and certainly neither children nor sex. Her husband had long since, perhaps from the first, accepted that the great benefit she was to his image had its necessary price but, since the price cost him no face, he paid it gladly and kept both mistress *and* concubines; that gave him even more face in certain quarters. Had Lady Pan the common humility to consider others, she might have asked herself whether P.K. Pan had married her to possess her for herself or only because Matthew Ellimore had wanted her; she had never asked the question: her world, beyond a doubt, and latterly beyond need of proof behind the shelter of Pan's great wealth, had always revolved around her as its centre. The centre asked no questions: it had dedication and faith, it received homage. That was natural.

Lady Pan was therefore more than a little surprised, though she was too disciplined to let it show in a quirk of the mouth or a frown or even a narrowing of the eyes, when her husband entered her dressing-room where, five hours before dinner, she was sitting, bathed, in a peignoir, in front of her mirror, considering her face in each exquisite detail. Sir P.K. Pan had not seen her smile, unless there was a large and glittering audience present to make the sacrifice worthwhile or unless he had told her in advance that the guest was incredibly important (Kissinger had received a smile, Carter had not – Nancy Reagan neither), in all the time they had been married. Of course he had never seen her frown. But he could read the signs. She pulled the lapels of the gown together and inclined her head a millimetre to her two maids who immediately left the room.

Pan headed for the liquor cabinet. (Lady Pan had not told the decorator that she never, never took alcohol because nothing except sunlight ages your skin faster.) He poured himself a stiff Glenfiddich.

'You're looking murderous, my darling. What is it?'

Familiarity had blunted the shock of the lack of interest in her voice for any question that did not concern her directly. 'My ivory,' he said.

'Oh dear.' Even she had gathered the importance to him of the ivory: it was how he had first come by her. 'Don't tell me *that Spanish widow*' – each word separately emphasized – 'is selling to someone else?'

He shook his head. 'It's worse than that. Someone's had my ivory warehouse burned.'

'Then you must have her and her adventurer killed.'

Even in his distress he looked up at her sharply. 'I'm P.K. Pan. Such things are not discussed in my house.'

'But she will have a monopoly on all the world's ivory! Something you've worked so long for! That's intolerable, that such a woman – ' Jennifer Pan realized anger was contorting her face and stopped to look in the mirror for the damage the anger had done to her skin. There were no lines on her face. 'You must not make me angry.'

'She will not have a monopoly on all the world's ivory. You see, I sent Henry Chew to burn all her ivory. Now nobody will have any ivory.' He raised the glass to his lips but it was empty. He looked at the glass in his hand, then

318

let it drop to the floor. In the lush carpet it made no sound. 'Nobody.'

She was not listening. She was looking into the mirror, waiting for lines. He left the door open behind him.

Daniel Drang now knew why Lance Weber had come this far from Lake Kivu before crossing into Kenya. He owned the commander at the sleepy little border post beyond Mtandikemi. As they rushed up to it, they could see a customs official check the load on the truck in the gate by lifting the tarpaulin and letting it fall again.

'Faster!' Drang shouted. 'Faster!' He heaved forward with his whole body as if that would make the truck run faster. The goddamn cheek of that Weber, *turning back into Tanzania* to fight a rearguard action on foreign soil while calmly sending the ivory north to cross at a bought border post. It was just too fucking much and the crazy pilot and Frank were helping zilch by flying head on at him and waving their arms. The truck was going as fast as the dumb Tanzanian could make it go.

They came to the border post just as the last truck disappeared up the road into Kenya.

'My ivory gone bush,' said the Tanzanian captain, tears in his eyes. 'Now I kill you, you fucking Yankee.'

That hurt almost more than the loss of the ivory. While the captain was still fumbling with the flap on his holster, Drang was out of the truck and running towards the border post. He grabbed the first man he saw by the shirt and shook him.

'That was ivory in those trucks. Africa's ivory, you stupid black bastard!'

'You stupid black bastard yourself. That was paddle pool for children.'

Frank grabbed Drang by the shoulder and spun him around. Drang had not heard the plane land on the road

319

though it was now standing only ten paces behind him, the engine running.

'Come on, Daniel! He's bluffed you out. The ivory's on a ship heading East.'

'But those trucks! They – '

'They're loaded with inflated rubber rafts, you dumb asshole. Now come on before somebody kills you!'

'I wish they would.'

'The Tanzanian Navy is chasing Weber and a Kenyan gunboat is standing by in case he tries to escape into their waters,' Frank shouted as he dragged his superior towards the small plane.

Immediately Daniel Drang scrambled aboard.

Wong stood on a rock and watched the tail end of the Tanzanian gunboat. He could not see Lance's MTB because the Tanzanian gunboat was immediately behind it. He was satisfied with a job well done. His orders had been to follow the ivory until it left Africa or, if it was parted from the white man, to send subordinates after the ivory while he followed the white man himself. It would be a pity if the Tanzanians killed Weber and in the process sent the ivory to the bottom of the sea but his orders did not cover that eventuality. Nevertheless, it would have given him great satisfaction to kill Weber. The nearest reliable communications were across the Kenyan border at Mombasa. He would stay here a while to be able to report that the Tanzanians had sunk Weber's unarmed vessel, then he would drive to Mombasa and report. After that he would be free to return to the heart of darkness and kill the border commanders who had insulted him, called him a coolie. In the unlikely event that Weber should survive a running battle with the Tanzanian Navy fighting with the help of air cover, he would hurry to Mombasa to report and hope that his excellent service be rewarded by being allowed to kill Weber the moment

320

the man had been parted from the ivory. Against that prospect, the border commanders were a sad compromise . . . He hoped Weber beat the Tanzanian Navy as roundly as he had beaten the Tanzanian Army. He did not consider this wish illogical and contradictory.

'Who hit me?'

'You can hit me back later. We got company on the water.'

Lance shook his head and rose wearily. He had been dragged into the wheelhouse (he did not know enough about ships to differentiate between a wheelhouse and a bridge) and dropped on the floor. He fingered the bump on the back of his head and then his jaw. He saw a handle and grabbed it to pull himself upright. Esmeralda rose with him, still dabbing at the blood on his chin. Tanner touched her gently on the elbow and she stood aside.

'Didn't you say the Kenyans would stand off as long as we stay out of their territory?'

'But not the Tanzanians. Look the other way. We're in their territorial waters.

'What's that bloody noise?' Lance's head was throbbing and the playground blare of badly amplified sound was not helping.

'They're telling us to stop or they open fire.'

'Then they should learn to speak English. We didn't understand them. Carry on.'

'Britannia rules the waves,' Christine said from the door. 'Even Lance can't fight cannon and torpedoes with bare hands.'

'Be quiet, woman,' Jimmy said.

'She's right, you know,' Esmeralda said. 'My husband wanted me to bring the ivory out of Africa. It's out. The duty fulfilled. Let them have it.'

'No!' Christine shouted. 'I've seen too much of them.

321

It'll go into Swiss bank accounts. Nothing for the animals. Please Lance, can't you do something?'

Lance took a moment to look at Christine and then at Esmeralda. 'Where are my Chinese?'

'They came just before you were brought aboard,' Jimmy said. 'They're standing ashore, watching. You can't see them because the Tanzanian boat is between us and them. Forget them. Bruun will be waiting when we land, wherever we land. If we land.'

'Men who kill so brutally shouldn't be allowed to live.'

'We'll find them for you later, Lance,' Boo said.

'Sambo's friends can find anybody in their line of work,' Pierre added. 'We have other problems now.'

Lance shook his head again. Esmeralda gave him a mug and he drank the lukewarm tea in it. 'Can we outrun them, Tanner?'

'Sure.'

'Then let's do it, man!'

'We are. They were waiting for us outside the inlet. Since then we've opened up a gap of several furlong.'

'Can we go any faster?'

'No. The throttles are wide open, the engines revving just short of the red.'

'Then when do we get out of the range of their weapons?'

'Ah, the correct question at last. When we're approximately seventeen miles from them. That's seventeen nautical miles, longer than land miles, you know.'

'I didn't.'

'The further we get, the more trouble they have hitting us. But with a spotter plane . . .'

'Why aren't they shooting now?'

'Because we're too near. They'll go down with us.'

Lance studied the pilot for a moment. Tanner's eyes were clear and guileless and there was no liquor on his breath. He was neither shaking nor sweating. 'You've done this before?'

'It was a bit touch and go when I brought Ruby out of South Africa. But I haven't actually ever had a torpedo up my ass before.'

'Language, Tanner.' Ruby was carrying a tray. She handed the mugs around.

'Don't you have coffee?' Nasheer said.

'Oh, sorry!' She turned to the door. 'I'll go get it.'

'I'll do it,' Nasheer said and disappeared.

'This isn't a tea party,' Lance said, wondering if the blow on the head was going to be fatal as well as making him insane. 'People are shooting at us.'

'They'd have to be awfully lucky to hit any of us with small-arms fire,' Pierre said judiciously.

'I'm talking about the cannon and the torpedoes,' Lance said, sinking more and more with each passing minute into the morass of unreality that rose stagnant about him. 'Are you all crazy for death or is it just me?' He looked around their faces.

'I'm too tired to worry,' Esmeralda said.

'I'll show you somewhere you can lie down,' Ruby offered immediately.

'Everybody out of the wheelhouse except Tanner, me and Jimmy!' Lance roared.

'What do you want Jimmy for?' Boo asked.

'To help me think.'

Boo went, laughing. When everybody had gone, Tanner said, 'Phew! It was getting like a houseparty. Only, I didn't want to tell them to bugger off while the owner was present. I hope they can all swim. The lifeboats are in good order.'

'That serious, eh?' Lance said.

'We're gaining on them,' Jimmy said from where he stood looking astern.

'Yeah. About this range they can hit us without doing themselves any harm. Jimmy, use those glasses and watch her sides and bows. I don't know where the torpedo tubes

323

are but they probably make a white line on the water. Warn me immediately you see something.'

'Yes sir, Skipper sir.'

'Slow down,' Lance said.

'Are you serious?'

'Yes. Slow down to whatever their top speed is and make sure we're just enough in front of them so they will be damaged if they torpedo us.'

'They'll start shooting rifles at us again.'

Lance shrugged. 'That's better than torpedoes or cannon.'

'It's your ship, pal.' Tanner closed the throttles slowly, watching the revolution counters.

'She's gaining on us,' Jimmy said.

'You could get some of your hotshots to take a rifle to them,' Tanner suggested. 'I'm a man of peace but it seems to me it's okay to shoot back at people who shoot first.'

Lance had to laugh. 'Yeah. But this lot are shooting at us in their official capacity. If we shoot back we attract official interest. From Brigadier Burger of the Bureau of State Security, BOSS to you – '

'DONS to you, pal. They now call it the Department of National Security.'

'Whatever they call it, he's got a neat little paramil section called, when I last heard, the State Security Police. They drop in on people like us who attract too much attention. Burger warned me before this caper started.'

'Sheet! You didn't tell me that when you hired me! Burger himself, eh?' Tanner's outrage fled before awe.

'They're only a couple of hundred metres from us now,' Jimmy said.

'Come away from the window, Jimmy,' Lance said. 'You're inviting a potshot.'

'It's armoured glass all around,' Jimmy said, pointing to the grey splotches on the outside. 'Once I took this girl to London Zoo and she put her face right up to the glass and a puma came and smacked his paw against her face. On the other side of the glass. In the night she had a nightmare and brought up her dinner.'

'Charming!' Lance and Tanner said at the same time.

'How far will they follow us?' Lance asked. 'Twelve miles?'

'Theoretically. More probably two hundred. Remember also what I said about sea-miles being longer than land-miles.'

'How long before we get to twelve miles?'

'Fifteen minutes.'

'Okay, tell me when we get there.'

Lance watched the clock creep slowly round. Jimmy counted the bullets splattering directly in front of his face.

'Get the hell away from the window, Jimmy!' Lance looked at the clock again. 'You don't know the glass doesn't suffer fatigue from too many bullets. You don't want to die at eleven twenty-five in the morning, do you?'

'It's not only that they don't want to damage their own ship,' Tanner said. 'They're probably hoping to catch us whole. That way they don't have to dive for the ivory and the Tanzanian Navy gets to confiscate a perfectly good ship.'

Jimmy said, 'They're falling back. They've caught on and are slowing down to give themselves some breathing space.'

'I can see them on the radar,' Tanner said. 'Come away from that bloody window. It won't stand up to cannon fire or a rocket.'

Jimmy reluctantly stepped aside. He too watched the radar. 'It's so impersonal, green dots against a green background, shooting torpedoes and things at you.'

Fifteen minutes were up. Lance asked, 'Is their sea-border twelve miles out or two hundred?'

'I don't know,' Tanner replied.

'What about Kenya?'

'I don't know that one either.'

'Fuck!' Jimmy exploded. 'We've come halfway across Africa and now we're going to drown for lack of an elementary piece of knowledge.'

'Sorry,' Tanner said. 'I'm a pilot. It never occurred to me to ask.'

'It's not your fault. We're landlubbers. We should have stayed ashore,' Lance said. 'Are we twelve miles out?'

'Oh yes. And a bit.'

'Then head north east.'

'Huh?'

'Enter Kenyan waters.'

Tanner pointed to the second green dot on the radar. 'That's a Kenyan gunboat. He's the one that came to warn us to stay clear.'

They heard the rumble of a heavy-calibre weapon at the same moment as a spout of water rose well in front of them.

'The Kenyan told you he didn't want to fight. These Tanzanians have just demonstrated they mean to fight. We *can't* fight. Let's see if the Kenyan will give us the benefit of the doubt. Okay?'

'Those Kenyans shoot a lot more accurately than the Tanzanians, I've heard.'

The Tanzanians fired again. This time there was a spout of water less than fifty metres off the bow.

'Those aren't warning shots,' Jimmy said. 'They're bracketing us.'

'Christ, I've met some high rollers in my time,' Tanner said, turning the wheel, 'but you guys play the limit all the time.'

'That'll be enough,' Lance said evenly.

The chill in Lance's voice caused Tanner to look at him in consternation and then, getting no response from Lance's set features, at Jimmy.

'He's a reformed gambler,' Jimmy said, jerking his thumb at Lance.

'Well, fuck me with a hot stone!' Tanner turned his eyes back to the radar. 'Those are range marks, those circles. The Kenyans have been falling back a bit. But, unlike the Tanzanians, they can catch us if they want to. Their ship is newer and faster.'

'If they do, we'll head back into Tanzanian waters,' Lance said, watching two spouts of water on either side of their path. The water was still settling when they passed through between the two craters in the sea.

Tanner turned a switch and a circular wiper started working on the windscreen. The charges had fallen near enough to splash them with water. Tanner put his hand on the throttles. He looked over his shoulder at Lance. 'Can I take her into the red for a bit?'

Lance nodded. Tanner knew more about ships than he did. From his behaviour so far, Lance judged that the pilot was not panicking: they were in real trouble.

Tanner slammed the throttles against the guard. There was a steady surge of power. Lance could feel they were going faster. The whole floor was vibrating.

'Never mind that gunboat,' Tanner said. 'You two just watch those oil pressure and temperature dials in that block there. They'll show if we're running the bearings hot.'

With great effort Lance kept his eyes on the dials while he heard the Tanzanians firing at them. He heard water splashing on the windscreen again and sensed Jimmy looking up from the dials.

'Leave the driving to me,' Tanner said.

'What about the Kenyans?'

'They're not shooting. But we're still well within their range and in their waters.'

'Goddamnit, then why are the Tanzanians still shooting?'

'Because they lack your Brigadier Burger's fine talent for border-spotting, the international version of the hairsplitting game,' Jimmy chuckled.

Nobody replied. There was almost a minute with no splashes of water reaching out for them. Tanner closed the throttles. The rev-counter needles came out of the red. Tanner inspected the oil pressure and temperature gauges carefully.

They looked at each other and laughed aloud, stopped abruptly and turned to study the radar's screen.

'Green movies,' Jimmy said.

'Somewhat apt,' Lance said. 'That water that came aboard was green. I always thought the sea was blue.'

'Really heavy water is green,' Tanner said.

'Is that Kenyan gunboat gaining or losing?' Jimmy asked.

'It doesn't matter,' Lance said. 'If it can hit us miles and miles away, the question is, Is it shooting at us or Does it intend calling up air cover.'

I'm in no hurry to find out,' Tanner said, steering straight east. 'Those Tanzanians are falling in parallel to us. They're calling up air cover.'

'No, that spotter belongs to the Organization for African Unity,' Lance said.

'Them too? Christ, you're popular. No wonder Burger himself comes to warn you. You know, don't you, that guy's heavy metal? As heavy as they come.'

Lance waved a hand. He was not worried about Burger right now. 'I have a good mind to make a diplomatic complaint about the Tanzanian Navy firing on me while I was in Kenyan waters. We even have a witness, that Kenyan gunboat back there.'

Tanner's mouth gaped at Lance for the merest fraction of a second before he shut it with a click of teeth. 'You're serious!'

'Lance is a solid citizen,' Jimmy said. 'He pays a lot of

taxes. He's entitled to the protection of the law just like everybody else.'

Tanner reached for the mike above his head.

'No,' Lance said. 'Later, if they start shooting again. Let's not attract attention to ourselves right now.'

Esmeralda brought them coffee twice before Tanner said, 'They're turning back.' He pointed to the radar. 'We must be two hundred miles out.' He punched some figures into a keyboard. Seconds later their position flashed on the screen. Lance marked the latitude and longitude on the map on the chart table and measured.

'Is this ruler marked in nautical miles?'

'Yes. You're pretty suspicious.'

'People have just been shooting at me with cannons. What do you expect me to do, break out in song?'

'Is it two hundred miles?'

'Quite a bit over.'

'Okay. Now where?'

'How far can we go?'

'Almost anywhere in the world, though we might have to refuel. This isn't some pleasure boat, chum, this is a blue-water fighting ship.'

'Then take us to Singapore.'

'Yes, sir. That plane's turning back.'

'Probably out of fuel. Can they find us again?'

'Very unlikely.'

'Okay. Then Jimmy and I are going to sleep. You want to be relieved up here in the wheelhouse sometime, I take it?'

'Yeah. And incidentally, pal, on a ship this size it's not a wheelhouse, it's a bridge.'

'Mr Lestronge, is it possible to – '

'My boy, people have been asking questions about you. Don't tell me where you're calling from.'

Lance was calling from Colombo. He had not wanted to use the radio even though Tanner had assured him almost nobody would be able to intercept his one message among the thousand on air at any one time.

'That's what I was calling about. I wanted to know if I could retain your services to find out who's been asking questions about me.'

'No, no, no,' Lestronge laughed. 'My services are not for hire. For you they are free in the memory of your brother. Other people, not so fortunate in their relatives, don't pay either but one day I may call on them for a return favour. Money is too crude a commodity – as you will find out now you have so much of it.'

'Thank you. I think I'm starting to know what you mean about money. Who's been asking these questions about me?'

'Not on the phone, boy. Come to me and bring your friends with you. Do not go to Singapore before you have spoken to me.'

'He doesn't know I have the . . . the . . . the – '

'Valuables.'

'Right. He sent a man to destroy them.'

'A man who failed. There's been a rumour that your valuables are now the only ones in the world. His got burnt. Very clever, my boy, also very dangerous.'

Lance thought for a moment. Pan's ivory burnt! 'I didn't do it, you know.'

Lestronge laughed disbelievingly, an obscene sound. 'Come to Hong Kong, my boy.' He rang off.

Lance looked at the phone in his hand for a moment . . . *bring your friends with you*, Lestronge had said. Lance shivered. Now it was not only Bruun but Pan after him as well. And after Esmeralda. And Jimmy. And Pierre and Boo and Tanner and Ruby and Nasheer. And Christine. Instead of freeing himself from Bruun by going after the ivory, he was sinking deeper and deeper into the quagmire with each of his frantic efforts to save himself.

* * *

'You have export papers for all this ivory, Mr Weber?' the customs inspector asked.

'This is my business manager, Mr Nasheer Habakuk Hussein el Hussein.'

Nasheer bowed sweepingly, then flourished permits. 'I think the permits issued in Paris will be acceptable in Hong Kong.'

'Except for ivory sourced in the Central African Republic,' the man said. He took the papers from Nasheer and studied them. 'Was any of this ivory in fact sourced in the CAR?'

Nasheer looked at Lance, who looked away. Nasheer shrugged. 'The papers say not.' Another shrug. 'I wouldn't want to tell you lies.'

'Yes. I know. With ivory you never can tell. What about East Africa?'

'Same answer, sir. But I shouldn't be surprised. After all there were once a great many elephants in East Africa. But as for proof . . .' Nasheer shrugged again.

'You're familiar with the regulations regarding animals under conservation orders and their skins, tusks, etcetera?'

'Indeed.'

'There have been stories . . . Your ship is somewhat scarred. Gunfire?'

'Yes sir. There are men on the seas who have little respect for the property or territory of others.'

Lance smiled. Nasheer had a talent for staying very close to the truth yet misleading his interlocutors: the Tanzanian Navy had indeed damaged his property, the ship, and while in the territory of 'others', the Kenyans.

'Acts of piracy should be reported. You have armament on board?' The customs official studied the men he could see. They looked capable of using any arms they could lay their hands on. But then they had women with them. Men do not usually take their women fighting.

'Sporting rifles,' Lance said. 'We outran the attack.'

331

'Suitable for hunting elephants?'

'I should think so,' Lance said, 'though you'd have to be a very good shot to put such a light bullet through an elephant's eye into his brain. You need heavy stuff for elephants, man, not sporting rifles.'

The customs officer smiled for the first time. Despite the chilly air around these men, they were simply healthy outdoor specimens unused to dealing with officialdom; they were not dangerous. He raised his clipboard and scribbled his signature on a sheet of paper. 'I don't see why you shouldn't sell your ivory here if you can find a buyer. Good day, gentlemen. And good luck.'

When the customs officer was back on board his launch, Tanner sighed aloud. Nasheer sat down on the deck. Lance whistled his relief. It was the final hurdle. Before, in every port, they had told customs they were in transit on a pleasure cruise. But sooner or later they had to find a place to land the ivory without breaking any laws; that had been clear even before they had set out, which was why Nasheer had obtained the perfectly genuine 'Certificates of Origin' from a mercenary French official.

'Well done, Nasheer,' Lance said. 'Your part of our expedition is finished. Cash up, take your commission and pay the rest into the local Barclays if there is one or – '

'There's bound to be a Barclays in a British Colony, Mr Weber. But perhaps I should stay and help to negotiate the sale of the ivory?'

'I did that before we fetched it, Nasheer, thank you all the same.'

'Except he sent Henry Chew to destroy the ivory and so forfeited his deposit,' Esmeralda said.

'Oh, yes. Hmm. All the same, we'd better give Pan another chance,' Lance said. 'We don't want to add him to our list of enemies.'

A launch bumped against the boarding ladder. Lance looked over the side. It was the Chinese Lestronge had sent before, as ever neatly dressed in dark suits and white shirts with sober ties. They politely asked permission to come aboard.

'Mr Lestronge has sent us to guard your ship while you visit him.' He saw Pierre and Boo and Tanner and Nasheer. 'He did not realize you had your own men.'

'I'd like to go shopping,' Esmeralda said. 'Would it be an imposition to ask you instead to accompany me?'

The leader of the Chinese bowed. 'No Madam. It will be a pleasure.'

'I'll come too,' Christine said.

'When is Mr Lestronge expecting us?' Lance asked.

'Whenever you are ready sir.'

'We are ready now.'

'Then he waits for you now. There is a car on the dock to take you.' He called something over the side in Chinese. 'The launch will come back to fetch us for the shopping expedition.'

When they reached the dock, Daniel Drang was standing there, looking cool in a white seersucker suit despite his glowering frown. A little further along the quay, Lance spotted Wong – Bruun's butcher!

'Do you see what I see?' he asked Jimmy.

Nasheer said, 'Once you've feared one in particular, the yellow men no longer all look the same. That one was at Lake Kivu with us.'

'Right,' Jimmy said. 'Let's go get him.'

Lance put his hand on Jimmy's arm to restrain him. 'No. He'll be here when we get back. Let's first find out from Lestronge who else has been asking questions about us.'

'Yeah, that makes sense, getting rid of all distractions before going after Bruun.'

In Lestronge's office, Sir P. K. Pan sat glowering at them while Lestronge took Lance in a bear-hug and kissed him on both cheeks. 'What a nice tan you have. And you, Jimmy.'

'Thanks,' Jimmy said drily. 'Nobody can accuse you of racism.'

'Tch! A prejudice for children. There are worthwhile people and others. You two have just become multi-millions worthwhile. If you survive, of course.' Lestronge laughed. It was a joke.

Lance smiled a little, Jimmy broadly, Pan not at all.

'Mr Lestronge tells me you believe I burnt your ivory,' Lance said to Pan.

Pan made no reply.

Lestronge said, 'While you are in Hong Kong, you are under my protection. I have explained that to our mutual friend here. Let me say at once that I believe you. But why should he? After all, his little bonfire has made your ivory worth much, much more than it was before. Is that not so?'

Lance shrugged and sat down opposite Pan. 'That is so. Except for one small thing. That ivory is not mine, but his. He bought it from me before I left for Africa.'

Pan looked up at Lance, who was reminded of a beaten dog now patted. Still the Chinese tycoon said nothing but Lance knew what was in his mind: Henry Chew. Well, let him sweat!

'Secondly, I was on my way to Singapore when I called you, Mr Lestronge, from Colombo – and you told me to proceed directly to Hong Kong because I was suspected of this outrage.' Behind Pan, Lance could see Jimmy smiling broadly. Lestronge, who could also see Jimmy, was looking at Lance as if seeing him for the first time, a small smile playing around the corners of his mouth, running oddly into the scar Bruun had put on the ex-mercenary's face.

'Thirdly, I am a game-reservation keeper, not some kind of international crook. How do you account for the fire being started while I was in Africa? Only a fool would suspect me of having the kind of international organization one would need for such an act.'

Pan, still saying nothing, took out his chequebook.

'Hold on a minute,' Lance said. 'You broke our contract when you sent Henry Chew to napalm the ivory we were supposed to be fetching from Africa. Our arrangement – '

'Ah-hah!' Lestronge said explosively. 'The biter bit.'

Pan cast him a distracted glance, probably having heard the sounds without registering the import of the words.

'What I have in mind is a new arrangement, Mr Weber,' Pan said, leading forward to Lance.

'Well, all right. But – ' Lance was about to say Pan would have to forfeit his deposit of two million for his treachery and pay the full agreed price of twenty-five million, when the tycoon interrupted him: 'It will be worth your while, Mr Weber. That ivory is now, because of its greater rarity, worth more. I recognize this. I will therefore be happy to offer you forty million for it.'

Lance, who had forgotten that Pan did not know about the price threshold for making artificial ivory, felt his mouth drop open.

'If it's open to bids, I offer forty-five million,' Lestronge said. 'It seems to me a matter of principle not to sell to a man who first tried to cheat you and then ran around saying you cheated him.'

Behind Pan, Jimmy shook his head violently at Lestronge. The information broker waited until Pan's venomous look had passed from him to Lance, then tapped the side of his nose meaningfully.

'Let us not forget that I financed your operation when its chances of success were negligible, Mr Weber,' Pan said earnestly. There was sweat, two drops of it, on his forehead; Lance had never seen such naked lust. 'Fifty million.'

'Done!' Lance said before Lestronge could open his fat mouth again. He did most emphatically not want to land Lestronge with ivory worth less than half what he had paid – he had enough enemies already. 'That is, if you really want the ivory, Sir – '

'Of course I do,' Pan said. 'You've agreed. Now let us act in a businesslike manner.' He opened his cheque-book.

'Not a cheque,' Jimmy said. 'A telex transfer from your bank to Mr Weber's account at Barclays in Singapore would be more appropriate.'

'I shall be happy to provide facilities,' Lestronge offered. 'It is usual to specify delivery details as part of the sale contract.'

'The ivory's on a ship in the harbour out there,' Lance said.

'I'll take the ship as well,' Pan said. 'How much?'

Lance shrugged. He had become attached to that converted MTB. 'She's got new engines.'

'One million?' Pan said impatiently, writing a telex message on a sheet of paper he had taken from Lestronge's desk.

'Wouldn't you like to see her first?'

'No.'

'Well, if you think it a fair price.' Lance was reluctant to let the ship go but he knew the ostentation of such a huge yacht was not his style and the fuel bills every time they had filled the tanks had staggered him. But if Pan wanted to think in round millions . . .

In less than half an hour, Barclays in Singapore telexed to say they had received a deposit of forty-nine million to Lance's joint account with Esmeralda. Lestronge had meanwhile been attending to his paperwork and Pan had made calculations on the back of an envelope while Jimmy occasionally choked on his efforts not to laugh out loud. Lance napped. He had stood radar watch in the early hours of the morning while Tanner had guided the ship into the busy lanes entering Hong Kong's harbour.

With the deal done, Pan did not offer to shake hands.

'My people will be on the ship in half an hour,' he said and left without goodbyes.

'The same men he had brought to kill you,' Lestronge said when the Chinese tycoon had gone. Then he sat shaking silently in his chair for five minutes while Jimmy roared with laughter and Lance sat staring from the one to the other in total amazement.

'Oh my boy, did you have him on the run!' Lestronge at last choked out. 'Never mind jobs toting guns, I can get you a seat on our board!'

'Thank you.' Lance wished the man would talk sense. But he was not going to tell him to cut the bullshit, he still wanted to pick Lestronge's brains – or, to be exact, his computer.

Jimmy picked up the phone on the little table next to him and asked one of Lestronge's secretaries to get the ship on the ship-to-shore and tell Pierre to clear everybody off. Lestronge was still shaking and Lance waiting patiently when Pierre rang back to find out if the instructions were bona fide.

'We will of course pay you a commission for arranging the sale,' Lance said. 'A finder's fee, so to speak.' He had run across the practice in buying his game reservation. 'What would be fair?'

'A token one per cent,' Lestronge said, waving five hundred thousand dollars away with a manicured hand. 'You must never let Pan know by word or deed that you knew the ivory was not worth more than twenty-five million.'

Lance nodded.

'Understand?' Lestronge insisted. 'An honest mistake . . . But if it became public that you knew . . . He would lose so much face, he would have to have you killed if it was the last thing he ever did.'

'All right.' Lance looked at Jimmy, who nodded his head. 'I'll tell Esmeralda too. She's the only other one

337

who knows.' Lance paused to be sure he had Lestronge's full attention. 'Who else has been asking questions about us?'

'Nobody and everybody. Do you know people called Fitzmeikle from Sydney, Australia? Of course you do! We had an unfortunate accident to one of their lesser luminaries in Macao last time you passed through.'

'Don't worry about them. The eldest brother got chopped up by Bruun's men in Zaire.' Lance paused, then asked, 'Who else?'

Lestronge's face did not change at the mention of Bruun's name. 'More nobodies. Minor adventurers. Nobody to worry about. And two other feelers.'

Aha! Lance thought but said nothing. Lestronge liked playing cat and mouse. Let him.

'Brigadier Burger's agency has been following your movements closely. They put in a request to the American satellite tracking facility to trace your ship every inch of the way.'

Lance felt a drop of sweat fall from vertebra to vertebra. 'Is that all they have done?'

'That is enough. Don't let me find, after all, that you are too stupid to be frightened, my Lance.'

'I'm not. But I've done nothing to excite Burger. We were very careful to kill only when it was necessary in Africa and never to shoot at any officials in the performance of their duties. Burger's no fool: he's not going to come after us for killing a few freelancing soldiers who were trying to rob us.'

Lestronge spread his hands. 'All right. But Burger doesn't act idly. What is his interest if not the ivory?'

'Bruun. He came to tell me Bruun is probably alive after Bruun killed my parents and the widow of Colonel Jacques Roux. I told you all that when I was here last.' Lestronge nodded and Lance continued, 'Burger warned me then not to do anything in pursuit of Bruun that would get in the papers or stir up anybody. He said that, if I did, he would have to come after me.'

'He came himself?'

'Sure. I told you.'

'No, you didn't make that clear. I assumed he had sent you a message.'

'Sorry.'

Lestronge looked at Lance for a long time. Lance met his glare, wondering what the hell he had done now. Finally Lestronge spoke: 'I don't suppose it would do any good to tell you to crawl into a hole and pull the hole in after you. But that is what I would do if Rocco Burger started taking an interest in my every movement even out on the Indian Ocean.'

'He's not so bad,' Lance said. 'He's all right,' he added after searching for a moment for a more appropriate word and finding 'compassionate' meaningless in this context.

Lestronge snorted. 'If you want to be friends with mambas, don't complain when you die of snakebite.' Then he smiled and punched his computer. 'Do you know what it says on his personnel file? It says, here it is: This officer is no more brutal than he has to be.'

Lance nodded, impressed by Lestronge's information system. 'You said there were two feelers of importance.'

'Yes.' Lestronge sounded resigned and somehow ashamed. 'You remember a phantom, a joke?'

'J. Arthur Rank,' Lance said immediately. 'I remember, though I still don't see the joke.'

'Never mind that now. The point is, maybe he's not a phantom. You see, the reason I know Burger asked the NSA for daily checks on your ship is because the CIA told this phantom another source had made the same request as he and could he account for it. Do you see it?'

Lance nodded. There was bile rising in his throat.

Lestronge told him anyway. 'Phantoms, ghosts, don't demand information. All of a sudden J. Arthur Rank comes to life. Mind now, I'm still not agreeing with you that it is Bruun. But, according to my files you have no enemies except Bruun – and perhaps Pan.'

'That's what I've been saying all along, Mr Lestronge. Only nobody would believe me.'

'Except Brigadier Burger. Who is – '

'Not him either, actually. He was there when Bruun was given over to the tribeswomen – ' here Lance watched with interest as Lestronge shivered convulsively and turned to see Jimmy rippling too ' – and in fact Burger was the one who made the decision not to rescue Bruun. So he thinks Bruun is dead. But, just like everybody else who didn't believe me, he had no alternative candidate to offer. Where do I find this J. Arthur Rank joker?'

'In the Opium Triangle.'

'Huh?'

'It's the area where Burma, Thailand and Laos meet.' Lestronge pushed some buttons on his console and tore a sheet off the printer next to the screen. He slid it across the desk to Lance. 'It is a place that even you cannot go to, my boy.'

Lance read the printed sheet. It reported a pitched battle between Thai narcotics police and opium smugglers. The police had lost eighteen dead and over forty wounded; they claimed to have killed forty-seven smugglers and wounded one hundred and fifteen. He gave the paper to Jimmy.

'A few weeks ago we beat out the Tanzanian Navy,' Jimmy said. 'Before that the Tanzanian Army, the armies and police of several other States, bandits, Australian Mafia, the OAU . . . listen to the man, Lance. Our luck can't last forever. Let us instead make some plan to get Bruun down here. Or somewhere else. Africa. Our own ground.'

'He didn't come to Africa for the ivory, did he?'

'I want Bruun too,' Lestronge said. 'But going after him in the Triangle is suicide. That piece of paper reports a regular run-of-the-mill police action against a minor drug chieftain. Sixty-three dead. The police never dare to attack this J. Arthur Rank or even mention his operation. You would need a regular army to take him on and you would need air support. And, if by some luck you succeeded, the CIA would come after you because he's their kingpin in the world's heroin trade.'

'Where exactly is he?' Lance asked.

'I thought you weren't going to listen,' Lestronge said, pushing a map across the desk. 'Where he is nobody knows. But he has a communication headquarters here, where the cross is marked. Logically, he cannot be far from there.'

Lance stood. 'Thank you, Mr Lestronge.'

'You're going?'

'After we double-check the information against another source.'

'Call me if you need weapons, sources for reliable men, anything. I hope you get back alive. If you do, Lance, don't call me again. You're too dangerous to know.'

This time Lestronge did not come out of the building to see them off. He stayed in his office, seated behind his desk.

'Where's Christine?' Jimmy asked.

'She wandered off on her own to do some personal shopping,' Esmeralda said. 'She insisted.'

'Christ! What were Lestronge's Chinese bodyguards doing meanwhile?'

'Their orders were to protect us, not restrain us.'

'She won't come to any harm.' Lance looked up from his figuring. 'The ivory now belongs to Pan.'

Jimmy burst out laughing. After a moment he saw their confusion and explained. 'She's gone after the ivory, of course. I wonder who she teams up with, Drang or Bruun?'

There was an uncomfortable silence. Jimmy, no longer laughing, poured himself a drink. Pierre, after waiting a moment to be offered a drink, pushed himself up from his chair and made drinks for everybody else.

Esmeralda said, more for the sake of saying something into the silence after everybody had told Pierre what they wanted to drink, 'Nasheer brought his accounts and the deposit receipt for the balance. Every penny is accounted for. He said he was at your service at any time, and his whole family too,' she added, looking at Lance.

Lance looked up from his sheet of paper. 'We received a total of fifty million dollars for the ivory. The costs of the expedition were about one point seven million, which I agreed to carry out of my share – '

'And most of which you recovered rather nicely by the profit on selling the ship to Pan,' Pierre said.

'Right. So there is in fact a round fifty million to calculate the shares on.'

Esmeralda laughed and raised her glass. 'A toast to round figures.'

'Thank you, my darling. So my fifth is worth ten million and Jimmy's tenth is five million. Esmeralda's three-fifths is worth thirty million. That leaves five million for Pierre and Boo to split between them and the tribe.'

There was a moment of awed silence.

Boo said, 'You don't have to pay us, you know. Jimmy was going to take care of us out of his share. That had always been understood.'

Pierre laughed. 'I was going to ask, as a special favour, that you keep your money in my father-in-law's bank.'

'It's settled,' Lance said. 'I didn't know you kept cheque accounts, Pierre – I thought you were investment bankers.'

There was a moment of stunned silence. Then Pierre said, 'For a man who just distributed fifty million dollars like it was fifty cents, that's a silly remark, Lance. For that kind of money, *any* bank will break its own rules whole-sale.'

Lance shrugged. 'Every bootmaker to his last.' He distributed the cheques he had written. 'What are you going to do with the money?' he asked Jimmy.

'Give Christine a million for animal conservation. She'll know where best to spend it now she's seen Africa. Some of the rest to Pierre's bank, some into electronics firms out here. What are you going to do?'

'Why, I think I'll give Christine another million. After that I'll see. Pierre can look after mine meanwhile.'

Esmeralda laughed throatily. 'I'll make your two million to Christine up to a round five. Matthew would have considered it the final irony. So would Christine, except she lacks a sense of humour where the animals are concerned.'

There were more drinks.

'All right,' Jimmy said, raising his voice. 'What are we going to do about Bruun?'

'You're going home to Sambo,' Lance said firmly.

'Not us,' Boo said before Jimmy could answer. 'Sambo's orders were not to come home until Bruun is dead. Sambo gets very upset when people attack his family.'

'There's a problem,' Lance said reasonably. 'We're too few to attack Bruun. What we – '

'With so much money, we could build a wall around ourselves,' Esmeralda interjected fervently.

Lance ignored the interruption. 'What we can do is tell somebody with no shortage of trained men where Bruun is.'

'Burger,' Jimmy said.

'Yes.'

'And we'd be an embarrassment to him,' Pierre said.

Lance shrugged apologetically. 'Not just you. Me too.'

'But you're sending us to Brussels and going with Burger yourself,' Jimmy said in a tight voice.

'I was going to ask you to take Esmeralda with you until I can come myself.'

'Drang was right: Whitey sticks together.'

'Jimmy!' Pierre said sharply.

'Jimmy, you know it isn't like that,' Lance said, pain clear in his voice.

'Sorry.' Jimmy hung his head. 'How're you going to persuade Burger to let you go along?'

'I don't tell him where to go unless he lets me come.'

'You don't tell him where to go unless he lets *us* come.'

'Come on, Jimmy! Use your head. If it gets out, he'll be accused of using mercenaries, the very last thing he wants.'

'We could use Lestronge's men,' Boo said.

Lance shrugged again. 'Who knows where their loyalties lie?'

'What makes you so sure Burger will come after Bruun halfway across the world?' Pierre asked.

'Because Bruun killed on South African soil. And because Burger thinks Bruun is evil, to be killed at all costs.'

'There you are,' Jimmy said. 'Burger will have to accept us if he wants to find Bruun.'

After that no one felt like celebrating any more. When it was clear that Christine was not going to return, they went out to dinner, picking up Tanner and Ruby on the way.

When they returned from dinner, Wong was no longer in the reception area. Nor did he appear the next morning. Lance burnt with rage at this further proof of Bruun playing cat and mouse with him. Or had Wong been working for someone else altogether; had Wong's interest genuinely been in the ivory? He tried to shrug off the depression of fear. He had another lead to Bruun now. But everything was so tenuous. Wong would have been able to supply confirmation by directing them to another link in the chain . . . 'I like clearcut facts,' Lance told Esmeralda. 'This business of working in the dark with nothing but threadbare inferences to guide us . . . It frightens me. I feel out of my depth.'

Late in the afternoon Burger returned his call. Lance, unused to the long-distance phone, conscious of the expensive seconds ticking by, came straight to the point.

'Brigadier, we'd better meet.'

'Why?'

'Remember that you asked American friends to trace my ship?'

If Burger was surprised that Lance had found out, he took care not to let it show in his voice. 'Yes.'

'Somebody else also asked the same people to keep track of my whereabouts. When I docked here, his sidekick was waiting for me. The same sidekick who followed me around in Africa and chopped up people with a meatcleaver.'

'Very succinct. I'll be in Hong Kong tomorrow morning.'

'Singapore. We'll be at Raffles.'

'Too obvious.'

'Mrs Ellimore travels only first class.'

'Be careful, Lance.'

Burger rang off. Lance dialled the desk and asked them to make air bookings to Singapore on the first available flight.

Later Tanner and Ruby came to say goodbye. 'I have another job for you,' Lance said. 'Flying this time.'

'Let's hear about it. And how much,' Tanner laughed.

'No,' Ruby said firmly. 'If you'll excuse us, Mr Weber, you're a man who attracts danger like honey calls to ants. I want my Tanner whole and well. We'll take the generous

345

amount you've already paid us and settle in South America.'

Tanner blushed and was about to say something sharp to her when Lance said, 'I quite understand. If I was in your place I'd do the same. I wish Esmeralda and Jimmy and his brothers would show as much sense.' It was inconvenient, not having his own pilot. It meant he would have to fly with Burger. But he wholeheartedly meant what he said to Ruby. Even with Burger behind him, attacking Bruun's mountain fastness could be a spectacular way of committing suicide. 'It is something I have to do. Sorry I mentioned it.'

'That's the second job Ruby's turned down for me in two days,' Tanner said ruefully. 'Guess who was waiting with a job offer last night when we got home from dinner?'

'I give up. Not Pan?'

'Christine. She wanted a chopper pilot to drop some people on a ship. I explained to her that they still execute people for piracy. Ruby said no. So I told Christine she'd find lots of out-of-work pilots hanging around the airport and off she went. Guess who with?'

'Obviously not Pan. It's his ship she wants to pirate.'

'You sold out just in time, didn't you? Daniel Drang was waiting in the taxi outside. Where are Jimmy and the others?'

'Shopping. You left most of Esmeralda's luggage behind in Africa.'

'Sorry. People were shooting at me.'

'At us,' Ruby corrected him gently. But Lance knew how he felt: it is difficult not to take people shooting in your direction very personally indeed.

'Tell me, Tanner, if I hired a chopper pilot at the airport, could I rely on him?'

'To fly, sure. To risk his life, you'd like to know a little something more about him. Where are you going?'

'The Opium Triangle. It's up between – '

'Yes, pal, I know. I wouldn't like to take any chances on a casually hired chopper pilot not running for his life the minute the shooting started. It's a plenty rough place to walk out of. I know a Yank pilot who crashed a Phantom there: he got off without a scratch but after he walked out he had to spend six months in hospital and they cut one foot off and he still sees a shrink.'

'Look at this,' Pierre said.

Lance took the paper. 'Where?'

'Stop press.'

Lance read the piece aloud. 'UPA reports armed hijack China seas ship carrying one billion US dollars ivory belonging Singapore financier Sir P. K. Pan. Pan warehouse with similar amount ivory burnt Tokyo last month in military style attack. Beautiful blonde woman and several African mercenaries implicated hijack.'

'Hurrah for Christine!' Jimmy said. For the first time since she had disappeared, his old smile was back.

Esmeralda was not so sure. 'Drang will betray her. He is quite as fanatical as she but for a different cause. And Pan will have them both killed. If Bruun doesn't get them first . . .'

The rest of their breakfast was silent. Lance wondered about Christine. The newspaper had the amount wrong. Perhaps they had the other details wrong too.

Bruun . . . If he wanted that ivory . . . And Lance and Esmeralda . . . and Jimmy and Pierre and Boo . . . Bruun had only to send men to do what Christine had done: drop on the ship out of the sky. He had known where it was, just like Burger had known. Lance wondered if goldfish ever had nervous breakdowns in their bowls.

Burger came at noon, dapper and spruce as ever. Lance

347

wondered if he had stopped off somewhere to change the clothes he had slept in on the plane.

'I see your ivory is still causing trouble,' Burger said to Esmeralda after the introductions had been made.

'Coffee, tea, or something stronger, Brigadier?'

'Campari and soda, please.' Burger shook hands with Pierre, Boo and Jimmy. 'I breathed a sigh of relief when you lot retired to Brussels. Now it seems – '

'After dealing with Bruun we shall return to Brussels and the gentle pastime of gracefully growing old and rich,' Pierre said.

Burger waited until he had a drink before he replied. 'You will not be dealing with Bruun. I shall attend to it. Do not misunderstand me, I have nothing but respect for you as fighting men of great ability and intelligence. But it would be political suicide for me to take you with me on a punitive expedition in a country where none of us can claim citizenship or even ties.'

Pierre looked at Lance.

'Then you wasted a journey, Brigadier. We intend going after Bruun with or without your help.'

'Lance, stop trying to convince everybody you're stupid. People have long since caught on. You must have known what I would say, so why waste my time and yours by asking me to come here?'

'You're as keen to see Bruun dead as we are. You have trained, reliable men capable of doing the job. You could probably get a dispensation from the Thai government to move armed men through their country – they've been having so much trouble with the opium smugglers that they will welcome any help.'

'All of that's true. But, now that I know Bruun's in the Opium Triangle and has CIA connections, I can probably find him. I do not need you to tell me where he is.' Burger stood.

Lance spread a map on the table. Esmeralda took the

tray and gave it to Boo, who put it on the sideboard. 'By the time you've made your enquiries, Brigadier, he'll be gone. He has virtually unlimited funds.'

'It's been a pleasure meeting you, Mrs Ellimore. Allow me to say you are the most beautiful woman I have ever met.' Burger bowed over her hand.

'On the other hand,' Lance said stubbornly, not looking up from the map, 'I have a map reference that'll drop us right on him like Judgement Day.'

Burger sat down again. 'I do not judge. I simply deal with evil men.'

'That's a judgement. Whether they are evil. If so, whether they are evil enough to merit your particular attentions.'

'Bravo my Lance!' Esmeralda exclaimed.

Burger inclined his head to her. 'You also have excellent taste in your men, Madam. All right, Lance. What can you offer me except a time saving? Not your undoubted skill with a rifle. I've plenty of fighting men.'

For the first time since Burger had come, Lance smiled. 'Bait,' he said. 'I don't suppose you want a bloodbath.'

Burger smiled ever so slightly. 'You suppose right. Chop off the head . . . By comparison to Bruun, a bunch of poppy-growing peasants are lilywhite. So you think you can lure Bruun out of his stronghold?'

'Yes.'

'It's possible. But it will have the same effect as my enquiries – it would be a warning and we could lose him. No thank you. What does this stronghold of his consist of?'

'You're taking us?'

Burger sat for nearly a minute, considering. (Esmeralda would later tell Lance she had never seen a man who could sit so totally still.) At last Burger said, 'Yes. I'll take you. You've earned the right.'

* * *

Two days later, the converted MTB that Lance had sold to Pan and that Christine had then pirated was found drifting off Taiwan. There were a number of dead bodies, African and Chinese. One of them was Frank, identified in the news bulletins as a 'sometime OAU employee' and by *The New York Times* as an ex-CIA man whose name they had had cause to publish before, during the Vietnam war. Of Christine and Drang there was no sign. The ivory had been transferred in mid-ocean.

Pan came to visit Lance. The Chinese tycoon had white lines around his eyes.

'Mr Weber, if you did not burn my ivory in Tokyo, who did?'

'I don't know. I can guess.'

'Do you know why Miss Rawls took my ivory?'

'Yes. She wants the money for animal conservation. Her associate, a Daniel Drang, wants the ivory for Africa.'

'For Africa?'

'To alleviate poverty, to fight imperialism. He is a soured idealist but nonetheless a dangerous man.'

'So whoever took my ivory from him and Miss Rawls must be even more dangerous.'

'Yes.'

'Do you know who this man is?'

'Yes. The knowledge will do you no good.'

'It is worth a considerable amount of – '

'No. I don't want your money. The man is protected.'

'Tell me his name.'

Lance considered. He did not like Pan. But Pan had come as a supplicant. However, if Pan started looking for Bruun, he could spook him before Burger could finish his preparations. On the other hand, it might distract attention from Lance and Burger's preparations.

'His name is J. Arthur Rank. Once, I believe, it was Theodore Bruun. He is something important in the opium trade.'

350

Pan had gone dead white.

'Are you all right?' Esmeralda asked him anxiously.

'Yes. It is nothing. Thank you for the tea, Mrs Ellimore. Mr Weber, this man Rank is not "something in the opium trade", he *is* the opium trade.'

Lance walked to the door with Pan. The Chinese suddenly seemed old. At the door he said, 'My ivory and the ship were insured, of course. But I have lost face quite intolerably. I shall make some enquiries and then perhaps I shall wish to employ you.'

Lance made no reply. He did not know whether to laugh or cry.

Forty-five minutes later they flew out to Bangkok to meet Burger, who had meanwhile come to an arrangement with the Thai narcotics authorities – a continually shifting melange of customs, police and army commands no Westerner will ever make sense of.

'You're going to attack Bruun with forty men?' Lance could not believe he had heard right. 'Brigadier, the Thai lost that many men just attacking one of Bruun's minor henchmen. Bruun dictates policy to the governments of three countries and sends messages to the President of the United States offering to end the heroin trade for one billion dollars.'

'Forty men is my total paramil establishment,' Burger said calmly. 'These men are handpicked, well motivated and trained to a T.'

'I'm in no doubt as to their ability, sir. I'm talking about their numbers. Can't you call in some men from the South African Army?'

'The Thai have bent as far as they can, Lance. Anyway, if I ask the Army, it'll be months before the red tape clears.'

Lance nodded. By then it would be too late. Bruun would have disappeared again.

Pierre was interested in something else. 'You mean you keep peace in South Africa with forty men, Brigadier?'

Burger smiled. 'These are shock troops, used only in the most dire emergencies. I also have my policemen, who generally suffice. But you are right, my total department is not very large. Security is a matter of brains rather than brawn or numbers. I have fewer men, for instance, than the security division of Anglo-American Corporation or even their De Beers diamond division.'

Pierre whistled. 'Some men would pay for that knowledge.'

Burger said nothing. Pierre knew as well as he did the fatal cure for loose mouths.

Lance was not interested in Burger's administrative and budgetary problems. (Lance had not in fact distinguished 'establishment' as a civil service allocation of money or men from a building or some other fixed property.) 'All this is irrelevant. We're going to commit a sick, silly suicide. Bruun can squash forty men like a pimple.'

'Then we'll have to outsmart him, Lance. With the impetuosity of your youth, it's amazing you're still alive.'

'Don't patronize me, Brigadier. All that patience has brought me so far is fear. And you and your forty men. In Hong Kong I could have recruited a thousand men for the asking.'

'And how far could you trust them?'

Lance had no answer to that. After a moment to let it sink in, Burger changed the subject. 'Lance, we simply cannot take a woman.'

'You tell Esmeralda.'

'She's your – '

'She's a free agent. Her servant was killed by Bruun's men on his orders. She has a right to – '

'Justice. We will serve Bruun his desserts on her behalf.'

Lance smiled in genuine enjoyment.

352

Jimmy said, 'Brigadier, we've been there before with her.'

Lance said, 'She has a right to revenge.'

'Damnit man, this is nineteen eighty – '

'She's Spanish. You really mustn't discriminate against her because of her ethnic origin or her sex, Brigadier.'

Burger looked up at Lance. The younger man was mocking his conservatism. 'Chivalry, not conservatism.'

Lance, properly rebuked and aware of it, spread his hands. 'Look, I don't want her to come. But, way back when we needed her help, I made a promise. I've talked to her but she won't listen. If you want to reason with her, you don't need my permission.'

'We could restrain her.'

'No. She must give up her right to come voluntarily or I'll go after Bruun with mercenaries.'

'I could ask the Thai to extract the information from you.'

Boo chuckled roundly. 'And then you kill us all, after which you go to Brussels and kill Sambo and the other brothers before they come after you.'

'That's a somewhat impetuous suggestion, Brigadier,' Pierre said, also chuckling.

'I'll talk to her. We leave in one hour,' Burger said.

When Burger had walked away, Jimmy laughed. 'There are very few men alive who have ever seen that man lose his temper.'

'It's not so funny,' Pierre rebuked his younger brother. 'He is a bad enemy.'

'Who wants to kill Bruun so much he takes insults from black men,' Boo said.

'We'll worry about his feelings later,' Lance snapped. 'Right now we've to decide whether to tell him it's off and go back to ask Lestronge for help recruiting men, or to go with Burger and his inadequate force.'

'He'll kill us if we back out now,' Pierre said.

'Pierre's right,' Boo said.

'He wants Bruun so badly, he can taste it,' Jimmy added.

'If he's unbalanced, all the more reason to stay well away from him.'

The three brothers stared at Lance, Boo's mouth gaping open, Jimmy's smile slackening at the lower lip.

'And you're perfectly rational on the subject of Bruun?' Jimmy finally asked.

Lance ignored the question and turned to look out of the window of the hut at the four helicopters. They were at an airfield in north-western Thailand, no more than fifteen kilometres from the border with Burma. They had been flown up in a Thai military plane from Bangkok that morning, to find Burger and his men installed and ready to leave in short order. Burger had asked Esmeralda to check the food supplies; then he had tackled Lance about leaving her behind. Lance hefted his rifle in his hand. It had been cleaned by someone, probably one of Burger's men. Their firearms had been left behind in Hong Kong because of the strict regulations in force in Singapore. Burger had arranged for the weapons to be brought directly to Thailand.

Lance did not think he was unbalanced on the subject of Bruun. Obsessive perhaps, but Bruun had that effect on many people. He, Lance Weber, was certainly still sane enough on the subject of Bruun not to wish to commit suicide in the attempt to kill him. The question was, was Burger?

'Forty men,' Lance said neutrally.

'They're very fine men,' Pierre said.

'But will training be enough?'

'Your brother used to say training and numbers are useful adjuncts to morale. We don't know the morale of Bruun's men.'

'Oh yes, we do,' Lance said. 'They know there's a death

354

sentence for opium pedlars in Thailand – those the police don't just shoot out of hand. There's no morale-builder like fighting for your life.'

Burger came back into the hut. His mouth was set in a straight line. His lead pilot was with him. The Thai had supplied the gunships out on the tarmac, glistening in their new, unmarked paint. Burger had brought his pilots with him. This was not a joint operation: the Thai were simply turning a blind eye and supplying a modest amount of equipment. Burger spread a map on the table in the centre of the hut. Besides the scarred table, there were two hard wooden chairs and a filing cabinet. On the wall hung a Coca-Cola calendar. There was no other furniture.

'Where is he, Lance?'

'Where's Esmeralda?'

'She's coming.'

Esmeralda came through the door and stood against the wall. Lance glanced at her: her full lips were compressed in a straight line of anger but her eyes shone with triumph.

Lance took the sheet of paper from his pocket and gave it to Burger. The pilot looked over Burger's shoulder and then plotted the co-ordinates on the map. Burger looked at the map, then at the sheet of paper, then at the map again. Finally he took the pilot's ruler and laid it on the map to be sure the co-ordinates were correctly plotted against the scale on the edges of the map.

'It's in Burma,' he said to Lance.

'Yes.'

'Damnit, Lance! We're in Thailand by courtesy of the Thai government!'

'Which courtesy the Burmese would never extend to Brigadier Rocco Burger of the South African Department of National Security.'

'You knew all along?'

'I didn't tell you he was in Thailand. I said – '

'I know what you said!' Suddenly Burger laughed, an

355

abrupt snort of sound, from him somehow obscene but, more, frightening. 'We're here. What's the invasion of a third country? If we succeed in killing Bruun, that will be its own reward. If we fail, we'll never know.'

'You don't believe in life after death, Brigadier?' Esmeralda asked from the wall.

Burger glanced at her but did not answer.

The pilot said, 'If that reference is accurate and we don't have to search too long for the exact place, we can be there in twenty-five minutes at the outside.'

'That reference was pinpointed from a large number of radio transmissions over a period of six years,' Lance said.

The pilot nodded. 'I'll drop you right on top by dead reckoning. But a reconnaisance flight would be better.'

'No,' Burger said. 'See if there's anything on the satellite photos we brought.'

The pilot took the photographs out of his briefcase and spread them on the table. They covered northern Thailand but the area of the map reference was right on the edge of one of the sheets.

'A native village,' the pilot said.

Lance sighed his disappointment.

'What did you expect?' Pierre asked. 'Of course there will be camouflage.'

'With more heavy-vehicle traffic than one would expect,' the pilot said, reading the streaks on the sheet. He traced a line with his finger and Burger nodded, tracing another line with his finger.

Lance watched the pilot sweat. Burger, still wearing the jacket of his brown suit, did not seem to notice the heat or the humidity.

'We'll be there at quarter past one,' Burger said. 'Perfect timing, right in the middle of their siesta. Lay off the course on a dogleg there and another course straight out,' he told the pilot. 'I'll brief the team leaders out there. Are the helicopters armed yet?'

'They finished an hour ago.'

Burger left. The pilot sat down at the table with his maps and instruments. The other three pilots came into the little hut, crowding it. Lance and the others walked outside.

'You should bring Christine and Brigadier Burger together,' Esmeralda said. 'He's the last Neanderthal male chauvinist hog.'

'Pig.'

'That's what I said, darling.'

They listened to Burger briefing his men. Lance exchanged glances with Jimmy, Pierre and Boo. Esmeralda looked thoughtful as her eyes ran over Burger's men. 'They look so young, she said to Lance, 'just off the farm.'

To Lance they looked hard and competent, but still too few.

When Burger had finished his briefing, Lance caught him by the elbow. Burger shook his arm loose.

'Brigadier, what happened to outsmarting Bruun, to finesse? What you're planning is nothing better than a frontal attack.'

'Do you have a better plan that can be put into operation in the next hour?'

Lance shook his head. 'This is stupid. We're on the same side.'

'You can still stay here. We'll pick you up on the way home.' Burger walked on.

'Wow!' Jimmy exclaimed. 'Right off his head with hatred of Bruun.'

'This is where we should get off the roller-coaster,' Pierre said. 'It is out of control.'

'I'm going,' Esmeralda said. To Lance, in a softer voice, she added, 'It is my last duty.'

He knew what she meant. The little Spaniard had been her husband's servant as well as her own. Once the butler was revenged, she would be all Lance's.

'If Burger fails, Bruun will never let us near him again,' Lance said. 'Our lives won't be worth living. But everyone should decide for himself. Pierre, Boo, you have wives and children. Jimmy, there's your duty to the future of the tribe.'

'Don't you read me lectures about duty, Lance. I get enough of that in Brussels.' Jimmy laughed self-consciously. 'You can't go after Bruun without me. I bring you good luck.'

Pierre said, 'It is exactly to make sure my children will grow up that I must come with you.'

Boo, strapping on the grenades one of Burger's men was offering, did not deign to reply.

Before he climbed up into the helicopter after Esmeralda, Lance had a brief, sensuous moment, a glimpse out of time and out of purpose, enjoying the thick air and the lush green vegetation that would overwhelm the airfield in a month if not checked. Then he was pushed from behind by one of Burger's men and swung himself up. Inside the helicopter he sat holding Esmeralda's hand. Boo had a rosary and was muttering a prayer. Lance had not known he was religious. Perhaps this was a time to make any man religious though Lance did not feel like talking to God. He was thinking that he wanted sons by Esmeralda.

'Don't be in too much of a hurry to kill Bruun,' Jimmy said. 'Especially if Christine isn't there. We must make him tell us where they are keeping her. First.'

The engines started up. There was no further talk.

Jimmy had his own demons and obsessions, Lance thought. Christine. They had been careful not to mention her name. She was dead and that was it. They had all seen men tortured by Bruun. When he had had Briony Roux in his power, he had given her over to his African soldiers to rape until she was deranged and only saved her from being raped to death because he thought the despot he worked for might appreciate a white woman. All that had happened within less than twenty-four hours. If Bruun had taken Christine with the ivory to question her about Lance and Jimmy and the brothers, she would have told him all she knew and died within at the very most forty-eight hours. She was a memory. Lance hoped her memory would not fog Jimmy's eye when the shooting started. There was no time and no place for sentiment here. He took the sidearm from Esmeralda's belt and inspected it. 'If you are captured, kill yourself,' he shouted against her ear. She nodded. He had told her several times. He hoped she understood that it was not that he would rather have her dead than possessed by another or others – even against her will – but because of the certainty that she would die anyway in Bruun's hands and far more painfully than by a self-inflicted bullet through the palate into the brain. The noise of the blades overhead was palpable, claws tearing at their skulls and their unspoken thoughts. Even in dead silence and in private he could never have explained. He saw greenery flying past the open door of the helicopter. It was almost near enough to touch.

The surprise was complete. Burger's pilots brought the helicopters in so low that they could be heard before the radar picked them up; the very next moment they were overhead and firing their rockets. All four helicopters made a pass across the village, firing eight rockets each, the heavy .50 calibre machine-guns firing continuously.

Lance, seeing the running men, women and children being mowed down, hoped fervently they were at the right place. If they had made a mistake . . .

There were more men than women, many more. Some of the men were firing machine-pistols at the helicopters. Lance saw at least two portable rocket-launchers being carried out into the open by two-man teams moving with the precision of trained soldiers.

That was no guarantee that they would find Bruun here but in these mountains the only men armed with rocket-launchers were the opium smugglers: the Burmese authorities' writ did not run here.

They had come to the right place.

After the explosive rockets, fire.

The four helicopters made another pass, then hovered over the corners of the square. The resistance was virtually broken. Men were throwing away their weapons and trying to run through the flames, any direction, just away from this sudden, ruthless, total firefight that had dropped on them from the sky without warning. The machine-guns mowed down the runners and the resisters impartially.

It took perhaps thirty seconds while the four helicopters hung still and vulnerable in the air over the square, dead centre in the flames. Then nothing moved in the village except the flames, reaching for the sky, for oxygen, for more combustibles to feed their greed.

The helicopters settled almost gently. Lance held Esmeralda, who was poised to jump out, while Burger's men streamed efficiently past her, fanning out on the ground, facing an attack that could come out of the flames. Burger stepped out behind them. Lance let Esmeralda go and she jumped out. They stood watching the wall of flame. Lance saw a nerve twitch in the neck of one of Burger's younger men.

'Bruun had better be here,' Burger said tightly. 'Otherwise this mass slaughter will be for nothing.'

One of Burger's men threw a piece of equipment at his master's feet. 'Sam 7 missile-launcher. They fired it but we were too close and it went out of control, crashing in the forest.'

Burger touched it with the toe of his immaculately polished brown lace-up shoe. 'That little toy can take out a helicopter all by itself. Amateurs do not usually have such fine armament.'

'You're feeling better now?' Esmeralda asked.

'A little, thank you,' Burger replied. 'Killing innocent people is a trade I prefer to leave to the soldiers. A policeman should be precise. Like a rifle, not like a shotgun.'

The men had finished clearing a break through the fire with the extinguishers. As he ran after Burger, Lance was beginning to feel more optimistic about the operation. Even Burger's frontal attack had had a certain subtlety about it. There were two zones untouched by the fire and they were now running towards the second one. Nobody could get at their helicopters except from the air or by coming through this corridor first, in which case they would run smack into the owners of the helicopters. It was straightforward and foolproof, yet clever. He noticed with approval that Jimmy, Pierre and Boo had positioned themselves around Esmeralda so that, with his own body, they formed a square of flesh around her.

From ahead of them there was some firing. Burger kept his stride, not quite running but walking very quickly with the longest strides his not overly long legs could make. Lance and the others, all taller than Burger, found it easier to lope than to lengthen their stride to keep up. Lance supposed Burger's dignity would not allow him to be seen to run, even when he was running towards the firing.

Two of Burger's men were down. Burger looked into the staring eyes of the dead one for a moment, then closed the eyes. Immediately they sprang open again. Burger raised the other man's shoulders from the burning hot ground and held him until the medic arrived. Esmeralda pressed a bandage from her pocket across the graze in the man's skull. How well he would recover depended on how bad the concussion was, Lance knew. The small amount of blood indicated nothing: the skin around the top of the skull does not bleed profusely. Lance could feel that Esmeralda, having done what she could, was impatient to go and find Bruun. But he waited calmly for Burger to proceed. They had come for Bruun. They would get to Bruun when Burger's men had cleared a path. Until then they would only be in the way of men trained to fight as a group, would in fact stand a good chance of being killed by Burger's men in the confusion that always attended a firefight. Jimmy noticed Esmeralda's impatience and winked broadly at Lance. The medic came and Burger rose. He proceeded at the same pace as before.

The second unburnt area was linked to the other area, where the helicopters were, by the corridor the extinguishers had made but was otherwise totally surrounded by fire. Lance, still at heart a wild-life keeper, glanced up at the trees to see if the fire would spread: it would not, the trees were lushly green, loaded with water.

The open area was about a hundred paces to a side and bare, except for the squat pagoda in the centre. Even here the style of architecture looked somehow out of place, too Chinese. It was exquisitely proportioned and obviously beautifully constructed by the finest materials, but for all of that it was not very big and there was no obvious reason why, in a crowded village which already had a square, so much space should have been left around it. As many as fifty men lay dead in the square. Three more of Burger's men had died and one lay wounded seriously. Some of the others were going around making sure all the men on the ground were dead, shooting the wounded in the head. Esmeralda gasped at the brutality.

'Standard procedure,' Lance told her. 'Burger leaves no survivors.'

'He's quite as neat in his own way as your late brother,' Pierre said.

Lance walked over to watch the sappers at work on the small pagoda. They ignored the locks on the door and were putting plastique on the protruding hinges. Thinking that it was too easy and too obvious, Lance walked around the building. On the other side he found what he was looking for, the glint of metal where the veneer had worn thin.

The engineers blew the doors just as Lance walked around the corner. Burger's face was grim as he looked at the sheet of steelplate behind the decorative doors. There was no break in it; it was obvious the doors had been put there to mislead someone. Them.

'It's this side,' Lance said. 'Steel sliding doors big enough to take a truck through.' He traced the outline of it on the veneer for the explosive expert.

'It's nothing but the head of a big lift,' Burger said as they stood watching the explosives being set.

'What worries me is that there is no mast for the communication he's supposed to have sent.'

'They send up a balloon every time, shackled to that ring. You can see the line where the roof opens and the little platform for the balloon handler to stand on. Very clever. The underground complex must be huge. Bruun will burn in hell for the women and children he kept upstairs for camouflage. And I shall have nightmares until it comes my turn to burn in hell for killing them.'

'So you do believe in an afterlife, Brigadier?' Lance said before he could stop himself. It was an impertinent question.

'In the exact sense Mrs Ellimore does. As a time of accounting, of reckoning, of payment of dues, of settling of accounts.'

'Stand back, will you!' the engineer shouted at them. He watched them walk away, then pressed the button on the small transmitter in his hand. The whole building seemed to rise about a foot into the air, then collapsed lopsidedly.

The dust was still settling – some of it was still wafting upwards, Lance noticed – when Burger's men swarmed into the hole, a burly red-faced lieutenant in the lead.

363

After a moment, his face appeared above the rubble and kept rising. When his feet were clear of the ground, he jumped to one side. A steel cube rose above the ground. The doors opened. Lance had his rifle pointing at the man's heart and was already squeezing the trigger when he recognized the grinning face as one of Burger's men.

'Want a ride, friends,' the lieutenant said in heavily Afrikaans-accented English. It was a joke, directed at Lance and his friends. Even Burger laughed shortly.

'See if you can blow it out rather than in,' Burger said to the demolitions man.

'As a matter of fact, I do want to go for a ride,' Lance said, stepping boldly into the lift. Esmeralda immediately followed him. Jimmy, Pierre and Boo stepped in too.

'This is not the time for games,' Burger said tightly.

'While you're fiddling around with explosives, Bruun is escaping by the back door,' Lance said. 'Let us go then. You can blow the lift and climb down the hole when we send it back up.'

'Doesn't it strike you as suspicious that the lift is there waiting for us in full working order?' Sarcasm dripped from the lieutenant's clipped accent.

'It strikes me as part of catching them by surprise,' Lance said. 'Someone forgot to turn the electricity off. If they're waiting for the lift, they'll also be waiting at the bottom of the shaft to pick you off while you play mountaineers.'

Jimmy had his finger on the button. He was looking at Lance.

'Into the lift,' Burger said. He led his men in. They filled the lift. He had left only one man to secure their retreat.

Lance was crushed at the back of the lift with Burger and Esmeralda. 'If they have to send up a balloon to radio out, he can't call for reinforcements.'

'The bigger part of this force is still downstairs and now

warned,' Burger said shortly. 'It is we who have need of reinforcement.'

'I wonder if this lift is booby-trapped?' Jimmy asked no one in particular.

'You've been watching too many American films on television,' Boo said. 'If you had a wife and children, you would watch a more wholesome manner of programme.' To one of Burger's farm-fresh young men who was staring at him, Boo added, 'Even us blacks have television now, you know. In colour, too.'

The lift bumped against its stops. The door slid open. Before them was a whitewashed passage, anti-climactically empty. Burger's men surged out, weapons at the ready. One looked a little foolishly at the armed grenade he had ready in his hand. Lance raised an eyebrow at him, then hurried to grab Esmeralda's arm.

'Stay with Burger,' he told her.

'But – '

'Don't get in the way of the men. Do you see me or Jimmy or Pierre or Boo doing anything but staying behind Burger?'

She nodded.

'You'll get your turn at Bruun. I promise. For now, do as I tell you.'

'How masterful you are when it suits you,' Burger said.

Esmeralda shot the policeman a sharp glance but Lance chose to ignore the barb.

Burger's men were throwing open the doors of each room they passed. They were in some kind of underground barracks, with six bunks to a room. There was every sign that the rooms were inhabited but they met nobody.

'How many floors does this place have?' Lance asked Jimmy. 'How many buttons on the board in the lift?'

'Four. We're on the top floor.'

'Tch!' Burger said. He spoke into his radio. 'Find the stairs. We want to be on the lowest level.'

Fifteen seconds later they came upon more lifts but Burger refused to use them for transporting men. 'There must be stairs for so many men. You can retreat up stairs. In a lift you're a sitting target the moment someone switches off the electricity.'

'The lifts are dead anyway,' a tinny voice on the radio reported.

'Find the stairs,' Burger ordered.

In another fifteen seconds, they found the stairs. They went down one floor at a time. Lance feared Burger would go by the book and insist on searching each floor before proceeding to the next but Burger seemed to be as aware of the danger of Bruun escaping as he was. On each of the two floors they left two men to guard the stairs. It was pitifully inadequate but it was all they could spare.

'Shooting ahead,' said the leader when he came to the bottom of the stairs. 'Far off.'

Burger thought for a moment but all he said was, 'Advance.'

Down the length of the single flight of stairs, Lance saw the man with the live grenade still clenched in his hand throw it around the corner at the bottom of the stairs. There were no shots in reply. Another man threw another grenade in the other direction. Still nothing. The lieutenant clicked his fingers and four men dived out into the passage to crash flat on their stomachs, automatic arms pointing and ready.

'Die verdomde gang is leeg, man,' one of them said, turning over on his back. The damn passage is empty, man.

Lance, who understood Afrikaans, went with Burger to look. It was very strange. Faintly, at the end of the passage, they could hear a furious firefight. Lance and

366

Burger simultaneously looked back at the doors at the other end of the passage.

'Go,' Burger said. Lance ran to the double doors. They swung open easily. He had a flash of memory: the inside of a hospital. Through the doors was a kitchen. Beyond there were no further exits. The kitchen too reminded Lance of a hospital: all stainless steel. It was too small to cater for the number of men whose bunks they had seen higher up. Running down the passage, he heard a mewling, like a kitten. He flung open the door from which it had come and stood to one side pointing his rifle into the room. There was a smell, sickening in its clinging thickness before he even identified it as the smell of urine and faeces.

Lance steeled himself to enter the darkness and put on the light.

A hand appeared at the bottom of the doorpost. Lance nearly fired but from behind the hand came the sound of a kitten mewling again. He stepped over the hand and felt on the wall for the switch. A second after the light came on, he was out in the passage, vomiting on the white floor, which, he noticed in that sanity-saving detachment that always comes to the survivors in such moments of extreme pain and horror, was carpet instead of the bare concrete of all the other floors. And in that same detachment he felt himself disgraced for the weakness of vomiting when he should have had the strength to do something useful.

The others came running. Lance had the strength to catch Esmeralda around the waist to prevent her going into the room. But she was heading for him.

In the door, Burger gasped.

Even Burger . . . Lance thought.

The floor was filthy with faeces and urine and blood and vomit. In one corner lay the naked body of Daniel Drang. His eyes had been rudely poked out, his fingers and toes cut off. He had been emasculated, his ears sliced away.

His nose had been split, then squashed. There was hardly an inch of his skin that had not received the attention of some instrument before he had been disembowelled. His body was already starting to decompose. Burger wondered why they had shaved his head so meticulously: it was virtually the only unscarred part of him.

Burger looked down at Christine at his feet, her hand still on the doorpost, her voice still mewling. He hoped she was insane, beyond the pain of her mutilated body. Her head too was shaved, he noticed. Her face was untouched except for the lines of terror newly etched on it. But her nipples had been pierced, the toenails of her left foot had rude bamboo splinters broken off under them. From the blisters on the insides of her thighs he concluded that she had been violated with an electrically heated instrument. He was pushed aside as Jimmy scooped Christine up in his arms.

'They had only started on her,' Burger said. 'They were saving her for later.'

Jimmy looked at Drang's body, then down at Christine in his arms.

'That's Bruun's work all right,' Lance said. He was still kneeling on the floor, Esmeralda wiping his mouth. 'Go attend to her.' Esmeralda left him. Jimmy laid Christine out on the floor.

'Jimmy,' she whispered weakly. 'I knew you would come.'

Burger shivered convulsively. She was still sane. And probably in the most excruciating pain. His men were standing around, looking this way and that, embarrassed to be present at the evidence of such inhumanity to man. The medic came forward to Christine's body.

'Why are your heads shaven?' Burger asked.

'To attach electrodes because the thing can't hear or see pain,' Christine said clearly. 'Kill him for me, Jimmy.'

'Where is he?' Burger asked.

368

There was a long silence before she answered. 'He gets his kicks through electrical impulses from the brains of the people he tortures.'

'Tell us where he is. We'll kill him for you,' Burger said, bending over her.

'In the glass cage.'

'Where is it?'

She shook her head. A clot of blood dribbled from her mouth. There was internal damage. Burger nodded at the medic, who pushed the poised needle into her flesh. Burger pointed at the blood clot to be sure the man knew to handle her carefully.

'Small kitchen, carpet on the floor,' Lance said. 'That's a dead end down there.'

They turned the other way, past the stairs. As they waited for Burger's men to secure the passage directly beyond the next set of communicating doors, Lance asked, 'Where's Esmeralda?'

'She stayed with Christine,' Jimmy said. 'I told Boo to stay too.'

The sound of fighting was now nearer yet further away. Soon they understood why. The passage made a right-angle turn. Ahead of them was a single wooden door. It did not budge when Pierre pushed his shoulder against it. He shot the hinges off and pulled the door from its lock and the wall. Beyond was a steel plate. 'Hey, here!'

The spearhead was already a hundred paces down the right-angle passage towards the fighting. Burger halted the advance and came back. He studied the steel door.

'It is used very often,' the engineer said.

'So they don't keep rarely used valuables behind it,' Burger said. 'Open it.' Burger spoke on the radio, giving orders to maintain a cautious advance towards the fighting but to stop short of it.

Three minutes later the door blew. The group down the passage out of reach of flying debris consisted of Burger,

369

his engineer, Lance, Jimmy and Pierre. The engineer went forward through the hole in the wall, his FN at the ready. He screamed only once. He came staggering back through the door. The acid in his face had caused him to scream, until it filled his mouth and burned his tongue away. His face and head was already a skull and bone was sticking through the ragged pieces of cloth and pinkish-turning-to-white-flesh on his chest. He was dead of massive trauma before he hit the ground.

Pierre flung a grenade through the thinning rain of acid while Lance and Jimmy fired a steady stream of bullets into the murk. Burger talked calmly on the radio, calling some men back by name. One of those he called had a flamethrower.

'Burn that entrance clean,' Burger told him.

After five minutes, the plaster on the wall had long since burnt away and the metal framing of the door glowed cherry-red. The man ran out of fuel for his infernal machine. Before Burger could order his men through the gap, Lance and Jimmy looked at each other, then dived through side by side. Inside they rolled and came up, rifles at the ready. Then they rose, slapping at the small fires that had started on their clothes.

'It's just like the movies,' Jimmy said.

'Boo won't believe you,' Lance said when he recovered. 'You can come in now,' he called to Burger.

Burger and Pierre came to stand with them. It was not a very large room. The glass cage and its paraphernalia took up most of the space. There were electrical wires and clear glass and plastic tubes for the life-support systems.

But what held their attention was the thing inside the glass cage. It looked like a seated man clumsily modelled by a careless child. The head was bald and eyeless, the nose just two large holes in the middle of the face under the holes indicating the putative position of the eyes. The mouth was lipless, the gaping gums toothless. The arms

370

ended in blunt palms without fingers, the feet had no toes. The elbows and knees were immensely thick and oddly angled. All over the thing had small delicate scales like some rare and wonderfully vicious fish from the unimaginable depths of the sea; it was the result of being flayed alive. A closer look, on overcoming the first necessary revulsion, revealed that in place of genitals under the folds of flab there was only a transparent plastic tube in the rolls of fat; the gaping gums revealed no tongue.

'Who enters so rudely?' The voice was a bass rumble, thunderous.

Lance and Jimmy both put shots into the loudspeakers in the corners of the wall and the ceiling before turning to look sheepishly at Burger, then at the thing in the cage.

'How does he speak?'

'Through that hole in his throat,' Burger said, pointing. He moved daintily on the fire-blackened floor to look into the hole at the side of the hairless, scaled head. 'I can't see a thing but the tribeswomen would have pierced his eardrums. He probably hears through that diaphragm on which his hand rests.'

'You are right,' said the eerie voice. 'You must speak louder. I cannot make sense of what you say.'

Lance said, loudly, 'J. Arthur Rank? Theodore Bruun?'

'Yes. Who are you?'

'Lance Weber. Come to – '

Lance was cut off by the gleeful cackle. Then, abruptly it became a wheeze and stopped. 'With Brigadier Burger and the faithful Jimmy?'

'Yes. We're going to kill you for the murder of my parents, of Briony Roux and her child, of my employees on my reservation, of Esmeralda Ellimore's butler, of the various Fitzmeikles, of – '

'Don't weary me with menials and petty criminals. I tire very easily.'

'All right. Then you will just die,' Lance said. He

371

opened fire on full automatic, knowing Jimmy and Pierre would do the same. Almost immediately the three of them fell to the floor.

'Jesus Christ,' Pierre said when the ricochets stopped whining. 'That's all armoured glass.'

Burger was already up, pursing his mouth with distaste as he brushed down his suit with his handkerchief. When he had done all he could, he dropped the soiled silk handkerchief on the floor.

'Do you have any gas, Brigadier?' Lance asked.

'Something better.' Burger whispered in the ear of his man who had come in to see if he was all right. The man went out.

Lance could not see why Burger was whispering. The horrid shivery laughter was still booming out in the room.

'I shall enjoy killing you slowly. Or perhaps I shall keep you alive forever. Gunfire cannot kill me and gas can't get at me and tasters taste my food and my – '

'Shut up!' Burger shouted.

There was a moment of uneasy silence. Lance looked at Pierre and Jimmy. It could be bad if Burger cracked up now. They still had to get out of here with what sounded like a pitched battle approaching closer by the second.

Burger's radio broke the silence – or rather sounded over the cackling of the loudspeakers.

'We're behind them now, sir. They're being strenuously attacked from the other side. What do you want us to do?'

'Who's attacking them?'

'I don't know.'

'Keep your distance. Don't get involved.'

'Sir, they're retreating fast. Soon they'll retreat right over your position.'

'Then hold just before you get here. We don't need much time.'

'Yes sir.'

Burger's messenger returned with a canister. Burger

took the canister from him. He raised his voice. 'Listen to me, Bruun.'

'Soon I'll listen to you beg.' Again the cackling.

'What's that?' Lance asked Burger.

'White phosphorus. There is almost nothing it will not burn, short of some space-age metals.'

Lance looked doubtfully at the glass cage. It was perfectly possible that Bruun, with all his power, had obtained fireproof glass as well.

Burger handed Lance the canister. 'The flamethrower must have exhausted his fire precautions.' He pointed distastefully to some white powder on his sleeve, then at the water on the floor. 'None of these things are any good against white phosphorus. Wait till we're all out, then pull the tag and get out within three seconds.'

Lance looked at the tag Burger indicated, then held the canister out between Jimmy and Pierre.

'It was your parents,' Pierre said. 'I wouldn't presume.'

'You lost a brother to Bruun. I'll understand, Pierre.'

A look of pain passed across Pierre's face and he reached for the canister but Jimmy said, 'No, let Lance do it. He believed in Bruun when all around him thought him insane.'

They went out. Lance felt he had to say something. He had a sense of desembodiment, of not being in the same room with Bruun or even himself. He raised his voice.

'Goodbye, Bruun.'

'For a little while. You can't get out.' Cackle, cackle, cackle.

'For Esmeralda,' Lance said softly, grateful that she was not there after all. He pulled the tag and backed out of the room. There was not even the slightest temptation to stay and see Bruun burn. Behind him there was a flash of light and heat that singed the fluff on the back of his neck.

They stood down the passage, listening to the sound of the fighting on one side and the amplified laughter of the mutilated maniac on the other side. Shortly the cackling turned to querulous shouts about the air conditioning and then, almost immediately, to anguished screams.

Lance started forward with his rifle.

Burger put a hand on his elbow. 'Where are you going?'

'To put him out of his misery.' When his brother Ewart had burned, he had been too slow and Sambo had had to fire the bullets of mercy.

'No. Let him suffer for those women and children up there that he used for a shield. Let him burn for your parents, for Briony Roux and her child, for Peter and Magda Brazenose, for the others.'

Lance shook his arm free but made no further move to take his rifle to the gaping hole in the wall through which the eerie white light and the screams emanated. Burger was right. Bruun had killed innocent people simply to prod others into behaviour patterns desired by him. Now he must pay the price.

Presently the flames fused something in the amplifier and the screams ended.

Burger's men came bursting through the door down the passage. They were pursued by a hail of bullets. Beyond the door, with the slow-seeming speed of professionals who had been under fire before, they lined up against the walls, waiting for whoever looked through the door first.

Lance recognized the face immediately. He fired three shots from the hip into his chest before Burger's men fired one. Then he stopped firing. One of Burger's men grabbed the grenade as it fell from the lifeless fingers of Wong, who had followed Lance halfway across Africa and back. He threw the grenade through the closing door and received for his pains a bullet through the upper arm.

Then the door was closed again, the riddled body of Wong lying this side of it.

'Bruun's meatcleaver messenger,' Jimmy said.

Burger was turning to organize a retreat. The new amplified voice froze them in their tracks.

'Mr Weber?'

Lance remained silent. Burger gestured to his men to hurry around the corner.

'Mr Weber, don't shoot. It is I. Pan.'

'All right, come on,' Lance shouted.

Pan peered through the doors. He looked down to see what was blocking the door. He grimaced with distaste at the smell of the juices the body on the floor was dripping, then heaved at the door.

Several stocky Chinese carrying automatic weapons followed him through the door. They looked warily at Lance, Burger, Pierre and Jimmy. Burger's men were just around the corner.

'We meet in the middle,' Pan said. 'He's gone then?'

Lance shook his head. 'He's in there.' He was standing directly in front of the door. 'What's left of him.'

Pan came forward to look. He rubbed his eyes and looked again. He seemed less old than when Lance had last seen him but no less defeated. 'Where?'

'That puddle on the floor,' Burger said behind him. 'He lived in a cube of armoured, gas-proof glass. We burnt his glass and him with white phosphorus.'

The puddle on the floor breezed a delicate white smoke as if it had a life of its own. It was eating into the floor at the rate of an inch a minute. All that was left of Theodore Bruun, beyond the indelible memory of the evil he had done, was a few of the instruments that had kept him alive, products of space-age man's urge to explore outer darkness.

Kenya

Gerrit Jansen had visited Lance Weber's game reserve every year since it opened; when it had come on the market, he had outbid an American consortium for the property. Now, nearly a year later, he had come to check that the contractors had rebuilt the buildings exactly as they had been before the inexplicable tragedy of the still unresolved attack. He was a large, florid Dutchman, apparently abrupt in his manner but kindly in the results of his actions; his consuming passion was wild-life conservation. He was also a good businessman, a man who had pulled himself up the wheel of fortune from being a barefoot orphan when the Nazis retreated from Utrecht to where he could now afford to indulge this expensive passion with the best game reserve in the world. It was this 'best' that was concerning him now as he stood on the porch in front of the main building. What with one thing and another, the gap in the fence had not been mended at once after he had bought the reserve; soon he had learned that more animals would enter the fence than would leave through it and, deliberately, he had decided to leave the repair of the fence until last. His rational mind had told him it was perverse to invite the ire of his fellow gamekeepers for what was in fact an involuntary theft of their stock; deep down, irrationally, he felt it was not yet time to close the gap, although it would have to be mended soon. He wanted to retire here and to live in peace with his neighbours.

'Massa, Massa! Come quick!'

Jansen looked down at the black man before him. The man had been running, sweat gleamed on his heaving chest. 'All right, what is it?'

'You come, Massa.'

'To see what?'

The black man had come up the steps and was pulling at Jansen's sleeve. The white man was so slow! 'Massa, you come see. You not believe me I tell youi.'

Jansen, who knew he had much to learn here, started down the steps towards the Landrover standing there. He did not know the man's name, but he had been pointed out to the new owner as a man who, after many years in the city, had returned to his tribe on the game reserve a very rich man. This, Jansen felt, gave them something in common. Jansen chose to drive; the black man was too excited for his liking, his breath coming in gasps to a greater extent than the exertion of running a few miles – or all day – could account for in one so obviously at the peak of fitness. The black man gave directions by pointing, accompanying each pointed finger with 'Massa!' Jansen was surprised when he was directed out of the main gate and into the bush along the outside of the fence: there was no road there; he had been expecting to be led to some disaster at one of the black settlements inside the game reserve. The black man directed him around this tree and that. Now and again they glimpsed a shining strand as they came near the fence; for some reason they were following it.

'Here, Massa, we stop here, Massa.'

Jansen brought the Landrover to a halt. As far as he could make out, they were in the middle of nowhere. 'Now what?'

'We walk, Massa. We not frighten them then.'

'Animals?'

'You wait and see, Massa. You not believe me I tell you.'

The black man was tugging at his sleeve again, trying to push him out of the Landrover. Jansen started opening the door. Now the black man was pulling him back, pointing to the rifle on its rack behind the seats.

'No,' Jansen said. It was the rule, made by him, that the

380

rifle was to be carried – a standard precaution on every game reserve – but he did not feel at ease with rifles, he had no skill with them, the thing would only get tangled in his legs if he ever had to run for his life; he was the boss, he could break the rule.

The black man shrugged. He had no faith in the new owner's skill with the rifle. The elders of the tribe told of a time when every white man had skill with the rifle, even as recently as the previous owner, He Who Runs With The Ball, the one he had missed while he was away making his fortune. But that was no longer.

Jansen followed the black man through the long grass; from the Landrover it had looked merely long, here it was over their heads by a good margin.

'Shh, Massa.' The black man half turned to show his finger on his lips.

Jansen was aware of the grass waving ever so gently in front of them, *where they had not yet been*. The thrill of fear possessed him but he kept a steady pace behind the other man; he had not come this far without considerable nerve, even if he had no skill with a rifle.

The black man turned and put his hand against Jansen's chest. Jansen had been in Africa long enough to know tugging at sleeves was permissible in times of stress but that such familiarity as a hand firmly against the chest from a man who was in essence a sort of feudal retainer would be permitted only in times of extreme danger. The Dutchman froze in his tracks and tried not to breathe. Still the grass waved gently, the frequency of the oscillations becoming longer. Something large, he felt, was coming nearer.

The grey shapes lumbered out of the long grass, looming over the two men, near enough to reach out a hand and touch the loose grey skins. The smell was overwhelming. Then they were gone.

Jansen felt faint with joy and incredulity. 'Elephants,'

he whispered hoarsely. He would have started after the elephants immediately but for the black man's hand holding him back by the elbow.

'Now you believe me, Massa. Not too close, Massa. They go for hole in fence. They know they safe here.'

'Shh!' Jansen said, then, breaking his own injunction, 'How many were there . . . it went so fast.'

'Four, Massa. A bull, a cow, a female half-grown and a baby – he'll grow a fine bull.'

A new breeding herd, Jansen whispered to himself in his mind, afraid that if he spoke aloud he would wake up and find it only a dream.

'They know they safe here,' the black man said, half expecting the white man to ask the stupid question, How? and hugely relieved when Jansen smiled believingly and nodded his bluff head.

They stood in the tall grass to which still clung the odour of elephants passing and watching the elephants amble amiably through the gap in the fence, the half-grown female 'nurse' nudging the baby bull through into his new, safe home.

'I fetch tools and mend fence now, Massa?'

'Yes, you do that.' The man was excellent foreman material. Jansen jerked his mind back from the elephants, already between the first trees in his game reserve, to business. 'Tell me, what is your name?'

'Mpengi, Massa. Mpengi the Watusi.'

The most chilling horror stories – now available in Panther Books

Max Ehrlich

The Cult	95p	☐
The Edict	£1.95	☐

Mendal Johnson

Let's Go Play at the Adams'	£1.50	☐

James Kahn

Poltergeist	£1.95	☐

David Seltzer

Prophecy	£1.50	☐

Charles Veley

Night Whispers	£1.95	☐

William K Wells

Effigies	£1.95	☐

Jay Anson

666	£1.50	☐

Peter Loughran

Jacqui	£1.75	☐

H P Lovecraft

Omnibus 1: At the Mountains of Madness	£2.50	☐
Omnibus 2: Dagon and other macabre tales	£2.95	☐

Brian Lumley

Psychomech	£1.95	☐
Psychosphere	£1.95	☐
Psychamok	£2.50	☐

Whitley Strieber

Black Magic	£1.95	☐
The Night Church	£1.95	☐

Miles Gibson

The Sandman	£1.95	☐

To order direct from the publisher just tick the titles you want and fill in the order form.

GF3181

All these books are available at your local bookshop or newsagent, or can be ordered direct from the publisher.

To order direct from the publisher just tick the titles you want and fill in the form below.

Name _____

Address _____

_____

Send to:
Panther Cash Sales
PO Box 11, Falmouth, Cornwall TR10 9EN.

Please enclose remittance to the value of the cover price plus:

UK 45p for the first book, 20p for the second book plus 14p per copy for each additional book ordered to a maximum charge of £1.63.

BFPO and Eire 45p for the first book, 20p for the second book plus 14p per copy for the next 7 books, thereafter 8p per book.

Overseas 75p for the first book and 21p for each additional book.